*F*yodor *D*ostoyevsky

Fyodor Dostoyevsky

Selected Works

Fyodor Dostoyevsky

Notes from the Dead House

Translated by *Guy* and *Elena Cook*

Raduga Publishers · Moscow

Translation from the Russian
Edited by *Olga Shartse*
Designed by *Vladimir Kireyev*

Ф. М. ДОСТОЕВСКИЙ

Избранное

ЗАПИСКИ ИЗ МЕРТВОГО ДОМА

На английском языке

Copyright © Raduga Publishers 1989

Printed in the Union of Soviet Socialist Republics

ISBN 5-05-001668-1
ISBN 5-05-002441-2

NOTES FROM THE DEAD HOUSE

PART ONE

Introduction

In the remote regions of Siberia, in the middle of the steppe, the mountains or the impenetrable forests, you sometimes come across small unattractive wooden towns, with one or—at the most—two thousand inhabitants, and two churches—one in the town and the other at the cemetery. They are really more like the big villages in the vicinity of Moscow, than towns. As a rule they are amply supplied with police officers, members of the local court, and all the other lower ranks of officialdom. A civil servant in Siberia is very snug, despite the cold. The inhabitants are simple and conservative people; the way of life is old, solid and consecrated by the centuries. The officials, who rightly play the part of the gentry in Siberia, are either natives—Siberian born and bread—or people who have come from Russia, mostly from the capitals, attracted by the double pay, by the generous allowances for travel, and by tempting hopes of future promotion. From this number, those who can solve life's riddle almost always stay in Siberia forever, gladly striking root there, eventually to bear rich and sweet fruit. Others, of a more light-minded disposition, who are unable to solve the riddle of life, soon become bored with Siberia and ask themselves despondently why on earth did they come here at all. Impatiently, they see out their official term of three years, and—as soon as it expires—begin petitioning for a transfer, and return to the place they came from, cursing Siberia and laughing at it. They are wrong. One can be blissfully happy in Siberia, not only from the point of view of a career, but in many other respects too. The climate is excellent; there are many wonderfully rich and hospitable Russian merchants, as well as many well-to-do people of indigenous not Russian nationalities. The girls blossom like roses, and their morals are immaculate. Game comes flying down the streets in search of a hunter. Champagne is drunk by the bucket-ful. The caviar is superb. The crops yield a hundredfold. It is—when all is said and done—a most blessed land. One must only know how to make use of it. And in Siberia they do know how to make use of it.

It was in one of these cheerful and self-satisfied little towns (one with the most charming inhabitants, the memory of whom will remain forever imprinted on my heart) that I first met Alexander Petrovich Goryanchikov, who had been born into the landed gentry and nobility in Russia, but was now meekly and quietly living out the remainder of his days as an exile in the town of K. after serving his sentence of ten years' hard labour, for the murder of his wife, as a second category convict. He was in fact registered somewhere in the surrounding region, but he lived in the town where he could make at least some kind of a living by giving lessons to children. In Siberia, one often comes across exiles who live by tutoring, nobody has any qualms about employing them. They usually teach French, a language which is essential for getting on in life, and about which, if it were not for them, people in these remote regions of Siberia, would not have the faintest idea. I first met Alexander Petrovich at the house of Ivan Ivanovich Gvozdikov, an honoured and very hospitable official of many years' standing, whose five daughters all showed excellent promise for the future. Alexander Petrovich taught them four times a week, and charged thirty silver kopeks for each lesson. His appearance excited my curio-sity. He was extraordinarily pale and thin, not yet old—about thirty-five—small and frail. He always dressed very neatly, in the European style. If you engaged him in conversation, he would look at you very fixedly and attentively, listening to each word with exaggerated politeness, pondering over it, as though what you were asking had posed a problem for him, or you were seek-ing to extract some secret from him; then, finally, he would give his answer, clearly and laconically, but weighing each word with such extreme care that you suddenly started to feel uneasy for some reason, and were quite relieved when the conversation drew to a close. Straightaway, I asked Ivan Ivanovich to tell me something about Goryanchikov, and found out that his lifestyle

7

was moral and beyond reproach (had it been otherwise, Ivan Ivanovich would never have invited him to teach his daughters); that he was a terrible recluse, he kept away from everybody, was extremely learned, read a lot, but spoke very little, and was in general rather difficult to engage in conversation. There were those who insisted that he was definitely mad, though they would also agree that this was not necessarily such an important drawback; there were many respectable members of the community who were quite willing to bestow their benevolence on Alexander Petrovich, and he could even be quite useful in drawing up petitions and so forth... It was thought that he must have a good many relatives in Russia—and no mean ones at that—but it was known that he had resolutely broken off with them from the very moment he was sentenced, to his own detriment, actually. His story, moreover, was known to everyone in our town. Everyone knew that he had killed his wife out of jealousy during the first year of their marriage, and then gone to the police to give himself up—a fact which had considerably lessened the sentence that he was given. Crimes such as his are always regarded almost like mishaps, and viewed with pity. Yet, in spite of this, this strange man stubbornly avoided people, and would appear in public only in order to give lessons.

At first I took no particular notice of him. Little by little, however, for a reason I do not fully understand myself, my curiosity about him was roused. There was something mysterious about the man. There seemed to be not the slightest possibility of starting up a conversation with him. To be sure, he always answered my questions, and did so in a way which even suggested that he regarded this as his primary duty. Yet once he had answered, I hesitated to continue with my questions; and besides, at the end of such conversations, his face wore a look of suffering and exhaustion. I remember, on one fine evening in summer, walking away with him from the house of Ivan Ivanovich I suddenly had the idea of inviting him to my place for a cigarette. I cannot describe the terror that showed in his face. In his utter confusion he started mumbling some disconnected phrases, then suddenly he gave me a spiteful glare and rushed off in the opposite direction. I was quite astonished. From then

on, when he met me, he looked at me with something like fear.
I did not leave it at that though; something drew me towards him,
and a month later, without any pretext, I went to call on him
myself. I was no doubt acting in a foolish and tactless manner.
He had lodgings on the very outskirts of the town, in the house
of an old woman whose daughter suffered from consumption and
had—in her turn—an illegitimate child: a pretty and cheerful
little girl of about ten. When I went in, Alexander Petrovich
was sitting beside the girl, giving her a reading lesson. When he
saw me, he became as embarrassed as if I had caught him committing a crime. He was completely at a loss, he jumped up from
his chair and stared at me wide-eyed. At last, we both sat down.
He followed my every glance, as though suspecting that it held
some particular and mysterious meaning. I realised that he
was suspicious to the point of insanity. He looked at me with
hatred, all but asking me: "Won't you ever go?" I started to talk
to him about the town, about current events. He remained silent
and smiled maliciously. It not only transpired that he did not
know any of the most ordinary town news which was known to
everybody else, but that he was not even interested to find out.
Then I talked about our region and its needs. He listened to me
silently, looking into my eyes in so strange a manner, that at last
I began to feel ashamed of this line of talk. I did, however,
almost manage to arouse his interest with the new books and
magazines I had brought straight from the post office. I offered
them to him, as they were, with their pages still uncut. He
looked at them greedily, then at once changed his mind and
declined them, giving his lack of time as an excuse. Finally, I
bade him good night, and when I stepped outside the door, I
felt as though some unbearable weight had been lifted from my
heart. I was ashamed of myself, and indeed it did seem extremely silly to have pestered a man whose primary aim was to hide
himself away from the world as far as possible. But there was no
going back. I remember noticing that there were hardly any
books in the house and thinking that those who said he read a
lot had been mistaken. However, when I passed his lodgings very
late at night on a couple of occasions, I noticed that a light was
still burning in his windows. So what could he be doing, sitting

9

up so late? Was he perhaps writing something? And if so, what?

Circumstances kept me away from the town for about three months. When I returned, it was already winter, and I was told that Alexander Petrovich had died in the autumn—died alone, without even having called in a doctor. He was already almost forgotten in the town. His lodgings were standing empty. Immediately, I made it my business to make the acquaintance of the deceased's landlady, with the intention of finding out from her what it was that her lodger had been so busy with, and whether or not he had been writing something. In return for twenty kopeks, she presented me with a whole basketful of papers which the dead man had left behind him. The old woman confessed that she had already disposed of two of his notebooks. She was a grim, taciturn woman, and it was difficult to get anything out of her. She could not tell me anything particularly new about her former lodger. According to her, he had almost never done anything, and had gone for months on end without opening a book or setting pen to paper, but instead he had spent the nights pacing about his room, as though he were endlessly thinking something over, sometimes even talking to himself. He had grown very fond of her granddaughter and treated her very tenderly from the first when he learned that her name was Katya. On St. Katherine's Day he always went to church and had a memorial service sung for somebody. He could not stand visitors, and only left the house to give lessons. He even used to look suspiciously at the old woman herself when she came once a week to tidy the room up a bit, and he had hardly exchanged a word with her during the whole three years. I asked Katya if she remembered her teacher. She looked at me without saying a word, then turned her face to the wall and burst into tears. So this man had been able to inspire love in at least one person.

I took his papers away, and spent a whole day sorting them out. Three quarters of them were useless pieces of writing, or pupils' calligraphic exercises. There was among them, however, one notebook—a rather thick one—the pages covered with fine handwriting, but the notebook unfinished, and perhaps neglected and forgotten by the author himself. This was a description—rather a muddled one—of the ten years of penal servitude that Alexander Petrovich had served. In places, the description was interrupted by some other story—strange, terrible memories, jotted down unevenly as though under compulsion. I read these fragments over several times, and I felt almost certain that they had been written during bouts of insanity. The prison diaries on the other hand— "Scenes From the Dead House" as he himself called them at one point in his manuscript— seemed to me to be not entirely without interest. A completely new world, unknown until now, the strangeness of some of the facts, some particular notes about that human wreckage, fascinated me, and I read some of the things with curiosity. I may be mistaken of course. I have chosen two or three chapters at random... Let readers form their own judgement.

I

Dead House

Our gaol building stood at the far end of the fortress, right up against the ramparts. Sometimes you would look through the chinks of the fence into the blessed world outside—maybe there was something to be seen out there? But all you would see was a patch of sky and the high earthen ramparts overgrown with weeds, and the sentries pacing up and down those ramparts day and night; and you would be struck by the thought that years would pass, and you would go up to look through the chinks of the fence just as you were doing now, and see the same rampart and the same sentries and the same tiny patch of sky—which is not the sky above the gaol, but another sky: different, distant and free. Picture a large courtyard, about two hundred paces long and about a hundred and fifty across, an irregular hexagon, completely enclosed by a high stockade, a fence made of tall posts (pales) deeply embedded in the earth, fitted tightly against each other, held in place by planks nailed to them transversally, and with their upper ends sharpened into points—and you will have a pretty good idea of what the outer wall of our gaol was like. Strong gates had been put into one of the sides of this fence, always locked and always—day and night—guarded by sentries; they were opened only when an order was given to let people out to work. Beyond these gates was the bright world: the world of freedom, where people went about their ordinary lives. Yet to those on this side of the fence, that world appeared like something from a fairytale. This side was a world to itself, bearing no resemblance to any other, with its own laws, its own style of dress, its own mores and customs: a Dead House, alive, with a life like nowhere else on earth, and people of a special sort. It is this particular corner of the world that I shall now set about describing.

As soon as you step within the confines, you will see several buildings. There are two long, one-storey cabins stretching along either side of the wide inner yard. These are the barracks where the prisoners are billeted according to their various categories. At the far end of the compound, there is another wooden cabin. This is the kitchen, which is divided into two artels; beyond that there is yet another building, in which, under one roof, are housed the larders, barns and stores. The central part of the yard is empty, presenting a flat, fairly large open space. This is where the prisoners line up for the checks and roll calls which are carried out in the morning, afternoon and evening, and sometimes several more times during the course of the day, depending on how mistrustful the guards are and how fast they can count. There is another fairly large space around the edge, between the buildings and the fence. It is here, along the backs of the buildings, that some of the more unsociable and morose prisoners like to walk, out of sight, in their free time thinking their sad thoughts. Coming across them during these promenades, I liked to search their sullen, branded faces, trying to guess what these thoughts might be. There was one prisoner whose favourite pastime was counting pales. There were about one and a half thousand, and he had his eye on each and every one of them. Each pale stood for one day; and each day he added another pale to the count so that, contemplating the number of uncounted pales left, he could have a visual idea of how many days he had left in gaol till the end of his sentence.

When he finished one side of the hexagon, he was truly happy. He still had many years to go; but there was plenty of time to learn patience in gaol. On one occasion I saw how a prisoner, who had done twenty years hard labour and was about to be released, was saying goodbye to his fellow prisoners. There were some among them who could remember what he was like when he first arrived: young and carefree, unconcerned about either his crime, or his punishment. And now he was leaving: a grey-haired old man, with a glum, sad face. He went around all six barracks in silence. On entering each one he crossed himself in front of the icon, made a sweeping bow to all his friends and begged them to remember him kindly. I can also recall how one prisoner, who had been quite a prosperous Siberian peasant in his time, was called over to the gates one evening. Six months earlier, he had received word that his wife had married another man, and he had fallen into the depths of despair. Now she had come to the prison herself. She called him out, and gave him the food she had brought him. They spoke together for a couple of minutes, shed a few tears, and said goodbye forever. I could see his face, as he was coming back towards the barrack... Yes, one really could learn patience in this place.

When it got dark, we were all taken into our barracks and locked up for the whole night. I always found it very hard to go back into the barrack from the open air. It was a long, stuffy room with a low ceiling, dimly lit by tallow candles, and reeking with a heavy, suffocating smell. I do not know now, how I survived ten years there. Three planks on the bed-shelf was all the space I got to sleep on—and this same bed-shelf, in our room alone, had to make do for about thirty people. In wintertime we were locked in early. It took nearly four hours for everyone to go to sleep. And until then—shouting, coarse laughter, swearing, the clanking of chains, smoke-laden air, shaved heads, branded faces, clothes made from odd pieces of fabric, everything befouled, disgraced ... how tenacious of life man is! Human beings are creatures that grow accustomed to anything. That is probably the best definition of them.

All told, there were around two hundred and fifty souls in our gaol. The number was fairly constant. One lot would be just arriving, a second lot would be finishing off their sentences and leaving, a third lot would be dying. And the people could not be more varied! Every gubernia and every region of Russia was represented, I reckon; and there were non-Russians too; and even some convicts from the Caucasus. The whole lot were divided according to the seriousness of their crimes—according, that is, to the number of years laid down for those crimes. At a guess I would say there was not a single crime that was not represented. The bulk of the gaol's population were convicts who belonged to the civilian category. These were convicts completely deprived of all their civil rights, cast adrift from human society forever, their faces branded as a permanent testimony to their outlawdom. They were sentenced to hard labour for terms of eight to twelve years, and then sent somewhere into the various districts of Siberia to settle as exiles. Then there were con-victs in the military category who—as in Russian military penal companies in general—had not been deprived of all their civil legal rights. They were sent out to us for short terms and when these were over, they were returned as privates to the places where they had been serving in the army—in other words, to the Siberian line battalions. Many of these returned to prison almost immediately for some second serious offence—but this time it would not be for a short spell, but for twenty years. This category of prisoners was known as 'lifers'. Yet these 'lifers' were still not deprived of all their civil rights. Finally, there was one special category, quite a large one, composed mostly of soldiers, for those who had committed the most atrocious crimes. They were known as the special category. These criminals were sent to us from all over Russia. They described themselves as 'permanent', not actually knowing the length of their sentence. According to the rules they had to be given double and triple 'corrective lessons' to do. They were to stay in our gaol until a special type of labour camp was set up in Siberia—which had the hardest penal servitude of all. "You're here for a term, and we're forever," they used to say to the other inmates. Some time later, I heard that this category had been abolished. In addition, the civilian category was also abolished in our fortress and one all-embracing military penal company was established.

14

That, of course, meant that the prison authorities changed too. What I am describing here, in other words, took place a long time ago, things long past and over...

It is a long time ago now. It comes back to me as though in a dream. I remember how I first arrived at the gaol. It was an evening in December. Dusk was already falling; the prisoners were returning from their day's labour and making ready for the roll call. A mustachioed sergeant opened the doors for me into this strange house, where I was to spend so many years, and live through so many emotions, about which—if I had not experienced them myself—I would not have even the most approximate of ideas. For example, I could never have imagined just how awful and torturing it would be never once to have even a minute of privacy during the whole ten years of my penal servitude. At work—always under supervision of guards; at the barracks—always in the company of two hundred fellow prisoners. And never, not once, alone! However ... if only that had been the worst thing I had to get used to.

Among the prisoners there were killers by chance and killers by profession—bandits and bandit chieftains. There were just plain crooks, thieves and burglars. There were also those about whom it was difficult to make any decision. You wondered what on earth they had done to end up here. Yet everyone had his history: something vague and heavy, like a hangover from last night's drinking. They were not, in general, prone to recounting their histories; they did not like talking about the past, and clearly, they tried not to think about it. Some of the murderers I knew among them were so cheerful, so untroubled by thought, that you could bet your life their conscience never gave them a pang. There were some gloomy individuals, on the other hand, who hardly ever spoke. It was a rare event, on the whole, for anyone to tell his life story: curiosity was not exactly in vogue, not the done thing, not what was expected... Just occasionally, the odd person who had nothing better to do, would get carried away by what he was saying, and one of the others would listen to him, with a kind of sullen indifference. Nobody could surprise anyone here. "We've all got a good education," they used to say, with a strange kind of complacency.

I can recall a time when one of the bandits, who was rather worse for drink (because it was occasionally possible to get drunk in our prison), started recounting the story of how he had stabbed a five-year-old boy to death; how he first won him over with some toy or other, then enticed him somewhere into an empty shed, and stabbed him to death—just like that. Everyone in the barrack, who up to that moment had been laughing at his jokes, started shouting at him, and the bandit had to shut up. They were not shouting from any sense of outrage at what he had done but just because people *weren't supposed* to talk *about that*, because it was *not done*. I should mention, incidentally, that these men really were educated—in the literal sense of the word, as well as in the broader sense of knowing about life. Probably half of them were able to read and write; and where else, from a mass gathering of ordinary Russian folk would you be able to take out a chunk of two hundred and fifty people and find that half of them were literate? I heard somewhere at a later date, that someone, given similar statistics, had reached the conclusion that education had a detrimental effect on the common people. But that is not right. The causes are entirely different—though it is hard not to agree that education does develop a sense of self-assurance in the common people. But, after all, there's nothing wrong with that. These different categories of convicts could be told apart by their clothes. Some wore jackets of which one half was dark brown, and the other half was grey. Their trousers were the same, with one grey leg and one dark brown. On one occasion, while we were working, a bread girl who had come in among the convicts, peered at me very intently, and then suddenly started cackling. "Just look at him! He's come out all wrong!" she shouted. "They must've run out of grey, and run out of black too!" Then there were those whose jackets were entirely grey—though the sleeves were dark brown. The heads were shaved differently too. Some had half their head shaved from front to back; others had been shaved from side to side.

From the moment when one first saw this strange family, one could detect a striking common characteristic. Even the most striking, the most original individuals, who dominated the others naturally, even they tried to adjust to the general tenor of prison life. I have to say that, on the whole, these people—with the odd exception of some who were inexhaustibly cheerful (and accordingly despised)—were sullen, envious, vain in the extreme, boastful, quick to take offence, and all to a man were terrible formalists. The highest virtue was the ability never to show surprise at anything. They were all crazy about preserving appearances. Yet very often the most conceited air changed in a flash into the most craven. Still, there were a few truly strong people, who behaved straightforwardly, and never put on any airs. How odd it was though: even among those truly strong ones, there were some who were vain to excess, almost to the point of illness. Vanity and keeping up appearances, were in general the most important things. The majority had sunk to the depths of depravity and baseness. The backbiting and the gossiping were endless—it was like living in the murkiest darkness of hell. No one dared to rebel against the prison's regulations and established ways. Everyone submitted to them. There were some striking, strong characters who did not submit easily, and then only after a long struggle—but still, in the end, they submitted. Then there was another kind who came to the prison: people who had gone to extremes and stepped right beyond the pale while they were still at liberty, committing their crimes unaccountably, without seeming to know why they acted as they did, in a kind of delirium, a daze, often motivated by vanity incited beyond reason. In our place they were put down immediately—and never mind if some of them, before coming to prison, had terrorised whole villages and towns. A newcomer, taking a quick look round, soon saw that this was not the right kind of place, that here there was no one to astound; and imperceptibly he would submit, and adjust to the general tenor of prison life which was manifested outwardly by that peculiar dignity which characterised almost every inmate of the gaol. It was as though the title of 'convict', of 'a sentenced person', was a rank, and a high-standing one at that. And there was no sign of shame or repentance! Yet there was also a kind of outward submissiveness on an official level, so to say, a calm philosophy: "We are finished people," they used to say. "Since we couldn't

17

live properly in freedom, we've got to run the gauntlet now, down the line." "You didn't listen to what your mum and dad told you, so you'll have to listen to the drum now." "You didn't want to work at home, so now you're breaking stones." This sort of thing was frequently heard, put forward either as a moral admonition or in the form of straightforward sayings and proverbs—but it was never meant to be taken seriously. It was words only. There was hardly a man among them who admitted his own criminality to himself. And just let anyone, who was not a prisoner himself, try to reproach them with their misdoings, or revile them—although it is not typical of Russian people to reproach wrongdoers—and you would not believe the swearing it would provoke! And how expert they all were at swearing. They swore artistically and with real style. With them, swearing had been elevated to the level of a science; it was not so much through the use of an offensive word that they strove to get under your skin, it was more by the offensive meaning, spirit, or idea of what they said—and this is far more refined, and more poisonous. This skill of theirs was developed even further in endless squabbles. All these people worked only under compulsion, consequently they preferred to do as little as possible, and as a result grew depraved. If they had not been depraved before they came to prison, they grew depraved while they were inside. They had all been brought here against their will, and they were all strangers to each other.

"Old Nick wore out three pairs of boots, getting us together!" said the convicts about themselves—and so no wonder that gossip, intrigue, backbiting, jealousy, squabbles, bitchiness and viciousness were always in the forefront of this blighted life. There isn't a woman in the world who could have equalled these cut-throats in their bitchiness. I must repeat that there were also some strong, self-controlled characters among them: hardened, fearless individuals, who all their lives had been used to directing and breaking in others. Such people somehow commanded automatic respect; though they were, on their part, often very jealous of their reputation; they tried not to impose on any of the others, never took part in petty squabbles, and conducted themselves with extraordinary dignity. In their relationships with the prison authorities, they were reasonable, and almost always obedient—not out of any sense that it was right to be obedient, not out of any sense of duty, but as though obeying the rules of a pact which both sides had realised was to their mutual advantage. And, indeed, they were treated with caution. I recall how one of these convicts—a fearless and determined man whose tendency to savage violence was well known to the authorities, was summoned to be punished for some offence. It was a summer's day. Work was over. The officer who was most immediately and directly in charge of the prison, came over in person to the guardhouse—which was right up against the gates—to witness the punishment. This Major was the personification of doom to the prisoners; he had reduced them to such a state that they quaked in their shoes at the very sight of him. He was strict to the point of insanity; he 'pounced on people' as the convicts put it. The thing they feared most about him was his lynx-like eyes, from which nothing could be hidden. He seemed able to see things without looking at them. When he came through the gaol gates, he already knew what was happening at the far end. The convicts called him 'eight-eyes'. His methods were quite erroneous. With his violent, spiteful actions he only further aggravated the already embittered men, and had it not been for his superior, the Commandant, a man of noble and reasonable character who sometimes restrained the Major's excesses, he would have caused a great deal of trouble with his kind of administration. I find it hard to understand how he came through it all unhurt; but he retired alive and in good health, though after having been tried in court.

When he heard his name called, the prisoner turned pale. Usually he lay down to be flogged resolutely, without a word, endured his punishment silently, and then stood up smartly, taking his mishap coolly and philosophically. Nevertheless, he was always treated with caution. This time though, for some reason or other, he considered himself in the right. He had turned very pale, and when the guards were not looking managed to hide a sharp English cobbler's knife in his sleeve. Carrying knives and sharp tools was strictly forbidden. There were frequent surprise and thorough searches for them, and the punishments were severe. But as it is no simple matter to discover anything on a thief when he has made a particular point of hiding it, and as knives and tools were in constant need, they were always in good supply, despite the searches. And when they did happen to be taken away, new ones immediately appeared in their place. The whole gaol rushed over to the fence and watched with bated breath through the chinks between the pales. Everyone knew that on this occasion Petrov would not submit to the flogging and that that would be the end for the Major. Just at the crucial moment, however, the Major climbed back into his droshky and drove away, delegating the disciplinary action to another officer. "Divine intervention!" the prisoners used to say about it afterwards. As for Petrov, he took his punishment with extreme calm. His anger had departed with the Major. A prisoner is obedient and submissive only up to a certain degree; there is a limit that should not be crossed. Nothing, by the way, could be stranger than these occasional eruptions of contumacy and impatience. For years, a person puts up with everything that happens to him, accepts it, lives through the cruellest punishments, and then suddenly blows up over some trifle, some silly little thing. It could be described as a kind of madness, and that is—actually—how many people view it.

I have already mentioned that in the course of several years I did not see in these people a single sign of repentance or of painful brooding about their crimes, and that the majority of them inwardly considered themselves to be completely in the right. And that is a fact. To a great extent, of course, this can be explained by vanity, bad example, bravado, and a false sense of shame. Who, on the other hand, can say that he has fathomed the depths of these lost souls and saw what was hidden away from the whole world? Yet surely it should have been possible, in all these years, to notice something, to detect if only a sign indicating the suffering or anguish in their hearts. But there was nothing, definitely nothing. Apparently, a crime cannot be comprehended from any preconceived or established point of view, and its philosophy is rather more complicated than people tend to think. It is beyond doubt that prisons and the forced labour system do nothing to improve a criminal; they just punish him, and protect society from any further attempts to disrupt its peace and quiet. Within the criminal himself, prison and hard labour develop only hatred, a craving for forbidden pleasures, and a terrible irresponsibility. I am firmly convinced, moreover, that the notorious system of solitary confinement in cells is deceptive, erroneous and superficial in its results. It sucks out a man's inner juices, devitalises his soul, weakens and frightens it, and then yields up a half-crazed and morally shrivelled mummy, as an example of repentance and reform. A prisoner who is in rebellion against society obviously hates it, and almost always considers himself as right and society as wrong. Besides, he has been punished by it, and so considers himself cleansed, and quits with that society. There are points of view judging from which you would have to absolve the criminal of his crime. Nevertheless, despite the existence of many different points of view, everyone will agree that there are crimes, which always and everywhere, according to all the different law codes have been considered as indisputable crimes since the creation of the world, and will go on being considered as such so long as people remain human. It was only in prison that I heard stories of the most horrible and unnatural atrocities, of the most monstrous murders, recounted with irrepressible and childishly merry laughter. In particular, there was one patricide who remains in my memory very vividly. He was of noble birth, had held an official position, and was something of a prodigal son for his sixty-year-old father. He led a completely dissolute life, and he ran into debt. His father restrained him, tried to reason with him. The old man owned a house and a homestead, he might also have had money ... and so his son murdered him for the inheritance. It was a whole month before the crime was discovered. The murderer himself had reported to the police that his father had disappeared. He passed that month in extreme debauchery. Finally, while he was out one day, the police found the body. There was a cessditch, running across the courtyard, covered over with planks. The body was found lying in this ditch. It was clothed and laid out neatly. The grey-haired head had been severed and then put back against the body, and under this head the murderer had placed a pillow. He did not plead

21

guilty. He was deprived of his title, stripped of his official rank, and sentenced to twenty years hard labour. Always, during the whole of my time with him, he was in the most excellent, cheerful frame of mind. He was unbalanced, light-minded and irresponsible in the highest degree, though not at all stupid. I never noticed any signs of cruelty in him. He was despised by the other prisoners—not for his crime which was never mentioned—but for his foolishness, for his simply not knowing how to behave. He would remember his father in conversation sometimes. Once, when he was telling me about the robust physique which was a family feature, he added: "*My old Pater*, for example, he never complained of any aches or pains till the day he died." Such inhuman callousness is impossible of course. It was phenomenal: there must have been a deficiency of some kind in him, a moral or physical freakishness, as yet unknown to science. I did not believe in this crime, of course. Yet fellow townsmen of his, who must have been fully familiar with his story, told me about the case in great detail. The facts were all so clear, you had to believe them.

The prisoners heard him one night, shouting out in his sleep: "Hold him! Cut his head off, his head, his head..."

Almost all the prisoners talked and raved in their sleep. Usually it was swearwords and thieves' argot, talk of knives and axes. "We're folk who've been through the fire," they used to say. "Our innards have been burnt out of us. That's why we shout in our sleep."

The hard labour prescribed for us was not a job, but a duty. A prisoner fulfilled his 'task' or did his stint, and then returned to the gaol. This work was regarded with hatred. Without some private, personal occupation to which he could devote all his ingenuity a human being could not have survived in the gaol. I really do not know how else these men, who had lived life to the full and wanted to go on doing so, would have been able to get on together quite normally and correctly of their own free will and agreement, when they had been forcefully herded together in a place like this, and forcefully wrenched away from society and the normal way of life. In a place like this, the idleness alone would have been enough to develop criminal qualities of which they had previously not even dreamed. A man cannot live without work and something he can legitimately, normally call his own: he grows depraved and brutalised. And that is why from a natural necessity and instinct for self-preservation every person in the gaol had his own trade and occupation. The long summer days were almost always filled up with prescribed labour, and the nights were so short that there was hardly time to get enough sleep. In winter, however, in accordance with the regulations, the prisoners had to be locked up as soon as it started to get dark. What was there to do during those long tedious hours of winter evenings? So, despite the ban, almost every barrack changed into a vast workshop. The work itself, the possession of a trade, was not banned; but it was strictly forbidden to have any tools about you in the gaol, and without tools it was impossible to work. People worked quietly though, and apparently the authorities, in some instances, chose not to pry. Many prisoners came to the gaol without any trade, but learned one from the others, and left as proficient craftsmen. We had cobblers and shoemakers, tailors and joiners, locksmiths and engravers, and gilders. There was one Jew, Isai Bumstein, who was a jeweller and a money-lender besides. All of them worked hard to make a bit of money. They got their orders for work from the town. Money is minted freedom—so for a human being deprived of freedom, it is ten times dearer. Just to hear it jingling in his pocket is comforting enough, even though he cannot spend it. But then money can always be spent, in all places and at all times; especially as a forbidden fruit is always twice as sweet. You could even get liquor in the gaol. Pipes were strictly forbidden, yet everyone was smoking them. Money and tobacco saved people from scurvy and other illnesses. And work, for its part, saved them from crime—for without work, the prisoners would have devoured each other like spiders in a glass jar. Yet, despite this fact, both work and money were forbidden. Quite often, sudden night searches were carried out, and all banned articles were confiscated, and the money, however well hidden, sometimes fell into the hands of the searchers. That is one of the reasons why it was not saved, but spent quite quickly on drink instead; that is why liquor found its way into

23

the gaol. After each search a guilty prisoner, as well as being deprived of all his possessions, would also be rather painfully punished. Yet after each search, the losses were at once made up, new possessions at once acquired, and everything went on in the same old way. The authorities knew about this, and the prisoners meekly took their punishment, although this sort of life was rather like settling down on Mount Vesuvius.

The ones without a skill earned their living in a different way. Some of these ways were quite original. There were men, for example, who dealt in rags and junk. Some of the stuff sold here would not have been regarded as things at all outside the prison, and it would never have occurred to anyone to buy or sell them. The gaol was very poor and incredibly mercantile. The rottennest rag had its price—it might always come in handy somewhere. And poverty gave money a completely different value from that which it had in the outside world. A thing that took time and skill to make was bought dirt cheap. Some people turned successfully to money-lending. A prisoner who had frittered everything away would bring his last possessions to the money-lender and get a few copper coins for them at a frightening rate of interest. If he did not redeem these things in time, they were sold—quickly and heartlessly. Money-lending flourished so much that even articles of prison issue were accepted into pawn: things like prison underwear, boot leather—uppers and soles, etc.—things which a prisoner might find himself in need of at any moment. When such things were pawned, however, matters sometimes took a different turn, though not a particularly unexpected one. Having pawned his articles of prison issue and pocketed the money, the man went at once to report it to the senior sergeant, his immediate superior who at once confiscated the things from the money-lender without even advising the higher authorities. Curiously enough, a quarrel did not always follow; the money-lender would silently and sullenly give up the articles as though this was how he had expected it to turn out all along. Perhaps, he could not help admitting to himself that if he had been the pawnee, he would have done the same. That was why, if he ever swore about it later, it was not out of any ill will but just for form's sake.

By and large everyone stole from everyone else terribly. Almost everyone had his little trunk with a padlock, for keeping the different articles of prison issue. This was allowed, but the trunks were no protection. I do not think I have to tell you what skilful thieves the prisoners were. One prisoner, a man who (I can say without any exaggeration) was deeply devoted to me, stole my Bible: the one book which we were allowed to have in the gaol. That same evening he confessed as much to me—not out of any sense of repentance, but because I had been looking for it all day and he felt sorry for me. We had our vintners too, who traded in liquor, and got rich quickly. I shall go into more detail about this some other time. It was quite incredible. A lot of the prisoners were in gaol for smuggling, so it was hardly surprising that liquor was brought in, even with all the searches and escorts. Smuggling, by the way, is a very special kind of crime, by its very nature. It is hard to realise, is it not, that for some smugglers money and profit are of only secondary importance? Yet that is just how it is, in fact. Smugglers work for the love of the game, it is a vocation. A smuggler has something of the poet in him. He risks everything, braves the most terrible danger, he uses all his cunning and inventiveness to come through safely, and on occasion, works with a kind of inspiration. It is a passion with him, as strong as gambling. There was one prisoner I knew, a man who was of monumental size, but so meek, quiet and resigned that it was hard to imagine how he had ever ended up in gaol. He was utterly without malice and he got on so well with everyone that during the whole of his term he never had a single argument. He came from the Western border, he had been sent out to us for smuggling, and so, of course, he could not resist the temptation, and he began sneaking liquor in. He was forever being punished for it, and he was frightened to death of these floggings. Sneaking liquor in earned him only the most miserable pittance. Only those who ran the business grew rich from the stuff. This oddball did it all for the love of the art. He was a real cry-baby and time after time, when the punishment was over, he would vow never to smuggle anything in again. With tremendous self-control, he would resist the temptation for as much as a month, until finally he succumbed again...

Thanks to characters like him, the gaol was never short of liquor.

Last but not least there was one other income which, though it did not enrich the prisoners, was at least steady and benevolent. That was charity. In our society, the upper classes do not have the faintest idea how much the middle classes and the tradespeople, and our common folk in their entirety, care for 'the unfortunates'. The charity goes on unceasingly, almost always in the form of bread—cottage loaves and buns—and, rather less frequently, in the form of money. In many places, without the sustenance, it would have been just too hard for the prisoners, especially those awaiting trial, who are kept in much worse conditions than those already under sentence. The bread is religiously shared out in equal portions among the prisoners, and if there is not enough to go round, it is cut up into equal lots—sometimes into as many as six—to make absolutely sure that each inmate has his piece without fail. I can remember the first time I received money as alms. It was not long after I first came to the prison. I was returning from the morning's work alone, under guard. A woman was coming towards me with her daughter—a girl of about ten, a pretty little angel. I had seen them on a previous occasion. The woman was a soldier's widow. Her husband, a young soldier, had died in the prisoners' ward of the hospital while waiting to stand trial; I'd been in there, ill, at the same time. His wife and daughter came to pay their last respects to him; both of them cried terribly. Now, catching sight of me, the little girl blushed and whispered something to her mother, who stopped immediately, found a quarter kopek in her bundle and gave it to her. The child started to run after me.

"Here, take this copper in the name of Christ!" she shouted, running in front of me, and shoving the coin into my hands. I took the coin, and the girl returned to her mother, completely happy. I treasured this coin for a long time.

II
First Impressions

I can picture my first month and the beginning of my life in gaol very clearly, even now. The years that followed flicker past in my memory much more dimly. Some seem even to have become completely erased, merged into one another, leaving behind them a general impression—oppressive, monotonous and stifling.

Everything I went through during the first days of my sentence, however, stands out in my mind like something that took place only yesterday. But that is only to be expected.

I distinctly remember how the thing that amazed me from my very first entrance into prison life was that there was nothing I found particularly startling, unusual or—better to say—unexpected about it. It was as though I had pictured it all before, when, going to Siberia, I tried to guess what lay in store for me. But very soon I was brought up short at almost every step by the strangest, most unexpected things, by really monstrous facts. And it was only later, when I had lived in the gaol for a considerable period of time, that I fully comprehended the utter uniqueness of such an existence, and its totally unforeseen nature, and I was more and more staggered by it. This amazement, I must confess, stayed with me through all the long years of my hard labour to which I was never able to reconcile myself.

My first impression could not have been worse, and yet, funny thing, it seemed to me that life in gaol would be easier than I had imagined on the way. The prisoners, though wearing shackles, could walk freely around the whole gaol; they swore, sang songs, did their own work, smoked their pipes, and some (though a very few) even drank liquor; and cards were played at night. The work itself did not seem too hard, and it was only much later that I realised that it was *hard labour* not because it was arduous and never-ending, but because it was *forced*, compulsory, done under constraint. A peasant probably works much harder, and even at night, especially in summer, but he is working for himself, working with a rational purpose, and it is incomparably easier for him than for a convict to do his enforced and—as far as he is concerned—completely useless work. It once crossed my mind that to crush and destroy a man completely, to punish him in a manner so terrible that even the worst of murderers would shudder at the punishment and fear it beforehand, it would be enough to make him do work of an utterly

27

useless and meaningless nature. Whereas the present form of hard labour is uninteresting and boring for a convict, the work itself at least is sensible: a prisoner makes bricks, digs the earth, does some whitewashing and building. Work like that has both meaning and purpose. The prison labourer even gets carried away with his work sometimes; he tries to make a quicker and better job of it. But if he were made, for example, to pour water from one wooden pail into another and then from that one back into the first, or to pound sand, or to shift a pile of earth from one place to another and back again, then I think that within a very few days the prisoner would have hanged himself, or committed a thousand new crimes to escape, if only through death, from this humiliation, shame and torture. Such a punishment, of course, would be just torture and vengeance, nonsensical because it would have no rational purpose. But since an element of torture, nonsense, humiliation and shame is an essential part of any forced labour, prison work is incomparably more agonising than any free work, precisely because it is forced.

I had, however, entered the gaol in winter, in December, and I had as yet no idea of summer work, which was five times harder. On the whole, there was little work to be done in our fortress in winter. The prisoners were sent down to the Irtysh to break up the old prison barges there, they did various job in the workshops, or shovelled the snow which had been piled up in drifts around the prison buildings, or heated up alabaster and powdered it, etc., etc. The winter days were short. Work was soon over, and the whole lot of us would come back early to the gaol, where there was nothing to do—unless one had some private job to do. Yet out of all the prisoners, perhaps only one third occupied themselves with their own work. The rest just frittered their time away, wandered idly around all the barracks, cursed, picked quarrels with one another, and if they happened to have some money—got drunk. At night they played cards, gambling away everything down to their last rag. And all this was out of frustration and idleness and having nothing to do. I realised later that apart from having one's freedom taken away, apart from the forced labour, there is another agony in prison life which is

28

perhaps the worst of all. And that is *enforced communal living*. This living together communally happens in other places too of course. But in gaol you get the kind of people you'd never choose to live with and I am certain that all the convicts felt the agony of this, though—most of them—subconsciously.

The food seemed sufficient too. The other prisoners assured me that nothing like it could be found in the military penal companies of European Russia. I am no judge—I have not been there. Besides a lot of people were able to get their own food. Beef, in our place, cost a half-kopek a pound—and three kopeks in summer. True it was only those who were always in pocket who could buy their own food, the majority ate prison food. In boasting about the food, the prisoners meant only the bread, and the thing they were most thankful for was that it was allocated by the barrack and not issued in individual rations by weight. The very possibility filled them with horror: if the bread had been distributed in individual rations, one third of them would have gone hungry; sharing it as they did, there was enough for all. The bread in our prison was famous throughout the town for its wonderful taste which was ascribed to the happy construction of the prison ovens. The cabbage soup, on the other hand, was very poor. It was cooked in one common cauldron, thickened slightly with cereal, and it was very thin and watery especially on weekdays. I was disgusted by the enormous number of cockroaches in it. This did not seem to bother the other prisoners though.

I did not go to work during the first three days. This was the usual procedure for new arrivals, who were allowed to rest after their long journey. The very next day, however, I had to go to be reshackled. My shackles were not the regulation type, but were joined by rings (the 'jingle-jangle' kind as the prisoners called them) and they were worn on the outside. The regulation shackles, specially adapted for working, were not made of rings but of four iron rods, each one almost as thick as a finger, connected by three rings. These had to be worn under the trousers. A strap was tied through the central ring and this in turn was fastened to a belt around the waist, worn over the shirt.

I remember my first morning in the gaol. The drum beat

reveille in the guardhouse near the gaol gates, and about ten minutes later the sergeant on guard duty started to unlock the barracks. People were waking up. In the dim light of the tallow candles, the prisoners, shivering with cold, began to get up from their bed-shelves. The majority of them were silent and sullen after sleep. They yawned, stretched, and scowled at the world with their branded brows. Some crossed themselves; others had already begun squabbling. It was unbearably stuffy. The fresh winter air burst in through the door as soon as it was opened, and swept through the barracks in billows of vapour. The prisoners crowded around the water buckets; they passed the ladle along from one to another, filling their mouths with water which they then spat out again to wash their faces and their hands. The water was laid up the previous evening by the *parashnik*. In accordance with the rules, there was one prisoner in each barrack who was selected by the entire artel to be responsible for upkeep. He was called the *parashnik* and was not sent out to work. This man's job was to keep the barrack clean, wash and scrub the bed-shelves and the floors, empty the night bucket, and fetch in two bucketfuls of water—for washing in the morning and for drinking during the daytime. Arguments started up immediately on account of there being only one ladle.

"Where d'you think you're going, scarface?" growled one morose and swarthy prisoner with a shaven and strangely bumpy skull and a lean, tall body as he shoved a fat, ruddy-faced, cheerful little man out of his way. "Hold your horses!"

"What are you shouting about? Holding horses has to be paid for, you know! Get lost will you! Just look at him. Stuck up there like a bloody monument. I'll tell you what, mates! He's got no 'offiness' about him."

The word 'offiness' created an effect, quite a few people started to laugh. That was just what the jolly little fat man wanted. He was clearly the barrack's self-appointed clown. The tall prisoner surveyed him with the utmost contempt.

"You fat slob!" he muttered. "Look how fat the prison bread's made him. Pleased as punch I suppose! He'll probably give birth to twelve piglets for Easter."

The little fat man lost his temper at last.

"Well what kind of bird do you think you are?" he shouted suddenly, going red in the face.

"That's just what I am—a bird."

"Yes, but what kind?"

"That kind!"

"What d'you mean—that kind!"

"Just that kind! That's all."

"Yes, but tell me what kind?"

They glared at each other fixedly. The little fat man was waiting for an answer. His fists were clenched as though he was about to rush into attack. I really thought there was going to be a fight. It was all new to me and I watched it with great interest. Later I discovered that scenes like this were absolutely harmless, performed as in a comic play, for everyone's entertainment, and hardly ever came to a fight. It was all very typical—a good introduction to the way things were in prison.

The tall prisoner stood there calm and majestic. He could feel that all eyes were on him, waiting to see whether he would disgrace himself with his answer. He had to hold his own, prove that he really was 'a bird', and demonstrate exactly what kind. He squinted his eyes at his opponent with the utmost contempt, trying to cause the greatest possible offence by glancing at him over his shoulder, down at him as though examining some species of insignificant insect, and then said slowly and distinctly:

"The Oracle Bird!"

The prisoner's ingenuity was greeted by a loud burst of laughter.

"You're no Oracle Bird—you're just a scoundrel," the little fat man roared in a fury feeling that he had lost on all scores.

As soon as the argument showed signs of becoming serious, however, our heroes were immediately put in their places.

"Stop yelling!" everyone started shouting at them.

"Why didn't you have a fight instead of just yapping at each other," came a shout from the corner.

"That'll be the day—when you get a proper fight out of those two," came an answer. "We're a swaggering, cocksure lot, there's never seven of us afraid to lay into one..."

"They're a fine pair. One of them wound up in gaol over a

31

pound of bread, and the other one pinched a jug of milk from a village wife and got thrashed for it."

"Hey, you! Pack it in," shouted the invalid soldier who was stationed in the barracks with us to keep an eye on discipline and, to that end, slept on a special bunk in the corner.

"Trouble, fellows! Old Mister *Ninvalid*'s awake! How d'you do, brother *Ninvalid* Petrovich!"

"Brother, huh! I'm no brother of yours! We've never had a drink together and you call me brother," the soldier grumbled, pushing his arms into the sleeves of his greatcoat.

The men were getting ready for the roll call. Day was breaking. A dense crowd thronged in the kitchen. The prisoners, dressed in their sheepskins and their two-tone hats, were swarming around near the bread, which one of the mess hands was cutting up for them. These mess hands were elected by the whole artel—two for each kitchen. It was they who had charge of the kitchen knife which was used for cutting bread and meat—one for the whole kitchen.

The prisoners sat down at the tables and on all the benches. They kept their hats and their belted sheepskins on, and were ready to go out to work at the moment's notice. In front of some of them there were wooden bowls of kvass; they crumbled their bread into it and then spooned it up. The din and the shouting were terrible, but there were some people in the corners who talked quietly and decently.

"A very good day to you, Antonych," said one young prisoner, sitting down near a sour-faced and toothless prisoner.

"The same to you—if you mean it," said Antonych without looking up, and trying to masticate the bread with his toothless gums.

"Do you know what, Antonych? I thought you were dead! I could have sworn you were!"

"No, you go ahead and die first. I'll come along later."

I sat down beside them. To my right two sedate prisoners were talking, both apparently trying to keep up appearances in front of one another.

"It won't be them as steals from me, I can tell you," one of them was saying. "It's more likely I'll do the stealing myself."

32

"Same with me. If they try anything with me, they'll get burnt."

"That's what you think! You're a convict same as everyone else. There's no other name for us... She'll fleece you without so much as a curtsey. My money went down the drain too. She came over here the other day. But where could I get with her? I started asking Fyodor the Flogger, you know, the one who had a house at the edge of the town, he bought it from Lousy Solomon—the Jew that went and hanged himself..."

"I know. He was the vintner in our place the year before last. They used to call him 'Grishka the Gloomy Pub'. I know the one."

"No, you don't, that was another character."

"What d'you mean another? You think you know too much. I could bring you any number of witnesses..."

"You could! Who d'you think you are anyway?"

"Who am I? I've given you many a licking but I don't go bragging about it and you ask me who I am!"

"You! You gave me a licking! There isn't a man yet born who could give me a licking! And the one who tried it now lies under the sod."

"The plague on you!"

"Pox you!"

"May a Turkish sword chop your head off!"

And they were off and away.

"Hey you, stop it," everyone shouted. "You couldn't live properly outside; now eat the good prison bread and like it."

They were quietened down straightaway. Swearing at someone—'tongue lashing' was permitted. It was also a bit of entertainment for everyone. Fighting, on the other hand, was not always tolerated. So the adversaries would come to blows only in the most exceptional circumstances. A fight would be reported to the Major at once. Investigations would start. The Major would turn up in person. In other words, it meant trouble for everyone, and so fighting was not allowed. And the adversaries themselves would swear mostly for the fun of it, as a practice in eloquence. Sometimes it was self-deception, they'd start off at a terrible pitch, in a frenzy... Now they'll go for each

33

other, you'd think. Nothing of the sort. They would get to a certain point, and then part company. At first I found this really incredible. I have deliberately given a perfectly unremarkable piece of prison conversation here as an example. At first I could not imagine how anyone could quarrel for the pleasure of it, for a nice bit of fun. One shouldn't forget, however, the vanity involved. Skill in the dialectics of swearing was held in great respect, and its practitioners were all but applauded like actors.

I had already begun to notice, the night before, that people were looking askance at me.

I had already intercepted some dark looks. Some other prisoners, on the other hand, were hanging round me, thinking that I might have brought some money. They immediately started fawning on me, teaching me how to wear my new shackles. They procured for me—at a price of course—a small trunk with a padlock, in which I could keep my prison issue, together with the underwear I had brought with me. The very next day they stole my belongings and spent the proceeds on drink. One of these people later became a most faithful companion to me—though it did not prevent him from continuing to steal from me whenever an occasion arose. He would do it without the slightest compunction, almost mechanically, as though it was his duty. It was impossible to be angry with him.

They taught me, among other things, that I had to have my own tea, that it would not be a bad idea for me to find myself a kettle, and—for the time being—they acquired somebody else's for me. They also recommended a cook for me, saying that, for around thirty kopeks a month, he would cook me whatever I wanted, if I wished to eat separately and to buy my own victuals... I don't need to add that they borrowed money from me, and that each came three times to borrow from me on the first day alone.

Former noblemen were, in general, regarded unfavourably in prison.

Despite the fact that they had been deprived of all their rights and made in every way the equals of the other prisoners, these prisoners would never recognise them as their fellows.

There was no deliberate discrimination in their attitude, it was quite ingenuous and instinctive. They quite sincerely recognised us as noblemen, and yet they liked taunting us with our fall.

"You've had your say! Now leave off for a bit! Pyotr once hobnobbed with the King, now he sits here weaving string," and other similar remarks were made.

They loved to watch our sufferings—which we tried not to show. In particular, we had a hard time at work in the beginning, because we had not the strength that they had, and were not quite able to pull our weight. Nothing could be more difficult than gaining the confidence of the common people (especially people of this type) and winning their affection.

There were several former nobles in the prison. To start with there were five Poles. I'll go into their stories some other time. They were especially disliked by the prisoners, even more than the exiled Russian noblemen. The Poles (I am only talking about the political prisoners) treated the other prisoners with a sort of refined, offensive politeness. They were unsociable in the extreme, and incapable of disguising from the other prisoners the disgust they felt for them. The prisoners understood this only too well, and paid them back in kind.

I had to live in the gaol for two years before I was finally accepted by some of the prisoners. Most of them got to like me in the end though, and reckoned me to be a 'good' fellow.

There were four other Russian nobles apart from myself. One was a particularly vile and mean little creature, who was unbelievably corrupt, a spy and informer by profession. I had heard of him before I came to the gaol, and I refused to have anything to do with him from the very first. The second was the patricide I've already mentioned elsewhere in my notes. The third one was Akim Akimovich. He is sharply imprinted in my memory. He was tall and thin, feeble-minded, terribly illiterate, very fond of philosophising, and punctilious like a German. The other prisoners used to laugh at him; but some of them were afraid to have anything to do with him on account of his rigorously fault-finding and cantankerous character. From the outset he treated them as equals, quarrelled with them, and even had fights with them. He was phenomenally honest. If he considered anything unjust, he would immediately become involved, even if it was none of his business. He was also extremely naive. While exchanging insults with the other prisoners, for example, he would start lecturing them and earnestly trying to persuade them not to steal. He had been an ensign in the army in the Caucasus. We took up with each other on my very first day, and he immediately told me his story. He had started off as a cadet—also in the Caucasus—in an infantry regiment. He had slogged it out for a long time, until, finally, he was commissioned, and given the command of some fort or other. One of the local princes who had pledged allegiance to the Russian throne attacked his fort at night and set fire to it. The attack was repulsed. Akim Akimovich did not let on that he knew the identity of the malefactor. The incident was laid at the door of the hostile tribes, and one month later, in the most hospitable manner, Akim Akimovich asked the prince over to visit him. The prince came along, without suspecting anything. Akim Akimovich lined up his troops. He denounced and reproached the prince publicly, explaining that it was reprehensible to set fire to fortresses. He then proceeded to read him a very detailed exhortation on how a loyal prince should behave himself in future, and, by way of conclusion, had him shot. He immediately filed a detailed report about the matter to the authorities. For all this he was tried and sentenced to death, but the sentence was later commuted and he was sent out to Siberia for twelve years second category hard labour in the fortress. He was fully aware that he had acted wrongly; he told me that he had known as much even before he executed the prince, known—that is—that loyal princes had to be brought to trial within the processes of law. And although he knew all this, he still could not quite understand what he was convicted for.

"For goodness sake!" he remonstrated with me. "He set fire to my fortress, didn't he? Should I have just touched my cap to him!"

And yet, despite the fact that they made fun of him, the prisoners still respected him for his punctiliousness and ability.

There was not a single trade Akim Akimovich did not know. He was a carpenter, a cobbler and a shoemaker, a house painter, a gilder and a locksmith—and he had learned every one of these skills in the gaol. He was entirely self-taught: he just watched someone doing a job once and then did it himself. He also made all kinds of boxes, baskets, lanterns and toys, and sold them in the town. In this way he always had a bit of money coming in which he used immediately to buy extra underwear, to get a pillow which was slightly softer, to acquire a bed-roll for himself. He was assigned to the same barrack, as I was, and he rendered himself of considerable assistance to me during my first days in gaol.

Before leaving the gaol for work, the prisoners formed up in two rows in front of the guardhouse; the soldiers on escort duty lined up in front of them and behind them with loaded rifles. Then out came the officer of the engineers, the sergeant and several lower ranks who would be supervising the work. The sergeant counted the prisoners into groups and sent them off where they were needed.

I went along with some of the others to the engineering workshop. It was a low stone building in the middle of a large courtyard, cluttered with various materials. There was a smithy there, a metal workshop, a carpenters' workshop, a painters' workshop etc. Akim Akimovich came out here and worked in the painters' boiling the linseed oil, mixing the paints and graining the furniture in imitation of walnut.

While I was waiting to be re-shackled, I got into conversation with Akim Akimovich about my first impressions of the gaol.

"Ah, yes, they're not too fond of the gentry here," he remarked. "And especially if they're political prisoners. They'd gladly eat them alive. And small wonder. You're a different class of people for one thing. Not like them in the slightest. For another thing, all of them have either been the property of some landowner or had been soldiers. Judge for yourself, how can they like you? It's difficult to live here, I can tell you that. But it's even harder in the military penal companies in Russia. We've got people out of them here. They're as pleased as punch with this gaol, as though they'd moved into heaven out of hell. The problem is not the work. I've heard that in the first category there the people in charge are not all military, in any case they behave differently from the ones here. I've heard a prisoner is allowed to have his own small household there. I haven't been there, you know. But I've heard as much. Their heads are not shaved. They don't wear uniforms. Still, it's a jolly good thing they have this uniformed appearance here, and their heads shaved. Makes things more ordered, more pleasing to the eye, my dear sir. It doesn't go down too well with them though. You can see what riff-raff they are. One is from the soldier class, another is a Circassian, the third is some religious dissenter or other, and the fourth is your godfearing Russian peasant who has left his wife and dear family at home behind him. The fifth is a Jew, the sixth is a Gypsy, and the seventh is God knows what. And they have to learn to live together in some sort of agreement, eat out of the same bowl, and sleep on the same bed-shelves. What kind of freedom do you get here anyway? All extra tit-bits have to be eaten in secret, any spare money has to be hidden in your boots. It's just prison and prison, day in, day out. No wonder foolish notions come into your head."

All this, however, I already knew. I particularly wanted to ask about the Major. Akim Akimovich did not keep anything back, and I remember the impression I gained from him was far from pleasant.

But for two more years I was doomed to live under the command of this Major. Everything which Akim Akimovich had told me about him turned out to be absolutely true, except, of course, that the impression made by reality is always much stronger than that gained from merely hearing about it. He was a man to be feared—precisely because he held practically unlimited power over two hundred souls. Otherwise, he was just a disorderly, nasty man, and nothing more. He regarded the prisoners as his personal enemies, and that was his prime error. He actually did have some abilities, but everything, even the good things in him, came out wrong. Vicious and lacking in control, he would sometimes come tearing into the gaol, even at night, and, if he noticed a prisoner sleeping on his back or on his left side, he would punish him in the morning. "You must sleep on your right side, as I've stipulated." He was hated in the gaol, and feared like the plague. His face was red and spiteful. It was well known that he was under the thumb of his batman, Fedka. Above all, he loved his poodle, Trezorka, and when once this Trezorka fell ill, he almost went mad with grief. He was said to weep over him as though over his own child. He kicked one vet out of his house, almost coming to blows with him as was his way; then, hearing from Fedka that there was a prisoner in the gaol who was a self-taught vet and was very successful at treating animals, he at once summoned the man before him.

"Cure my Trezorka! I'll make it well worth your while!" he shouted to the prisoner.

The man was a peasant, a muzhik from Siberia. He was cunning and clever, and really good at treating animals, but very much the shrewd, calculating type of muzhik.

"There I was looking at this Trezorka," he told the other prisoners later, quite some time after his visit to the Major, when the whole affair was already long forgotten. "I was looking at this dog lying on the sofa on a white pillow, and I could see there was an infection, and if I gave it a bit of bleeding the dog would have recovered, I swear. Then I said to myself: 'But what if the cure doesn't help and the dog dies?' 'No, your honour,' I said, 'you have called me too late. If you had called me yesterday or the day before, at the same time as this, I could have cured the dog. But now I cannot, I can't cure him...'"

So Trezorka died.

I heard in great detail how this Major of ours was nearly murdered once. There was a prisoner in the gaol, who had been there for several years, and was well known for his meek behaviour. It was also noticed that he hardly ever spoke to anybody at all. For this reason he was considered a kind of holy fool. He could read and write, and during the whole of the previous year he had been constantly reading the Bible by day and by night. He would get up at midnight, when everyone had gone to sleep, light a wax church candle, climb on to the stove, open the book, and read till the morning. One day he went to the sergeant and announced that he did not want to go out to work. The Major was immediately informed; he flew into a rage and came riding over to the prison at once. The prisoner lunged at him with a brick which he had prepared beforehand, but missed. He was

39

seized, tried and punished. It all happened very quickly. He died in hospital three days later. His dying words were that he bore none any ill will, he had only wanted to partake of suffering. Not that he belonged to a dissenting religious sect, either. In the prison he was remembered with great respect.

At last I had my re-shackling done. In the meantime, several bread girls had come into the workshop. Some of them were mere children. Their mothers baked the buns and the girls brought them to sell, year after year. When they grew up they still came to the gaol, but no longer bringing any buns. That was almost always the way it went. There were also ones who were no longer young girls. The buns cost half a kopek, and almost all the prisoners bought them. I saw how one prisoner, a carpenter by trade, who still had a lot of colour in his cheeks though he was already grey-haired, started smilingly making advances to the bread girls. Just before they came, he donned a red calico neckerchief. There was one fat and badly pockmarked young woman who put her bread basket down on his workbench. Then a conversation started up between them.

"Why didn't you come there yesterday?" the prisoner asked with a smug little smile.

"I like that! I came all right, only you'd gone," the young woman retorted.

"We were called away. Otherwise I'd have certainly been there. All your lot came to see me the day before yesterday..."

"Who d'you mean?"

"Maryashka came, and Khavroshka came, and Chekunda came, and Twopenceha'penny came..."

"What on earth is he talking about?" I said, turning to Akim Akimovich. "Do things like that really?.."

"Yes, they do," he said, modestly lowering his eyes. He himself was very chaste.

These things did happen, of course, though very seldom and in the face of immense obstacles. Generally speaking there were more people going after drink than after this sort of business, despite all the physical privations of so compulsory a way of life. It was difficult to come by any women. A time and place had to be chosen, a rendezvous fixed and settled, a secluded spot found (which was very difficult), the guard talked round (which was even more difficult), and, by and large, a great deal of money, relatively speaking, spent. Nevertheless, I still witnessed a few love scenes, as it happens, later on. One time, I remember, in summer there were three of us in a shed on the bank of the Irtysh, burning wood to heat up some kiln or other. The guards escorting us were the friendly kind. A couple of 'pullets'—as the prisoners call them—turned up.

"What made you stay there so long? Over at the Zverkovs' I bet!" said the prisoner they had come to see in greeting. He had been waiting for them quite some time.

"Who, me? Why, a magpie sat longer on a post than I stayed at that place," the girl retorted cheerfully.

She was the dirtiest-looking wench in the world. This was Chekunda, and Twopenceha'penny had come along with her. That one was quite beyond the powers of description.

"And we haven't seen you for a while either," said the old beau, turning to Twopenceha'penny. "You seem to have lost weight somewhat."

"Maybe I'ave. I used to be ever so fat, and now look at me—thin as a rake."

"Going with soldiers all the time, eh?"

"Some nasty person's been putting ideas in your head. Why shouldn't I though? Oh, a girl like me would give her life to live with a soldier as his wife!"

"Never mind them, love us instead. We've got money..."

To complete the picture, you should visualise this gallant to yourself: standing there shackled, with his head shaved, in striped prisoner clothes, and under guard...

I said goodbye to Akim Akimovich and, when I was told that I could now return to the gaol, I took one of the guards and returned home. People were already returning in groups. The first ones to return were the ones who worked 'tasks'. The only way a prisoner could be made to work conscientiously was by giving him a 'task'. Sometimes the 'tasks' were enormous, but still they took only half as long as the other work, which continued right up until the drum was beaten for the midday meal. When they had finished the 'task' the prisoners were allowed to return home without any hindrance, and nobody would prevent them.

The prisoners did not eat their midday meal together, but just whoever came first. The kitchen could not have accommodated everyone at one time anyway. I tried the cabbage soup, but being unused to it, I could not eat it, and I made myself some tea. I sat down at one end of the table. I had a companion with me—also someone from the nobility.

There were prisoners coming and going. There was plenty of room though; not everyone had arrived yet. A group of about five people sat down separately at a large table over to one side. The cook poured out two bowls of soup for them and then placed a whole platter of fried fish on their table. They were having some sort of celebration and eating things of their own. They glanced at us out of the corners of their eyes. One of the Poles came in and sat down beside us.

"I may have been out all day but you can't fool me!" a tall prisoner shouted out loudly, coming into the kitchen and running his eye over everyone who was there.

He was about fifty, and lean and muscular. There was something sly and cheerful in his face. The most remarkable thing about him was his fat and drooping lower lip; it made his face extremely comical.

"Well, hello there! Won't you give us a hello? Hello my hearties from Kursk," he added, sitting down near the people who were eating their own food. "And a very good lunch to you! Move up and make room for another!"

"We aren't your 'hearties from Kursk', mate."

"Well, you must be my mess-mates from Tambov then?"

"No, we're not from Tambov either. You won't get anything from us. Go find a rich man and ask him."

"And I've got nothing but gripes and belchers in my belly today, mates. Tell me where he lives, this rich man."

"That fellow Gazin is a rich man, go over to him!"

"He's on a drinking bout today, mates, drinking away every kopek he's got."

"He's got about twenty roubles," remarked somebody else. "You can make a lot of money as a vintner, mates."

"So you won't make a place for me. Never mind then—there's still prison food."

"Go and ask for some tea. You can see how their lordships are drinking it, over there."

"What do you mean 'lordships'? There's no 'lordships' here. They're the same as us now," another prisoner said gloomily from his place in the corner. He had not uttered a single word up to this point.

"I wouldn't mind having some tea, but I don't like to ask. We've got our pride too, you know," said the prisoner with the fat lip looking at us good-humouredly.

"You're welcome to have some," I said, inviting him to join us. "Would you like some?"

"Would I like some? 'Course I would. Who wouldn't?" He came up to our table.

"Look at him! At home he ate gruel out of a boot, and here he wouldn't mind some of their lordships' drink," came the gloomy voice from the corner again.

"Why? Does nobody drink tea here then?" I asked him, but he did not deign to answer me.

"Here they come with the buns. Would you please buy me one too?"

The buns were brought in. A young prisoner was carrying an armful of them and selling them around the entire prison. The woman who baked these buns let him have every tenth one, and it was this tenth bun that he was counting on now.

"Buns for sale!" he shouted out, coming into the kitchen. "Moscow buns! Hot buns! I'd eat them myself, but they cost money! Here you are, mates! Just one left. You all had mothers, so have a heart!"

This appeal to mother's love made everyone laugh, and some people bought several buns from him.

"And I'll tell you what, mates," he said. "Gazin'll get what's coming to him with his drinking today. Yes, by Christ, what a time to hit the bottle. Old eight-eyes'll get him if he doesn't look out."

"They'll hide him. Why, has he really had a skinful?"

"And some! He's mad drunk, laying into everyone..."

"He'll get a fight then, if that's what he is asking for..."

"Who are they talking about?" I asked the Pole sitting next to me.

"About Gazin, one of the prisoners. He trades in liquor. And when he's made enough money, he drinks it all away. He's a cruel, mean character. He's quiet when he is sober, but when he's drunk it all comes out. He goes for people with a knife. Then they have to put a curb on him."

"How do they do that?"

"About ten prisoners jump on top of him and beat him senseless till he's half dead in other words. Then they lay him on the bed-shelf and cover him with sheepskin."

"But they could kill him like that, couldn't they?"

"Anybody else would be killed, but not him. He's incredibly strong—stronger than any other person in the gaol, and he's got a powerful constitution too. The next morning he gets up feeling absolutely fine."

"Can you tell me something please," I continued my questions to the Pole. "They are eating their own stuff, and I'm drinking tea. Yet they glare at me as though they envied me my tea. Why is that?"

"It's nothing to do with the tea," the Pole answered. "They resent your being a nobleman and so unlike them. A lot of them would like to pick on you. They'd love to humiliate you and insult you. You've got a lot of troubles to come in this place. It is really awfully difficult for people like us here. It's hardest on us in every respect. One must learn to be very indifferent to get used to it. You'll still have a lot of unpleasantness and be sworn at for having tea and special food, despite the fact that plenty of others here often eat their own food, and some of them always drink tea. It's all right for them to do it, but not for you."

Having said this, he got up and left the table. And a few minutes later, the truth of his words was borne out...

III

First Impressions

Just as M—tsky (the Pole who had been talking to me) left, Gazin burst into the kitchen, blind drunk.

The sight of a drunken prisoner in broad daylight, on a weekday when everyone had to be out at work, with a commander as strict as the Major—who might arrive in the gaol at any minute—with the sergeant, who never left the gaol for an instant and who was in charge of all the convicts, with the sentries and the invalid soldiers—in other words, with all the strict controls that there were around us—completely confounded every impression of prison life which had been forming in me. Indeed, I was to live a long time in that gaol before I could begin to find an explanation of all these facts, which baffled me during the first days of my sentence.

I have already mentioned that the prisoners always had work of their own, and that in prison life such work is a natural necessity; that apart from it being a necessity, a prisoner passionately loves money and values it above everything else, setting it almost on a par with freedom, and that he feels comforted just by the sound of it jingling in his pocket. If he has no money, he feels sad, depressed and fretful, and starts to lose heart; then he is ready to steal or do anything just to get some. Yet despite the fact that money was held so precious in the gaol, the fellow who was lucky enough to have some, never hung on to it for very long. It was, for one thing, very hard to keep it safe from theft or confiscation. If the Major got his clutches on it during one of his surprise searches, he confiscated it immediately. Maybe he used it to improve the prisoners' food; in any case, it was always taken to him. More usually it was stolen. Nobody could be trusted. Eventually a way of keeping the money in perfect safety was found. It was given into the keeping of an elderly prisoner, one of the Old Believers, who had come to us from the Starodubye Settlement, formerly known as Vetkovtsy...[1] I cannot resist the temptation to say something about this man, even though it means deviating from my subject.

He was a small grey-haired man of sixty or thereabouts. I was deeply impressed the moment I set eyes on him. He was so unlike the other prisoners. There was something so calm and serene in his glance that I remember the special pleasure it gave me to look at his bright clear eyes with fine crow's feet radiating outward from them. I often talked to him, and I can say I have seldom encountered such a kind and good-humoured creature in my whole life. He had been sent to us for an extremely grave crime. Converts to the Orthodox faith had started to appear among the Starodubye Old Believers. The government gave them great encouragement and did everything in the power to convert the remaining dissenters. The old man, together with other fanatics, decided to 'stand up for the faith' as he put it. So when the construction of an Orthodox church was started, they burnt it down. The old man, as one of the ringleaders, was sentenced to hard labour. He had been a well-to-do tradesman, and he left a wife and children behind him, but he went into exile with great fortitude because—in his blindness—he considered it to be a 'martyrdom for the true faith'. After living with him for sometime I could not help wondering: how could so peaceful a man, as meek as a child, be a rebel. Several times I started to discuss 'faith' with him. He stuck to his convictions, but as he argued his cause there was never any malice or hatred in his words. Still, he had razed a church and did not deny it. One would have expected him, with his convictions, to regard his act and the 'martyrdom' he was suffering for 'the faith' quite a glorious affair. But no matter how closely I observed him, or how much I studied him, I never noticed a single sign of vanity or pride in him. There were other Old Believers in our gaol, mostly from Siberia: worldly-wise people, crafty muzhiks, who were dogmatic in their reading of the Bible, and pedantically doctrinaire, though good at disputation in their own way too, and as haughty, arrogant, cunning and intolerant as it was possible to be. The old man was a completely different type of person. Perhaps more doctrinaire than any of them, he avoided arguments. A very sociable character, he was cheerful, and laughed a lot, though not in the rude, cynical way the convicts laughed, but quietly and sincerely, with a child's simple-heartedness that went especially well with his grey hairs. I may be mistaken, but it seems to me that you can come to know a person from his laughter, and if the laughter of a perfect stranger appeals to you the very first time you hear it, you can say with certainty that that person is good. The old man gained the general respect of the whole gaol, but he was not at all conceited with it. The prisoners called him 'grandad' and they never did anything to hurt him. This did give me some idea of the influence he must have had on his fellow believers. Although he endured his years of hard labour with apparent fortitude, there was a deep and incurable sadness in him, which he tried to keep hidden from everyone. I lived in the same barrack as he did. On one occasion, at about two in the morning, I woke up and heard a quiet restrained sobbing. The old man was sitting on the stove (that same stove where the prisoner who read himself silly and intended to kill the Major used to pray at nights) and saying his prayers over his handwritten book. He was crying, and I could hear him saying from time to time: "Oh Lord, do not forsake me. Oh Lord, give me strength. Oh, my little children, oh, my dear children, we will never see each other again." I can't tell you how sad I felt, and so it was to this old man that the prisoners, one by one, started to give their money for safekeeping. In prison almost everyone was a thief, but suddenly, for some reason, everyone became absolutely sure that the old man would not steal under any circumstances. They knew that he hid the money that was given to him somewhere, but in so secret a place that nobody could find it. Eventually he divulged his secret to me and to some of the Poles. There was a knot in one of the pales, which seemed to have grown together with the wood very solidly. It could be removed revealing a big hollow. That's where he hid the money, and then put the knot back, so that nobody could ever find anything.

However, I am wandering away from my story. I left it at the point where I was explaining why the prisoners never hung on to their money very long. Apart from the difficulty of keeping it safe, there is all the anguish and heartache here, in gaol; a prisoner is, by nature, a creature who craves freedom terribly, and who is, by virtue of his social position, so irresponsible and feckless that he naturally longs to 'blow the lot', have a boisterous spree and forget, for a moment at least, his heartache. It was strange to see how a prisoner would work without stint for months on end, solely for the sake of being able to blow all his earnings—down to the very last kopek—in one day, and then again start sweating his guts out for several months, until the next spree. A lot of them liked to get some new clothes—civvies of course: black trousers of some kind, Russian *poddyovkas*, half-length caftans. Cotton shirts and belts with brass buckles were also popular. They used to don their finery on holidays, and then go round all the barracks, showing themselves off to the whole world. The self-satisfaction felt by a well-dressed person was really childish, but then the prisoners were just like children, in many ways. All these good clothes, however, soon disappeared—they were either pawned or sold for next to nothing, sometimes on the very same evening. Drinking bouts unfolded themselves gradually though. They were usually timed for a holiday or the name-day of the reveller. As soon as he got up, he would light a candle before the icon and say his morning prayers; then he would dress up and order himself a meal. Beef would be bought, and fish; Siberian *pelmeni* would be made; the prisoner would stuff himself like a pig, almost always on his own, rarely inviting any of his comrades to partake. Then the drink appeared. The reveller would get as drunk as a lord, and walk around the barracks, swaying, staggering and tripping over his own feet, trying to show everyone just how drunk he was, how he was out 'on a spree', and thus win their respect. Everywhere among the people of Russia a certain sympathy for a drunk is always felt, and in gaol he even enjoys a kind of reverence. There was something aristocratic about these prison sprees. The reveller, when he became happily drunk, would almost certainly hire some music. There was a Pole, a deserter, a very nasty fellow, but he could play the violin and had it with him—his only property. He had no trade of his own; and he got a bit of money only by hiring himself out to play some jolly dances for the drinkers. His duty was to follow his drunken master from one barrack to another, never leaving his side, and scraping away at his violin for all he was worth. Often an expression of boredom and misery appeared on his face. But the cry of: "Play, damn you, you've got your money!" would keep him scraping away endlessly. A prisoner starting out on his drinking spree could feel absolutely confident that, should he get too drunk, he would be well looked after, put to bed on time and always hidden away somewhere if the authorities turned up. None of this would be done out of self-interest. For their part, the sergeant and the invalid soldiers who lived in the gaol to keep an eye on us could rest assured that the drunk would not cause any trouble. The whole barracks would look after him should he become rowdy or start any kind of disturbance. He would immediately be silenced, maybe even simply tied down with ropes. That was why the lower ranks of the prison authorities turned a blind eye to drinking. They simply did not want to take any notice of it. They knew all too well that if liquor was forbidden, the situation would be even worse. Still where did the liquor come from?

The liquor was bought right inside the gaol from the people who were known as vintners. There were several of them, and they plied their trade unceasingly and with great success, although on the whole there were few drinkers and sprees, because drinking sprees needed money, and prisoners' money was come by only with great difficulty. This trade started and was allowed to continue in a very original manner. Suppose, for example, there is a prisoner who has no trade and does not want to work (there were such people) but wants money and is moreover one of those impatient types who want to get rich fast. He has a bit of money to start off with and he decides to begin trading in liquor: a bold undertaking with a lot of risk involved. One can easily end up paying for it with one's back, and lose both the goods and the capital. But the vintner takes a chance. He does not have a lot of money to begin with, so the first time he smuggles the liquor into the gaol himself, and naturally, sells it off at the best price possible. He tries this out again on the second and third occasions and, if he is not caught by the prison authorities, he expands his business, and only at this point really sets up in trade on a grand scale. He becomes an entrepreneur, a capitalist, keeps his agents and assistants, takes fewer and fewer risks, and makes more and more profit. His assistants take the risks for him.

49

In gaol there are always a lot of people who have squandered everything in gambling or drink—miserable, ragged people who have no trade but are endowed in certain measure with boldness and resolution. The only thing they have left, their only capital is their back. This may still be of some service. So this wretch who has squandered everything decides to put this last piece of capital into circulation. He goes to the entrepreneur and gets himself hired to sneak liquor into the gaol. A wealthy vintner would have several employees. Somewhere outside the goal there is somebody—a soldier, a tradesman, or even a wench, who with the entrepreneur's money buys liquor at the pub—charging a commission, which is quite a lot, actually, in relative terms—and then hides it in some place where the prisoners come to work. He or she would almost always try the quality of the vodka himself, making up the difference by watering it down savagely. Take it or leave it, a prisoner can't be too choosy. At least his money is not completely wasted and he gets some vodka—a rather strange variety perhaps, but vodka nevertheless. The smugglers, who have already been pointed out by the vintner, come to this delivery man with ox intestines. These are thoroughly washed first, and then filled with water which preserves their original moist and elastic state and, in time, makes them suitable receptacles for vodka. Having filled these intestines with vodka, the smuggler winds them round his body where they would not show. In so doing, needless to say, he demonstrates all his cleverness and all his smuggler's cunning. His honour is at stake: he has to get round both the guards and the escort. And he does get round them. A good thief can always hoodwink the escort—very often a new recruit. He has made a study of this escort in advance, of course. The time and place where they are working are also taken into consideration. A prisoner who is a stove-maker, for example, can climb up on to one of the stoves. And who can see what he is doing up there? An escort can't be expected to climb up there after him! As he approaches the gaol, the smuggler has a coin in his hand— fifteen or twenty silver kopeks—just in case, and he waits near the gates for the corporal. Any prisoner returning to the gaol from work is searched by the corporal on guard, who examines him very thoroughly, and frisks him, and only then unlocks the gates and lets him in. The smuggler usually hopes that the corporal will have the decency not to feel him too thoroughly in certain places. Yet there are times when the sly old corporal gets into those places too, and feels the liquor there. Then there is only one way out of it. Silently and without letting the escort see, the smuggler thrusts the coin he has ready for emergencies into the corporal's hand. Sometimes this ruse enables him to pass through safely with the liquor, but there are also times when the ruse fails and he has to pay for it with his last piece of capital—his back. The matter is reported to the Major; 'the capital' is then flogged very painfully, the liquor is confiscated and the smuggler assumes the blame for everything, never betraying the entrepreneur—though we should remark at this point that this is not because he feels an aversion for informing, but simply because informing would not do him any good, as he would be flogged anyway. His only consolation would be that they would both be flogged together. He still needs the entrepreneur, even though according to custom and to their initial agreement the smuggler is not to get a single kopek from him for his flogged back. As for informing on people, it is something that flourishes in prison, generally speaking. An informer is not despised in any way; it would not occur to anyone to feel indignant towards him. Nobody cold-shoulders him or stops being friends with him, and if, in the gaol, you were to try proving to people that informing was a vile, disgusting thing, nobody would understand what you were talking about. That prisoner I mentioned earlier, the depraved and evil nobleman with whom I had severed all relations at once—was friends with the Major's batman, Fedka, and acted as his spy, while Fedka, for his part, passed on all the information he obtained from him about the prisoners to the Major. This was common knowledge in the gaol. Yet it never crossed anyone's mind to punish this scoundrel, or even to reproach him.

But I am digressing again. Needless to say, there are times when the liquor is smuggled in without a hitch: the entrepreneur takes delivery of the vodka-filled intestines, pays the agreed amount, and begins to reckon up. It turns out, according to his calculations, that the vodka has already cost him too much, and so, to reap a higher profit, he decants it once more, waters it down again, almost by half, and is then quite ready for his customer. With the very first holiday, and sometimes even on a working day, the customer appears: a prisoner who, for several months, has worked like a horse, and has put by a bit of money to be blown on the day which he has especially selected for that purpose. Long before this day dawns, the thought of it warms this poor toiler's heart, appears to him in happy daydreams at work and in his sleep at night, keeping his spirits up with its magic through the tedious everydays of prison life. This radiant day dawns at last. The money has been saved, it has not been confiscated or stolen, and he takes it to the vintner. This latter, to start with, gives him some vodka, as pure as possible—watered down only twice, that is. But what he pours out of the bottle, is at once made up with water. A glass of vodka costs him five or six times the price he would have paid at the pub. You can imagine how many such diluted glasses are needed, and how much money has to be spent, to get drunk. Yet because he has lost the habit of drinking, and because of his long abstention before this, the prisoner gets tipsy very quickly, and goes on drinking until he has spent all his money. Then he goes through all his new clothes—the vintner being also a pawnbroker. First to go are the recently acquired civvies, then the old rags, and finally the prison issue. When he has pawned everything down to the last rag, the drunk lies down to sleep, and next day, when he wakes up with the inevitably splitting head, he vainly begs the vintner for at least a mouthful to cure his hangover. Sadly, he bears this misfortune, and the same day he gets back to work, and works again for several months, without stopping for breath, remembering the happy day he went drinking, and little by little, he begins to cheer up and look forward to the next one—still a long way off but sure, in its own due course, to come round.

As for the vintner who has now made an enormous sum of money with his trading—tens of roubles—he lays in his last lot of liquor, but this time without watering it down, because this lot he has put by for himself. Enough trading. High time he celebrated for himself! The carousing begins: drinking, feasting and music. The money is plentiful: enough even to ingratiate himself with the most immediate, junior prison officers. The carousing sometimes continues for several days. The stock of liquor, needless to say, is soon exhausted. Then the reveller goes to the other vintners who are already waiting for him, and drinks until he has not a kopek left. No matter how well the prisoners try to take care of the person on a spree, he does sometimes attract the attention of the higher authorities, the Major or the guard officer. Then he is taken to the guardhouse, fleeced of any money which is found on him, and then whipped, by way of conclusion. When he has shaken that off, he comes back into the gaol, and in a couple of days starts up his vintner's trade again. Some of the revellers—the rich variety needless to say—start dreaming of the fair sex. Sometimes, instead of working they slip away from the fortress into the suburbs, accompanied by a guard who has been bribed. Out there, in some secluded little house or other at the very edge of the town, they feast and make merry and then really big sums of money are spent. Even a prisoner will not be rejected if he has ready money; as for the guard, he is picked out beforehand, he must be someone experienced in such clandestine arrangement. Guards of this sort are themselves future candidates for gaol, as a rule. Anything can be done for money though, and such excursions almost always remain secret. It should be added, however, that they happen rather rarely; they take a lot of money, and lovers of the fair sex resort to other means, ones which are completely safe.

During the very first days of my life in gaol, I felt an especial curiosity about one young prisoner, an extremely pretty young boy. His name was Sirotkin. He was in many respects a rather mysterious creature. The first thing that struck me about him was his beautiful face. He was no more than twenty-three years old. He was one of the special category, with no fixed sentence, which meant that he was listed among the most important military criminals. Meek and quiet, he spoke very little, and laughed only rarely. His eyes were blue, his features regular, his face clean and smooth, and his hair very fair. Even his half-shaven head hardly spoiled him, he was such a pretty lad. He had no trade, but he managed to get hold of some money—not very much, but rather frequently all the same. He was distinctly lazy and slovenly. Occasionally somebody would dress him up, perhaps even in a red shirt, and then Sirotkin seemed very happy with his new attire, and would go parading himself all around the barracks. He did not drink, he did not play cards, he hardly ever argued with anyone. Usually, he walked up and down behind the barracks—calmly and pensively, with his hands in his pockets. What could he have been thinking about? It was almost impossible to imagine. Sometimes you might call out to him, out of curiosity, ask him some question about something. And he would answer immediately, quite respectfully too, not in the usual prisoner's manner, but always briefly and indistinctly, looking at you all the time, like a ten-year-old child. If he did come by some money, he spent it not on something he needed, like new boots, or taking his coat to be darned; instead, he bought himself a bun or a honey cake and ate it up—exactly as though he was seven years old. "Oh, what shall we do with you, Sirotkin!" the prisoners used to say to him. "A real waif and stray, you are." During time off work he went wandering around the other barracks—almost everyone was busy with something, and he alone had nothing to do. If the men said something to him, almost always something mocking (he and his friends were very often mocked at) he turned round, without saying a word, and went to another barrack; and sometimes, if they laughed at him too cruelly he blushed. I often wondered what this mild, simple-hearted creature could have done to end up in gaol. Once I was lying ill in the prisoners' ward in the hospital. Sirotkin was ill too, and had the bed next to mine. One evening we fell into conversation. Without realising it, he grew quite carried away, and in passing he told me how he was recruited, how his mother, bidding him farewell, had wept over him, and what misery it was to be a soldier. He added that he could not bear the life of a recruit; everyone was so bad-tempered there, so strict, and the commanders were almost always displeased with him...

"So how did it all end?" I asked him. "How on earth did you wind up here? And in the special category, of all things. Ah Sirotkin, you poor chap!"

"Well, you see, Alexander Petrovich, sir, I was in the battalion only one year, I came here for killing Grigory Petrovich, my company commander."

"That's what I heard, Sirotkin, but I simply can't believe it. Now how could you have killed anyone?"

"It just happened, Alexander Petrovich. It was just too hard for me there..."

"But how do the other recruits manage? It's hard at the beginning, of course, but they get used to it, and make fine soldiers. Your mother must have spoilt you; she probably fed you on honey cakes and milk till you were eighteen."

"Oh, my mother did love me very much, it's true. When I went away she took to her bed, and I hear she never got up again... I felt more wretched than ever in the recruits. The commander took a dislike to me, and was always punishing me for everything, but what for? I did everything I was told, and was always on best behaviour. I didn't drink, I didn't steal—it's a bad thing you know, Alexander Petrovich, sir, if a person starts stealing. Everyone around was so hard-hearted. There was nowhere to have a good cry. I used to go around the corner sometimes, to have a weep there. Anyway, I was standing on guard. Night had fallen. They had put me on duty in the guardhouse near the gun room. There was quite a wind up. It was autumn, and so dark, you couldn't see a thing. And I felt so miserable, so miserable, I can't tell you. I laid the musket up against my leg, unfixed the bayonet and laid it down beside me. I pulled off my right boot, pointed the muzzle against my chest, leaned up hard against it, and pulled the trigger with my big toe. And guess what! It misfired. I examined the musket, cleaned out the priming, added some more powder, sharpened up the flint, and aimed it at my chest again. And do you know what? The gunpowder blazed up, but still there was no shot. What's going on here, I thought. I put my boot back on, refixed the bayonet, and started walking up and down. And that's when I made up my mind: I'd go to hell itself only to get out of the recruits. Half an hour later, our commander came riding by, on sentry inspection. And he rode straight up to me. 'What kind of sentry duty do you call this?' I took my musket in the advance position and plunged the bayonet into him right up to the muzzle. They gave me four thousand lashes for that, and then I got sent out here, to the special category..."

He was not lying. And really, what else could they have put him into the special category for? Ordinary criminals are punished far more lightly. Out of all his fellows, Sirotkin was the only handsome man. As for the others in the same lot, about fifteen of them in all, they were a strange sight: only two or three of the faces were passable, the rest were so lop-eared and ugly and slovenly; some even had grey hair. If I get the chance later, I shall go into greater detail about the whole of this bunch. Sirotkin was often with Gazin, the man in connection with whom I began this chapter, mentioning how he came bursting drunkenly into the kitchen and how this had upset my early conception of prison life.

This Gazin was a terrible creature. He produced a frightening and harrowing effect on everyone. I always thought that nothing could be fiercer or more monstrous than he was. In Tobolsk I had seen the bandit Kamenev, notorious for his evil deeds, and later I saw Sokolov, an army deserter and terrible murderer, awaiting trial, but neither of them produced such a revolting reaction in me as Gazin. There were times when I thought I was looking at an enormous, gigantic spider as big as a man standing in front of me. He was a Tatar, terribly strong—stronger than anybody in the gaol—taller than average, built like Hercules, but with an ugly and disproportionately large head. He walked with a stoop, glowering at everyone around him. There were strange rumours going around the gaol about him. It was known that he had come from the military, but the word was going about among the prisoners—I do not know if it was true or not—that he was a fugitive from the Nerchinsk mines,[2] that he had been sentenced to hard labour in Siberia many times, escaped many times, changed his name, and finally ended up in our gaol, in the special category. They also said that he used to love slitting the throats of young children, just for the fun of it. He would take the child off to some suitable place. There he would first frighten and torment the child, and when he had relished to the full the sight of his poor little victim trembling before him he would slit his throat quietly, slowly, with pleasure. Maybe all this had been invented, and stemmed from the generally unpleasant impression which the person of Gazin produced in everyone, but all these inventions seemed somehow to suit him. Here in the gaol, however, he behaved quite well, in the normal run of things, when he was not drunk. He was always very quiet, never argued with anyone and avoided quarrelling, but more as if out of contempt for the others, as if he considered himself above the rest. He spoke very little, and he was rather deliberately antisocial. His movements were all slow, calm and confident. That he was not at all stupid, and in fact extremely cunning, was clear from his eyes. Yet in his face and smile there was always something superciliously mocking and cruel. He traded in liquor, and he was one of the most successful vintners in the gaol. Once or twice a year he got drunk himself. It was then that the brutality of his nature revealed itself to the full. He got drunk slowly, at first just going for people with jeering, terribly spiteful and calculated comments that seemed to have been prepared in advance. Finally, completely sozzled, he flew into a terrible rage, grabbed hold of a knife and started lunging at people. The prisoners, who knew how fantastically strong he was, scattered out of the way and hid. He lunged at anybody and everybody. A way of coping with him was soon found though. About ten men out of his barrack would jump on him suddenly and all together, and start beating him up. You could not imagine anything more cruel than this beating: they beat him in the chest, and under the heart, in the gut and in the pit of his stomach; they beat him hard for a long time, and only stopped when all his senses had left him and he seemed like a dead man. They would not have dared beat anyone else like that; that kind of beating is meant to kill—and it would have killed anyone other than Gazin. After the beating, completely unconscious, he was wrapped in a sheepskin and carried over to his bed-shelf. "He'll get over it." And true enough, the next morning he would wake feeling almost well, and go out to work, silently and sullenly. So on every occasion when Gazin got drunk, everyone in the gaol was aware that the day would inevitably end with a thrashing for him. He knew it himself, but still got drunk. It went on like that for several years; and then everyone noticed that Gazin had started to surrender. He began complaining of various aches, he grew perceptibly more sickly. He went more and more often to the hospital. "He's giving up," the prisoners used to say among themselves.

He came into the kitchen in the company of that nasty little Pole with the violin—the one the drinking parties used to hire to round off their festivities—and stopped in the middle of the kitchen, silently and carefully examining everyone who was there. Everyone fell silent. In the end, noticing my friend and me he looked at us spitefully and mockingly, smiled complacently as though he had worked something out for himself, and came towards our table, reeling violently.

"Might I be permitted to ask you," he started off—he spoke Russian— "what kind of income you have, that you should sit here drinking tea like this?"

I exchanged glances with my companion, knowing that it was best to keep silent and not to answer him. At the first sign of opposition he would have flown into a rage.

"So you've got some money, have you?" he went on interrogating us. "Heaps of money, eh? Is that what you've come to prison for—to drink tea here? Eh? Tea drinking you've come for, is it! Well come on, tell us, blast you..."

Then, seeing that we had decided to keep silent and take no notice of him, he turned red and started shaking with rage. In the corner next to him there was a big tray where they put out all the sliced bread for the prisoners' midday and evening meals. It was so big that it could hold bread for half the population of the prison. At this time it was standing empty. He grabbed it with both hands and swung it above our heads. Just a second more, and he would have smashed our skulls with it. Murder, or attempted murder, meant trouble for the entire population of the gaol—there would be investigations and searches, discipline would be tightened up, and that was why the prisoners tried to avoid going to such extremes. Despite all this, however, everybody present held their breath at this moment, waiting to see what would happen. No one spoke up in our defence! No one shouted at Gazin to stop him. So strong was their hatred for us! They seemed to be enjoying the dangerous situation we were in. But we came through safely. He was on the verge of bringing this enormous tray down on our heads, when a voice from the entrance shouted:

"Gazin! The liquor's been stolen!"

He dropped the bread tray with a crash, and rushed out of the kitchen like a madman.

"Divine intervention that was," the prisoners said between themselves. And they repeated these words many times afterwards.

I was never able to find out whether the news about the stealing of the liquor was true, or made up just in time, for our salvation.

In the evening, just before the barracks were locked up, when it was already dark, I went walking along the pales, and a heavy sadness descended on my heart. I never, never experienced such misery as this again during all my time in gaol. The first day of imprisonment is hard to bear, wherever you are: in gaol, in the political prison or penal colony. I remember that there was one thought that tormented me above all others, a thought that was to dog me through my entire time in prison, one which seemed largely insoluble to me, and remains insoluble to this day—the inequality of punishments for identical crimes. I know that crimes cannot be compared, of course, even roughly. For example: two people both kill someone; all the circumstances surrounding each case are considered; almost the same punishment is given for each. Yet look at the difference between the two crimes. The first man, let us say, murdered somebody just like that, without a second thought, for nothing, for an onion. He went out on the road and murdered a passer-by, who turned out to have nothing on him but an onion. "What's this then, dad? You sent me out for plunder. I've murdered a peasant, and all I found on him was an onion." "Listen, idiot! One onion—that's a kopek for you! One hundred souls—one hundred onions—and you've already got a rouble!" (This was part of the prison folklore.) The other man, however, killed while defending the honour of his bride, or his sister or daughter, from a lecherous tyrant. One, harassed by a whole army of police agents, killed someone while he was living the life of a tramp, defending his freedom and his life, quite probably dying from hunger too; another slaughtered little children for the pleasure of it, just to feel the warmth of their blood on his hands, to relish their fear, their last dove-like tremor under the blade. So what happens? Both are sent to the same hard-labour prison. There are variations in the length of sentence, of course. Even so, these variations are comparatively few, whereas there is a countless number within one and the same type of crime. Each character represents a different variation. But let's assume that this difference cannot be levelled out, cannot be balanced—it is one of those insoluble problems, like squaring the circle. Let's assume that. But even if the imbalance did not exist, let's look at another difference: the difference in the effect of the punishments... On the one hand we have a man who, in gaol, pines and melts away like a candle; then on the other hand we have a man who, before coming to gaol, did not even know that there was such a jolly life anywhere on earth, or such a pleasant society of braves. Yes, there are people of that kind coming to the gaol too. Or again, for example, you have an educated person with a developed consciousness—a person of feeling. The torment of his aching heart will kill him more surely than any punishment. He will sentence himself more ruthlessly, more cruelly than the most merciless of judges. Then next to him is someone else, who through his whole prison term will not even think twice of the murder he committed. He even considers himself in the right. There are also people of the type who commit crimes deliberately, just to be given hard labour and thus to escape their free life, which is even harder. Out in the free world, such a person lived in the most humiliating conditions, he never had enough to eat and worked for his employer from dawn till dusk—while in prison the work is much easier than at home, there is enough bread to go round—and bread of a quality he has never even seen before; on holidays there is beef, and there is charity, and a chance to earn a kopek or two. And the company? The men are mostly the cunning, crafty type who know everything there is to know; and this fellow regards his companions with a kind of deferential amazement. It is the first time he has met such people; he reckons them to be the best society that can be found anywhere on earth. So can both of them really be said to be equally sensitive to their punishment? However, why bother with insoluble questions? They are beating the drum; it's time to go into the barracks.

IV

First Impressions

The final roll call for the day began. After this roll call, the barracks were locked, each with its own special lock, and the prisoners were left locked in until dawn.

The roll was called by the sergeant and two soldiers. For this the prisoners were lined up in the courtyard sometimes, and waited for the officer on guard to come. More often than not, however, the whole ceremony was less formal, and took place inside the barracks. And that is how it was on this occasion. The men calling the roll got mixed up in the count, they went away and came back again. Finally the poor guards got the count right and locked the barrack. As many as thirty prisoners were housed inside it, packed rather tightly together on the bed-shelves. It was still too early to sleep. Obviously everyone had to find something to occupy himself with.

Only the invalid soldier, whom I have already mentioned, was now left to represent the authorities in the barrack. There was also, in each barrack, a head prisoner, personally appointed by the Major himself, for good behaviour, of course. It frequently turned out that these head prisoners were caught committing serious misdemeanours themselves. Then they would be whipped, demoted to ordinary prisoners again, and replaced by someone else. It turned out that in our barrack the head prisoner was Akim Akimovich, and to my surprise, he often shouted at the other prisoners. The prisoners' usual response to this was mockery. The invalid soldier was cleverer; he did not meddle in anything, and if he did start nagging, it was just for form's sake, a duty done. He would sit there on his bench in silence, stitching boots. The prisoners took hardly any notice of him at all.

61

There was one observation I made on this very first day of my life in gaol, which subsequent experience convinced me to have been absolutely correct: namely, that escorts, guards and in general everyone who is associated, however remotely, with prison life, all have an exaggerated conception of what prisoners are like. They seem to be on the alert all the time, fearfully expecting a prisoner to suddenly go for one of them with a knife. Even more remarkable than this, is that the prisoners themselves are aware that they are feared, and this gives them Dutch courage. The best person to be in charge of prisoners is someone who is not afraid of them. And for all their swaggering, the prisoners themselves like it much better when they are trusted, and they can even be won over that way. During my time in gaol, it sometimes happened—though very rarely—that one of the people in charge would come into the gaol without an escort. You should have seen how happily amazed the prisoners were by this. A fearless visitor like that always inspired their respect, and if anything nasty was really likely to happen, it would not be in front of him. The fear which prisoners inspire is universal; it happens wherever there are prisoners, and I actually have no idea what causes it. There are some grounds for it, of course; there is a prisoner's appearance for one thing, which marks him out as a bandit, for another thing, anyone approaching the prison feels that nobody in this entire crowd has come here voluntarily, and that no matter what measures are taken a living being cannot be turned into a living corpse—he will retain his feelings, his craving for vengeance and for life, and his passions and the need to satisfy them. Still, I am absolutely sure that there is no reason to be afraid of prisoners. One human being does not go for another with a knife so easily or so fast. To put it briefly: though there is a possibility of something dangerous happening, and indeed it sometimes does happen, yet, from the rarity of such occurrences, one can conclude that the risk is negligible. I am only speaking about the prisoners who are serving a term; many of them are actually glad to have finally arrived in gaol (that's how good a new life seems!), and they are disposed, as a result, to lead a quiet and peaceful existence; besides, the really troublesome kind are prevented from doing too much bullying by their mates. Every convict, however daring and brave, is afraid of everything in the prison. Now a prisoner awaiting sentence is a different matter. He really is capable of going for someone at the drop of a hat—not for any reason, but just because he is due to be punished the next day, and if a new case starts at this point, then his punishment will be put off. In an instance like this, there is a reason and a purpose for the attack. It is 'to change one's fate'—at any cost and as soon as possible. I even know of one strange psychological case of this kind.

In the military category in our gaol, there was one prisoner, a former soldier, who had not been stripped of his rights and by court verdict committed to gaol for about two years. He was a terrible braggart, and unbelievably cowardly. Generally speaking, boastfulness and cowardice are very rarely found among Russian soldiers. They are kept too busy to boast, even if they wanted to. Yet when someone is a braggart, he is almost invariably an idler and coward as well. Dutov (as this particular prisoner was called) eventually finished his short sentence and was posted back to serve in his regular battalion. But as all men of this type who are sent to gaol to be reformed become only worse idlers than ever, it generally happens that after two or three weeks at large, they come up before the courts again, and then reappear in the gaol, though this time not just for two or three years, but as one of the 'lifers', sent down for fifteen or twenty years. That is precisely what happened with Dutov. Three weeks after his release, he picked a lock and stole something, and on top of that behaved in an insulting and disorderly manner. He was tried and sentenced to a very harsh punishment. Scared out of his wits by the impending punishment, as only the most abject coward could be, the night before he was to run the gauntlet, Dutov went for the officer of the guard with a knife as he was entering the prisoners' room. Dutov knew very well that he would bring upon himself a much harsher immediate punishment and a longer period of hard labour. But he was thinking only of postponing the dread moment when he would be punished, even for just a few days, or even just for a few hours. He was such a coward that he did not even wound the

63

officer he had gone for with the knife. He only did it for appearances' sake to create a new crime for which they would have to bring him back to trial.

The moment before the punishment is, obviously, terrible for the prisoner under sentence, and I chanced, over the years, to see plenty of people in this situation awaiting their fatal day. I usually came across them in hospital, in the prisoners' wards, while I was confined there—as happened to me rather often. It is a well-known fact to prisoners all over Russia that the people who behave most compassionately to them are doctors. They do not shrink from prisoners as almost all outsiders do involuntarily—all except the common people, perhaps. The common people never reproach a prisoner for his crime—however awful it may be—but forgive him everything in the light of the punishment he has suffered and because of his general misfortune. Hardly surprisingly, the common people all over Russia refer to crime as 'misfortune' and to criminals as 'unfortunates'. There is a deep significance in this definition: all the more important because it is made instinctively and intuitively. To return to the doctors—they are, in many cases, a real haven for the prisoners, especially for those awaiting sentence, who are kept in worse conditions than those whose fates have been decided. A prisoner awaiting sentence, after he has worked out when the dread day is likely to be, will often, wishing to put off the awful moment if only for some time, get himself admitted into hospital. When he is discharged, however, knowing almost certainly that the fatal day is tomorrow, he is almost always in a terrible state of nervous agitation. There are those who try to hide their feelings out of pride, but their clumsy affectation of bravado does not deceive their comrades. Everybody understands what he feels, and keeps quiet out of humaneness. There was one prisoner I knew, a young man, a murderer who had been in the army, who was sentenced to the full number of strokes.[3] He got so scared that the night before the punishment he decided to drink a mug of liquor infused with snuff. By the way, any prisoner is sure to have some liquor on hand the night before... It is brought into the gaol a long time in advance, procured for big sums of money, and the man awaiting punishment is prepared to deny himself the barest necessities for half a year beforehand to save up the price of a bottle to drink a quarter of an hour before the punishment. There is a widespread belief among prisoners that a person who is drunk feels less pain from the whip or the sticks. But I am wandering away from my point. The poor lad, having drunk his mug of liquor, was taken seriously ill at once; he started vomitting blood, and he was taken to hospital almost unconscious. The vomitting upset his chest so badly that within a few days he had developed symptoms of consumption, which he died from six months later. The doctors who treated him for consumption remained unaware of how it had originated.

On the subject of this frequent faintheartedness of prisoners before punishment, I should add that there were, on the other hand, some who amazed an observer with their unbelievable fearlessness. I can remember a few examples of such courage, which reached the point of insensitivity; and such examples were not so rare. I remember particularly well my encounter with a most frightful criminal. One day in summer a rumour spread through the prisoners' wards that a famous bandit, an army deserter called Orlov, was to be punished that evening, and—after the punishment—to be brought into the wards. The patients, while awaiting Orlov, all maintained that he would be punished with the utmost ruthlessness. Everyone was in a state of agitation, and—to tell the truth—I also waited with extreme curiosity for the appearance of the famous bandit. I had heard a lot about him. He was a cut-throat second to none: a man of extraordinary will-power and proudly conscious of his own strength, he had murdered old people and children in cold blood. He confessed to many murders and was condemned to be punished with sticks as he ran the gauntlet between the two rows of guards. Evening had already fallen when he was brought into the hospital. It was dark in the ward, and the candles had been lit. Orlov was practically senseless, horribly pale, with thick, dishevelled jet black hair. His back was swollen and was a bloody, blue colour. The prisoners nursed him the whole night through, giving him fresh water, turning him from side to side, giving him medicine, as if they were tending some close relative, or benefactor. The very next day, he completely recovered his senses and was able to walk the length of the ward twice. I was astounded. He had come to the hospital so utterly weak and exhausted after taking a good half of the strokes assigned to him at one go. The doctor called a halt to the punishment only when he saw that continuation threatened imminent death. Orlov, moreover, was short, slightly built, and emaciated after being kept a long time awaiting his sentence. No one, I think, who has ever met prisoners awaiting sentence will easily forget their thin, emaciated, pale faces, and their feverish expressions. Despite this, Orlov was making a speedy recovery. Apparently, his natural faculties were greatly aided by the energy of the spirit within— and indeed this man was someone out of the ordinary. From curiosity, I made myself more closely acquainted with him and was able to study him over the course of a whole week. I can say without hesitation that I have never, in my whole life, met a man with a stronger character and iron will. I had already come across another celebrity from the same mould, one of the bandit chieftains, while I was in Tobolsk. That man was really a wild animal, and when you met him, even before you knew his name, you instinctively felt that it was some terrible beast standing there next to you. What horrified me in him, was his moral and spiritual stultification. The flesh had triumphed so completely over all the qualities of heart and mind, that it was apparent from the very first glance at his face that there remained in him only a wild thirst for bodily pleasures, for voluptuousness, for the satisfaction of the most carnal desires. And I am certain that this Korenev (as the bandit was called) despite being capable of murdering someone without batting an eyelid, would have lost all his confidence and even started to tremble with fear before punishment. Orlov was just the opposite. In him a complete victory of spirit over flesh was truly displayed. It was evident that he could control himself to the limit, that he despised all punishments and tortures, and was afraid of nothing on earth. In him there was only boundless energy, a thirst for action, for revenge, and a desire to attain the goal he had chosen. Among other things, I was struck by his extraordinary superciliousness. He viewed everything with a kind of immense disdain, not as though he were trying to put himself up on stilts, but just like that—quite naturally. I do not think there was anyone in the world whom he would have accepted as an authority. He viewed everything with unexpected calm, as though there was nothing in the world that could surprise him. And though he was well aware that the other prisoners looked up to him, he never put on airs in front of them—and this despite the fact that vanity and arrogance are the rule among prisoners, almost without exception. He was anything but stupid, and he was open, in some strange ways, though not at all garrulous. When I asked him he answered quite frankly that he was waiting to be well again, so he could take the rest of his punishment as quickly as possible, and that at first he had been afraid that he would not survive it. "This time though," he added with a wink, "everything is clear. I'll get through the sticks; they'll send me off immediately in a convoy to Nerchinsk; and I'll skip off on the way there. Yes, I swear I will! I'm just waiting for my back to heal—the sooner the better." All the five days he was there he waited impatiently for his discharge from the hospital. There were times when he was cheerful and rather given to laughter while he was waiting. I made several attempts to talk him into telling me of his exploits. A frown would pass across his face during these interrogations of mine, but he would always answer honestly. When at last he realised that I was trying to reach into his conscience and awaken some glimmer of repentance in him, he looked at me in the most supercilious and disdainful way imaginable, as though suddenly, in his eyes, I had turned into some silly little boy with whom it is impossible to discuss things sensibly, as one can with grown-ups; there was even something rather like pity in his expression. The next minute he burst out laughing at me, and his laughter was of the heartiest kind, without a hint of sarcasm. I feel sure that when he was alone, and going over my words again in his mind, he most likely burst out laughing to himself. Finally, he was discharged from hospital, though his back was not completely healed. I was discharged at the same time, so we happened to return from the hospital together—I to the gaol and he to the guardhouse nearby, where he had been kept under custody earlier. As we parted he shook hands with me—a sign, on his side, of a deep pledge of trust. He did it, I think, because he felt very pleased with himself and with the moment. Actually, he could not but despise me, considering me a very submissive creature: weak, pitiful, and inferior to himself in all respects. The next day he was taken through the remaining half of his punishment...

As soon as our barrack was locked, it immediately took on a different air—there was now something really homely and domestic about it. It was only then that I saw the prisoners, my comrades, as they were at home. In the daytime, the sergeants, the sentries, and any of the people in charge, were likely to enter the gaol at any moment, so all the inmates behaved rather differently and nervously, as though they were constantly expecting something to happen. As soon as the barrack was locked though, they all immediately settled down into their places, each in his own special spot, and almost everyone embarked upon some handicraft. The barrack was suddenly brightly lit. Each prisoner had a candle and candlestick—usually a wooden one—of his own. Here, one of them sat down to stitching boots; there, another to sewing clothes. And the mephitic quality of the air grew stronger with every hour. In the corner a bunch of loafers spread out their rug and squatted down for a game of cards. In almost every barrack there was a prisoner who owned a small threadbare rug, a candle and a pack of incredibly greasy cards. All this together was known as a *maidan*. The owner took a payment from each player: all told about fifteen kopeks for the night. That was his trade. The gamblers would usually play 'Three Leaves', 'Hill' and so on. They were all played for money. Each player would put a pile of copper coins—the entire contents of his pocket—down in front of him, and he would only get up from his squatting position when he had gambled away everything he had, or won everything from his friends. The game would go on late into the night and sometimes last until dawn, until the very moment when the barrack was unlocked. In our quarters, as in all the other barracks in the gaol, we always had our share of beggars and *baigushi*, impoverished nomads, who had either gambled or drunk everything they had away, or were just plain beggars by nature. I call them beggars *by nature*, and stress that that is just what they were. It is true that, wherever you go among our people, there will always be some odd characters who, whatever the circumstances, whatever the conditions, even though they are not at all lazy, are nevertheless destined to be beggars their whole life through. They are always solitary men, always scruffy, always have a downtrodden, woebegone look, and they are always being pushed and ordered around by someone else—usually by one of the drinkers or by someone who has suddenly become rich and powerful. Any new start or new initiative they take as a misfortune, a sore trial. It is as though they have been born already conditioned never to start anything themselves, but only serve others, without any will of their own, dancing to a tune called by somebody else: their destiny being only to fulfil the will of others. And what is more—no changes of circumstances, no sudden windfalls, can ever make them any richer. They are always beggars. Such personalities are not, I have noticed, found only among the common people, but among people belonging to all societies, classes, parties and associations. And so in every barrack, in every gaol, as soon as a *maidan* was formed, one of these characters would immediately offer his services. In fact, no *maidan* could exist without such a servant. The players usually hired him jointly for about five silver kopeks, and his main task was to stand on guard through the whole night. In most cases that meant standing in the unheated anteroom, freezing for six or seven hours in the darkness and cold, sometimes thirty degrees below zero, on the alert for any sound, tinkling or footstep outside. The Major or the sentries sometimes came to the gaol late at night, sneaking in quietly and catching red-handed both the gamblers and the craftsmen, whose additional candles had already been spotted from outside. When the lock started to rattle on the door it was already too late to hide, to put out the candles and to lie down on the bed-shelf. But since the watchman hired by the *maidan* caught it very badly from the players for failing in his duty, the instances of such failures were very few and far between. Five kopeks is a pitifully small amount, of course—even in gaol. And I was always surprised by the hardness and heartlessness of the employers, in this and in all other cases.

"You've taken the money haven't you? Now do as you're told!" This was a line of reasoning that brooked no objections. For this miserable pittance the employers demanded their due—even more than their due if possible, and still considered they were doing the employee a great favour. A reveller, when he was drunk and throwing his money about, would always short-pay the toady he employed; this was something I noticed not only in prison, and not only among gamblers.

I have already mentioned that all the inmates of our barrack got down to some craft or other as soon as we were locked up; apart from the gamblers, there were not more than five men among us who were completely idle—and these went to sleep immediately. My place on the bed-shelf happened to be right up near the door. On the opposite side of the bed-shelf, head to head with me, was the place of Akim Akimovich. He worked till ten or eleven, cutting out and glueing together a bright-coloured Chinese lantern, commissioned for a fair amount of money by some customer of his in town. He made these lanterns very skilfully, working very methodically and without pause. When he finished his work, he tidied everything up, laid out his trim little mattress, said his prayers and—in a very decorous manner—settled himself for sleep. He seemed to have developed this preoccupation with decorum and orderliness to the finest degree of pedantry; he clearly believed himself to be extremely clever, as most dull-witted and narrow-minded people usually do. I took a dislike to him from the very start, though I remember that on my first day, I pondered over him a great deal and was, more than anything, amazed that a person such as he, instead of prospering in life, should have landed in gaol. I shall return to him again on many later occasions.

But let me give a brief description of the inmates of our barrack. I was to live in it for many years, and these people were to be my mates and comrades. Naturally enough, I studied them with an avid curiosity. To my left the bed-shelf accommodated a group of Caucasian mountain dwellers who were serving different terms, mainly for robbery. There were two Lezgins, one Chechen, and three Daghestan Tatars. The Chechen was a gloomy, morose character; he hardly spoke to anyone, and constantly looked around with hatred, glowering at everyone with a malevolently mocking smile. Of the Lezgins, one was already an old man; he had a long thin, aquiline nose, and looked like a real bandit... The second one, however, Nurra by name, produced the nicest impression on me from the very first. He was not yet old, rather short but built like a Hercules, absolutely blond, with light blue eyes and an upturned nose which made him look like a Finnish woman. He had bandy legs from being constantly in the saddle. His body was a mass of scars, bayonet cuts and bullet wounds. He belonged to one of the Caucasian tribes which had pledged allegiance to the Russian throne, but was forever sneaking off to join forces with the hostile mountain tribes, and carry out raids on the Russians. Everybody in the gaol loved him. He was always cheerful, friendly to everyone, he worked without complaining, was calm and good-natured, though he was often outraged by the squalor and nastiness of prison life, and was infuriated by thieving, cheating, drunkenness, or—in general—by anything dishonest. He never started any quarrels over this, however—he just turned away indignantly. For his part he never stole a single thing, nor did any wrong during his whole term in prison. He was extremely pious. He performed his prayers very devoutly, and during the fast periods before the Moslem festivals, he fasted fanatically, standing whole nights in prayer. He was loved by everybody, and everybody believed in his honesty. "Nurra's a lion," the prisoners would say, and the name 'lion' stuck. He was absolutely convinced that, at the end of his term, he would be packed off home, back to the Caucasus, and this hope kept him alive. If he had been suddenly robbed of this hope, I believe he would have died. He made a striking impression on me on my very first day. I could not help noticing this kind, sympathetic face among the malicious, gloomy and mocking faces of the others. Within half an hour of my arrival, he had patted me on the shoulder as he passed by me, smiling kindly right into my eyes. At first I was unable to make out what it meant. He spoke very bad Russian. Not long afterwards he approached me again, still smiling, and slapped me on the shoulder in the most friendly way imaginable. Then he did it again and again. This continued for three days. It was intended to show, as I rightly guessed and later found out for sure, that he was sorry for me, that he felt how hard it must be for me to get used to life in the gaol, and that he wanted to show me his friendship, to cheer me up, to assure me of his protection. Kind, simple-hearted Nurra!

There were three Daghestan Tatars—three brothers. Two were already advanced in years; the third, Alei, was no more than twenty-two, and looked even younger. His place on the bed-shelf was alongside mine. His face—handsome, open and intelligent, good-humoured and innocent—instantly won my heart, and I was very glad that fate had sent him and no one else to be my neighbour. His entire soul was there to see in this handsome, even beautiful face. His smile was so trusting, so childlike and innocent, his big black eyes were so soft and tender, that I always experienced a particular pleasure, even relief from my own grief and sadness when I looked at him. I say this without any exaggeration. Once, when he was still living at home, one of his elder brothers (he had five in all, the other two had been sent into some factory prison) told him to take his sabre, mount his horse, and come with him on some expedition or other. So great is the respect for one's elders among the mountain dwellers, that the boy not only did not dare to ask where they were going, the thought did not even occur to him. And for their part, his brothers did not see any need to tell him. The truth was that they were off on a raid to hold up a rich Armenian merchant on the highway and to rob him. And that is just what they did: they slaughtered the escort, murdered the Armenian and plundered his goods. The crime was disclosed; all six of them were arrested, tried, convicted, punished and sent to Siberia for hard labour. The only mercy the jury showed to Alei was to give him a shorter term. He was exiled for four years. Alei was adored by his brothers, with a love which was more paternal than fraternal. He was a consolation to them in their exile, and though generally they were gloomy and morose, they always smiled looking at him, and when they talked to him— which they seldom did, as though they still considered him too young to discuss anything serious with—their stern faces brightened up, and I guessed that they were talking to him of something lighthearted and almost childishly funny, because they always glanced at each other and laughed good-naturedly after hearing his answer. He himself hardly even dared to speak to them first—that's how deferential he was. It was difficult to imagine how this boy could preserve such gentleness of spirit through all his time in prison, to remain so uncompromisingly honest, sincere and nice, and not become hardened or corrupted. He had a strong and stalwart personality, however, despite his apparent gentleness. I was to get to know him very well. He was as pure as an innocent girl, and any nasty, cynical, dirty, unjust or violent deed in the gaol would light a flame of indignation in his beautiful eyes, making them even more beautiful. He kept away from arguments and abuse, yet he was not one of those people who would let anyone insult him with impunity, and he was well able to stand up for himself. He had no quarrels with anyone; everyone loved him and treated him affectionately. At the beginning he was merely polite to me. But little by little I started to talk to him, and within a couple of months he had begun to speak Russian excellently: a thing his brothers never achieved during the whole length of their prison term. He seemed a very clever boy to me, extremely modest and tactful, and even rather deep for his age. I think I ought to say straight-away that I consider Alei to be no ordinary creature, and I always recall my encounter with him as one of the most gratify-ing encounters of my life. There are people born with such fine souls, so graced by God, that even the thought that they might ever change for the worse seems incredible to you. You always feel certain of them. And I still do of Alei. Where is he now, I wonder.

On one occasion, already quite a while after my arrival, I was lying on the bed-shelf, preoccupied with some very painful thoughts. Alei, who was usually so industrious and hard-work-ing, was on this occasion not doing anything, though it was rather too early to lie down to sleep. It was one of their Moslem holidays and they were not working. He was lying with his hands behind his head, also thinking about something. Suddenly he said:

"Tell me. Are you feeling very miserable?"

I looked at him with curiosity. It seemed strange that a question so blunt and direct should come from Alei, who was always tactful, discreet, and wise in his soul. But when I looked at him more closely, I saw such anguish in his face, so much torment from his own recollections, that I realised at once that he himself was feeling very miserable and exactly at that moment, too. When I told him this, he sighed and smiled sadly. I loved this smile, always so tender and so heartfelt. More than that, when he smiled, he revealed two rows of pearl-white teeth, beautiful enough to arouse the envy of the world's greatest beauties.

"Tell me, Alei, you must be thinking of how this festival is being celebrated in your home in Daghestan. It's good there, isn't it?"

"Yes," he answered delightedly, his eyes flashing. "How do you know that is what I am thinking of?"

"How! How could I fail to know. Tell me, is it better there than here?"

"Oh. Why are you talking like this?"

"There must be so many flowers out there now, in your homeland—like paradise!"

"Oh please! It is better not to talk of these things." He was very agitated.

"Listen, Alei! Have you got a sister?"

"Yes, I have. Why do you ask?"

"If she looks like you then she must be very beautiful."

"Like me! She is so beautiful ... there's no one more beautiful in the whole of Daghestan. She is so beautiful, my sister. You've never seen anyone like her. My mother was very beautiful too."

"Did your mother love you very dearly?"

"How can you ask! She must be dead with grief for me by now. I was her favourite son. She loved me more than she loved my sister, more than anybody... She came to me in a dream last night crying over me."

He fell silent, and did not say any more that evening. From that time on, however, he always looked for a chance to talk to me, though, owing to the reverence he felt towards me for some

74

mysterious reason, he never started a conversation first. He was very glad to be addressed by me though. I used to ask him all about the Caucasus and about his earlier life. His brothers did not mind his talking to me; they even seemed to be pleased by it. In fact, seeing how I grew fonder and fonder of Alei, they even treated me more kindly themselves.

Alei would help me in my work; in the barrack he tried to be of service to me wherever possible, and I could see that he was very happy to be able to make life easier for me in some little way or other, and to please me. There was no servility or self-interest in this at all, only a warm and friendly feeling towards me which he now made no secret of. He was, by the way, very skilled at handiwork. He learned how to sew underwear, how to make boots, and, later on, as much carpentry and joinery as he could. His brothers praised him and were very proud of him.

"Listen, Alei," I said to him one day. "Why don't you learn to read and write Russian? Do you realise how useful it might prove to be later, out here in Siberia?"

"Yes, I would love to—I really would. But who is going to teach me?"

"There's no shortage of literate people here! I could teach you myself if you want!"

"Would you! Oh please." He even raised himself on the bed-shelf and looking straight at me, joined his hands together in entreaty.

So we started the very next evening. I had a Russian translation of the New Testament which was not banned in the gaol. And without any kind of alphabet book, but using this book alone, Alei learned to read very well within several weeks. Within three months he could understand the language of books completely. He loved his studies passionately, and was quite carried away by them.

On one occasion we read the whole of the Sermon on the Mount. I noticed how there were certain parts of it that he pronounced with particular feeling.

I asked him if he was pleased by what he read.

He glanced at me quickly and blushed.

"Oh yes," he answered. "Isa was one of the Holy Prophets.

He spoke the Word of God. It is wonderful."

"So which bit do you like best?"

"I like the part where he says: forgive, love, don't cause offence and love your enemies. He speaks so wonderfully."

He turned to his brothers, who had been listening to our conversation, and started to explain something to them very passionately. For a long time they talked very seriously among themselves, nodding their heads in agreement. Then with a proudly benevolent smile—a typically Moslem smile that is, the kind I love so much, particularly for the feeling of pride it conveys—they addressed me, confirming that Isa was a Prophet of God, who had worked miracles and on one occasion had made a bird of clay, breathed into it, and it took wing ... and that this was written in their books too. In saying this, they were quite certain that they were causing me the very highest degree of satisfaction by praising Isa, and Alei was very happy that his brothers had decided to try to please me in this way.

Alei's writing also progressed very well. He managed to come by some paper (he would not let me use my own money to buy any), some quills and some ink—and within two months or so he had learned to write perfectly. Even his brothers were amazed. Their pride and satisfaction knew no bounds. They could not thank me enough. At work, if it happened that we were together, they competed with each other to see who could be of most help to me, and considered it a great pleasure to do so. Alei's behaviour does not need describing. He loved me, perhaps even as much as he loved his brothers. I shall never forget the day he left the gaol. He took me behind the barrack, flung his arms around my neck and burst into tears. It was the first time he had ever kissed me or cried in front of me. "You did so much for me, so much," he said. "My own father and mother could not have done more; you have made a real person out of me. God will reward you for that, and as for me, I shall never forget you..."

Where, oh where are you now, Alei? My dear, kind Alei!

In addition to the Circassians, there was also a large group of Poles in our barrack, who formed a completely separate community, and hardly communicated with the other prisoners at all. I have already mentioned that because of their distance and their hatred towards the Russian prisoners, they in their turn were hated by everyone else. They were sick, tortured souls: six of them in all. Some of them were educated men whom I shall say something about later—separately and in greater detail. It was from them, during my last years in gaol, that I managed to obtain some books. The first book I read produced a strong, peculiar, and a very special impression on me. I shall talk about these experiences separately later. They seem to me too curious, and I am sure that to many people they will be completely incomprehensible. There are some things, which unless you have experienced them yourself, it is impossible to judge. For the moment I shall say only one thing: mental deprivation is much harder to bear than any physical suffering. A commoner who enters a prison, comes into his own society, perhaps even into a more developed one than the one he left. He has lost a great deal, of course—his family, his home town or village, in fact everything—but his milieu remains much the same. An educated person, on the other hand, while receiving what the law regards as the same punishment as a commoner's, often loses incomparably more. He must suppress all his needs and all his habits, and move into a milieu which, for him, is lacking in everything. He must learn to breathe a different kind of atmosphere. He is a fish, pulled up out of the water on to the sand... Very often a punishment which is the same for everyone according to the law, becomes for him ten times more tormenting. This is simply a fact ... even if only in terms of the physical habits that have to be abandoned.

The Poles, however, were a separate and exclusive group.[4] There were six of them and they stuck together. Out of all the other prisoners in the barrack, the only one they liked was the Jew, and probably that was only because he amused them. All the prisoners liked our Jew too, though everyone without exception used to laugh at him. I could not look at him without being reminded of Yankel, the Jew in Gogol's story *Taras Bulba*,[5] who looked like a plucked chicken when he got undressed to get into some sort of cupboard or other for the night with his wife. And our Jew, Isai Fomich, was the spitting image

77

of a plucked chicken. He was a man, no longer young, about fifty, short and weak, cunning, yet positively stupid. He was arrogant, impudent, and at the same time a terrible coward. His face was covered all over with tiny wrinkles, he had been branded on the public scaffold and there were scars left on his forehead and his cheeks. I was never able to understand how he could have survived sixty lashes. He came into the gaol accused of murder. He had a prescription hidden on him, which his fellow Jews had brought him from the doctor as soon as he was taken down from the scaffold. With this prescription an ointment so powerful could be procured that any brand marks would disappear within two weeks. He did not dare use this ointment in the gaol, however; he was waiting for the end of his twelve-year sentence of hard labour, after which, when he was sent to one of the settlements, he was most definitely going to make use of the prescription. "Unless I do," he once told me, "I won't be able to get married. And I've got to get married whatever happens." We were great friends. He was always in the most excellent spirits. He found it very easy to live in the gaol. By trade he was a jeweller and he was swamped with orders from the town, where there was no other jeweller, and in this way he managed to wriggle out of his hard labour. Needless to say, he was also a moneylender, and supplied the whole gaol with money, charging interest or taking things in pawn. He had arrived before I did, and it was one of the Poles who told me the details of his arrival. It is a hilarious story and I am going to tell it later; I shall come back to Isai Fomich on more than one occasion.

The remaining men in our barrack were as follows: four Old Believers, all ancients and terribly dogmatic, including one elderly man from the Starodubye Settlement; two or three Ukrainians, all very gloomy people; a young prisoner of about twenty-three, thin-faced and thin-nosed, who had already killed eight people; a group of counterfeiters, one of whom was the barrack clown, and—last but not least—a bunch of grim and gloomy characters, with shaved heads and disfigured features, silently and enviously glowering around with hatred, and obviously intending to go on glowering, keeping silent and hating in this way for many years to come, throughout their term.

All these things merely flashed in front of my eyes during this first hapless evening of my new life—flashed by amidst the smoke and the soot, through the cursing and the inexpressible cynicism, through the mephitic air, the clanking of the shackles, the swearing and the immodest laughter. I lay down on the bare bed-shelf, put my clothes under my head—I did not yet have a pillow—and covered myself with my sheepskin. Though broken and exhausted by all the hideous and unexpected impressions of my first day, it was a long time before I could sleep. My new life was only just beginning. Many things lay ahead of me, which I had never conceived of, or even guessed at...

V

The First Month

Three days after my arrival, I was ordered out to work. Considering how extraordinary my situation was to start with, there was nothing particularly extraordinary in the first day of labour—yet it remains in my memory very vividly. It was a part of my first impressions, and I was still studying everything avidly. Throughout those three days my spirits were very low. "This is the end of my journey," I kept telling myself every few minutes. "Here I am in prison. This is going to be my home for many long years—this place which I am entering with such a mistrustful, such a painful feeling. Yet who knows? Maybe in years to come, when I have to leave it, I shall miss it." I added these last words with that self-mockery which at times becomes an urge to rub salt into your own wounds, as though wishing to feast your eyes on your own pain, almost as if there was a perverse pleasure to be had in the contemplation of the magnitude of the disaster. The thought that I might in time come to miss this place appalled me: I could already feel the horrifying extent to which a human being is capable of getting used to things... But that was still in store for me. In the meanwhile everything around me was hostile and terrifying ... not everything, of course, but so it seemed to me. The savage curiosity with which

I was being sized up by my fellow-prisoners, the extra hardness with which they regarded me, a newcomer from the nobility who suddenly entered their midst, this hardness, bordering on hatred, wore me down so much that I myself wanted to be sent out to work as soon as possible, to find out and savour the whole extent of my disaster at once and start living like everyone else, merging into the common pattern as soon as I could. There was much that I did not notice or suspect then, of course, although it was right under my nose. I remained unaware of the positive features that were there among the hostile ones. Even during those three days, however, I had already met some welcoming and friendly faces, and they had already cheered me up. Akim Akimovich was more friendly and kind to me than anyone; and I could not help noticing some kind and cheerful faces among the gloomy and resentful ones. "There are bad people everywhere, and then good ones among them." I hurried to console myself with this thought. "And who knows? These people are perhaps not so much worse than the *remainder*, those who *remain outside* the gaol." This was the drift of my thoughts, and I shook my head in doubt at them. Dear God! If only I had known how much truth there was in those thoughts of mine!

For example, there was one fellow there, whom I really got to know well only many years later, though he was actually with me and near me almost always during my time in prison. This was Sushilov. As soon as I mentioned those prisoners who were *no worse* than anyone else, I remembered him automatically. He used to run errands for me. I had another person for errands as well. Right from the beginning, during my very first days, one of the prisoners called Osip was recommended to me by Akim Akimovich, who said that for thirty kopeks a month—if the prison food really disgusted me and I had the means to buy my own—this man would dish up a separate meal for me every day. Osip was one of the four cooks appointed to our two kitchens on the prisoners' own recommendation, though I must add that the final decision rested with the cooks themselves, and if they agreed to take up the post, they were free to turn it down again the very next day. The cooks did not go out to work with the other prisoners, and their only duty was to bake bread and make the soup. In our place they did not even call them *cooks*, but *stryapkas* (word applied only to women cooks)— though not out of contempt for them, seeing that clever, and if possible, honest chaps were chosen for the kitchen—but just for fun. Our cooks never took offence at this. Osip was almost always chosen. He was a *stryapka* for several years running, only temporarily refusing to accept the post when he succumbed to despondency, and at the same time a strong desire to smuggle in liquor overtook him. He was a man of rare honesty and meekness, though he had been put into prison for smuggling. He is the smuggler I have already mentioned—the tall hefty young lad. He was a coward about everything, especially about being whipped, and obedient, mild and kind to all. He *never* argued with anyone. Yet, despite his cowardice he could not help sneaking in liquor to satisfy his passion for smuggling. Like the other cooks, he also traded in liquor, not on the same scale as Gazin, of course—he did not have the courage to take such large risks. I always got along very well with this Osip. As for having the means to provide one's own food, very little money was needed. If I remember correctly, it cost me about one silver rouble a month; I ate the prison bread, of course, and occasionally the cabbage soup, too, if I was very hungry, in spite of my disgust for it—a disgust which eventually disappeared almost completely. I usually bought a piece of beef, about one pound for a day. In winter, beef cost next to nothing. One of the invalid soldiers who lived in with us—there was one in each barrack, to keep things orderly—usually went to the market to buy food for the prisoners, undertaking this daily duty of their own free will and expecting no payment for it, nothing worth mentioning anyway. They did it for their own peace and quiet, otherwise they would never have been able to keep on good terms with the prisoners. They brought tobacco, tile tea, beef, buns, etc etc. Probably the only thing they did not bring was liquor. They were never asked to do this, but if there was some liquor around they would be offered a glass. For several years running Osip made one and the same dish for me: a piece of fried beef. The *way* it was fried is another matter, and that is not really the point. What is quite remarkable is that for several years I did not so much as pass the time of day with Osip. I often used to strike up a conversation with him, but he was somehow unable to keep it up: he would smile, or answer 'yes' and 'no', and that was that. How strange, that this Hercules of a man had the mind of a mere seven-year-old.

Apart from Osip, I also had Sushilov to help me. I never asked his help or sought him out. He found me himself in some odd way, and stuck to me. I cannot even recall when or how it all started. He began doing my washing for me. There was a big pit, specially dug behind the barracks to pour the soapy water in. Above the pit, there were troughs in which the prisoners' clothes were washed. As well as doing the washing, Sushilov invented thousands of other duties, just to please me: he would brew my tea, run various errands, help me to buy something or other, take my coat to be mended, grease my boots four times a month; he did all these things zealously, fussily, as though God knows how important these tasks were. In other words, he wove his life in with mine, and made all the things I had to do his own. For example, he would never say: "You've got so many shirts" or "Your coat is torn", and so on, but always "*We*'ve got so many shirts at the moment" or "*Our* coat is torn". He was always trying to catch my eye—it seemed to be his main purpose in life. He had no trade of his own, or 'handicraft' as the prisoners usually call it, and I seemed to be his only means of earning a couple of kopeks. I paid him as much as I could afford, next to nothing really, and he was always content. He could not help being a servant to someone, and it seemed that he had picked me out mainly because I was more considerate than the others, and more honest when paying. He was one of those people who can never grow rich and improve their lot, and who acted as watchmen for the *maidans* standing out on the porch all night in the cold, straining their ears for any sound of the approaching Major, taking five kopeks in silver for being there practically all night, and losing the money if anything went wrong—as well as getting a thrashing. I have already described such people. Their most typical feature is that always, everywhere, and in practically all their dealings with people they obliterate their own individuality, playing not second but third fiddle to others. They were born like that. Sushilov was a miserable sort of fellow, humble, submissive, and even downtrodden; not that anyone in our barrack ever beat him: he simply was like that. I always felt sorry for him. I could not look at him without pity, but why I could not say. And I could not talk to him either. He was incapable of conversation, it was obviously too great an effort for him, and he only cheered up when—in order to bring the conversation to a close—you gave him something to do, or asked him to run somewhere for something. In the end I became convinced that running errands made him quite happy. He was neither tall nor short, neither ugly nor good-looking, neither stupid nor clever, neither young nor old, slightly freckled and rather fair-haired. It was impossible ever to say anything very definite about him. There was just one thing. He belonged, it seemed to me, and as far as I could make out, to the same category as Sirotkin, and came to be there solely through his natural downtroddenness and meekness. The prisoners made fun of him sometimes, mainly for *swapping over* on the trudge in a convoy to Siberia, and, what's more, swapping over for just a red shirt and one silver rouble. It was the paltriness of the sum for which he had sold himself that made him the object of ridicule. 'Swapping over' means changing names, and consequently fates, with somebody else. This is a fact—however amazing it may seem—and in my time it was still being practiced among convicts on the way to Siberia, sanctified by tradition and possessing its own specific etiquette. I simply could not believe it at first, but in the end, of course, I had to.

This is how it is done. A party of prisoners is going under escort to Siberia. There are all sorts on their way there: some going to hard-labour prisons, some to factories, some into exile, all herded together. Somewhere along the way, say in Perm Gubernia, one of the men wants to swap over. A convict sentenced for murder or some other major crime—let's call him Mikhailov—thinks he can do better for himself than go to prison for so many years. Say he's a cunning, experienced character who knows the ropes. He goes looking for someone in the same party: someone who's a little bit on the simple side, someone downtrodden and submissive, and who has been given a comparatively mild sentence, either to work for a few years at one of the factories, live in exile, or even do a shorter term of hard labour. At last he lights on Sushilov. Sushilov is a former serf, and is simply going into exile. He has already covered one and a half thousand versts on foot, without a kopek to his name, of course, because Sushilov is the sort who never has any money. And he has been plodding on, dog-tired and footsore, existing only on the prison rations he is issued, without ever a tastier morsel for a change, dressed in prison garb, and doing odd jobs for each and every person to earn just a few miserable kopeks. Mikhailov strikes up a conversation with Sushilov, becomes acquainted with him, makes friends with him even, and then at one of the journey's stages, he offers him some liquor. Finally, he makes a suggestion: would Sushilov like to 'swap over'? He says that he, Mikhailov, is on his way to prison, well not exactly prison, but into some special category. Even though it's a prison, it's a special one, so it must mean a better one. Not even all the authorities knew about this special category at the time of its existence, not even the people in St. Petersburg. It was such a separate and special nook in one of the quieter corners of Siberia, and so small in number (there were only up to seventy people in it in my time) that it was difficult even to track it down. I later met people who had been officials in Siberia and knew quite a bit about life there, but the first they ever heard about the existence of this special category was from what I told them. There are only about six lines concerning it in the Criminal Code: "From this date until the institution of severer penal servitude in Siberia, there is established for the most serious offenders a special category affiliated to the prison of X." Even the prisoners who were in the special category themselves did not know: did it mean they were there for life or only for some period of time? No period of time was laid down for them. It just said "until the institution of severer penal servitude in Siberia" and that was all; so in that case, it must mean 'forever'. It was not surprising then that neither Sushilov nor anyone else in the convoy knew about it, and that included Mikhailov himself, who had perhaps only a vague idea of this 'special category', deduced from his crime—which was a very grave one—and the fact that he had already gone through three or four thousand sticks for it. So it could hardly be a good place they were sending him to. Sushilov, on the other hand, was on his way to one of the settlements. What could be better? "Do you want to swap over?" Sushilov is by that time quite tipsy and, being a simple soul, he is filled with gratitude to Mikhailov for showing so much kindness to him, and consequently he dare not refuse. What is more, he has already heard say in his party that it is possible to 'swap over', that there are others who do indeed 'swap over', and there is nothing either unusual or unheard of about it. They come to an agreement. The shameless Mikhailov, taking advantage of Sushilov's exceptional simplicity, immediately buys his name for a red shirt and a silver rouble, which he hands over to him straightaway, in front of witnesses. The next day Sushilov is sober, but Mikhailov gets him drunk again. And then, he can't very well back out now. The silver rouble has already been spent on drink, the red shirt too. If he refuses to swap, Mikhailov will want his money back. And where will Sushilov find a whole silver rouble?* And if he does not give the money back then the chain-gang will make him give it back: convicts are very strict about such things. Once you've made a promise, you've got to keep it—the chain-gang will see to that too. Otherwise, they'll eat you alive, beat you up, or just kill you. At the very least they will frighten you to death.

Actually, if the chain-gang showed leniency just once, the practice of swapping over names would cease. If someone could refuse to keep the bargain after he had already taken payment—who would ever stick to the agreement in future? In short this is a matter of common concern, and that's why the chain-gang watches it so strictly. Well, then Sushilov sees that there is no getting out of the bargain and accepts it. This is announced to the entire gang, and if necessary a drink or a bit of money is given to some of the men. It is all the same to them, of course, whether it's Mikhailov or Sushilov who goes to hell. They've

*In mid-nineteenth century there was both silver and paper money in Russia. One silver rouble equalled 3 roubles 50 kopeks in banknotes.—*Ed.*

had their drink, and so they'll keep their mouths shut. During the very next stop on the journey there is a roll call. When it comes to Mikhailov, "Here!" answers Sushilov. And when Sushilov is called "Here!" shouts Mikhailov, and the party continues on its way. Nobody mentions it again. In Tobolsk the men are sorted into categories. 'Mikhailov' is sent to one of the settlements, while 'Sushilov' is taken off under double escort to the 'special category'. After that it is no longer possible to protest; what proof has Sushilov? How many years would such a case drag on for? And what would he get for the swap-over? And where, when all is said and done, are the witnesses? Even if there were any, they would deny all knowledge of it. So the fact remains that Sushilov, for a silver rouble and a red shirt, entered the special category.

The prisoners used to laugh at Sushilov: not so much because he had swapped over (though they do despise people who have swapped lighter for harder labour, as they look down on any idiot who has let himself be duped), but mainly because he had only taken a silver rouble and a red shirt for it. It was too negligible a price. Swapping over is usually done for large sums—again relatively speaking, of course. Tens of roubles, sometimes. Sushilov, however, was so submissive, so lacking in personality, and so insignificant in everybody's eyes, that they did not even bother to laugh at him too much.

I lived together with Sushilov for a long time—for several years. Little by little, he grew very attached to me. I could not help noticing it, and I became very used to him too. One day though—I will never be able to forgive myself for this—he did not carry out some duty I had given him despite the fact that he had just received some money from me, and I was heartless enough to tell him:

"Right, Sushilov! You've taken the money, and you've not done what I asked you to..."

Sushilov did not say anything. He ran my errand for me, and then a sort of despondency came over him. Two days passed. I thought it could not possibly be a result of what I said to him. I knew that one of the prisoners, Anton Vasilyev, was insistently demanding the repayment of some paltry debt from him. It must be, I thought, that he did not have the money for it, but was afraid to ask me for some. So on the third day I said to him:

"Sushilov, I was wondering whether you wanted some money for Anton Vasilyev. Here you are."

I was sitting on the bed-shelf at the time. Sushilov was standing before me. He appeared to be astonished that I should offer him some money of my own free will, that I should myself have remembered his being in a tight corner, especially, as he had, by his own reckoning, recently taken too much from me anyway, and did not, therefore, even dare to hope that I would give him any more. He looked at the money, then at me, then suddenly turned on his heel and left. I was amazed by the whole affair. I followed him outside and found him behind the barracks. He stood leaning against the pales, with his forehead pressed to the wood. "What is the matter with you, Sushilov?" I asked him. He did not look at me, and to my surprise, I noticed that he was on the verge of tears.

"You, Alexander Petrovich ... you think..." he started in a faltering voice, trying not to look at me, "that I do it for money ... while I ... I ... oh God!" And with that he turned back towards the fence so abruptly that he banged his forehead on it, and burst into tears. It was the first time I had seen a man cry in the prison. With great difficulty I managed to comfort him, and although, from that time onwards, he began to serve me and 'keep an eye on me' even more zealously, if such a thing was possible, still there were some almost imperceptible indications which told me that in his heart he could never forgive me for my reproach. The others laughed at him, bullied him, and swore at him—very nastily sometimes, yet he lived on good, even friendly terms with them and never took offence. Ah yes, it can be very difficult to make somebody out, even when you have known them for many years.

That is why the gaol could not appear to me, at first glance, in its true colours, in the way that it was to appear to me later; and that is why I said that even though I looked at everything with an avid, intense attention, I could not make out a lot of things that were going on right under my very nose. Naturally, the first things that impressed me were large-scale events, which stood out sharply, yet even these, perhaps, I perceived wrongly, so that all that was left in my heart was an impression of heavy, hopeless sadness. This was largely due to my meeting A—v, a prisoner who had arrived at the gaol shortly before I did, and who made a particularly painful impression on me during my first days in the gaol. I must say, however, that I had known, even before my arrival in gaol, that I would meet A—v there. He poisoned those first difficult days for me, and added to the torment in my soul. I simply must tell you about him.

This was the most repulsive example of the depths to which a man can sink and become debased, killing all his sense of right and wrong without any difficulty and without any repentance. A—v was the young man, a former nobleman, whom I have already mentioned in passing, telling how he reported everything that was going on in the gaol to the Major, and was friend with Fedka, the Major's batman. Here, briefly, is his story. After dropping out of the university, and quarrelling with his Moscow relatives, who had grown frightened of his debauchery, he arrived in St. Petersburg, and—in order to make some money—he decided to falsely inform on ten people, to sell their life-blood for the immediate satisfaction of his unquenchable thirst for the most bestial and lewd pleasures for which, his head turned by the big city with its cafés and notorious Meshchanskaya region, he developed so great a weakness that, although he was by no means a stupid man, he embarked upon this mad and senseless venture. He was soon exposed. He had involved some innocent people in his report, deceived others, and as a result was sent to Siberia, to our gaol, for a term of ten years. He was still very young, and life was just beginning for him. One would imagine that such a dramatic change in his fortune would have affected his nature, awakened some resistance, brought about some crisis. Yet he accepted his new fate without the slightest sign of discomposure, without the slightest disgust, without any sense of moral outrage, and nothing frightened him in it, except, perhaps, the necessity to work and forget the cafés and the three Meshchanskaya streets. To him, the label of convict even seemed to free his hands for even dirtier and meaner actions. "Convict it is then! Well, if that's how it is, there'll be foul play and no shame about it—none at all." This, quite literally, was the way he thought. I recall this repulsive creature as something phenomenal. I spent several years among murderers, debauchees and utter villains, but I can say most definitely, that I had never in my life before encountered such total moral degradation, such depravity and brazen vileness as there was in A—v. There was the patricide in our gaol, the former nobleman whom I have already mentioned, but many facts and many of his traits convinced me that even he was incomparably more honourable and human. Throughout my life in the gaol, A—v remained for me a chunk of beef, with a set of teeth, with a stomach, and with an unquenchable thirst for the most crude and bestial physical pleasures, capable of killing in cold blood, of murdering, of doing anything in other words, simply in order to satisfy the smallest and most whimsical of his pleasures, so long that he might cover his tracks afterwards. I am not exaggerating at all. I got to know A—v very well. He showed the lengths which the physical part of a person will go to when left alone, unrestrained by any internal standards or laws. And how repellant to me was the sight of his unceasingly derisive smile. He was a monster, a moral Quasimodo. Add to this the fact that he was cunning and clever, good-looking, even somewhat educated, and not lacking in ability. No! Fire, plague, and famine are better than a man such as this in society! I have already mentioned that baseness had so contaminated the whole prison that spying and informing naturally flourished and aroused no anger whatsoever in the inmates. On the contrary, they were all very friendly with A—v and treated him much, much better than they did the rest of us. The favours bestowed upon him by our drunken Major, just gave him additional importance in their eyes. He had, by the way, convinced the Major that he could paint portraits (while he had convinced the prisoners that he had served in the army as a guards lieutenant) and so the Major demanded that he should be sent to work in his house, to paint his portrait. That was when A—v made friends with Fedka, who had a tremendous influence on his master, and consequently on everybody and everything in the gaol. A—v spied on us, ordered to do so by the Major who, for his part, when he was drunk, would slap A—v on the face and call him a spy and an informer. Quite often, having just slapped him, the Major would sit down again and order A—v to continue with his portrait. Our Major apparently believed A—v to be a truly remarkable painter, something of a Briullov,[6] whom even he had heard of; still he considered it his right to slap his face, as if to say, "You may be a painter, but you're a convict, and be you the Briulliest of Briullovs, still I'm in charge, and I'll do with you just as I want." He actually used to make A—v pull his boots off for him, and empty his chamber pots, but all the same, for a long time he could not abandon the idea that A—v was a great painter. The painting continued endlessly, for almost a year. At long last the Major realised that he was being made a fool of and when he became absolutely sure that the portrait was not being finished but was growing less and less like him with every day, he grew angry and beat the painter up, sending him back to do hard, dirty work in the gaol. Clearly A—v was very sorry about this. It was very hard for him to give up his days of idleness, his tit-bits from the Major's table, his friend Fedka and all the plea-sures which the two of them had invented for themselves in the Major's kitchen. At least it could be said that after A—v's removal the Major stopped harassing M., a prisoner whom A—v had continually slandered to him. Let me tell you why. M. had been alone when A—v arrived in the gaol. He was feeling very depressed. He had nothing in common with the other prisoners, whom he regarded with horror and revulsion, missing and fail-ing to notice everything which might have reconciled him to them; and so he kept aloof from everyone. They repaid his hat-red in kind. The position of people like M. in gaol is, generally speaking, terrible. He was unaware of the reason for A—v's imprisonment. And A—v, once he understood whom he was dealing with, quickly convinced him that the reason for his imprisonment was something completely other than informing, and, in fact, something rather similar to the offence M. had been sentenced for. M. was very happy to have found a friend and a comrade. He looked after A—v, comforted him during his first few days in the gaol, and, assuming that he must be suffer-ing most terribly, he bestowed his remaining money upon him, fed him, and shared all the most essential things with him. A—v, on the other hand, felt a loathing for M. from the first, precisely because he was so noble and looked with such horror at any baseness—because he was so different from him, in other words. Everything that M. had told him about the prison and about the Major, A—v hastened to report to the Major as soon as an opportunity occurred. As a result, the Major came to hate M. and started persecuting him terribly, and, if not for the intervention of the Commandant, he would have driven him to some desperate action. A—v, for his part, did not feel in the least embarrassed, when M. later found out about his baseness. Quite the contrary—he even enjoyed meeting M. and giving him mocking looks. Clearly this gave him pleasure. This was pointed out to me, on several occasions, by M. himself. A—v later managed to escape with another prisoner and one of the guards, but I shall tell about this later. In the beginning A—v tried playing up to me too, thinking that I had not heard his story. I can only say again that he succeeded in poisoning my first, miserable enough days in the gaol. I was appalled by the terrible vileness and baseness into which I had been plunged, in which I suddenly found myself. I thought that everyone around me here was as vile and as base as he was. I was wrong though. I was judging everybody by A—v.

During these first three days I wandered around the gaol in terrible dejection, lay on my bed-shelf, made arrangements with one reliable prisoner, who had been pointed out to me by Akim Akimovich, for some shirts to be made for me—at a price, of course, of so many kopeks for each—out of the prison material that had been issued to me; also on the insistent advice of Akim Akimovich I acquired a folding mattress (made of thick felt, covered with canvas), an extremely thin one and flat as a pancake; I also procured a pillow, stuffed with wool, which felt terribly hard to me, as I was not used to such things. Akim Akimovich went to great lengths to see that I acquired everything, and took part in the procedures himself, sewing a blanket for me with his own hands from pieces of prison broadcloth, cut out from the worn out trousers and coats which I had bought from the other prisoners. The prisoners were allowed to keep articles of prison issue which had served their time. They immediately sold them in the gaol, and—however worn out a thing might be—there was still a chance that it would fetch something. At first I was amazed by all this. Generally speaking, it was my first encounter with the common people. And here I suddenly became one of them, a convict like they were. Their habits, ideas and opinions, their way of doing things, were all mine now—formally, according to the law at any rate, even if I did not share them actually. I was surprised and embarrassed, as though I had never before even suspected the existence or heard of any of these things, though I had in fact both known of them and heard of them. But reality produces an entirely different impression than does second-hand knowledge and hearsay. How could I ever have imagined, for example, that these old things could be regarded as *things*? Yet here I was, with a blanket made for me out of such rags. It was difficult to name the sort of cloth laid down for the making of prison garb. In appearance it did resemble thick, military broadcloth; but when it had been subjected to even the most temporary wear, it turned into some sort of old fishing net and tore at a touch. True, a garment made from this broadcloth was issued for a period of only a year, but it was difficult to make it last even that long. A prisoner has to work, to carry heavy things on his shoulders, and his clothing rubs and tears through very quickly. The sheepskins, on the other hand, were issued for a period of three years and usually served throughout the whole of this period as overcoat, bedding and blanket. A sheepskin is strong; even so, towards the end of the third year, when the period they were issued for had almost expired, you often saw one all patched up with pieces of cotton cloth. In spite of this, they were still sold, at the end of the three years, for around forty silver kopeks—even the ones that were very worn out. Those that had lasted better, fetched sixty or even seventy silver kopeks—a large sum by prison standards.

On the subject of money ... I have spoken of it already. In gaol it took on a terrible power and importance. Quite definitely, one could say that a prisoner with at least some money would suffer ten times less than one who had nothing, even though the latter, like the former, was provided with everything by the prison. So what, one might ask, did he need money for? That was how the reasoning of the prison authorities went. I cannot repeat often enough that if the prisoners had been forbidden to have any money of their own, they would either have all gone mad, or they would have started dying like flies (although they were provided with everything they needed), or would have perpetrated unheard-of crimes, one out of despair, another to be executed or destroyed as quickly as possible, or somehow 'change his fate' (a technical expression). But if a prisoner who had contrived to get a bit of money by practically sweating blood for it, or running risks, or doing incredibly cunning things which often involved theft or swindling, and then spent it recklessly and as senselessly as a child, it did not prove that he did not value it, even though that is how it might appear at first sight. A prisoner's greed about money can bring on a fit of convulsions or insanity, and if he does throw it about when out on a spree, that is because he is throwing it about for something which he considers a degree higher than money. What is it that a prisoner considers one degree higher? Freedom or—at least—a dream of freedom. And prisoners are great dreamers. I shall have some more to say about that later, but as it has cropped up now... Would my readers believe me when I tell them that I have seen people who have been sentenced to hard labour for *twenty years*, very calmly telling me such things as, for instance: "Just wait till, God willing, I finish my term, then I'll..." A 'prisoner' is a person without free will; whereas, in spending money he is acting *of his own free will*. Despite the branding, the chains, the hateful pales of the gaol that hide God's World from him and fence him in like an animal in a cage, he can procure some liquor—a terribly forbidden pleasure, do a bit of philandering, and sometimes (though not always) he can bribe his most immediate superiors, the invalid soldiers and even the sergeant, to turn a blind eye to the way he is breaking the regulations and the rules; he might even, over and above the bargain, put on a show of bravado for them, and prisoners love doing this. It means he can show off in front of his comrades and convince even himself, at least *for a little while*, that he has much greater freedom and power than anyone might think. In short, he can get drunk, rowdy, really rile somebody, and thus prove to this person that he is *really capable* of all this, that it is all 'in his hands'—to convince himself, that is, of something a moneyless man cannot even dream of. Perhaps, that is why one notices in prisoners, even when they are sober, a general tendency to bravado, to swagger, and comically and naively glorify their own personalities—even if it is only illusory. Lastly, there is an element of risk in all this, extravagance, and that means there is in it at least some glimmer of life, some distant glimmer of freedom. And what won't a man give up for freedom? What millionaire, when the rope is tightening around his neck, will not give away his millions for just one gulp of air?

The authorities are sometimes surprised when a prisoner who has lived an extremely decent and quiet life for several years, and perhaps, even been given a position of responsibility for good conduct, will suddenly, and positively without any reason—just as though a devil had got into him—start misbehaving, throwing his money about, running riot, even risking a criminal charge, perhaps, either by doing something which is clearly in defiance of the authorities, or killing someone, raping someone, etc. They look at him and wonder. Yet perhaps the very reason for this sudden eruption, in just the person one would least expect it from, is a despairing, frenzied manifestation of personality, an instinctive longing to be himself, a desire to announce himself and his humiliated being—a desire that suddenly comes and builds up to a climax of rage and madness, of mental derangement, of a fit, of convulsions. In this same manner a person who has been buried alive and then comes round, must bang on the lid of the coffin and try to prise it open, even though, of course, his mind must be telling him that all his efforts will be in vain. But this is no time for reasoning. This is the time for convulsions. We should also take into account that almost any unsanctioned display of personality by a prisoner is considered a crime; and, that being the case, it is naturally all the same to him whether the display is a big one or a small one. If you are going to go on a spree—you might as well go on a big one; if you are going to run risks—then risk everything, even a murder, perhaps. And all you have to do is start; after that, a person gets so carried away, there is no stopping him. And that is why everything should be done not to drive people to this. It would make life safer for everybody.

Indeed it would. But how can it be done?

VI

The First Month

I had some money when I entered the gaol. I had very little actually about my person, for fear of it being taken away from me, but—just in case—I had several roubles hidden, that is, glued into the binding of my Scripture, which we were allowed to take into the gaol. This book and the money inside it had been given to me as a present while I was still in Tobolsk. The people who gave it to me had also been suffering in exile, already reckoning the time in decades and they had long come to regard any 'unfortunate' as a brother. In Siberia there are almost always a few people, who see it as their mission in life to take brotherly care of the 'unfortunates', comfort and condole with them, as they would with their own children, doing it as a sacred duty, completely devoid of any self-interest. I cannot help giving a brief account at this point of just one such encounter. In the town where our gaol was situated, there lived a lady, a widow, by the name of Nastasya Ivanovna. Needless to say, none of us could be personally acquainted with her while we were in prison. It seemed that she had made it the purpose of her life to help those in exile, but it was for us, prisoners, that she showed the greatest concern of all. Whether some similar misfortune had befallen her own family, or whether one of those nearest and dearest to her had suffered for the same crime, I do not know, but whatever the reason, she apparently considered it her great good fortune to be able to do everything in her power for us. She was not able to do much of course, because she was very poor. But we, in our gaol, felt that there, outside, we had a most faithful friend. She often passed us news, which we very badly needed. After my release from gaol, when I was on my way to another town, I called on her and made her acquaintance personally. She lived somewhere in the suburbs, in the house of a close relative. She was neither young nor old, neither good-looking nor plain; it was even impossible to say if she was intelligent and educated. The only thing you noticed about her every moment you were with her was her endless kindness, an irresistible desire to please, to give relief, to do something nice for you, by whatever means possible. All this showed in her gentle, kind glances. Together with one of my companions from the gaol, I spent almost an entire evening at her house. She looked fondly into our eyes, laughed when we laughed, and hastened to agree with everything we said; and she fussed about, trying to find something, anything, that she might treat us with. She gave us tea, something to eat, and some sweet things too, and if she had come into thousands of roubles she would have rejoiced in her wealth only because she could then have done more for us and also relieved the lot of our comrades who were still in the gaol. As she said goodbye, she produced two cigarette cases—one for each of us—as a souvenir. She had made these cigarette cases for us herself out of cardboard (how well they had been made is another matter) which she had pasted over with some coloured paper, the kind of paper in which arithmetic books for primary schools are bound (maybe she did actually use some arithmetic books to make them). All round the edges of both these cigarette cases, for decoration, she had pasted a thin border of wispy gold paper, for which she had perhaps made a special journey to the shops. "You smoke rolled cigarettes, if I'm not mistaken, so perhaps they might come in handy," she said, as though apologising to us timidly for her present. Some people say (I have heard and read as much) that the highest degree of loving one's neighbour is also the highest degree of selfishness. Well, what selfishness there could be in this case is beyond my understanding.

Although when I first entered the gaol I did not have very much money, I somehow could not feel annoyed with those prisoners who—practically in the very first hours of my prison life—although having already deceived me once, came back again, four or even five times, in the most naive way imaginable, to try and borrow more money from me. I must confess to one thing, however, most sincerely. It distressed me very much that all these people, with their simple tricks, seemed to consider me an easy touch and a fool, and laughed at me, precisely because I did give them money the fourth and fifth time they asked. No doubt, they must have thought that I fell for all their tricks and ruses, and—on the other hand—I was sure that, had I refused them and sent them packing, they would have respected me a great deal more. Yet however vexed I felt, I could not find it in me to refuse them. I was vexed because during these first days I gave careful and serious thought to how I would establish myself in the gaol or, rather, on what footing I ought to be with the other prisoners. I felt and realised that this milieu was completely new to me, that I was completely in the dark, and that it was impossible for anyone to live for so many years in the dark. So I needed to prepare myself. Of course, I decided that above all I should be straightforward in my behaviour, as dictated by my inner feelings and my conscience. Yet I also knew that this was a mere adage; that in practice I was in for all sorts of surprises.

Therefore, despite all my petty cares about bedding and such things, of which I have already spoken (and in which I had mostly become involved through Akim Akimovich) and even though these arrangements did distract me a little, a terrible anguish began to gnaw at me more and more. "Dead House!" I would say to myself, as sometimes, in the dusk, I looked attentively from the porch of our barrack at the prisoners who had already gathered together after work and were lazily wandering around the compound backwards and forwards between the barrack and the kitchen. I looked at them closely, trying to make out from their faces and their movements what kind of people they were, with what kind of characters, as they walked about before me with knitted brows or else over-cheerful expressions (there two types are encountered most frequently and can be said to characterise hard-labour convicts in general). They would be bickering or just talking, or else strolling about on their own, quietly and unhurriedly as though deep in

97

thought. Some had a tired and apathetic air about them, others (even in a place like this!) wore an air of insolent arrogance, their hats at a rakish angle, their sheepskins flung casually across their shoulders, a superior and cunning look upon their faces, swapping jokes and insults with each other. "This is my milieu," I thought. "My world for the duration, and with it I have to live whether I like it or not..." I tried to find out about these people by asking Akim Akimovich, with whom I liked to drink tea, just to avoid being alone. I should mention in passing, that during this initial period, I lived almost entirely on tea. Akim Akimovich never refused to have tea with me and himself boiled the water in our funny home-made tin samovar which had been lent to me by M. As a rule Akim Akimovich had just one glass of tea (he had his own glasses too), drinking it in silence, very ceremoniously. Then he thanked me, and at once got back to work on the blanket for me. What I needed to find out, though, he was unable to tell me. He did not even seem to understand why I was so interested in the characters of the prisoners around us and listened to my questions with a knowing little smile, which I can still remember very clearly. "No," I thought, "it seems I have to experience these things for myself, and not just ask about them."

On the fourth day—just as they had on the day when I was reshackled—the prisoners lined up early in the morning in two rows on the square in front of the guardhouse near the prison gates. Soldiers lined up in front of them and behind them with loaded guns and fixed bayonets. A soldier had the right to fire at a prisoner if he tried to make a getaway, but at the same time he was answerable for the shot if he fired it when the need was not dire. The same applies if the prisoners riot. But who would even consider running away in full view? An officer of the engineers arrived, with a corporal, some non-commissioned officers from the engineers and the soldiers who were to supervise the work. The roll was called. One group of prisoners, who worked in the sewing shop, left before anybody else; they were no concern of the engineers in charge. These men did all the sewing for the prison and had their own superiors. Next to go was the party for the workshops, and after that the men who were going to the usual manual work. I went with them, together with some twenty other prisoners. Behind the fort, on the frozen river, there were two old wooden barges which had to be taken apart so the old boards at least would not go to waste. The whole lot apparently was worth very little, almost nothing. Firewood was sold for next to nothing in the town, and there was plenty of wood around anyway. As the prisoners knew all too well, we were sent there just to ensure that we did not sit around doing nothing. They always began a job like this indifferently and apathetically. If, on the other hand, the work itself was sensible and worthwhile, and in particular if it could be put down in the prisoners' record as a 'task fulfilled', their attitude became completely different. They tackled the job with something like animation, though they had nothing to gain from it, and as I saw for myself, they laid themselves out to finish it as soon as possible and to do it to the best of their ability. It was even a matter of pride for them. In this particular case, however, when the work was more a matter of form than need, there was little hope of getting it put down as a 'task', and there was nothing for it but to work right up until the drumbeat which sounded the return home at eleven o'clock in the morning. It was a warm misty morning and the snow was on the point of melting. The lot of us went around the back of the fortress to the river, our chains jingling slightly; even though they were under our clothes, they produced a thin, sharp metallic sound with every step. Two or three prisoners from our group went to fetch the tools from the military prison depot. I went along with all the others and I even began to feel a little livelier. I wanted to find out what sort of work it was going to be, as soon as possible. What was it going to be like, this hard labour? And how would it be for me, personally, to have to work for the first time in my life?

I can remember everything down to the finest detail. There was a bearded townsman we came across, who stopped and reached into his pocket. One of our lot immediately detached himself from the group, took off his hat, received the alms—five kopeks—and briskly re-joined the rest of us. The townsman crossed himself and continued on his way. That same morning these five kopeks were spent on buns which were divided equally between all the members of our party.

There were, as usual, in our lot, some who stayed sullen and silent, some who were indifferent and showed no feelings at all, and a third kind who chatted lazily among themselves. There was also one man who was awfully happy and cheerful about something. He was singing, and almost dancing the whole way there, setting his chains jingling with every hop. This was the short stocky prisoner, who during my first morning in the gaol, had got into an argument with one of the others during the washing routine, because the latter had arrogantly dared to claim that he was the 'Oracle Bird'. The name of this happy-go-lucky character was Skuratov. Finally he burst into some dashing song or other, the refrain of which was, as I remember:

I was not even at my own wedding
So hard in the mills I was working.

All he needed was a balalaika.

Needless to say, his too cheery mood irritated some of the others in our party and was taken as even a personal affront.

"Hark at him howling away," said one of them resentfully, though it was none of his business really.

"The wolf had just this one song to howl but you went and nicked it, my old mate from Tula," remarked one of the sullen ones in his thick Ukrainian accent.

"So what if I am from Tula?" Skuratov countered immediately. "It's you people from Poltava—choking on your curds."

"What do you know about it! Look who's talking! Yokel, slopping up your soup out of a boot!"

"And here it's the devil who feeds us," a third person joined in.

"I'm not joking, mates; I'm used to having it easy, I am," with a light sigh Skuratov addressed everyone in general and no one in particular, as though apologising for his own delicacy. "Right from birth I've been caught up (by which he meant "brought up"—he mixed up the words purposely) on the finest French buns and prunes. And my own dear brothers still have their own shop in Moscow, they buy and sell things that come their way. Real rich merchants they are!"

"And what was it you dealt in?"

"Oh, you know, different things. That, mates, is when I got my first two hundred."

"Roubles do you mean?" one curious listener asked; he actually jumped at the thought of so much money.

"No, not roubles, my dear old fellow, but strokes of the rod. Hey, Luka, old boy..."

"I may be Luka to some people, but to you I'm Luka Kuzmich," grudgingly answered a small, thin, sharp-nosed prisoner.

"All right, let it be Luka Kuzmich, if you're so damn partic'lar."

"Luka Kuzmich to some people—Uncle Luka Kuzmich to you."

"Oh damn you and damn 'uncle'—it's hardly worth talking to you. And I was going to say something nice to you. Well now, mates, it happens that I was not to be in Moscow for long. They gave me fifteen lashes and sent me on my way. So then I..."

"What were you sent away for?" interrupted one listener who had been following the story very carefully.

"Well, to teach me not to go a-jugging an' a-supping an' a-spluttering when I shouldn't. Oh mates! That's why I didn't manage to get rich properly in Moscow. Oh, but how I wanted to! I wanted it so badly—just how badly I could never tell you!"

A lot of people burst out laughing. Clearly Skuratov was one of those self-appointed jesters, or—I should say perhaps clowns—who seem to make it their duty to cheer up their miserable companions and, for their pains, get nothing, of course, but swearing. He belonged to a very special and remarkable type of prisoner, which I shall probably find occasion to mention again.

"Even now you're better game than a sable," remarked Luka Kuzmich. "To look at you here must be at least a hundred roubles worth of clothes on you."

Skuratov was dressed in the most threadbare and worn-out sheepskin imaginable, patched all over. Somewhat indifferently, but carefully, he surveyed himself from head to toe.

"Yes, but my old head is worth a bit, isn't it, mates, my old head is," he answered. "That was my only consolation when I left Moscow—that my old head would go with me. Farewell to you, Moscow, and thanks for the drubbing, for a free spirit, for wealing me nicely all over! And as for the sheepskin, there's no need for you to look at it, my good man..."

"Maybe I ought to look at your head instead?"

"Even his head doesn't really belong to him. He got given it by way of alms," said Luka, getting involved in the conversation again. "He got it given him in Tyumen as his party was passing through."

"Tell us, Skuratov, didn't you ever learn any craft?"

"Craft, you say! He used to lead blind folk around and steal their lolly," remarked one of the sullen ones. "That's the only craft he knew."

"Well yes, I did try my hand at a bit of cobbling," ansered Skuratov, ignoring this biting remark. "I only managed to make one pair though."

"And did anyone buy them from you?"

"Yes, there was one fellow, he evidently had no fear of God and no respect for his mother and father. So God punished him for it, and he bought my boots."

Everyone round Skuratov roared with laughter. "And one other time after that, when I was already here, I did a bit of work," Skuratov continued with the utmost composure. "I put some toe-caps on Lieutenant Stepan Fyodorovich's boots for him."

"Was he pleased about it?"

"No mates, he wasn't. He cursed me to eternity and kicked me up the arse. That's how mad he was. Oh yes, life was really let me down, it has ... this prison life has let me down.

"Oh and that was the moment
Akulina's husband returned."

Here, he burst suddenly into song again, jumping and stamping his feet in time.

"Look what a disgrace the man is," grumbled the Ukrainian next to me, narrowing his eyes maliciously as he looked at Skuratov.

"Absolutely useless!" remarked someone else in a very definite and serious tone of voice.

I simply could not understand why they were all so angry with Skuratov, nor why it was generally true—as I had already observed during these first few days—that anyone who was cheerful was regarded with a degree of contempt. I had thought that the anger of this Ukrainian, and the anger of the others as well, was something personal. But the anger was not aimed against a particular individual, what angered them was that in Skuratov there was no self-restraint, no put-on look of self-respect which the whole prison was infected with, and that he was in their own words a 'useless' person. Still, they did not get angry with everyone who was cheerful or treated them with the same contempt as they did Skuratov and others like him. It all depended on how an individual allowed the others to treat him. A good-natured, unaffected person who did not put on any airs would immediately be subjected to contemptuous treatment. This was something that struck me very forcefully. Yet even among the cheerful types, there were those who were quite capable and quite fond of snapping back; and they had to be treated with respect. There was just such a sharp-tongued character in this crowd. He was really a most cheerful and endearing person—though that was a side of his character which I only found out about much later. He was a tall, handsome lad with a big wart on his cheek and a really comic expression on his face, which was rather good-looking and clever all the same. They used to call him 'the sapper' because that was the regiment he had been in; he was now in the special category. I shall have more to say about him later.

True, not all the 'serious ones' were as forthcoming as this Ukrainian who was so scandalised by such cheerfulness. There were several men in the prison who aspired to be leaders: in craftsmanship, in resourcefulness, in strength of character, in brains. Quite a few of them were in fact clever people, of character, and they did indeed achieve what they aspired to:

leadership and a considerable moral influence over their fellows. These clever individuals were often at daggers drawn with each other—and they attracted a great deal of hatred too. They affected a very dignified—even rather condescending—manner towards the other prisoners; they never started unnecessary arguments, were in the authorities' good books, behaved at work as though they were the foremen, and not one of them would ever pick on anyone for singing—they would never sink to so trivial a level. To me, throughout my whole term in prison—they were all extraordinarily polite, though they did not communicate with me—that, too, seemed to be in keeping with their sense of dignity. I shall have to come back to them later, and talk about them in greater detail.

At last we arrived at the riverbank. Down below, frozen into the ice, stood an old barge—the one that had to be taken to pieces. On the opposite bank of the river was the blue expanse of the steppe: a gloomy and desolate sight. I had expected everyone to get down to work with enthusiasm, but the thought had not even occurred to them. Some sat themselves down on the logs that were scattered around the bank; practically everybody took out of their boots a tobacco pouch containing a local blend of tobacco—the kind that was sold in the market at three kopeks a pound—and home-made pipes with wooden bowls fitted on to short willow stems. The pipes were lit; the guards stationed themselves in a circle around us, and began to watch over us with an air of intense boredom.

"Whoever got it into his head to break up this barge?" said one of the prisoners, though he was speaking to himself, without addressing anyone in particular. "Do they need some sticks or something?"

"Someone who isn't afraid of us, anyway," remarked one of the others.

"Where on earth can all those peasants be going?" said the first speaker after a short silence, and without taking any notice of the previous remark. He was pointing towards the crowd of peasants who, in single file, were making their way somewhere through the untrodden snow. Everyone lazily turned to look at them, and, for want of anything better to do, began to make jokes at the peasants' expense. The peasant who brought up the rear was walking in a very funny manner, with his arms stuck out, and his head on one side. He was wearing a hat shaped like a tall cone, and his whole figure stood out sharply against the white snow.

"Just look at him, the village Yokel!" one prisoner said, imitating a broad peasant dialect. "Look at the way he's dressed!" It was remarkable that the prisoners generally regarded the peasants somewhat condescendingly, although a good half of them were from peasant families themselves.

"That last one's walking as though he's planting out radishes."

"Yes, he's a deep thinker that one! He's probably got plenty of money," a third voice chimed in.

Everyone laughed, though rather lazily and almost reluctantly. Meanwhile, one of the bread girls had come up to us—a brisk, saucy young woman.

We bought some buns from her with the five kopeks we had been given as alms, and at once divided them out evenly among ourselves.

One young lad, who used to sell buns inside the gaol, took about twenty of them and began to haggle for three instead of just two extra buns, which was the usual thing. But the bread girl would not budge.

"Well, will you give me a bit of the other then?"

"What 'other'?"

"What the mice don't eat."

"The pox on you!" shrieked the young woman—then burst out laughing.

Finally the overseer arrived—a sergeant carrying a cane. "Hey you, what are you sitting about for? Get working!"

"Come on, Ivan Matveich, put it down as a 'task', will you?" said one of those 'in charge' characters, slowly getting up from his place.

"Why didn't you ask for it this morning at the roll call? Just pull the barge to pieces and that will be that."

Reluctantly everybody got to their feet and dragged themselves down towards the river. Immediately some of the self-appointed 'foremen' began to make their opinions known in the crowd. The barge, it turned out, was not to be hacked up but, if possible, the logs had to be preserved and in particular the transversal *kokoras* (the knee-timbers were fixed along their whole length to the bottom of the barge with wooden nails)— a difficult and tedious task.

"Now, the first thing we must do is pull that here log free. Let's get started then, lads!" This remark did not come from one of the 'foremen' nor one of the 'in charge' characters, but from a quiet lad, an ordinary labourer of few words, who had said nothing up to this point, but who now, bending down, embraced a thick log with his arms, and waited for someone to come and help him. Nobody moved.

"Like hell, you'll lift that! Even if your grandad the bear was here to help you, he wouldn't have lifted it either!" someone muttered sullenly.

"So how shall we get started then, mates? I really can't see..." said the puzzled volunteer, abandoning the log and straightening up.

"There's no end to work, so what's the hurry to get started?"

"He couldn't figure out how much food to give three chickens, and here he is going first... The windbag!"

"Why, I didn't mean anything," the puzzled prisoner continued, trying to make excuses for himself. "I just..."

"And what am I supposed to do with you—put dust covers over you? Or maybe put you in moth balls for the winter?" shouted the overseer again, looking in perplexity at the gang of twenty that did not know how to start working. "Get going! Faster!"

"You can't go faster than fast, Ivan Matveich!"

"But you're not doing anything anyway. Hey there, Savelyev! Yes, I'm talking to you! Don't just stand there, gaping! Start working immediately!"

"What can I do on my own?"

"Come on, make it a 'task', Ivan Matveich!"

"I've told you, there isn't going to be any 'task'. Pull the barge to pieces and then get yourselves off home. Now get started!"

They did start at last, though ineptly, clumsily, and grudgingly. The sight of this large crowd of sturdy labourers, who really did not seem to know how to set about this work, was quite distressing. No sooner had they started to pull the nails out of the first and smallest of the *kokoras* than it began to split—"split all on its own", as they told the overseer, by way of justification. Well, if that was the wrong way of going about it, then they'd better try a different tack. A long discussion ensued about what this 'different tack' might be, and what to do. Naturally, it ended in swearing, and seemed likely to end in blows as well... The overseer shouted at them and brandished his cane, but the *kokora* split again. It turned out that we were short of axes, and that some other tools would have to be fetched. Two of the men were dispatched immediately, under escort, to fetch the tools from the fort, and the rest, while they were waiting for these tools to arrive, imperturbably sat down on the barge, took out their pipes and lit them.

At last the overseer threw in his hand.

"Seems we won't get any work out of you. Oh you, people..." he grumbled, gave a hopeless wave with a hand, and set off towards the fortress, swinging his cane.

An hour later the supervisor arrived. He listened calmly to what the prisoners had to say, then announced that he would record it as a 'task fulfilled' if they took out four more *kokoras*, but this time they must be whole and not split and if, in addition, they dismantled a considerable part of the barge. After that, everyone could go home. This was a lot of work for a 'task', but—good God!—how they set about it! No trace of laziness or bewilderment! They got busy with their axes, and started pulling out the wooden nails. Some of the others laid thick poles down underneath the *kokoras* and heaving at them with twenty hands, began briskly and skilfully prising them free, in a way which—to my surprise—brought them out completely whole and undamaged. Work was in full swing. Everyone had somehow grown remarkably clever. There were no wasted words, no swearing. Everyone knew what to say, what to do, where to stand, what to suggest. Exactly half an hour before the drum sounded, the designated 'task' was completed, and the prisoners went home, tired but completely satisfied, though all

107

they had gained from the allocated time was a measly half-hour. As far as I personally was concerned, there was one particular thing that I noticed. Wherever I tried to lend the men a hand, I was always out of place, always in the way, and told to get out almost with curses.

Even the lowest ragamuffin, who was himself a poor worker and who quailed before the other brighter and smarter prisoners, even he thought he had the right to shout at me if I stopped beside him to lend him a hand, to get out of his way and let him get on with his work. Finally, one of the smarter workers said to me, quite frankly and rudely:

"Keep out, and take yourself off. Can't you see you're not wanted."

"He's had it straight now!" one of the others immediately added.

"Better get yourself a poor-box and go begging, there's nothing for you to do here," a third one told me.

So I had to stand apart, and standing apart when everyone else is working is very embarrassing. But when I did walk away and stood alone at the end of the barge, they all started yelling at once:

"Look what kind of workers they've given us. What can you do with the likes of them? Nothing!"

All this was, of course, done deliberately, because it provided entertainment for everyone. They had to make sport of me, an ex-nobleman, and they naturally welcomed the chance.

So now it should be quite clear why—as I have said before—the first problem for me on my arrival in gaol was how to conduct myself, and on what footing to be with these people. I had a foreboding that there would often be confrontations such as this one now, at work. Yet in spite of all such confrontations, I decided that I would not change the plan of action which I had already formed in my mind. I knew that it was the right plan. I had decided to behave as simply as possible towards them and as independently, without making a special effort to get closer to them, yet not rejecting them either, should they themselves wish to establish a closer contact with me; not to be afraid of their threats and their hatred, and if possible to

108

pretend that I did not even notice such things; not to become matey with them in certain matters; not to pander to their habits and customs. I would not, in other words, seek their friendship. From the very outset, I guessed that they would have despised me if I had. However (as I later found out for certain), I ought really, in their opinion, to have observed the rules of behaviour due my noble birth. That is to say, I should have been more of a mollycoddle, I should have put on airs, turned up my nose at them, sniffed disdainfully at every step, and shirked work. That was what they understood a nobleman to be. They would then, of course, have cursed me for behaving like this, but in their hearts they would have respected me nonetheless. Playing such a role did not appeal to me. I had never been a nobleman in their sense of the word. Instead, I vowed to myself that I would never be a traitor to my education or my way of thinking in front of them, by making any concessions. If, wishing to please them, I started to play up to them, to agree with them, to become matey with them and to adopt all their 'qualities' just to curry favour with them, they would immediately jump to the conclusion that I was doing so out of fear and cowardice, and treat me with contempt. A—v was not a typical example in this case: he carried tales to the Major, and they were all afraid of him themselves. I did not, on the other hand, want to shut myself away behind a barrier of cold and inaccessible civility, as the Poles did. I could see clearly how they despised me for wanting to work like they did, and for not playing the pampered nobleman in front of them; and although I was sure that they would eventually have to change their opinion of me, yet the thought that in the meantime they seemed to have the right to despise me for apparently trying to win their favour at work—upset me very badly.

In the evening, when I returned to the gaol tired and exhausted from the afternoon work, a terrible feeling of depression came over me again. How many more thousands of such days are in store for me, I thought—all alike, all the same! It was already twilight, and I was walking about by myself along the paling behind the barracks, when I suddenly saw our Sharik, running straight towards me. Sharik was the prison dog, just as there are company, battery, and squadron dogs. He had been living in the gaol since time immemorial. He did not belong to anybody. He regarded everybody as his master, and lived on scraps from the kitchen. He was quite a big dog, black with white patches, a mongrel, not particularly old, with intelligent eyes and a fluffy tail. Nobody ever stroked him or took any notice of him. Already on my first day I had stroked him and fed him some bread out of my hand. While I was stroking him, he stood stock-still, gazing up at me tenderly and wagging his tail with pleasure. Quite a while had passed since he last saw me—the first person who had ever thought of stroking him in several years—and he ran around among all the prisoners looking for me. When he finally did find me behind the barracks, he dashed towards me, barking happily. I simply do not know what came over me, but I rushed forward to kiss him, to hug his head. He jumped up, put both his paws on my shoulders, and started to lick my face. So this is the friend that fate has sent me, I thought, and thereafter, during these first difficult and depressing months, when I came back from work, I first of all, before going indoors, hurried to the back of the barracks, with Sharik jumping in front of me and whimpering with joy, and then hugged his head and kissed it—and as I kissed it, my heart was wrung with a sweet yet tormentingly bitter pain. I remember that I even took perverse pleasure in the thought, priding myself upon my own pain as it were, that in the whole world there remained only one living creature who loved me, who was attached to me, who was my friend, my only friend— and this was my faithful dog Sharik.

VII

New Acquaintances. Petrov

Time, however, was passing, and bit by bit I began to settle in. With each day the everyday happenings in my new life bewildered me less and less. The incidents, the atmosphere, the people ceased to amaze me. Coming to terms with this life was impossible, but it was high time to accept it as an irrevocable actual fact. All my still lingering misconceptions I buried as deeply within myself as I could. No longer did I wander around the gaol like a lost soul, or wear my heart upon my sleeve. The convicts did not stop to stare at me with savage curiosity as often as before, nor did they watch me with such emphatic scorn. They too must have grown used to the sight of me, and I was very happy that it was so. I already walked around the gaol as around my own home. I knew which place was mine on the bed-shelf, and I suppose I even grew accustomed to things that I had thought I would never get used to in my whole life. Regularly, every week, I went to have half of my head shaved. Every Saturday, during our time off, we were called out in turn from the gaol to the guardhouse for that very purpose. (Anyone who failed to shave was answerable for it.) There were barbers from the battalions there. They soaped our heads all over with cold soap, and then scraped them pitilessly with the bluntest razor imaginable. A shiver runs down my spine, even now, when I remember that torture. A remedy was found soon enough though. Akim Akimovich pointed out a prisoner from the military category who made his living by shaving people with his own razor for one kopek. A good number of the convicts—people who were not, by any stretch of imagination, hot house plants—used to go to him in order to escape the prison barbers. This private barber of ours was known as 'Major'—I do not know why, nor can I see how he could be said to resemble a major. Now, as I am writing, this 'Major' comes before my mind very vividly: a tall, lean and silent lad, rather stupid, always preoccupied with his work, and always holding a razor strap in his hand on which he whetted his completely worn-away razor day and night, an occupation in which he was completely engrossed, thinking it the sole purpose of his entire life. He really was extremely pleased when his razor was good and sharp and when somebody came to be shaved: his soap was warm, his hand was light and his touch was like velvet. Apparently he enjoyed his craft and was proud of it, and he took the kopek he had earned very carelessly, as if the real point was his craft and not the kopek. A—v got a good trouncing from our Major when once in his current report he mentioned the barber, and referred to him mindlessly as 'Major'. The Major was terribly offended and flew into a rage.

"Do you know what a major is, you scoundrel!" he shouted, foaming at the mouth and laying into A—v as he was wont to do. "Do you understand what a major is! Some scoundrel of a convict, and you dare to call him a major in front of me, in my presence!"

Only A—v could get along with such a man.

From my very first day in gaol, I started to dream about freedom. Calculating how much longer I had left till the end of my term, with thousands of different variations, became my favourite pastime. I could not even think about anything else, and I am certain that it is the same with anyone who is deprived of freedom for a term. I do not know whether the other prisoners thought about their future freedom and did the same calculations I did, but the astonishing flippancy of their hopes struck me from the very outset. The hopes of a convict who is deprived of his freedom are completely different from those of a man who lives a normal life. A free man also has hopes, of course (for a change in his situation, or the successful outcome of some undertaking or other)—but he lives and he acts; and he is swept into the whirl of real life. Not so for a prisoner. It's life too, of course—prison life, hard-labour life. But no matter who the convict is, and for however long he has been sentenced, he instinctively and quite definitely cannot accept his fate as something positive and final, as a part of real life. No convict feels that he is at home, but rather as though he is *here for a stay*. He thinks of twenty years as two, and is perfectly certain that when he leaves gaol at the age of fifty-five, he will still be the same robust fellow he is now at the age of thirty-five. "We've got plenty of living to do yet!" he says to himself, and stubbornly drives away any doubts or unwelcome thoughts. Even those here for an indefinite period, like the prisoners in the special category, even they make calculations about the future sometimes, hoping that a reprieve might suddenly come from St. Petersburg: "To be sent to the mines in Nerchinsk, and given a fixed term." Then everything would be just fine. For one thing, Nerchinsk is almost a six-months' march away, and marching in a party of convicts is a hundred times better than being in gaol. For another, he would just finish the term in Nerchinsk, and then... To think that even grey-haired men could count on this!

In Tobolsk I saw people chained to the wall. A man like that sits on his chain, which is about two metres long, and he has his bedding there too. He has been chained up like that for something terrible, something quite out of the ordinary, and committed while he was already here, in Siberia. There are some who are chained like this for five years, some even for ten. Most of them had been bandits. I saw only one who appeared to be from a higher level of society. At one time he had been a civil servant somewhere. He spoke with such lisping humility, a sugary smile playing on his lips. He showed his chain to us, and demonstrated the most comfortable way of lying down to sleep with it. That bird must have been quite somebody in his time. In most cases these people behave very meekly and seem quite content, while they are actually all dying to be done with the chain. What then, one might ask? I will tell you. Taken off the chain the convict will then be able to come out of his stifling, damp room with its low brick vaults, and walk around in the prison yard ... and nothing more. He will never be allowed outside the gaol. He knows very well that a person released from his chain is kept inside the gaol, in shackles, for the rest of his life. He knows this very well, but just the same he can hardly wait to get off the chain. If not for this wish, how could he survive being chained to a wall for five or six years without dying or going mad?

I felt strongly that work could save me, and strengthen me in health and body. The endless emotional instability, nervous irritation, the stuffy air of the barrack could make a complete ruin of me. "Being in the fresh air more often, getting tired every day, growing used to carrying heavy weights—at least in this way," I thought, "I should be able to save myself, to strengthen myself, to leave prison a healthy, alert and strong man, without ageing prematurely." I was not wrong in this: work and movement had a very good effect on me. I watched with horror how one of my friends (a former nobleman) was fading away, burning down like a candle. He had entered the prison at the same time as I did, when he was still young, handsome, alert; and he left it a grey-haired ruin of a man, hardly able to walk, and short of breath. "No," I thought when I looked at him, "I want to live—and I shall live." At first, of course, I took a lot of unpleasantness from the other convicts for my love of work; for a long time they stung me with their contempt and jeering. I ignored them all, and I went off somewhere to burn or crush alabaster, for example, which was one of the first jobs I came to know. This was an easy job. The engineering authorities were, where possible, prepared to make work easier for noblemen, which was only fair actually. It would be strange to demand the fulfilment of the same task given to the real labourers or someone who was half as strong and had never really worked. Such 'pampering' was not always practised, however, and then rather secretly, because the higher authorities watched this with a stern eye. We were often given hard work, and then, of course, the nobles suffered twice as badly as the other labourers. Three or four people from among the old and weak ones, and that, of course, included us, were detailed to the alabaster job, plus one real worker who had the knack of it. For several years running, it was usually one and the same person who came: Almazov, a middle-aged austere, dark-skinned, lean character who communicated very little, and was extremely sour-tempered. He despised us from the bottom of his heart. He was so taciturn that he could not even be bothered to grumble at us. The shed where the alabaster was baked and crushed stood on a steep and empty bank of the river. In winter, especially on overcast days, it was very dispiriting to look out over the river and the opposite bank. There was something heart-rendingly depressing in that wild and desolate landscape. Yet it was even harder to bear when the sun shone brightly on the endless expanse of white snow; if only one could fly away somewhere into the steppe, which started on the opposite bank and rolled away southwards for one and a half thousand versts. Almazov usually got down to work silently and glumly. We were embarrassed that we could not really help, while he deliberately managed on his own, deliberately not asking for any help, as though he wanted to make us feel guilty and punish ourselves with our own uselessness. Whereas all that needed to be done was to get the stove heated up for baking the alabaster, which we had, as a rule, brought there for him ourselves. The next day, when the alabaster was baked, we had to unload it from the stove. Each of us took a heavy wooden hammer, filled his box with the alabaster, and started crushing it. This was a marvellous job. Fragile alabaster turns quickly into a white, sparkling powder, and crushes so easily and so nicely. We swung our heavy hammers and got such a crackling going that we enjoyed every minute of it. Of course, we felt tired afterwards, but better too: our cheeks were glowing, our blood was running faster. Almazov looked at us more condescendingly now, like someone who was watching little children, and smoked his pipe condescendingly too, though he could not help grumbling every time he opened his mouth. He was the same with everybody and, all in all, seemed to be a kind soul.

Another job I used to be sent to was turning the lathe in the workshop. The wheel was large and heavy, and it took a great effort to keep it revolving, especially when the turner (one of the engineering craftsmen) was shaping something like a baluster or the leg of a big table, out of almost a whole log, when he was making furniture for some official or other. One man could not manage the wheel then, and two of us were detailed as a rule—myself and B., one of the other noblemen. This work was given to us over the course of several years, whenever there was something to be turned. B. was a young man, but weak and frail, suffering from a bad chest. He had come to the gaol a year before me with two of his friends—one, an old man who prayed day and night throughout the whole of his time in gaol (a fact which won him the respect of the other prisoners) and who died while I was there, and the other, who was still a very young man, fresh, rosy-cheeked, strong and brave, and who, from the halfway stage of their journey, had carried the exhausted B. for seven hundred versts. This was a friendship to be witnessed. B. was a man of excellent education and noble heart, he was magnanimous by nature but his illness had made him irritable. We used to cope with the wheel together, and both found it interesting. This work kept me in excellent trim.

In particular, I liked clearing away the snow. This was usually done after a snowstorm and was not at all rare in winter. After a day and night of heavy snowfall, some of the buildings were drifted halfway up to windows, and some were completely buried under. When the snowstorm was over and the sun came out, we were driven out in large groups—sometimes that meant the whole gaol, to clear away the snowdrifts from the prison buildings. Each man was given a shovel, and everyone together was set a 'task'—so enormous sometimes that one wondered how it could ever be fulfilled. We got down to it all together. Huge lumps of the crumbly snow, which had only just settled and was slightly frosted over on top, were easily picked up by the shovels and then thrown away from the buildings, turning into a sparkling dust in mid-air. The shovels cut so nicely into the white mass, glistening in the sun. The prisoners were almost always in high spirits when doing this job. The fresh winter air and the exercise warmed them up. Everybody grew cheerful; there was laughter and shouting and jokes. They started playing snowballs, but a minute later, of course, the spoil-sports, resenting the laughter and happiness, shouted at them to stop it, and the general merriment usually ended in a row.

Little by little I began to broaden my circle of acquaintances. I did not actually think of making acquaintances myself, I was still too disturbed and morose and suspicious. My circle of acquaintances grew of its own accord. One of the first who started to visit me was the prisoner Petrov. I say 'to visit me' and I would like to emphasise this phrase. Petrov was one of the 'special category' convicts and lived in the barrack which was furthest away from my own. It did not seem as though there could be any links between us. We had positively nothing in common, nor could we possibly have. Still, during this first period of my sentence, Petrov seemed to consider it his duty to come and visit me in my barrack almost every day or stop me during our time off, when I went for a walk behind the barracks, out of sight if possible. At first I found it unpleasant. But he somehow contrived to make his visits even enjoyable for me, though he was neither a particularly sociable nor a particularly talkative person. In appearance he was of medium height, strongly built, agile, and fidgety. He had a rather pleasant and pale face with prominent cheekbones, a bold expression, fine small white teeth, and an eternal pinch of rubbed tobacco behind his lower lip. This habit of putting tobacco inside the lip was popular with quite a few prisoners. He seemed younger than his years. He was about forty, but he looked no more than thirty. He always talked to me very freely and naturally, behaved very much as my equal, that is to say, with extreme tact and dignity. If he noticed that I wanted to be alone, he left me after a couple of minutes, each time thanking me for my attention, which he did not do for anyone else in the gaol. Curiously, this kind of relationship continued between us not only during these first days but for several years running, and we hardly grew any more intimate than this, despite the fact that he was very faithful to me. Even now I cannot decide what was it that he actually wanted from me? Why did he stick to me every day? He did steal things from me later on, but in a way that seemed to be almost *by accident*. He hardly ever asked me for money, so he cannot have come for that.

Also—I do not quite know why—it always seemed to me that he somehow did not live in the gaol like I did, but somewhere far away in town, in a different house, and just visited the gaol in passing to find out what was new there, to see me, to find out how we were all getting along. He was always in a hurry, as though he had left somebody somewhere and they were waiting for him, or as though he had left something unfinished. At the same time, he did not seem to be too flustered either. He also had a strange sort of glance; it was intent, with a touch of courage and a certain irony in it, but he seemed to look off somewhere into the distance, through things, as if behind the object which was in front of his nose, he was trying to make out another one, which was further off. This gave him an air of absent-mindedness. Sometimes I watched him go, wondering where he went after he left me. Where was someone waiting for him so impatiently? But when he left me, he always hurried off to his barrack or the kitchen, and sat down there near someone who was talking, listening attentively, sometimes joining in the conversation himself, even quite heatedly, then suddenly cutting himself short and falling silent. Whatever he happened to be doing, whether speaking or sitting quietly, he always seemed to have stopped for just a moment, in passing, and that somewhere over there, there was something that needed doing, and people were waiting for him. The strangest thing was that he did not have anything to do at all—ever! He lived a life of total idleness (apart from the prison labour, of course). He did not know any trade, and was almost always out of pocket. He did not let himself worry too much even over money. And what did he talk to me about? His conversation was as peculiar as himself. He would, for example, catch sight of me walking somewhere at the back of the barracks, and suddenly swing round sharply towards me. He always moved swiftly, and always swung round sharply. He walked up to me, but it seemed somehow that he had run.

"Good day."

"Good day."

"I hope I am not disturbing you."

"No."

"You see, I wanted to ask you about Napoleon. He's a relative of the one from 1812, isn't he?" (Petrov was a soldier's son and had gone to military school.)

"They are related."

"And what kind of president is he considered to be?"

He always asked questions quickly, abruptly, as though he needed to obtain the information as quickly as possible, or as though he were making inquiries about some urgent matter that would not brook any delay.

I explained what kind of president Napoleon was, and added that he would perhaps be Emperor soon as well.

"How come?"

I explained as well as I could. Petrov listened to me attentively, quickly grasping my meaning, and even bending an ear towards me.

"Hmm! I also wanted to ask you, Alexander Petrovich: is it true that there are monkeys as tall as the tallest man with arms hanging down to their heels?"

"Yes, there are."

"Well, which kind of monkey are they?"

I explained as much as I knew.

"So where do they live?"

"In hot countries. There are some on the island of Sumatra."

"Where's that? In America? Why do they say that the people there walk upside down?"

"No, not upside down. Now you're talking about the anti-podes."

I explained what America was and what the antipodes were, as far as I could. He listened with the same rapt attention, as though his sole purpose in coming had been to find out about the antipodes.

"I see! And last year I read a book about the Countess Lava-lier,[8] Arefyev brought the book from the Adjutant. Is it true or is it just—well, a fiction? It's by Dumas."

"Just a fiction, of course."

"Well, fare you well. Thank you very much."

And Petrov would disappear. Our conversations always went something like this.

I began to make inquiries about him. M., who had discovered my acquaintance with Petrov, actually warned me against him. He told me that many of the convicts had filled him with terror, especially at the beginning, during his first days in the gaol, but that no one, not even Gazin, had produced such a horrible impression on him as this Petrov.

"This man," said M., "is the most resolute and fearless of all the prisoners. He is capable of anything. When he's taken a fancy to do something, he'll stop at nothing. He would cut your throat too, if the idea came into his head, just like that, he'd murder you without batting an eyelid and without any feeling of repentance either. I even think he is out of his mind."

This description intrigued me. M., however, could not account for his feelings. And, strange thing, though I kept up my acquaintance with Petrov for a number of years after that, I talked to him nearly every day, he was always sincerely attached to me (though I really do not know why) and though throughout these years he was on good behaviour in the gaol and never did anything terrible, each time I talked to him, and listened to him, I felt convinced that M. was right and that Petrov was perhaps the most resolute, fearless and unconstrainable of people. Why it seemed so—that I could not tell you either.

I must mention, however, that this Petrov was the very same man who wanted to kill the Major when he was called out for the whipping and from whom the Major was saved by 'Divine intervention' as the prisoners said, having left just a minute earlier. There was an earlier incident, before Siberia. His Colonel hit him during drill; Petrov must have been hit many times before, but this time he refused to take it lying down, and stabbed the Colonel to death quite openly, in broad daylight, in full view of the line formation. I do not know the whole story in detail; he never told it to me. These incidents were just explosions, when his nature suddenly revealed itself in its entirety. They happened very rarely, it must be said. He really was a very sensible, even quiet sort of person. There were passions hidden deep within him, strong, burning passions, but these hot coals were always covered by ashes, and smouldered underneath, quietly. I never perceived the slightest hint of braggery or vanity in him, as I did, for example, in the others. He rarely argued with anyone, though on the other hand he was not particularly friendly with anyone either—with the single exception of Sirotkin, perhaps, but only when he needed him. True, I once saw him really losing his temper. Something—some object—was being withheld from him; he had been done out of something. He was arguing with Vasily Antonov from the civilian category, a very strong and tall man, spiteful, pugnacious, much given to mocking and anything but a coward. They had already been shouting at each other for some time, and I thought that, at the most, the affair would end in a bit of a scuffle, because Petrov, though rarely, did fight and swear like the lowest of the convicts. This time, however, something different happened. Petrov suddenly turned pale, his lips began to tremble and went blue; he seemed to find it difficult to breathe. Slowly, he got up from his seat, and slowly, very slowly, on soundless bare feet (he loved to go around barefoot in summer) he went up to Antonov. Immediately, silence fell upon the noisy, yelling crowd. You could have heard a pin drop. Everyone was waiting to see what would happen. Antonov jumped up to meet him; the blood had drained from his face. I could not stand any more, and I left the barrack. I expected to hear the scream of a man being murdered before I had stepped down from the porch. Nothing happened. Before Petrov had even reached him, Antonov quickly and silently threw him the thing they had been arguing over. (The argument was over some pitiful piece of rag, a foot-cloth or something.) Two minutes later, of course, Antonov called him a few names again, just to salve his conscience and save face, to show he was not a complete coward. But Petrov took no notice of his swearing—he did not even bother to answer back. Swearing was not the issue, and it had all worked out in his favour. He was quite satisfied, and took the rag. A quarter of an hour later he was again wandering about the gaol with an indolent air as if looking for people who would talk about something really interesting so that he could join them and listen for a while. Everything, it seemed, amused him, but somehow nothing touched him, and he wandered around the prison without anything to do, blown here and there by the wind. He could even be compared to a hefty labourer who, ready to put his back into his work at a moment's notice, but not yet given anything to do, sits waiting and plays with the little children. Another thing I was unable to understand was why he stayed in the gaol, and did not run away. He would never have thought twice about running away if the desire had really caught hold of him. People like Petrov are controlled by their reason only until they start to want something very badly. Then there is nothing in the whole world that can stand between them and their desire. And I am sure he would have managed to escape very cleverly, fooling everybody, and sitting out the chase in the forest or the river rushes for a week or more without anything to eat. It seemed that the idea had not occurred to him yet, or perhaps he did not yet want to escape *badly enough.* I had never been aware of any great reasoning powers or common sense in him. People of his kind are born with one idea that operates upon them subconsciously, pushing them hither and thither without their knowledge; so they dash around all their lives, till they find something they like, and then they don't care if their heads go rolling. It surprised me sometimes that a man such as Petrov, who had murdered his commander for hitting him, took his whipping here without a murmur. He was flogged sometimes, when caught with liquor. Like all the other prisoners with no trade, he now and then had a go at bringing in liquor. Even for the flogging he lay down as if it was his own choice, knowing that he was getting what he deserved; otherwise he would never have lain down even if they had killed him for it. It also amazed me that, for all his apparent attachment to me, he sometimes stole from me. This came over him in fits and starts somehow. It was he who stole my Bible which I asked him to take somewhere for me. It was a distance of no more than a few paces, but even then he somehow managed to find a buyer for it on the way, sold it and immediately spent the money on drink. He must have had a sudden and irresistible craving for liquor, and if he wanted something really badly—he *had to get it* immediately. People of this sort will murder someone for twenty-five kopeks to buy a gill of liquor with, while at another time they will let a man with a hundred thousand roubles on him go safely on his way. He announced the theft to me himself on the very same evening, though without a hint of embarrassment or regret, absolutely indifferently, as though talking about some everyday event. I tried to give him a good talking to. Apart from everything else, I hated losing my Bible. He listened to me very meekly, without becoming at all irritated. He agreed that the Bible was a very useful book, was sincerely sorry that I no longer had it, but showed no regret for having stolen it from me. He looked at me with such self-confidence that I stopped telling him off at once. Apparently he put up with my scolding because he figured that one could not get away without some castigation for doing such a thing... "Let him get it off his chest and indulge himself in a bit of scolding, though actually it is all nonsense, a serious person would feel ashamed even to discuss it." I believe he regarded me as a child, almost an infant, who could not understand the very simplest things in life. If, for example, it was I who started talking to him about something other than science or books, he did answer me, but apparently only out of politeness and as curtly as he could. I often asked myself what there was for him in all this book learning he was always questioning me about. Sometimes I glanced at him out of the corner of my eye during these conversations. Maybe he was laughing at me? No, not at all. He usually listened seriously and attentively, though not—it must be noted—too attentively, and this last fact annoyed me sometimes. He formulated his questions precisely and clearly, but he did not seem too impressed by the information I gave him, receiving it almost absent-mindedly... It also seemed that he had decided, without bothering his brains too long over it, that he could not speak to me the way he spoke to others, that apart from conversations about books, I could not—and was even unable—to understand things, so there was no point in troubling me.

I am sure that he even felt fond of me, and this was something that made a deep impression on me. Could it be that he saw me as a person who had never grown up? Did he feel that special kind of compassion for me which a strong being instinctively feels for a weaker one, and did he in fact consider me to be such a weaker being?.. I do not know. And although all this did not prevent him from stealing from me, yet I feel sure that even in the act of stealing, he felt sorry for me. "Honestly, what kind of man is this, who cannot stand up for his own property!" he must have thought, while rummaging in my belongings. Yet I think it was exactly for this that he loved me. He once told me himself, just in passing: "You're too kind-hearted..." and "so very, very simple—I feel terribly sorry for you".

"Please don't take it wrong, Alexander Petrovich," he added a moment later. "I couldn't help saying it. It's what I really feel."

It does sometimes happen in life, with people such as Petrov, that they suddenly manifest their worth decisively and clearly at the time of some momentous general action or upheaval, and at such times they really come into their own. They are not men of words, and they cannot be the leaders or instigators of such actions; but they can be the main executors and also the first to act. They go into action simply, no fuss or blowing of their own trumpets: they are the first to take the main hurdle without really thinking, fearlessly charging the bayonets, and everybody else rushes in after them, following blindly, to the very last ditch, where they generally lay down their lives. I do not believe that Petrov will come to a good end; he will stake his life and lose it. If he has not perished yet, it is only because his time has not yet come. Who knows though? Perhaps he will live to a ripe old age, wandering about from one place to another without purpose, and die peacefully of senility. Yet in my judgement, M. was right when he described him as the most resolute person in the whole prison.

VIII

Resolute People. Luka

Talking about resolute people, it is hard for me to say anything. They are few and far between: in prison, as anywhere else. You would see someone who was rather frightening to look at, and you would suddenly remember the things that were said about him, and even start to avoid him and keep out of his way. At first, it was instinct that made me steer clear of these people. Later I changed my opinion, even about the most terrible murderers. There were people in gaol who had not murdered anyone, and yet were more terrible than those who had murdered six. It was even difficult to begin to form an idea of some of the crimes: there was so much that was extraordinary in them. I say this because, among the common people, there are murders that are committed for the most astounding reasons. There are, for example—and in fact they are very common— murderers of the following type. A man is living peacefully and quietly. His lot is a hard one, but he endures it. He might be a peasant, a serf, a townsman, or a soldier. Suddenly, something inside him breaks. He can no longer bear it, and he sticks a knife into his enemy and oppressor. And here the strangeness begins. The man suddenly oversteps the limit. His first victim was his oppressor, his enemy. This is a crime, but it is understandable, for there was a motive. But then he starts stabbing not only his enemies but anyone he comes along for the fun of it, just because this man was rude to him or gave him a dirty look, or simply to make it an even number, or else he yells: "Get out of my way! Step aside for me!" And that will be that. It is like inebriation or delirium. Once he has stepped over his limit, he immediately begins to delight in the idea that there is nothing sacred any longer; something goads him on to leap over all law and authority at one go and enjoy his boundless unbridled freedom to the full, to relish the sinking feeling of horror which he cannot possibly help inspiring in himself. He also knows there is a terrible punishment in store for him. All this is perhaps akin to that fascinating attraction of the abyss people look down into from a high tower, a fascination so irresistible that they are ready to plunge down head first: the sooner it will all be over, the better! This happens even to the quietest and until then quite inconspicuous people. In this dazed state, some even strike a pose. The more downtrodden the person was before, the stronger his desire to parade himself, to strike horror in the hearts of others. And he relishes their horror, he loves the loathing he inspires in others. He puts on an air of *recklessness*, and often this 'daredevil' himself is anxious to receive his punishment, *to be sentenced* as soon as possible, because this *recklessness* is too heavy a burden to bear any longer. Curiously, in most cases, this mood, this air, lasts until the moment he mounts the scaffold, and vanishes all at once. The duration of this mood may really have been preordained in some way, according to rules that have been set out in advance. On the scaffold he suddenly submits, and becomes a self-effacing weakling. He whines, and asks for people's forgiveness. And then he comes to the gaol, whimpering, sniffling, even cowed, and looking at him you can't help wondering: "Can this really be the man who murdered five or six people?"

There are some who do not become resigned quickly, even after they have come to prison. They still have some swagger left in them—some boasting. "Look at me, mates! I'm not what I seem, you know! Dispatching six souls, that's what I'm here for." But even they become resigned eventually. Only sometimes, for his own gratification, he will recall his grand doings, the spree that he went on a long time ago when he was a real *daredevil*, and his day will be made if he finds some simpleton before whom he can parade himself in full splendour, boasting and telling of his deeds, without letting on, however, that he is dying to tell someone about them. As much as to say: "That's the kind of fellow I was!"

And what a curious subtlety there is in this touchy vanity! What studied indolence in the telling of these stories! What artful affectation is revealed in the tone and every word of the narrator! Where on earth do these people learn such things?

During the long evening of one of my first days, while lying idly and miserably upon my bed-shelf, I heard one such story and because of my lack of experience, took the teller for a monstrous villain, a fantastic man of iron while at the same time I did not regard Petrov at all seriously. The story was about how the narrator, Luka Kuzmich, had *done in* a certain army major for no better reason than his own amusement! This Luka Kuzmich was the tiny, skinny young prisoner with a pointed little nose, who came from the Ukraine and whom I have already mentioned. He was actually Russian, born in the south as a serf, I think. There really was something very arrogant and boastful about him. A small bird, but with sharp claws, as the saying goes. The prisoners can see through a man instinctively. Very few people had any respect for him, or—as the prison jargon puts it: "No respect to that one." He was terribly vain. On this particular evening he was sitting on the bed-shelf stitching a shirt. His trade was sewing clothes. Next to him sat the prisoner Kobylin, his neighbour on the bed-shelf, a dull and slow-witted, though kind and affectionate lad, tall and thick-set. Luka, being his neighbour, was forever arguing with him, and treating him in a very arrogant, derisive and despotic manner—which Kobylin was too simple-minded to be fully aware of. He was knitting a woollen sock, and listening indifferently to Luka's tale. Luka spoke in a loud, clear voice, wanting everyone to pay attention to him, though pretending that his story was for the ears of Kobylin alone.

"It was when I was being deported from our place over to

Ch—v, you know, for vagrancy," he started off, picking with his needle.

"And when was that?" asked Kobylin. "A long time ago?"

"When the peas ripen again, it'll be two years. Anyway—we got as far as K—v and I was put into the prison there for a while. I took a look around. There were about twelve other men in there with me, all tall, hefty Ukrainian fellows as big as oxen. And all so obedient! The food was disgusting. The Major was on the fiddle, did just what he *fanzy-wanzied*." (Luka distorted the words on purpose.) "I was in there for one day, then another, and saw that these men in with me were a cowardly bunch. 'Why do you grovel before an idiot like him?' I asked them. 'Well you go and talk to him yourself,' they said, laughing at me. I didn't say another word.

"And one of these Ukrainians was so funny, mates," he suddenly added, forgetting Kobylin and addressing himself to everybody else. "He was telling us about his trial and verdict, and how he talked to the judge. Crying his eyes out all the time he was too. He had a wife, he said, and children, waiting for him. And he was such a tough fellow, fat and grey-haired, and mixing in bits of Ukrainian with everything he said. ' "*Ni, ni, ni,*" I told him, "no, it wasn't me!" And the damn fellow just sat there writing and writing. I wish you'd croak, and I'd watch, I thought. And still he goes on writing and writing. Then suddenly he lets out a screech. That's it, I said to myself, I'm done for.' Throw me some thread will you, Vasya. This prison stuff is rotten."

"This is from the market," said Vasya, handing him some.

"The ones from our sewing shop are better. We sent our invalid soldier for some the other day. God knows what kind of bloody woman he buys them off," continued Luka, threading his needle under the light.

"Some old crone of his!"

"I wouldn't be surprised."

"What happened then with this Major?" asked Kobylin, who had been completely forgotten.

That was exactly what Luka was waiting for. He did not go on with his story immediately though, and he even appeared to take no notice of Kobylin. Calmly, he stretched out his threads; calmly and lazily he shifted his weight from one leg to the other. Only then did he start talking.

"I got these Ukrainian fellows all worked up at last, and they demanded to see the Major. Meanwhile, in the morning, I had already borrowed a stabber from the fellow alongside me, and hid it, just in case. The Major came storming over in a rage. 'Hold steady,' I said to these Ukrainian fellows, 'hold steady now!' But all their courage had already evaporated. They were shaking in their boots. Here the Major burst in, drunk. 'Who is it? What is it? I'm the Tsar round here! I'm God!'

"And when he said this—'I'm the Tsar round here! I'm God'— I asked, moving closer and closer to him all the while, with the knife hidden up my sleeve: 'Your Honour, how can you be both the Tsar, and God?'

" 'Aha!' screamed the Major. 'So it's you, is it! You're the mutineer!'

" 'No,' I said (all the time moving closer and closer), 'no, Your Honour, as you yourself know perhaps, our omnipresent and omniscient God is one. Our Tsar is also one, placed over us all by the Lord God. He is a monarch. Whereas you, Your Honour, you are just a Major, put in authority over us, by order of our gracious Tsar, and for your merits.'

" 'How-how-how-how-how!' he just started cackling like that. He couldn't speak. He was just choking. It gave him such a shock.

" 'This is how,' I said, and I jumped on him and plunged the knife into his stomach up to the handle. I did it real proper. He just rolled over, thrashing his legs. I threw the knife away.

" 'So much for him,' I said to the Ukrainians. 'Pick him up, will you.' "

At this point I shall allow myself a digression. Such expressions as "I am the Tsar around here; I am God" and many other similar ones, were unfortunately in very frequent use among the commanders in the old times. It must be admitted, however, that there are now very few commanders of this type left—perhaps none at all. I should also add that the flaunting of expressions such as this was usually done by officers who had risen from the ranks. It is as though a commission turns their head. After drudging for a long time under the yoke, and going through every stage of subordination, they suddenly perceive themselves as officers, commanders, the nobility, and because they are not used to it, and in the first flush of delight, they overestimate their new-found importance and power, which they display only in front of the lower ranks, of course, people who are subordinate to them. In front of the higher ranks, on the other hand, they maintain the same servile behaviour—though it is no longer necessary and is actually sickening to many of their superiors. Some of these toad-eaters fall over backwards reminding their superiors, with great feeling, that they have worked their way up from the ranks, and even if they have now been commissioned, still they will 'always know their place'. With the lower ranks, they become almost complete despots. It is unlikely that this type of officer still exists, and unlikely that nowadays, you could find anyone shouting: "I'm the Tsar around here; I'm God!" I must nevertheless remark that there is nothing that annoys the prisoners, and all people of lower rank, more than this sort of expression being used by those in charge of them. Such arrogant self-glorification, such inflated opinions about one's own invulnerability, evoke hatred in even the most submissive of people, until finally it provokes them into losing their patience. Fortunately, I can say that this is now something of the past—and that even in the olden days it was always strictly punished by the authorities. I know of several examples.

What irritates the lower ranks generally is when they are treated with careless arrogance and fastidious disregard. Some people believe that if you feed a prisoner well, look after him well, do everything according to the law, then that is all there is to it. This is a delusion. Any person, whoever he may be, how-ever humiliated, still demands respect towards his human dignity, perhaps instinctively or subconsciously. A prisoner knows very well that he is a prisoner, an outcast, and knows his place—but no branding, no shackles can make him forget that he is a human being. And, because he is in fact, a human being, he should be treated as one. Good heavens above, treating someone as *a human being* can even make human those people in whom

129

God's image has already dimmed! It is with these 'unfortunates', one should be particularly humane. It is their salvation and their joy. I have known such kind, noble commanders. I saw the influence they had upon these humiliated people. A few kind words—and the prisoners almost underwent a moral resurrection. They cheered up in the way children do, and, like children, began to love again. And there is another strange thing I should mention. The prisoners do not like it when one of the officers in charge treats them with too much familiarity and kindness. They want to respect the officer, but when he treats them like this they somehow cease to do so. Prisoners like the officer in charge of them to have some decorations, to look impressive, to be favoured by someone higher up, to be strict and important and fair, at the same time to preserve his dignity. Prisoners like this kind of person more: he has preserved his dignity, he has not ill-treated them, and so everything is good and fine.

. . . .

"You must have got roasted alive for it," remarked Kobylin, quite calmly.

"Well yes, you could say they did just that—roasted me alive. Hand me the scissors will you, Alei! Aren't you playing cards tonight, mates?"

"All the money's gone on drink," Vasya replied. "If they had any left they'd probably play."

"If this and if that! If they gave you a hundred roubles in Moscow!" said Luka.

"So how many did they give you altogether?" Kobylin started up again.

"One hundred and five lashes, my dear friend. But listen to what I've got to tell you, mates. They very nearly killed me, you know," said Luka, forgetting Kobylin again. "They sentenced me to these one hundred and five lashes, and drove me to the scaffold with pomp and ceremony. I'd never tasted any lashes in my life before, not a single one. The world and his wife was there. The whole town turned out. 'There's a cut-throat going to be punished, one of them murderers.' They're so silly these

130

folks, so silly—I really can't tell you how silly they are. I was undressed by Timoshka,* and he laid me out and shouted: 'Hold on, it's coming!' And I lay there waiting, wondering what was coming. Then—One!—Jesus! How he laid into me with that first one! I wanted to scream. I opened my mouth, but I hadn't got any scream left in me. I mean I hadn't any voice. Then— Two!—how he laid into me with that second one—you know, believe it or not, I couldn't even hear them counting 'two'. And when I came round again—it was to hear them counting out the seventeenth. About four times they unstrapped me from that whipping bench, you know, and each time they gave me a half-hour's rest. They poured water over me. I just looked at them, all my eyes popping out of my head, and thinking: 'I'm going to die right now...' "

"But you didn't die, did you?" Kobylin asked naively.

Luka looked him over with the most contemptuous glance imaginable. There was an outbreak of laughter.

"Thick as they come, he is."

"Something wrong in the upper storey," remarked Luka, as if regretting that he had ever started up a conversation with such a person.

"His brains are addled, you mean," summed up Vasya.

Even though Luka had killed six people, there was no one in the whole gaol who was ever afraid of him—and that was in spite of the fact that he doubtless wanted very badly to be thought of as a holy terror...

IX

Isai Fomich. The Bathhouse. Baklushin's Story

Christmas was coming. The prisoners awaited it with some solemnity, and watching them, I too began to expect something unusual. About four days before the holiday we were taken to

*Author's note. An executioner.

the bathhouse. It was only very rarely, during my first years in gaol, that we, prisoners, were taken to the bathhouse like this. Everybody livened up and began to get ready. The time had been fixed for the afternoon, so there was to be no more work after the midday meal. In our barrack, the person most cheerful and excited about this was Isai Fomich Bumstein, the prison Jew, whom I mentioned in Chapter IV. He loved wallowing in the steam until he was almost senseless and unconscious, and now, as I recall these things long past, whenever I come to those prison steam baths (which are really something well worth remembering), then always in the forefront of the picture, I immediately see the blissful and unforgettable face of Isai Fomich, my prison comrade and barrack companion. Heavens, what a funny, amusing character he was! I have already said a few words about him: he was about fifty years old, puny and wrinkled, branded very badly across his cheeks and forehead, and lean and feeble, with a body as white as plucked chicken's. His face wore an expression of complete and unshakeable complacency, even of bliss. He did not seem a bit sorry that he was in gaol. As he was a jeweller, and the only one in the town, he was constantly employed by the town gentry and the authorities, and did nothing else apart from jeweller's work. So at least he earned something. He was not at all hard up and, in fact, even lived quite *prosperously*, saving his money and lending it out at interest to the whole prison. He had his own samovar, a good mattress, cups, and a complete set of crockery. The town Jews did not snub him and, on the contrary, patronised him. On Saturdays, as allowed by the rules, he would go out under guard to the town synagogue. By and large, he led an easy life, but even so he was impatient to finish his twelve-year term and get married. He was the most farcical mixture of naiveté, silliness, cunning, arrogance, innocence, timidity, boastfulness and impudence. To me it seemed very odd that the prisoners did not laugh at him nastily, and only occasionally made a joke at his expense for the sake of some entertainment. Isai Fomich was apparently just a pretext for a bit of everyday fun and entertainment. "We haven't got another like him here. Leave him alone. He's all right, is our Isai Fomich!" the prisoners used to say, and

Isai Fomich, though he understood what they meant by this well enough, was apparently proud of his importance—a fact which amused the prisoners no end. He had entered prison in the most hilarious manner imaginable. This was well before my time, but I was told about it by the others. Suddenly, one evening, during time off, a rumour spread through the gaol that a Jew had arrived, was just at that very moment having his head shaved in the guardhouse, and would be brought in at any minute. At that time there was not a single Jew in the whole prison. The prisoners eagerly awaited his arrival and formed a jostling crowd around him as soon as he came through the gates. He was escorted into the civilian barrack by the prison sergeant and shown his place on the bed-shelf. In his hand, he was holding a sack which contained his prison issue and some of his own possessions. He put down his sack, climbed on to the bed-shelf, drawing up his legs and not daring to raise his eyes. All around he heard laughter and jokes about his Jewish origin. Suddenly a young prisoner squeezed his ways through the crowd, carrying an old, filthy, ragged pair of summer trousers, together with some prison foot-cloths. He squatted down beside Isai Fomich and patted him on the shoulder.

"Well, dear friend, I've been waiting here for you for six years. Take a look at these and tell me how much you'll give me for them."

And he spread the rags out in front of the Jew.

Upon seeing the things brought to him in pawn, Isai Fomich (who had been in too much of a funk since setting foot in the gaol even to dare look up at this crowd of derisive, branded and frightening faces, and who had, up to this point, been too timid to utter so much as a word) suddenly roused himself and started feeling the rags with his fingers in a most business-like manner. He even held them up to the light. Everyone waited to see what he would say.

"I don't suppose you'd give a silver rouble for it, would you? That's what I reckon they're worth, you know," the pawnee continued, winking at Isai Fomich.

"No, they're not worth a silver rouble. I might give you seven kopeks for them however."

These were the first words Isai Fomich uttered in the gaol. Everybody roared with laughter.

"Seven! All right, I make it seven. Your luck. Mind you keep my things safe until I redeem them. You're answerable for them with your life!"

"Three kopeks interest will make it ten kopeks to redeem them," the little Jew continued in his jerky trembling voice, reaching into his pocket for the money, and casting a fearful glance at the prisoners assembled around him. He was both terribly frightened and keen to do business.

"You mean three kopeks' interest a year?"

"Three kopeks a month! Not a year!"

"That's a bit hard, isn't it? What name do you go by?"

"Isai Fomich."

"Well, you'll go a long way in this place, Isai Fomich. Goodbye to you."

Amidst the unbroken laughter of the prisoners, Isai Fomich re-examined the things he had taken in pawn, folded them carefully, and stowed them away inside his sack.

Everyone really seemed to be fond of him. No one was ever nasty to him, even though they were all in debt to him. Isai Fomich himself was a gentle soul, and when he saw how fond of him everyone was, it even put something of a swagger into his step, though in such a simple-hearted and comical way, that he was immediately forgiven for it. Luka, who had come across a large number of Jews in his time, quite often used to tease him, though not at all maliciously, just for a bit of fun, in the same way that people tease a dog or a parrot, trained animals and so on. Isai Fomich understood this only too well. He never took offence, and he answered back very skillfully with jokes of his own.

"Hey! Yid! I'm going to do you over!"

"I'll hit you ten times for every once you hit me," Isai Fomich would answer, pluckily.

"Bloody Jew!"

"So be it..."

"No-good, stingy Jew!"

"So be it... No-good we may be, but we've plenty of money just the same."

134

"You sold Our Lord Jesus."

"So be it..."

"You're doing all right there, Isai Fomich, good for you! And you leave him alone, will you! We haven't got another like him here," the laughing prisoners used to shout.

"Hey, Yid! You'll get yourself a whipping! They'll send you to Siberia!"

"I'm already in Siberia."

"Well, they'll send you even further."

"And is God there all the same?"

"Of course, he is."

"Well then, if the Lord is with you and you've got some money, you'll be all right wherever you go!"

"Well done, Isai Fomich, good for you!" shouted everyone around, while Isai Fomich, though he could see that they were laughing at him, still managed to put on a brave front. The unanimous praise clearly gave him great satisfaction and he would start to sing some silly and odd kind of tune in a shrill, high-pitched voice: "La, la, la, la, la!" This song without words was the only one he ever sang during the whole of his imprisonment. Later on, when I came to know him better, he gave me his word of honour that this was the very song and the very same tune that had been sung by every one of the six hundred thousand Jews as they crossed the Red Sea, and that every Jew was obliged to sing it in the moment of triumph over his foes.

Every Friday evening, on the eve of the Saturday, people from the other barracks came over, just to see how Isai Fomich would celebrate his Sabbath. Such was the extent of Isai Fomich's vanity and innocent love of showing off that this widespread curiosity also seemed to please him. With pedantic and affected self-importance, he would put up his tiny table in one of the corners, open the book, light two candles, and mumbling some sacred words, begin to dress himself in his chasuble. This was a many-coloured woollen cloak, which he kept carefully stored away in his trunk. Then he would tie cuffs on to both his wrists and a little wooden box on the middle of his forehead, which looked as if some strange horn was growing from it. Then the prayers began. He read them in a sing-song voice, shouting,

135

spitting, whirling around and gesticulating in a wild and peculiar way. It was part of the prayer ceremony, of course, and there was nothing either funny or peculiar about it. What was funny, was the way Isai Fomich showed off, flaunting his rites in front of us. Now and again he suddenly covered his head with his hands and sobbed out the prayer. He sobbed with mounting despair, until, exhausted and almost wailing, he lowered his head, with the wooden box on it, down on the book. And then, in the midst of his sobbing and shaking, he burst out laughing and chanting in a sing-song solemn voice, positively limp from a surplus of happiness.

"Hey, just look at him getting all carried away," the prisoners used to say.

I once asked Isai Fomich what all this weeping and the sudden transition to a state of bliss that followed it could signify. Isai Fomich enjoyed such questions immensely. He readily explained to me that the crying and the sobbing was a sign of thinking about the loss of Jerusalem, and that the law prescribed that, with these thoughts, one should break out into as strong a wailing and sobbing as possible, while beating one's breast at the same time. Then, at the moment of the most convulsive shaking, he, Isai Fomich, *should suddenly* and spontaneously (this 'suddenly' was also prescribed by the law) remember that there is a prophecy about the return of the Jews to Jerusalem. At that moment, he should immediately burst out into songs of joy and break into laughter, reciting the prayers in a way which expressed as much happiness in the voice, and as much solemnity and dignity in the face as possible. This *sudden* change, and the obligation to make this change, was something that Isai Fomich was most passionately fond of: he saw it as a very special and extremely clever trick, and he told me about this intricate rule of the law with an air of great pride. Once during the climax of these prayers, the Major entered the room, accompanied by the guard officer and several sentries. All the prisoners sprung to attention along the bed-shelves. Isai Fomich was left on his own, and he started shouting and grimacing even more than ever. He knew that prayers were allowed, and that no one had the right to stop them, and he ran no risk at all, shout-

136

ing in front of the Major. And he took enormous pleasure in doing his act in front of the Major, and showing off in front of us. The Major went to within one step of him. Isai Fomich faced away from his little table and, waving his arms, began to read his solemn sing-song prophecy right into the Major's face. As this was the moment at which he was supposed to express great happiness and dignity in his face, he did exactly that, screwing up his eyes in a very queer manner, laughing, and wagging his head at the Major. The Major was taken aback; then he gave a snort of laughter, called Isai Fomich a fool, and left, with Isai Fomich shouting even louder behind him. An hour later, when he had sat down to supper, I asked him what he would have done if the Major, out of stupidity, had lost his temper with him.

"What Major?"

"What do you mean 'what Major?'! Didn't you see him?"

"No."

"But he was standing right in front of your face."

Isai Fomich began to assure me most earnestly that he had *not* seen the Major, and that during prayers he entered some ecstatic state, in which he could not hear or see anything that was happening around him.

I can see him now, as plain as day, wandering idly around the barracks on a Saturday, trying as hard as possible not to do anything—in observance of the Sabbath law. What incredible tales he used to tell me when he came back from his synagogue, what amazing news and information from St. Petersburg, about things which could never have happened, assuring me that he had heard the news from his Jewish friends, and that they had all got it first hand.

But I have already gone on too long about Isai Fomich.

There were only two public bathhouses in the whole town. One, which was kept by a Jew, had separate rooms costing fifty kopeks an hour, and was intended for high-ranking people. The other bathhouse was for ordinary folk, and was correspondingly shabby, dirty and crowded. That was where the prisoners went. It was a frosty, sunny day, and the prisoners were pleased enough to be going beyond the fortress and taking a look at the town. There was no end to the laughter and the joking along the way. An entire platoon escorted us, with loaded guns at the ready, to the amazement of the town residents. In the bathhouse we were immediately divided into two shifts. The second shift waited in the cold changing room while the first shift was washing. This was because the bathhouse was so cramped. Even with only half of our people in there, it was difficult to imagine how they could have squeezed in. Petrov followed me in and of his own accord helped me to undress, and even offered to wash me. Along with Petrov, Baklushin, the prisoner from the special category who was known as the 'sapper' and whom I mentioned some time ago as one of the most cheerful and amiable of the prisoners—which in fact he was—also volunteered to help me. I had already got to know him slightly. Petrov did actually help me to undress, which would have taken me a long time, and it was very cold in the changing room, almost as cold as it was outside. I should mention by the way that it is very difficult for a prisoner to undress before he has really learnt how it should be done. For a start, you have to get the knack of quickly undoing the thongs worn under the shackles. These thongs are made of leather, about fifteen centimetres long, and are worn over your underwear, right under the iron ring which encircles your ankle. A set of these thongs costs over sixty silver kopeks, and each prisoner acquires them with his own money. He has to, as it is impossible to walk without them. The ring of the shackle does not fit too tightly around the ankle and it is possible to insert a finger between the ring and the foot. For this reason, the iron knocks against your foot, chafes it, and a prisoner without these thongs would develop open wounds within a day. Still, it is not all that difficult to take off the thongs. What is really difficult, is learning how to take off your underpants from underneath the shackles. This is quite a trick. When you have slipped it down one leg—let's say your left leg—you have then to push it through between the foot and the ring of the shackle. Then, when you have freed your leg, you have to pass this same piece of underwear back through the same ring. Then you have to pass everything that you have taken off your left leg through the ring around your right foot, and then finally, to pass everything through the right shackle back again. It's the same story when you have to put on clean underpants. For a newcomer it is difficult even to imagine how it can be done. The first person who taught me how to do it was Korenev in Tobolsk—the former bandit chieftain who had been chained to the wall for five years. The prisoners are used to this procedure, however, and they can manage it without a hitch. I had already given Petrov a few kopeks to buy me a sponge and a cake of soap. They did actually provide each prisoner with soap: one piece each, about as broad as a two-kopek coin and as thick as the slice of cheese you would be given as *hors d'oeuvres* in a middle-class home. They sold the soap right there in the changing room, along with a drink of spiced tea, buns and hot water. According to the arrangement with the owner of the bathhouse, each prisoner was allowed just one bucket of hot water to wash himself down with; anyone who wanted to get any cleaner could, for half a kopek, buy another bucketful, which would be handed in through the little window made in the changing room wall for exactly that purpose. When he had undressed me, Petrov, who had noticed how difficult I found walking in shackles, even went as far as to lead me in by the hand. "Pull them up, around your calves," he told me, holding me up as if he were my nanny. "Look out, mind that step there." I felt rather embarrassed about it. I wanted to assure Petrov that I could walk on my own, but he would not have believed me. He insisted on treating me like a clumsy young child, whom everyone must help. Petrov was far from being a servant—in fact, he was anything but a servant. Were I to give him offence, I am sure he would have known what to do to me. I had not promised him anything in the way of money for his services, and he did not ask me for money either. What could it have been then, that made him tend me like this?

When we opened the door that led into the bath proper, I thought that we had entered Hell. Imagine a room which is twelve paces by twelve, but into which a hundred people have been packed at the same time, at least eighty anyway, because we were divided into two shifts and there were two hundred of us altogether who had been brought to the bathhouse. Steam clouded my eyes, it was dirty there and so cramped I could not even find a place to put my foot down. I was terrified, and I wanted to go back, but Petrov immediately started reassuring me. Somehow, with the greatest difficulty, we managed to push our way through to the benches, stepping over the heads of those who had settled down on the floor, asking them to bend down to let us pass. All the benches were occupied. Petrov announced that we would have to buy a place, and at once began bargaining with the prisoner who had settled himself down beside the window. This man surrendered his seat for a kopek, receiving the money on the spot from Petrov, who had prudently brought it with him in his clenched fist. Straightaway this prisoner made a dive for the space right under the bench, a place which was dark, filthy, and covered all over with a sticky slime almost half a finger thick. Even under the benches all the places were occupied, and swarming with people. Nowhere on the whole floor was there as much as a hand's breadth of space where prisoners were not crouched, pouring water over themselves from their buckets. The remainder stood upright between them, holding their buckets, and washing while standing. The dirty water streamed off their bodies and straight on to the shaven heads of those sitting on the floor at their feet. On the steam-shelf, and on the steps that led up to it, there were more crouching people, squashed up together, and washing. Very few were really washing themselves. The common folk only rarely wash with soap and hot water. They love stewing on the steam-shelf and then dousing themselves with cold water. On the steam-shelf, about fifty bunches of birch twigs were rising and falling rhythmically as the men were all beating themselves with wild abandon. Water was continually being poured over the red-hot stones to create more steam. It was no longer just hot there, it was like an inferno. There was shouting and raucous laughter, accompanied by the clanging of a hundred chains being dragged across the floor... Those wanting to get through became entangled in the chains of the others, grabbed at the heads of those sitting on the floor, fell down, and cursed, dragging the person they had grabbed at down with them. Dirt was streaming everywhere. Everybody was in a sort of drunken, excited state, shouting and screaming. Around the little window through which the buckets with hot water were passed, there was a cursing, jostling mêlée. The hot water was spitted over the heads of those sitting on the floor, before it had even arrived at its destination. From time to time the moustachioed face of an armed guard would appear at the window or in the open doorway, looking to see if there was any trouble. The shaven heads and steaming red bodies of the prisoners were even uglier than usual. The weals left by all the lashes and sticks usually stand out very brightly on a steamed back, and now all these backs appeared to have been wounded afresh. Such horrible scars! A shiver ran down my spine when I saw them. As soon as water is poured over the hot stones, the whole room disappears in a thick, hot cloud. Everyone starts shouting and laughing uproariously. Scarred backs, shaven heads, bent arms and legs, would flash through this cloud. And on top of it all came the voice of Isai Fomich, laughing his head off from the highest steam-shelf. He was steaming himself all but senseless. It seemed that no heat was enough to satisfy him. For one kopek he had hired a bath attendant to beat his body with birch twigs, but this attendant could finally stand the heat no longer. He threw away the twigs and ran to revive his senses by pouring cold water over himself. Isai Fomich did not give up though. He hired another attendant, then another. For an occasion such as this he had decided to damn the expense, and he went through at least five attendants. "You sure like this steaming business, Isai Fomich! More power to you, Isai Fomich!" shouted the prisoners to him from below. At this moment Isai Fomich could feel that he was indeed 'on top' of all the others. He had outdone them all. It was his moment of victory, and over all the noise, his shrill, mad voice was heard shouting out his aria: "La, la, la, la." It crossed my mind, that should we one day all meet again in Hell, the scene would be very much the same. I could not resist the temptation of saying this to Petrov. He just looked around, and made no comment.

I attempted to buy a place for him near to my own, but he sat down by my feet and announced that he was just fine where he was. In the meantime, Baklushin bought hot water for us and brought it over when it was needed. Petrov announced that he was going to wash me from head to toe to 'make me clean all over', and he insisted on my climbing on to the steam-shelf with him. I did not risk it. Petrov soaped me all over. "And now I'll wash your little *footsies* for you," he added when he had finished. I was going to tell him I could do it very well myself, but decided not to refuse him and surrendered completely. There was nothing servile in his use of the word 'footsies'. It was just that Petrov could not somehow call my feet 'feet'. Perhaps it was because other, real people have 'feet', while I had just 'footsies'.

When he had finished washing me, he took me back to the changing room with the same kind of ceremony—supporting me, that is, and cautioning me at every step I took as though I were made of china—and helped me to put my underwear back on. Only when he had completely finished with me, did he dash back inside to steam himself.

When we came home, I offered him a glass of tea. He did not refuse, drank it down and thanked me for it: It occurred to me that I might do a bit of spending and offer him a glass of vodka. We managed to get hold of some in our own barrack. Petrov was most delighted. He drank it, grunted, and commenting that I had brought him back to life, he hurried off towards the kitchen as though there was some problem there which could not be solved without him. In his place, a new companion arrived: Baklushin, whom I had invited to come and drink tea with me while we were still in the bathhouse.

I do not know anyone with a disposition nicer than Baklushin's. True enough, he always gave as good as he got, he even quarrelled often, and did not like it when people stuck their noses into his affairs—in other words he could stand up for himself. However he did not quarrel with anyone for long, and I believe was liked by all. Wherever he appeared he was sincerely welcomed. He was even well known in the town as being one of the most amusing people on earth, one whose cheerfulness never deserted him. He was a tall lad of about thirty, with an open, simple-hearted look, and he was quite handsome, despite having a wart. The faces he made, imitating anyone and everyone, were so funny that you could not help laughing. He never tried to humour the sour-tempered men among us who hated a joke, and so no one ever called him a shallow good-for-nothing. He was full of fire and life. I made his acquaintance during my very first days, and he told me that, being a soldier's son, he had gone to a military school, then served in a sappers' regiment, and had even been noticed and favoured by people in high places—something of which he was still very proud, presumably from force of habit. He immediately started asking me questions about St. Petersburg. He was even quite well read. When he came to have tea with me, he made the whole barrack laugh by telling how our Lieutenant Sh. had that morning given our Major quite a wigging, and, sitting down beside me, announced with an air of great pleasure, that it seemed that the play was going to be put on after all. A show was planned in the prison for Christmas. There were quite a few actors, it transpired; the sets and props were put together bit by bit. Some of the townsfolk had promised to lend clothes for the actors, for those playing female roles too. It was even hoped through one of the officers' batmen to get an officer's uniform, complete with shoulder-knots. If only the Major did not forbid the performance, as he had the previous year! He had been out of sorts last Christmas: he had probably lost at cards, and, for another thing, the prisoners had been misbehaving, so he forbade the show out of spite. Perhaps this year he would let it go ahead. In short, Baklushin was terribly excited. He was obviously one of the main organisers of the play, and I promised myself then and there that I would definitely come to the performance. I found Baklushin's innocent happiness about the coming show very appealing. Little by little we fell into conversation. He told me, by the way, that he had not spent all his time in the army in St. Petersburg, he had committed some misdemeanour and been sent to the garrison in R. as a non-commissioned officer.

"That's where I was when they sent me here," he remarked.

"What for?" I asked him.

"What for? You'll never guess, Alexander Petrovich! It was for falling in love!"

"Well, that isn't really the kind of thing you're sent here for," I objected, laughing.

"True enough!" Baklushin added. "True enough! But in the course of this affair, I shot one of the local Germans with a pistol. You shouldn't really be sent to prison for killing a German though. What do you think?"

"Well, how did it happen? Tell me about it, it sounds most curious."

"It's a hilarious story, Alexander Petrovich."

"Well, that's even better. Tell it to me."

"Do you really want me to? Well, all right, I will..."

What I heard was not, as it turned out, particularly hilarious, but a strange tale of murder...

"It was like this," began Baklushin. "When I was sent to R., I could see it was a fine, good city. There was just one thing wrong with it—there were too many Germans. Well, I was still a young man in those days, of course, in my commanders' good books, and I walked round with my hat at an angle, you know, passing the time by winking at the German girls. There was one girl I fancied there, called Louisa. She and her aunt were both laundresses, they took in only the finest linen to wash. Her aunt was a huffy old woman, and they were quite well off. To start with, I just used to take a turn up and down the street under their windows—later I got to know Louisa very well. She spoke Russian well, with just a hint of a burr, she was such a darling, unlike any girl I'd ever met in my life before. At first I wanted this and that, you know. 'No, don't you dare, Sasha,' she told me, 'I want to keep my innocence and make a worthy wife for you one day.' So she just cuddled me, and laughed in a very ringing kind of way... And she was so neat, I'd never seen the like. She was the one who talked me into this marriage business. So could I not marry her? So I got all ready to go to the Lieutenant-Colonel with my request for permission to marry... When suddenly—can you believe it, Louisa failed to turn up one time, then another time, then a third time... I sent her a letter. No reply. What was going on? I mean, if she was cheating me, she would surely have answered my letter and come to our rendezvous. But she didn't even manage to lie. She just broke it off, just like that. So it's her aunt's doing, I thought. I had never dared go and see her aunt. She knew what was going on all right, but we'd still pretended there was nothing between us and met on the quiet. I went around like one demented. Then I wrote her my final letter, saying: 'If you don't come this time, I shall go and see your aunt myself.' She got frightened and came. She was crying. She said there was a German called Shultz—a distant relative of theirs, a rich and already middle-aged watchmaker who had expressed a wish to marry her. 'He would bestow this good fortune on me, and himself not be left without a wife in his old age. He loves me too, and says he has been intending to propose for a long time, but kept putting it off. And Sasha,' she said, 'he is rich, and marrying him will make me happy. Do you really want to deprive me of such happiness?' She was crying all the time, and embracing me... So, I thought, what she says is fair enough. What's so wonderful about marrying a soldier, even if he is a sergeant. 'All right, Louisa,' I told her, 'fare thee well, God bless you. Why should I deprive you of your happiness? And is he a handsome man?' 'Well, no,' she said, 'he's rather elderly really, and he's got a long nose...' She even laughed about this herself. I went away. 'That's how it is then, that's my luck,' I thought to myself. The next morning I went out to take a look at that shop of his—she had told me the name of the street you see. I looked through the window. There was a German sitting there repairing a watch, he looked about forty-five, he had a hook nose and bulging eyes, was dressed in a smock and a wing collar, a really high one, and seemed terribly smug. I couldn't help spitting at the sight. I had a mind to break the window then and there... But then I thought, why bother? No good crying over spilt milk. When I got back to the barrack it was already dark. I lay down on my bunk and—would you believe it, Alexander Petrovich?—I just burst into tears...

"Well anyway one day went past, then another and another, all in the same way. I had not seen Louisa. Meanwhile I heard from a gossipy old woman, also a laundress, whom Louisa went to see sometimes, that the German had found out about our love, and that was why he had decided to speed up his courtship. He had originally intended to wait a couple of years.

10-732

He had apparently made Louisa swear an oath that she would never hear any more of me. He was keeping both Louisa and the aunt on tenterhooks, reserving the right to change his mind, saying he was not definitely committed to the idea. She also told me that in two days' time, on Sunday, he had invited them both over for morning coffee and that there would be another relative there, an old man who had been a merchant in former days, but had now fallen on hard times, and was working as a watchman in some cellar or other. When she told me that they might finally decide everything on that Sunday, I was seized with such anger that I could no longer control myself. All that day, and all through the following day, I could think of nothing else. I could happily have torn that German limb from limb.

"On Sunday morning, I did not know what was going to happen, but when the morning service was over, I jumped up, threw a coat across my shoulders, and set out towards this German's. I thought I would find them all there. I could not tell you why I went there, or what I thought I would say, but I did put a pistol in my pocket, just in case. It was a useless kind of thing, that pistol of mine, with one of those old-style triggers. I used to do a bit of shooting with it when I was a boy. It wasn't really fit for shooting by this time. I loaded it all the same, thinking that if they started pushing me out or insulting me, I would pull out the pistol and scare them with it. So I got there. There was no-one to be seen in the workshop—they were all sitting in the back room. Apart from them, there wasn't a soul in sight, no servants or anyone. He only had one servant, actually: a German woman who did as cook as well. I walked through the shop. I noticed the door to the back room was locked, but it was an old door, held by a hook. My heart was beating fit to burst. I stopped, and listened. They were talking German. I kicked the door with all my might. It opened straightaway. I saw a big table in front of me. A big pot of coffee stood on this table and some coffee was boiling on a spirit lamp. There were some biscuits, and on a tray there was a decanter of vodka, some salted herring and sausage, and a bottle of wine. Louisa and her aunt, dressed up to the nines, were seated on the sofa. Opposite them, on a chair, sat the German—the future bridegroom himself—with his hair done, and his smock, and his wing collars jutting out from his neck. And next to him sat another German, a fat old man with white hair who didn't say a word. Louisa went as white as a sheet when I came in. The aunt started up but immediately sat down again. The German scowled. He was so furious! He stood up and started walking towards me.

" 'Vot do you vish?' he said.

"I was rather embarrassed to start with. Then my anger got the better of me again.

" 'What do I wish, you ask me! Ask your guest to come in, pour him a glass of vodka. I have come to visit you.'

"The German thought for a while, and then said: 'Sit down.'

"So I sat down.

" 'Well get me some vodka then!'

" 'Yes here is your vodka,' he said to me. 'Drink please if you vish.'

" 'No, get me some good vodka!' I had really lost my temper by then.

" 'Ziss is good vodka.'

"What really riled me was that he ranked me so low. All the more because Louisa could see that he did. I drank up, and said:

" 'Why are you so rude to me, German? You'd better try to make friends with me you know. I've come here out of friendliness.'

" 'Your friend I not can be,' he said. 'You are a plain soldier.' This made me wild.

" 'You dare say that to me, you scarecrow. Sauerkraut! Do you realise I can do anything I want with you right now! Do you want me to shoot you with this pistol?'

"I pulled out my pistol, stood right in front of him and held the barrel against his head at point-blank range. The others just sat there, frozen stiff, not daring to utter a sound, and the old man, who was shaking like a leaf, had gone pale as death.

"The German was startled, but he managed to take himself in hand.

" 'I not am afraid of you,' he said. 'As a decent honest man, I ask you to stop ziss nonsense. I not am afraid of you in ze slightest.'

" 'You're lying,' I told him. 'You are afraid.' And he really did not dare to move his head away from the pistol. He just went on sitting as he had done before.

" 'No,' he said, 'you not vill dare to do ziss in no vay.'

" 'And why won't I dare?' I said. 'Tell me why.'

" 'Simply because you are strictly forbidden to do so, and aftervards you vill be strictly punished for it.'

"What was this stupid German about, damn him? If he had not egged me on, he would still be alive now. Everything happened because of the argument.

" 'So you reckon I won't dare?'

" 'Yes.'

" 'I won't dare?'

" 'I am absolutely certain, you von't dare do ziss to me...'

" 'Well take this then, sauerkraut!' And I let him have it. He just rolled over where he was in his chair. The others cried out.

"I shoved the pistol back into my pocket and left. On my way back into the fortress, I threw it away into some nettles near the gates.

"I came home, lay down on my bunk and thought: so now they will come to get me. But an hour passed, and then another, and still nobody came for me. By dusk I was in the grip of such anguish, I went outside. Whatever happened, I wanted to see Louisa. I walked past the watchmaker's. There was a crowd outside, and the police. Then I went to see my old gossip. Call Louisa for me! I waited a bit and what do you think? Louisa came running to me and fell on my neck sobbing: 'It's all my fault. I shouldn't have done what my aunt told me.' She also said that immediately after what had happened, her aunt had come home, so frightened that she had fallen ill, and was keeping her mouth shut. She had not told anyone herself and she forbade Louisa to tell anyone either. She was afraid. Let them do what they like. 'Nobody saw us when we were there,' said Louisa. 'He'd even sent his servant away, he was so frightened of her. She would have scratched his eyes out if she had known of his marriage plans. He'd sent everyone away. None of the workers were there either. He had made the coffee and set out the dishes himself. As for that relative of his, he has kept silent all his life, he never talked and when this thing happened he just picked up his hat and left before anybody else. So he'll keep his mouth shut too,' said Louisa. That's really how it was. For two weeks, nobody came for me and nobody suspected me. In those same two weeks, if you can believe it, Alexander Petrovich, I had my full share of happiness. I saw Louisa every day. And she grew so attached to me, so attached. 'Wherever they send you, I shall go too,' she would say weeping brokenly. 'I will leave everything for you.' I thought I'd die there and then, my heart was so wrung! Anyway, two weeks later they came for me. The old man and the aunt had come to an agreement and informed against me."

"Hold on though," I interrupted. "You can only have got ten or maybe twelve years for it, the full term, that is, in the civilian category. Yet here you are in the special category. How is that?"

"Well, that was for something else altogether," said Baklushin. "When they brought me in front of the tribunal, the Captain suddenly started hurling abuse at me. I could not stand it, and so I said: 'What are you swearing at me like that for? Can't you see, you swine, that you are sitting in front of the *zertsalo*, the holy symbol of our sovereign's justice!' Well after that everything went differently, they started prosecuting me all over again for everything, and they sentenced me, first to four thousand rods, and then to hard labour here, in the special category. When they took me out for my punishment, the Captain was taken out too: me to run the gauntlet, and him to be stripped of his rank and dispatched to the Caucasus as a private. Well, goodbye, Alexander Petrovich. You will come to our performance then, won't you?"

X

Christmas

The holiday arrived at last. Even by Christmas Eve the prisoners were hardly going out to work at all, except for those in the sewing and other workshops. The rest only went out for the guards to check them. Although everybody had been detailed to some place or other, they almost all returned to the gaol immediately, either singly or in small groups, and after the midday meal nobody went out at all. The majority of those who had gone out in the morning had done so on their own business and not for anything laid down by the prison. Some had gone to make arrangements for liquor to be smuggled in, and order a new batch. Others had gone out to see their friends and acquaintances, to collect what money was still owed to them for work they had done earlier in the year, and which they now needed for the holiday. Baklushin and the others who were taking part in the play had gone to see their acquaintances, mostly among the officers' servants, to get the costumes they needed. There were some who walked round looking careworn and preoccupied just because the others did, and though there was no hope of their getting any money from anywhere, they looked as if they were about to receive some too. Everyone, in other words, wore an air of expectation as if something extraordinary, some change was sure to happen on the following day. By evening, the invalid soldiers, who had gone to the market on errands for the prisoners, had brought in all sorts of victuals: beef, sucking pigs, even geese. The prisoners—even the thriftiest and most unambitious ones who had been saving up their kopeks religiously all that year, considered it their duty to spend some money on that day, and celebrate the breaking of the fast properly. The next day was a holiday for the prisoners, of which they could not be deprived as it was formally laid down as such by the law. The prisoners could not be sent out to work on that day. There were only three such days in a year.

Finally, who can tell how many memories must have awoken in the hearts of these outcasts with the celebration of such a day! Great feast days sharply impress themselves on the minds of the common people from early childhood. These are the days when they rest from their daily labours, when their families gather together. In gaol, the memory of such holidays is no doubt tinged with pain and anguish. Among the prisoners, this respect for the solemnity of such a day developed into a staid uniformity in behaviour. Very few of them drank. Everyone went about looking very serious, as though busy with something; though in fact many of them had nothing to do at all. Both the ones with nothing to do, and those who did go drinking, tried to preserve an air of great gravity... Laughter, it seemed, was forbidden. The general mood became so pernickety and intolerant, that if anyone violated it, even without meaning to, he was immediately ostracised, with a great deal of shouting and swearing, and everyone would be very angry with him for what was regarded as a sign of disrespect towards the Festival itself. This general mood of the prisoners was remarkable, even touching. Apart from this inborn feeling of veneration for the great holiday, a prisoner subconsciously felt that by observing this Holy Day, he somehow came into contact with the whole world, that he was not, after all, altogether such an outcast or lost soul, cut off from the rest of the world, because in gaol, it was somehow the same for him as for the people outside. That was what it meant to them. It was apparent and understandable.

Akim Akimovich also prepared for the holiday. He did not have any family memories, for he had been brought up as an orphan in a strange house and started hard work when he was barely fifteen. There had been no especial joys in his life either, for he had passed it all in regularity and monotony, afraid to digress from the duties imposed on him. Nor was he particularly religious. His concept of 'proper behaviour' had apparently absorbed all other human gifts, individual features and passions that he might have possessed, either good or bad. As a result, he intended to meet this solemn day without too much fuss and worry, without being disturbed by useless memories that were full of anguish, but with quiet and proper behaviour, as required for the fulfilment of his duties and the observance of the ritual that had been laid down once and for ever. He was not, on the whole, too fond of reflecting upon a fact, and he never seemed to bother his mind about its significance, though once the rules had been pointed out to him, he would obey them religiously. If, on the very next day, he had been ordered to do the absolute opposite, he would have done so with the same

humble obedience and thoroughness, as he had done the opposite on the day before. Once, and only once, during his whole
life, had he tried to live by the dictates of his own mind—and it
had landed him in gaol. He did not let the moral of this pass
unheeded. And although he was not destined ever to understand
exactly what he had done wrong, he had at least, as the result
of his adventure, drawn one safe conclusion: that he must never,
under any circumstances, use his own judgement, because thinking was 'not his business' as the prisoners used to say in their
conversations. Blindly devoted to ritual, he even looked upon
the sucking pig which he had roasted and stuffed with buck-
wheat (with his own hands, because he knew how to do this)
with a kind of preliminary respect, as if it were not an ordinary
sucking pig which one could buy and roast any old day, but
some special, festive one. Perhaps, when still a child, he had seen
a sucking pig on the table on Christmas, and concluded that this
was somehow essential; and I feel sure that, had he not eaten a
sucking pig on that day—even if it were only once—he would
have been tormented by pangs of conscience ever afterwards,
for not having fulfilled his duty. Before the holiday, he had
been walking around in his old jacket and trousers, which were
very neatly patched, but nevertheless completely worn out. It
now transpired that he had been carefully saving the new ones,
which had been issued to him about four months earlier; he had
kept them in his trunk and never touched them, thinking con-
tentedly that he would solemnly put them on for the first time
on Christmas. And that is just what he did. He took out the new
clothes on the evening before, spread them out, examined them,
brushed them, blew away bits of fluff, and, having made sure
that everything was in order, he tried them on. They turned out
to be a perfect fit. Everything was just right. All the hooks fastened tightly all the way up; the stiff collar, which may have
been made of cardboard, propped up his chin. The waistline
even had something of the military frock-coat about it. Akim
Akimovich went so far as to grin with pleasure, and turned himself around, with a bit of a swagger, in front of his tiny mirror
(around which, in his spare time and with his own hands, he had
put a gilt edging). Just one little hook, right up near the collar,

seemed to be slightly out of place. Once he had realised this, Akim Akimovich decided to move it. He moved it, and tried the uniform on again. It was just perfect now. Then he folded everything in exactly the same way, and put the suit away in his trunk till tomorrow with an easy mind. His head had been shaved quite satisfactorily, but when he had examined himself scrupulously in his little mirror, he noticed that it was not, after all, absolutely smooth. There were some hairs that were just sprouting and hardly noticeable at all. He went straight to the 'Major' to be shaved properly, according to the rules. And although nobody would have inspected him the next day, still he had himself shaved for his own peace of mind, to come to the great day with every one of his duties fulfilled. Veneration for every button, epaulette and stripe had been impressed on him since his youngest days as an indisputable duty, and in his heart—as an image of the highest degree of beauty which a respectable person can achieve. Having observed everything he, as senior prisoner in the barrack, ordered some hay to be brought, and carefully watched how it was scattered on to the floor. They did this in all the barracks. I do not know why, but hay was always scattered around the barracks for Christmas. Then, when his day's labours were completed, Akim Akimovich said his prayers, lay down on the bed-shelf and fell asleep at once, his sleep untroubled as an infant's, in order to wake up as early as possible the following morning. The other prisoners did exactly the same. They lay down to sleep much earlier than usual in all the barracks. The customary night work was abandoned; there was no mention of a *maidan*. Everything was waiting for the morrow.

At last it arrived. Very early, before it was light, when the reveille was sounded, the barrack was unlocked, and the sergeant on guard, who had come in to count the prisoners, wished everyone a happy holiday. All the prisoners responded, in a welcoming and affectionate manner. When he had said a quick prayer, Akim Akimovich and many of the others who had their own geese and sucking pigs in the kitchen, hastily went off to see what was being done to them, how they were being roasted, how everything was coming along, and so on. Through our small windows, encrusted with snow and ice, in the darkness we could see the fires, which had been lit before dawn, burning brightly in each of our two kitchens' six ovens. The prisoners, wearing their sheepskins, or just flinging them on their shoulders, were already dashing about the yard in the dark. Everybody was making for the kitchen. A few, a very few, had already paid a visit to the vintners. These few were the most impatient. By and large, however, everybody behaved properly and quietly, with unaccustomed sedateness. There was none of the usual swearing and arguing. They all understood that it was a big day and a great holiday. Some had already been to the other barracks to wish their friends there a Merry Christmas. There was almost a show of comradeship. I should mention in passing that a feeling of comradeship was practically non-existent among prisoners. I do not mean general comradeship, which was completely out of the question. I mean personal comradeship—one prisoner making friends with another. In our place there was almost nothing of this sort, and this is something quite remarkable. It was not like that outside prison. On the whole, everybody treated everybody else in a very dry and callous manner, and there were very few exceptions. It was a formal tone, set once and for all.

I also went out of the barrack. It was just beginning to get light. The stars were growing pale. A fine frosty mist was rising from the ground. The smoke from the oven chimneys rose into the air in thick pillars. Some of the prisoners I passed wished me a Merry Christmas, eagerly and affectionately. I thanked them and wished them the same. There were some among them who had not said a single word to me during the course of the entire month.

Near the kitchen, one of the prisoners from the military barrack caught up with me. He had his coat thrown hastily over his shoulders. He had been calling out to me: "Alexander Petrovich! Alexander Petrovich!" when he still had half the length of the yard to go. He was running towards the kitchen in a great hurry. I stopped and waited for him. He was a young lad, with a round face and a quiet look in his eyes; he was very reserved with everybody and had not said a single word to me, or taken the slightest notice of me since my arrival. I did not even know his name. He ran up to me, gasping for breath, and stopped dead in front of me, gazing at me with a blissful but rather stupid smile.

"What do you want?" I asked with some surprise, as he was standing right in front of me, smiling, looking me full in the face, and saying nothing.

"Well, you know... It's a holiday today..." he mumbled. Then, himself realising that there was indeed nothing to talk about, he left me and hurried away towards the kitchen.

I should point out here that, after this incident, he and I had no more contact, and practically never spoke to each other for the whole of my term.

Around the ovens in the kitchen, which were now roaring away very fiercely, there was a most terrible crush. Everyone was busy watching what was his. The cooks were starting to prepare the midday meal which on this day was to be earlier. Nobody had started eating yet; there were some who wanted to, but were keeping up appearances in front of the others. They were waiting for the priest. The breaking of the fast was supposed to be after his visit. Meanwhile, the day was hardly under way, before the lance-corporal could be heard shouting, on the other side of the prison gates: "Fetch the cooks!" These shouts came almost every minute, and continued for about two hours. The cooks had to go and receive the donations brought to the prison from all over the town in huge quantities: buns, bread, cheese pies, flat cakes, potato and cottage cheese tarts, pancakes and other kinds of pastries. I do not think there was one single housewife, from the merchant and middle-class houses of the town, who had not sent her baking to wish 'the unfortunates' and prisoners a Merry Christmas. There were rich donations—rich, sweet breads, in large quantities and made from the finest flour—and there were poor ones—say a cheap roll and a couple of greyish potato tarts brushed lightly with sour cream. These were the gifts of one poor person to another, all that he could spare. Everything was accepted with equal gratitude, without any distinction being made, either among the givers or the gifts. The prisoners who went to receive them took off their hats, bowed, wished the giver a Merry Christmas and took the gifts to the kitchen. When a great heap was piled up, the senior prisoner from each barrack was summoned to divide everything up equally between all the barracks. There was no arguing, no cursing. The task was carried out honestly and fairly. The share for our barrack was then distributed among us by Akim Akimovich and one of the other prisoners. They divided it with their own hands, and with their own hands they distributed it to everybody. Nobody expressed the slightest disagreement or envy. Everybody was satisfied. There was no question of suspecting that anyone could conceal what had been given us, or not share it out equally. When he had settled his affairs in the kitchen, Akim Akimovich embarked upon his robing ceremony, attiring himself very solemnly and properly, leaving no single little hook unfastened. When he had finished, he began to say his prayers and continued for some considerable length of time. Many of the prisoners, mostly the older ones, were already saying their prayers too. The younger ones did not pray for long: they just crossed themselves when they got up in the morning, even on a holiday. When he finished saying his prayers, Akim Akimovich came over to me and, rather ceremoniously, wished me a Merry Christmas. I immediately invited him to drink tea with me, and he invited me to partake of his sucking pig. Somewhat later, Petrov ran in to congratulate me. He seemed to have already been drinking, and, although he must have come in great haste and still could not get his breath back, he did not say much. He just stood in front of me for a minute as though expecting something and then departed for the kitchen. Meanwhile, in the military barrack, preparations were made to greet the priest. That barrack was laid out somewhat differently from the others. The bed-shelves there ran along the walls, rather than down the middle as it did in the other barracks, making it the only one of the gaol buildings which had a free space in the centre. It seems likely that it was laid out in this way deliberately, so that the prisoners could be assembled there when necessary. A small table had been put in the middle of the room, spread with a clean dishcloth. An icon had been set on it and a lamp lit before it. Finally, the priest entered, carrying a cross and holy water.

After praying and singing in front of the icon, he faced the prisoners and they, with sincere reverence, came up to him one by one and kissed the cross. After this the priest went around all the barracks and sprinkled them with holy water. When he came to the kitchen, he highly praised our prison bread which was famous for its taste throughout the whole town, and the prisoners immediately expressed a desire to send him two freshly baked loaves. One of the invalid soldiers was at once dispatched with them. The priest, bearing the cross, was seen out as reverently as he had been greeted. The Major and the Commandant then arrived. The Commandant was liked and even respected by our people. He walked around the barracks accompanied by the Major, and wished everybody a Merry Christmas. Then he paid a brief visit to the kitchen and tasted the soup. On this occasion it turned out to be first-class. In celebration of Christmas, nearly one pound of beef had been issued for each prisoner. For a second course, there was millet porridge, with any amount of butter. When he had seen the Commandant off, the Major ordered the meal to be started. The prisoners tried not to catch his eye. They did not like his spiteful look and the way he was peering through his glasses—now as always—to right and left, in the hope of finding a sign of misconduct, or somebody to pick on.

Everybody sat down to eat. Akim Akimovich's sucking pig had been excellently roasted. I could not explain to you how exactly it happened, but as soon as the Major had left, within no less than five minutes, it transpired that there were an enormous number of drunks, though only five minutes earlier, they had almost all been completely sober. There were glowing, beaming faces all round. Balalaikas were brought out. The Pole hired for the whole day by someone who was having a drinking bout, followed his employer about, fiddling merry dances. The talk grew more fuddled and noisy. Still, the meal passed without any unpleasantness to speak of. Everybody was full. Many of the older and more sedate characters went away to sleep immediately afterwards, and so did Akim Akimovich—who apparently considered it obligatory to sleep after the midday meal on a big holiday. The old man, one of the Old Believers, had a quick nap and then climbed up on to the stove, where he opened his

Book and prayed until very late at night, almost without pause. It pained him to behold this 'shamelessness'—as he called the general merry-making. All the Circassians seated themselves on the porch steps and surveyed the drunks with curiosity and disgust. I came across Nurra. "*Yaman, yaman!*"* he said shaking his head in righteous indignation. "Allah will be most angry!" Isai Fomich had stubbornly and haughtily lit a candle in his corner and started work, making it quite clear that he thought nothing of this holiday. Here and there, in the corners of the room, *maidans* were forming. Nobody was afraid of the invalid soldiers, and watchers were sent out in case the sergeant should appear, though actually he himself was trying hard not to notice anything. The guard officer did stick his head in three times during the course of the day, but when he did, the drunks hid out of sight, the gambling stopped, although he seemed to have decided to pay no attention to such minor disorders. Drunks were considered 'minor disorders' on a day like this. Little by little our folk were beginning to let themselves go. Quarrels were started. The majority remained sober, and there were thus plenty of people to take charge of the drunks. Those having proper drinking bouts, meanwhile, drank without constraint. Gazin wore an air of triumph. He strutted complacently about, near his place on the bed-shelf. Underneath it, he had stored some liquor, which he had bravely brought in from its hiding place in the snow behind the barracks, and he was now laughing up his sleeve, looking at the customers who were coming to him. He himself was perfectly sober. He was planning a drinking bout for the end of Christmas week, when he had already relieved the other prisoners of their money. Men could be heard singing in all the barracks, but the drunkenness was already reaching the level of stupefied intoxication when songs might easily lead to tears. Many convicts were walking about with their own balalaikas, their sheepskins flung carelessly on their shoulders, plucking at the strings like the braves they once were. In the special category, they had even formed a choir of about eight people. They sang very well, accompanied by balalaikas

*Yaman (Tatar)—meaning bad.—*Ed.*

and guitars. Very few of these songs were pure folk songs. I can remember only one of them, sung very valiantly:

> *A maiden young, the other night*
> *I was at a feast...*

I heard a new variant of this song there, one that I had not come across before. Several verses had been added on to the end:

> *I have cleaned up the house,*
> *An obedient daughter,*
> *And made up the soup*
> *With the washing-up water.*
> *I have swept up the dirt, the crumbs and the flies*
> *And baked all the sweepings into the pies.*

For the most part the songs were the so-called prison songs, all very well-known. One of them—'*It used to be...*'—is a comic song telling how a man had lived in freedom and plenty and now found himself in gaol. In the old days he used 'to have champagne with his blanc-mange', and now:

> *They give me cabbage floating in water,*
> *But I guzzle it down all the same.*

Another very popular song, which is also very famous, goes:

> *As a young boy, I lived in joy and plenty,*
> *A capital of my own I possessed.*
> *But then, poor me, I lost my money*
> *And here I am in gaol instead...*

and so on. Only in this song they did not say 'capital' but 'keepitall', thinking that the word had something to do with saving up. There were also some very plaintive songs. One of them was most definitely a prison song, also a well-known one, I think:

159

> *The heavenly daylight will shine,*
> *The drum will beat the reveille,*
> *The officer will open the door,*
> *The clerk comes to ask for me.*
> *No one sees us inside these walls,*
> *Or knows how we really live.*
> *But God who made heaven is always with us*
> *And we will not perish here...*

One of the other songs, however, sung even more plaintively, had a wonderful melody. Presumably, it had been composed by someone in exile, and the lyrics were maudlin and somewhat illiterate. I can remember only a very few lines of it now:

> *My eyes will never see*
> *The home where I was born.*
> *And guiltless, I am doomed for life*
> *This torment to endure.*
> *The owl will give its forlorn hoot*
> *Out in the woods somewhere,*
> *Oh, how my heart will ache, because*
> *I have no hope of going there.*

They often used to sing this song in our place, as a solo rather than in a chorus. Someone could go outside to the porch during their time off, sit down, and falling deep into thought, with his cheek resting against his hand, start this song in a high falsetto voice. It made the heart ache to hear it. There were some very fine voices among us.

Dusk, meanwhile, was already gathering. Sadness, anguish and dazedness were becoming painfully evident in the drunkenness and the drinking bouts. A prisoner who had been laughing only an hour before, had now had too much to drink, and was already sobbing his heart out. Some of the others had already had several fights. A third lot, pale as death and hardly able to stand, were roaming from barrack to barrack, picking quarrels with everyone they met. There were others whom drunkenness only made the more miserable, and they were now vainly searching for a friend, someone to whom they could pour out their soul and sob out their drunken sorrows. All these poor men had wanted to make merry, to pass this Feast Day joyfully but—oh God!—what a hard, sad day it had turned out to be for almost all of them. Everyone felt as if the great day had betrayed some promise. Petrov came to drop in on me again, twice. He had been drinking very little the whole day through, and he was almost sober. All day, he had been expecting something, certain that something unusual was bound to happen, something festive, something terribly jolly. He did not say so, but you could see it in his eyes. He scurried around from one barrack to another, never growing tired. Nothing special was happening though, apart from drinking, drunken, stupid swearing, and heads completely fuddled with drink. Sirotkin, looking remarkably pretty and clean, also wandered through all the barracks in a new red shirt. He too seemed to be waiting, very quietly and innocently, for something. Little by little, the atmosphere in the barracks was becoming quite disgusting and unbearable. There were also a lot of funny things happening, of course, but I felt too sad and sorry for all these people, and being with them gave me a kind of uneasy and suffocating feeling.

Here are two prisoners, arguing over which of them should buy the other a drink. It is clear they have been arguing like this for a long time, and that they have had a quarrel earlier. One of them, in particular, seems to hold some long-standing grudge against the other. He is complaining, going on and on, trying to prove, with a very thick tongue, that the other man has treated him unjustly: some sheepskin or other was sold and he was cheated of part of the money, or something, in But-ter Week, last year. There was something else as well... The one with these grievances, is a tall, muscular and quiet fellow, by no means stupid, but with a strong tendency, when drunk, to make friends and pour out his troubles. And what he is really after now—cursing and complaining—is to be even closer friends with his rival afterwards. The other—a thick-set, stocky, rather short fellow with a round face—is cunning and squirmy. He has probably had more to drink than the other, but he is only slight-ly tipsy. He is a man who takes orders from no one, and he is

161

known to be rich, but for some reason it suits him not to irritate his emotional friend, and he takes him along to the vintner. His friend insists that he is under an obligation and should buy him a drink: "If an honest fellow is what you consider yourself."

Now the vintner, showing a certain amount of respect towards the person who is ordering the drink and a hint of contempt for his emotional friend because he is not paying for his drink himself but being treated to it—takes out his liquor and pours out a cupful.

"Well, Stepka, you've got to do it," says the emotional friend, seeing that he's come out on top, "'cause it's your duty."

"I'm not going to waste my breath arguing with you," says Stepka.

"No, Stepka, you're lying when you say that," insists the former, taking the cup from the vintner. "It's you as owes me money. You have not got any conscience. Everything's borrowed—even your eyes. You're a no-good scoundrel, Stepka! D'you hear me? A no-good scoundrel! That's the long and the short of it!"

"Stop whining ... look, you've spilt the liquor!" shouts the vintner at the emotional friend. "He's treated you and toasted you, so drink it up! I haven't got all night to stand round listening to you!"

"I'll drink it—don't yell. A Merry Christmas to you, Stepan Dorofeich," he says politely, with a slight bow, turning, cup in hand, towards Stepka, whom only a few moments before he has been calling a scoundrel. "Health and wealth for a hundred years, not counting those you've lived already." He empties the cup in one gulp, grunts, and wipes his lips. "I could take a few, mates, in the old days," he remarks with a very serious and important air, addressing his words to everyone and no-one. "I must be getting on in years a bit now. Thank you very much, Stepan Dorofeich."

"My pleasure," replies Stepka.

"Now let's go back to where we were before, Stepka. Besides being a no-good scoundrel as far as I'm concerned, let me tell you something else..."

"Let me tell you something, you drunken mug," Stepka, who has finally run out of patience, suddenly interrupts. "You listen to what I have to say, and make sure you mark every word of it. Here's the world cut in two: one half for me and one half for you. Now go away, and never cross my path again. Not ever! I'm sick to death of you!"

"So you won't pay me the money you owe me?"

"What money's that, you drunken slob?"

"In the next world you'll come yourself begging me to take it. And I won't take it! My money's hard work money! Sweat money! Blister money! It'll worry you no end in the next world."

"Go to tell, will you!"

"Scoundrel!"

"Jailbird!"

And they're off again, their mutual abuse much heartier than before one stood the other a drink.

Now let's look somewhere else. Two friends are sitting a little apart from each other, on the bed-shelf. One is a tall, stocky, beefy fellow with a red face, a perfect butcher. He is deeply moved and almost in tears. The other is a puny, thin, skinny fellow with a long nose which seems to have something dripping from it, and little pig's eyes, staring down at the ground. This one is an astute, educated man. He was formerly a clerk, and he treats his friend with a certain disdain, which the other one secretly resents. They have spent the whole day drinking together.

"He dared hit me, by Jove!" the beefy friend is shouting, rocking the clerk's head, which he has clenched under his left arm. This beefy one, a former sergeant, is secretly jealous of his puny friend, and that is why both of them are trying to outdo each other by adopting a very refined manner of speaking.

"And I must inform you that you too are in the wrong..." begins the clerk, very dogmatically, stubbornly refusing to lift his eyes to meet his friend's, and staring importantly down at the ground instead.

"He dared hit me, you hear me," interrupts his friend, pulling even more roughly at his dear friend. "You are the only person left to me in the whole wide world. Do you hear what

163

I'm saying? That's why I'm telling it for your ears and yours alone, that he dared hit me."

"And I must tell you again, my dear friend, that such a feeble justification of your own conduct only puts shame upon your own head!" objects the clerk in his high-pitched and very polite voice. "So you had certainly better agree, my dear friend, that this inebriation arises only from your own inconstancy."

The beefy friend sways backwards, gazing stupidly out of his drunken eyes at the self-satisfied little clerk, then suddenly, and completely unexpectedly, he lands his enormous fist full in the clerk's little face. That puts an end to the friendship that had lasted the whole of that day. The 'dear friend' is knocked under the bed-shelf—unconscious!

Now let's look somewhere else. One of my acquaintances from the special category has come into the barrack. He is an unfailingly kind and cheerful lad, quite intelligent and prone to laugh at things, quite without malice, and rather simple-looking: the one who on my very first day in gaol came into the kitchen during the midday meal, looking for the rich man, and drank some tea with me. He is about forty, with extremely thick lips and a big fleshy nose, covered in blackheads. In his hands he was now carrying a balalaika, which he was carelessly strumming. He was followed by some kind of hanger-on, a tiny man with a big head, whom I had previously had very little to do with. Actually, nobody ever payed much attention to this man. He was a rather odd and mistrustful character, always very silent and serious. He worked in the sewing shop and, apparently, wanted to remain aloof and not become involved with anyone. In his present drunken state, however, he stuck to Varlamov like a leech. He was following him around in a terrible state of excitement, waving his arms, banging on the walls and on the bed-shelves with his fist, almost weeping. Varlamov seemed to take no notice of him, as though he was not even there at all. The remarkable thing was that before this the two had never been anything like friends. They had absolutely nothing in common: neither in their work nor their personalities. They were in different convict categories, and lived in different barracks. The name of the little prisoner was Bulkin.

164

When he saw me, Varlamov started grinning. I was sitting on my bed-shelf near the stove. He stood some distance away, facing me, apparently making up his mind about something, then swayed and started towards me with unsteady steps. Swaggering and just touching the strings of his balalaika, he spoke, rather than sang, tapping his heels:

> *Apple-cheeked and fair of face,*
> *Singing like a happy bird,*
> *Dressed in satin, silk and lace,*
> *The sweetest girl in all the world,*
> *Full of loveliness and grace,*
> *She's my sweetheart, in a word.*

This song appeared to make Bulkin lose his temper once and for all. He started to wave his arms about, and, speaking to everyone, he shouted out:

"It's all lies, what he says, brothers, all lies! He speaks not a word of truth! It's all lies."

"Our best wishes to old Alexander Petrovich," said Varlamov, looking me in the eyes and laughing slyly. I thought he was going to give me a drunken kiss. He was really in his cups. The expression 'to old so-and-so...' is used by the common people throughout Siberia, even when they are talking to someone no older than twenty, and is a sign of respect, rather deferential and quite flattering.

"Well, Varlamov, how are things?"

"They change from day to day. Anyone who is glad of the holiday is drunk from early morning, so don't mind me." Varlamov was speaking in a sing-song voice.

"Lies, all lies!" Bulkin shouted banging on the bed-shelf with his hand in desperation. But Varlamov seemed to have made a vow to himself to take no notice of him, and there was a certain amount of comedy in the situation, for Bulkin had attached himself to Varlamov without any reason from early morning, simply because Varlamov's words were 'all lies'. He was following him around like a shadow, picking on every word he said, and wringing his hands, which were almost bleeding from beating them against the walls and bed-shelves. He seemed to be suffering—really suffering!—from the conviction that Varlamov's words were 'all lies'! If he had any hair left on his head, he would doubtless have torn it all out in despair. It was as though he had taken responsibility for Varlamov's actions upon himself, as though Varlamov's faults lay heavily on his own conscience. Yet the most striking feature of the situation was that Varlamov was not even looking at him.

"All lies, lies, lies! It doesn't fit the facts!" Bulkin was shouting.

"Well what's it to do with you?" the prisoners asked laughing.

"I'll tell you something, Alexander Petrovich. I was a handsome lad in my day, and the girls all took a fancy to me..." Varlamov suddenly started off for no reason at all.

"Lies, all lies again! Lies!" Bulkin interrupted him with a shriek.

The other prisoners were splitting their sides with laughter.

"And I swaggered before them: a red shirt on my back, velveteen trousers! Lying around all day, drunk as a lord! What can I do for you, ladies?"

"Lies!" said Bulkin, decisively.

"In those days my father had left me a two-storey stone house. Well, within two years I had frittered those two storeys away. All I had left were the gates without the gate-posts. Well, what of it? Money is like pigeons: flying in, flying out."

"Lies!" said Bulkin, more decisively than ever.

"So in gaol, when I sobered up, I wrote my folks a really tear-wringing kind of letter, hoping they'd send me some money. Everyone said I had gone against my parents' wishes, that I'd been disrespectful to them. It's six years now, since I sent that letter."

"And was there no reply?" I asked him, laughing.

"Of course not," he replied, suddenly starting to laugh himself, and bringing his nose down closer and closer towards my own. "Do you know, Alexander Petrovich, that I've got a mistress here?"

"You? A mistress?"

"The other day, Onufriev said: 'My girl may have a few pockmarks and be not much to look at, but she's got plenty of clothes of least. And yours may be pretty, but she's a beggar woman and goes round with a beggar's sack.' "

"Is that true?"

"Well yes, she is a beggar!" he answered, laughing soundlessly. Everyone else there also started laughing. It was well known that he had taken up with a beggar woman, and given her no more than ten kopeks in the whole of the last six months.

"So what if she is a beggar," I said, wanting to be rid of him at last.

He said nothing, but looked at me very sweetly, and said gently: "Just for that, would you stand me a weeny little tot? All I've had to drink today is tea, Alexander Petrovich," he added mawkishly, taking the money I held out to him. "I'm so filled up with that tea, I can hardly breathe. It's sloshing around in my belly like beer in a bottle..."

When he took the money, Bulkin's moral indignation reached its climax. He was wringing his hands as though distraught with grief and almost crying.

"You consider yourselves God-fearing folk, do you?" he shouted, addressing his words to the whole crowd of us. "Look at him! Everything he says is lies! All lies! Complete, utter lies! Lies, lies, and more lies!"

"And what's it to you?" the prisoners shouted, astounded by his fury. "You old duffer!"

"I will not allow him to lie!" shouted Bulkin, banging with his fist on the bed-shelf, his eyes flashing. "I do not want him to lie."

Everyone roared with laughter. Varlamov took the money, bowed to me, and minced hurriedly out of the barrack, on his way, no doubt, to the vintner. It was just at this point that he appeared to notice Bulkin for the first time.

"Well, come along," he said, stopping in the doorway as if he really did need him for something. "Square peg!" he added contemptuously, making way for poor, distressed Bulkin, and starting to pluck at the balalaika strings again.

But why describe this drunken scene? The oppressive day is drawing to a close at last. The prisoners fall into a heavy slumber on their bed-shelves, talking and ranting in their sleep even more than usual. There are still some people playing cards. Christmas day—so long waited—has now passed. Tomorrow is another weekday... Back to work.

XI

The Performance

Three days after Christmas, in the evening, was the first performance in our theatre. Organising it must have been a lot of trouble, but the actors had taken the whole brunt upon themselves, so the rest of us had no idea how things were progressing, or what was being done. We did not even know exactly what we would be shown. During these three days, the actors tried to get hold of as many costumes as they could, while they were out working. And Baklushin, when he saw me, just snapped his fingers, looking highly pleased. A quiet mood seemed to come upon the Major. True, we were absolutely in the dark as to whether he knew about the theatre, and if he did know about it, whether he had given it official permission or just decided to turn a blind eye to it, accepting the prisoners' whim, provided, of course, that everything would pass off without trouble. I think he must have known about the play. How could he not have known? But he had decided not to interfere, realising that if he forbade it, the prisoners would become unmanageable, start drinking, and things would be even worse, so better let them keep themselves busy with something. I am only hypothesising about the Major's thoughts on this subject, of course, because it seems to be the most natural and sensible way of thinking about it. I might even say that if the prisoners had not been allowed this play of theirs, or some other such distraction at Christmastide, the authorities ought to have invented something of the sort for them. Yet as our Major was notorious for reasoning in a completely different way from the rest of humanity, I am perhaps putting my soul in peril by suggesting that he knew about the theatre and allowed it to go ahead.

A person like our Major needs to squash somebody wherever he goes, to take something away from somebody, to deprive someone of their rights—in other words, to establish order. The whole town knew about this side of his character. Why should it bother him that the result of his restrictions was to make disorder more likely in the gaol? There is a punishment to match all varieties of disorder—goes the reasoning of people like our Major—and strict and swift enforcement of the letter of the law is all that is needed to keep these ruffians in order. These dull-witted executives of the law quite simply fail to understand—are in fact incapable of understanding—that enforcing the law to the letter, without making any sense of it, without any understanding of the spirit of it, is the direct cause of disorder, and has actually never led to anything else. "That's what the rules dictate, and that's all there is to it," they say, and they are genuinely surprised that they are also supposed to have sense and a sober mind. To many of them this last demand seems a particularly superfluous and outrageous luxury, restrictive and not to be tolerated.

Whatever the reason, the senior sergeant did not pester the prisoners, and this was just what they needed. I can say with absolute certainty that the theatre, and the feeling of gratitude for its having been allowed, were the main reason why there was not a single instance of serious disorder in the gaol during the holiday: not one single malicious quarrel, nor one single instance of theft. I saw with my own eyes how the prisoners calmed down some of those who were shouting and arguing most volubly, simply by persuading them that the play would be forbidden as a result. The sergeant had made the prisoners promise that everything would be quiet, and everyone would behave well. They had agreed with pleasure and kept their promise religiously, flattered to be taken at their word. It should be observed, however, on the other hand, that allowing the play did not cost the authorities anything, and did not involve any sacrifice on their part. No space was fenced off for the seats, and the stage could be erected and dismantled within a mere quarter of an hour. The play lasted for an hour and a half, and if an order to stop the performance had suddenly been received from on high, it could have been instantly obeyed. The costumes had been hidden in the prisoners' trunks. Before I go on to describe the costumes and the stage, however, I shall tell you about the playbill, which said what was to be shown.

Actually there was no written playbill. Baklushin did write something before the second and third performances for the officers and other noble visitors who had already graced the first performance with their presence. Of the gentry, it was usually the officer on guard duty who came, and once the guards commander himself dropped in. An officer of the engineers came too, and the playbill had been designed precisely in case of such visits. The prisoners expected the fame of the theatre to resound through the fortress and the town—especially as there was no theatre in the town. It was said that there had been one once, created for a single amateur performance, but that was all. The prisoners were happy like children at the smallest success, even rather vain. "Who knows?" they would say to themselves and to each other. "Maybe even the highest authorities will hear of us. They will come and watch us. Then they'll see what kind of people there are among the prisoners. This isn't one of those simple performances like you get in the army you know, with dummies and floating boats, and walking bears and goats. We've got real actors here staging the gentry's comedies. There isn't a theatre like this even in the town. They say General Abrosimov had a performance there once. Maybe some day he'll have another one. Well, his costumes might be better than ours, but when it comes to the *dialogue*—we may very well beat them there. It might even reach the ears of the District Governor and you can never tell—perhaps he himself will even want to come and see for himself. After all, there isn't a theatre in the town now, is there?" In other words, the prisoners' fantasies grew really out of proportion over the holiday, especially after the success of the first night, almost to the point of imagining rewards, or their sentences being reduced, but even so they were quick to laugh at themselves for this in a very light-hearted sort of way. In other words, they were children, real children—though some of them were well over forty. Despite the fact that there was no playbill I was already more or less aware of the programme of the coming performance. The first play was 'The Rivals Filatka and Miroshka'.[9] Even a week beforehand, Baklushin was already boasting to me about how the part of Filatka—which he was playing himself—would be presented in a way that would outdo anything people had ever seen even on the St. Petersburg stage. He would wander around the barracks, bragging shamelessly, though in a good-natured enough sort of way, and then suddenly he would recite a bit from his part 'like it ought to be read in the theatre'—and everyone would laugh, regardless of whether his words had really been funny or not. It must however be said that, in this case too, the prisoners knew how to carry themselves well, and preserve their dignity. Baklushin's antics and stories about the theatre were admired only by the youngest and greenest—who were also the least self-controlled—or else by those of the prisoners whose prestige was so well established and unchallenged, that they had no fear of expressing their emotions—however naive these might be (or, in the eyes of the gaol, undignified). The remainder, on the other hand, listened to this hearsay and gossip in silence, neither condemning it nor contradicting it, but trying as hard as they could to treat the news about the theatre indifferently, and even slightly contemptuously. It was only towards the very end, almost on the day of the performance itself, that everybody started to show interest. What was going to happen? How would we carry it off? What about the Major? Would they do as well as the year before last? And so on and so forth. Baklushin kept assuring me that all the actors had been perfectly cast, and were 'just right for their parts', that there was even going to be a curtain, that Sirotkin was taking the part of Filatka's bride. "You'll see for yourself what he's like in women's clothes," he said, narrowing his eyes and clicking his tongue. The Lady Benefactress was to have a dress with flounces, and a pelerine, and a parasol in her hand, while the Lord Benefactor would step forth in an officer's frock-coat with shoulder knots and a swagger stick. This would be followed by another play, a drama, 'Kedril the Glutton'. The name caught my interest, but however much I asked them about this play, I could find nothing out in advance. I discovered only that it had not been taken from a book, but was a handwritten play that had been obtained from a retired sergeant, now living in the suburbs, who at some time in his life must have taken part in the play in army theatricals. There really are such plays as these in our remote towns and provinces. They seem absolutely unknown to anyone, and have perhaps never been published, but they simply appear from no one knows where and make an integral part of local amateur theatricals, or the folk theatre. I have, incidentally, just now used the term 'folk theatre'. It would be a very good idea indeed, if some of our researchers were to undertake new and deeper research into this 'folk theatre' than they have done up to now, for it does exist, and is, perhaps, not completely insignificant. I cannot believe that everything I was to see in our prison theatre was invented by our prisoners. Such things can only be handed down by tradition. Devices and concepts, established once and forever, are passed from generation to generation, from ancient memory. One must seek them out among soldiers, among factory workers in manufacturing towns, and even among the lower middle classes of poor and little-known towns. In the villages and provincial centres, they have also been preserved by the servants in the town mansions and country seats of the landed gentry. It even occurs to me that many of the old plays were spread through Russia in handwritten copies solely by these servants of the gentry. The old Moscow aristocracy and the country squires maintained their private theatres with serf actors. And it was in these theatres that our folk drama, the characteristics of which are unmistakable, originated. As far as 'Kedril the Glutton' was concerned, however much I wanted, I could find out nothing about it in advance, apart from the fact that devils appear on the stage and carry Kedril off to Hell. What does the name Kedril mean, and why Kedril and not Kirill? Is it about an event in Russia or abroad? I could obtain no information about this whatsoever. To conclude, it was announced, there would be a 'Pantomime with Music'. This was all, of course, very curious. There were about fifteen actors, smart braves all. They hustled and bustled about, holding rehearsals very secretively, out of sight, sometimes behind the barracks. They wanted, in other words, to surprise us all with something unusual and unexpected.

On working days the gaol was locked up early, as soon as night began to fall. At Christmastide an exception was made and we were not locked up until the sun had really set. This concession was actually made for the performance. During these Christmas days, towards evening, someone would be sent to the guard officer with a humble request to allow the performance to go ahead, and not to lock the gaol up until as late as possible, adding that there had already been a performance the day before and the place had not been locked up until quite late, yet there had been no trouble of any kind. The guard officer would reason like this: "There really wasn't any trouble yesterday, and if they promise there won't be any today either. They'll take care of it themselves, and that's the most reliable way. And what is more, if I try forbidding the performance, then maybe—because who knows, they're convicts, after all—they might do some mischief out of spite and get the guards in trouble." Besides, it was boring to stand guard, whereas this way there was a chance of a bit of theatre—and not just a soldiers' but a prisoners' theatre, and prisoners were a curious lot: it would be fun to watch... And the guard officer always reserved the right to watch.

If someone higher up should come and say: "Where is the guard officer?" then a direct answer and excuse could be given: "He's gone to the gaol to count the prisoners and lock up the barracks." Thus the guard officers allowed the performance to proceed on every evening of the Festival and did not lock the barracks up until the sun had really set. The prisoners had known in advance that no obstacles would be put in their way by the guards—and they were confident and calm.

Just after six, Petrov came over to fetch me, and we set off together to see the performance. Almost everyone from our barrack went, apart from the Chernigov Old Believer, and the Poles. The Poles decided to go only for the last performance, and even then only after being assured that it was good, very jolly, and safe. The snobbishness of these Poles did not irritate the prisoners at all, they were greeted most politely and were even allowed to stand in front. As for the Circassians and particularly Isai Fomich, they enjoyed our theatre immensely. Isai

173

Fomich paid three kopeks every time he went, and on the last night he put ten kopeks on the plate with an expression of pure bliss on his face. The actors had decided to collect from each person present as much as he was able to give, and to put the takings towards the cost of the production, and their own *sustenance*. Petrov had assured me that, however packed the theatre might be, I would be allowed to the front, because being richer than the others, I would be likely to give more than they, and also because I knew more about these things than anyone else. That is exactly what happened. First, though, I shall describe the auditorium and the stage arrangement.

The military prisoners' barrack where the performance was held, was about fifteen paces long. Coming from outside, you stepped on to the porch, then went into the entry, and from there into the barrack. This long barrack was, as I have mentioned before, arranged differently from the rest. The bed-shelves lined the walls, leaving the centre of the room free. One half of the room—the part closest to the entrance—was given over to the audience; the other half, where this barrack joined on to the next, was reserved for the stage. What struck me first of all was the curtain. It stretched for a distance of about ten paces, across the whole barrack. Having a curtain at all was an unbelievable luxury, but what's more, it had trees and pavilions, lakes and stars painted on it with oil paints. It was made of bits of cloth, some old and some new—everyone had donated as much as he could—old prison shirts and foot-cloths—and these had been sewn together into one big sheet; the part for which there had not been enough cloth, had simply been made of paper, also obtained by begging—sheet by sheet—from the prison offices and various departments. Our painters, among whom A—v (our own Briullov) was prominent, had done their best to make it as picturesque as possible. The effect was amazing. A luxury like this gladdened the hearts of even the most morose and fussy prisoners who, when it came to the performance, all turned out to be the same excited children as the most eager and impatient of the spectators. Everyone was delighted, in a rather boastful way. The lighting was several tallow candles, cut up into pieces. In front of the curtain there were two benches, which had been taken from the kitchen, and then in front of these benches there were three or four chairs which had been found in the sergeants' mess. The chairs were there just in case, for any high-ranking officers. The benches were for the sergeants, engineering clerks, corporals and others who were in charge but were not officers—just in case they should happen to look in. That is exactly what happened. Throughout the holiday, there had been no end of outside visitors to the gaol. On some evenings there were more, on others less, but on the final night there was not a single seat on the benches left unoccupied. Last of all, behind the benches, there was space for the prisoners themselves, who remained standing as a sign of respect to the visitors, with their caps in their hands, and wearing their jackets and sheepskins, despite the suffocating, steaming heat. Too little space had been left for the prisoners, of course. They were sitting on each other's heads, particularly in the back rows, and they were also crowded on the bed-shelves and in the 'wings'. There were some people who came to every performance, they went behind the stage into the next barrack and watched the performance from there. The crush in the front part of the barrack was terrible, as bad perhaps as the crush I had recently experienced in the bathhouse. The door into the entry where it was about twenty degrees below zero, stood ajar, and there was also a crowd of people there. Petrov and I were immediately allowed up front, almost as far as the benches, from where we could see much better than from the back rows. To some extent they regarded me as a connoisseur, an expert, who had been to grander theatres. They had noticed Baklushin continually asking me for advice and deferring to me. That is why I was privileged. To be sure, the prisoners were all extremely vain, shallow people, but this was actually an affectation. They might laugh at me, when they saw what little help I was to them in their work. Almazov might look down on us, noblemen, with contempt while vaunting his skill in baking alabaster. However, in their jeering at us and their persecution of us there was something else too. Once we had been noblemen. We belonged to the same layer of society as their lords and their masters about whom they could hardly have preserved any good memories. Yet now, in the theatre, they made way for me. They recognised that in this matter I was a better judge, that I had seen more and knew more than they did. Even the ones who were (as I well knew) least well disposed towards me, now sought my praise for their theatre and, without any self-abasement, allowed me to stand in front. This is how I see things now, as I remember the impression made by those days. At the time, it also seemed to me (I can remember it well) that, in their fair judgement of themselves, there was self-respect and no belittlement at all. The highest and most striking characteristic of our Russian people is their sense of justice and their craving for it. The kind of cockiness that makes a person push himself forward at all costs, *whether he deserves it or not*, simply does not exist among the common people. You must only remove the outer husk and look at the seed inside more closely and attentively, and without prejudice, and you will see things which you had never expected to find. There is not much that our sages could teach the common people. In fact, I assert the opposite: it is they who should learn.

While we were preparing to leave, Petrov had told me, very innocently, that another reason I would be allowed to the front was that I was likely to pay more. There was no fixed price. Everybody gave what they could afford, or what they wanted to. When the plate came round, almost everyone put something in, even if it was only half a kopek. Granted that I was allowed to the front partly because of money, on the supposition that I would give more than the others, didn't this gesture speak once again of the prisoners' self-respect? "Go to the front. You're richer than we are. We're all equals here, but you'll give more money, therefore a spectator like you is more pleasing for the actors, so you get the best place. It's not the money that brought us here, but the respect, so it's up to us to sort ourselves out." How much genuine pride there is in such an attitude! This is not respect for money, it's self-respect. Generally speaking there was no particular respect for money or wealth in the gaol, especially when one looked at all the prisoners together, *en masse*, as a community, an artel. Even going back over them individually, I cannot remember a single man who would really humiliate himself for money. And this includes the spongers who came begging from me. They did this more for the fun of swindling someone than anything else; it was just a bit of innocent mischief. I do not know if I am expressing myself clearly... Anyway, I have forgotten about the theatre. So back to where we left off.

Before the curtain went up, the entire barrack presented the strangest and liveliest picture. First, the crowd of spectators, squashed up and squeezed in on all sides, waiting blissfully and patiently for the performance to begin. In the back rows, people were clambering on top of each other. A lot of them had brought thick logs from the kitchen, and having propped their log against the wall, they put their feet on it, placed both their hands on the shoulders of the person in front, and then stood like this, without shifting their position, for two solid hours, completely satisfied with themselves and with their place. Others found a foothold on the step round the base of the stove, and stood thus through the whole performance, supporting themselves against the men in front. This was in the very back rows near the wall. Along the side, above the heads of the musicians, there was a whole crowd of people who had climbed on to the bed-shelf. These were considered very good places. About five people climbed on to the stove itself and lying across the top of it, looked down. That must have been bliss! Crowds of late arrivals, who had no hope of finding a good place, made for the window-sills along the other side. Everybody behaved very quietly, with great self-control. They all wanted to make the most favourable impression on the gentry and other visitors. Every face wore an expression of the most ingenuous expectation. It was so hot and stuffy that every face was red and drained with sweat. What a strange light of childish happiness, of touchingly pure joy, shone on these furrowed, branded faces, in their glances which had hitherto been so gloomy and morose, and in their eyes which had been known to flash with such frightening fury! They were all bare-headed, and all the heads on my right appeared to be shaven. Now, at long last, there was some bustling about on the stage. The curtain was about to rise. The orchestra struck up... Now this orchestra is worth describing. Eight musicians had taken up their positions on the bed-shelves along one side. There were two violins (one from the gaol and the other, for which a player had been found among ourselves, borrowed from someone in the fortress), three balalaikas (all home-made), two guitars and a tambourine in place of a double-bass. The violins could only wail and scrape, and the guitars were absolutely no good, but then the balalaikas were marvellous. The nimbleness with which the fingers of the players ran up and down the strings was comparable only to a conjuring trick. Only dance tunes were played. During the fastest of these, the balalaika players would rap their knuckles against the sounding boards of their instruments. The tone, the taste, the rendering, the mastery of the instrument, the interpretation of the tune were all distinctly and originally the prisoners' own! One of the guitar players had superb command of his instrument too. This was the person—the ex-nobleman—who had killed his father. As for the tambourine player, he performed wonders: he would spin it on a finger one moment, then run his thumb across its skin, next he'd beat it rapidly and rhythmically or suddenly he would break up the strong, clear sound into thousands of tiny sounds, rattling and whispering together. Finally, two concertinas appeared. Quite frankly, I had no idea of what could be done with simple folk instruments: the harmony, the unity and, above all, the spirit, the understanding of the music and the rendering of the melody's very essence, were absolutely amazing. It was then, for the first time, that I clearly understood what it is that gives rakish and daring Russian dance songs their rakish and daring quality. At last the curtain went up. Everyone stirred, everyone shifted his weight from one foot to the other. The back rows rose on tiptoe. One person fell off his log. All the spectators without exception let their mouths fall open, as they fixed their eyes rigidly upon the stage. Complete silence descended. The performance began.

Alei was standing next to me along with his brothers and the other Circassians. They all became passionately attached to the theatre and came every time. I have often observed that Moslems, Tatars and others, are always very keen on any kind of spectacle. Huddling beside them, all eyes and ears, was Isai Fomich, full of ingenuous and avid expectation for the wonders and pleasures that lay ahead now that the curtain had gone up. It really would have been a great shame if his expectations had been disappointed. Alei's dear face shone with such childlike and radiant happiness that I must admit I found it a pleasure just to look at him, and I involuntarily turned and looked into his face every time there was a burst of laughter when one of the actors cut an especially skilful or funny caper. He did not see me. He was taken up with far more important matters. On my left, very close to me, there was a middle-aged prisoner who was usually cross about something, always frowning and grumbling. He, too, had noticed Alei, and I noticed him turning round, half-smiling, to have a look at him—the boy was such a heart-warming sight. They began with 'Filatka and Miroshka'. Filatka (Baklushin) was indeed superb. He played his part with extraordinary clarity. He had evidently given careful thought to each phrase and movement, and lent meaning and sense to each empty word and each gesture, perfectly in character with the part he was playing. Add to this preliminary hard work and deep study, an extraordinary and genuine cheerfulness, spontaneity, and lack of affectation, and you would have agreed—if you could have seen Baklushin for yourself—that here, beyond the shadow of a doubt, was a born actor of enormous talent. I have seen 'Filatka' many times on stage in Moscow and St. Petersburg, and I can tell you without hesitation that the actors there were not nearly as good as Baklushin. Compared to him they would be just swains in some pastoral, not real peasants at all. Their attempts to portray peasants were too laboured. Baklushin, moreover, was inspired by rivalry. Everybody knew that the part of Kedril in the second play would be taken by the prisoner Potseikin, an actor whom everybody for some reason considered to be better and more gifted than Baklushin—a fact from which Baklushin suffered like a little child. The times he came to me and poured out his heart! Two hours before the performance, he was shaking like a leaf. When the crowd laughed and shouted out to him: "Well done, Baklushin! Just right!" his face beamed with joy, and genuine inspiration sparkled in his eyes. The kissing scene with Miroshka, in which Filatka shouts to him: "Wipe your lips!" and then wipes his own, was hilariously funny.

179

The whole audience roared with laughter. But for me, the most entertaining part of it all was the audience itself. They opened up completely. They enjoyed themselves without reserve. Shouts of approval grew more frequent with every moment. Here would be someone nudging his neighbour to tell him his opinions, without even seeing or caring who it was that was standing beside him; there would be another, who in the middle of some comic scene or other, would suddenly turn round to the crowd in delight, looking around them all quickly, as though appealing for their laughter, and immediately turn back again towards the stage. A third would be clicking his tongue and snapping his fingers, too excited to stand still, but as there was nowhere for him to move to, all he could do was shift from one foot to another. By the end of the play, this general mood of cheerfulness had swelled to enormous proportions. I am not exaggerating in the slightest. Imagine a gaol, and chains, and being locked away, with long bleak years ahead, and a life as monotonous as a drizzle on a dark and gloomy autumn day, and suddenly all these repressed, imprisoned people are allowed to unwind for one hour, to make merry, and forget the nightmare, to set up and organise a theatre—and what a theatre too! To the pride and surprise of the whole town. Everything fascinated the prisoners, of course—the costumes, for one thing. Fancy seeing Vanka the Bad Egg or, say, Netsvetaev or Baklushin, in a completely different outfit from the one in which they had appeared every day for several years. "He's a prisoner, the same prisoner, you can even hear his shackles jingling—but take a look at him now, walking out in a frock coat, a bowler hat and a cape, a regular civilian. Stuck on a moustache he has—and hair as well. Look at that now! He's taken a red handkerchief out of his breast pocket, and is fanning himself with it. He's playing a lord for us, for all the world as though he really is one!" Everyone was delighted. The Lord Benefactor created a tremendous effect by appearing in the adjutant's full dress coat—which had seen better days—complete with epaulettes and a service cap with a cockade. There had been two contenders for this part and—would a reader believe it?—they had quarrelled terribly like children over who should have it: both of them had wanted so badly to appear in the officer's full dress coat complete with shoulder knots. They had been pulled apart by the other actors, and a vote had been taken which gave the role to Netsvetaev, not because he was smarter or better looking than the other man and thus more like a lord, but because he had assured them all that he would appear with a cane, and wave it and draw it along the ground just like a real lord, like the greatest dandy in the world—something that Vanka the Bad Egg would never be able to do in a thousand years, having never even seen a proper lord. And in fact, as soon as Netsvetaev did appear in front of the audience, along with his lady, he did exactly that, tracing something on the floor very quickly with his thin reed cane, which he had procured from somewhere or other, no doubt thinking that this was a sign of the height of lordliness, dandyness and fashion. In his childhood, as a servant's son, running about the place barefoot, he had probably seen some handsomely dressed lord with a cane, and been enthralled by the way this man could twirl it. This had made an indelible impression on him, so that now, at the age of thirty, he could recall it, just as it had been, and captivate and charm the whole audience with it. So deeply was Netsvetaev absorbed in this activity, that he could no longer even look at anyone, and he delivered his lines without lifting his eyes. All that interested him was to follow the movements of his cane and its point. The Lady Benefactress was also pretty remarkable—in her own way. She appeared in a threadbare muslin dress, which looked as though it had been made out of an old doormat. Her neck and arms were bare, and her face smothered in powder and rouge. On her head she wore a calico nightcap, tied under the chin, in one hand she had a parasol and in the other a painted fan with which she fanned herself without pause. She was greeted by a burst of laughter. She barely managed to keep a straight face herself, and occasionally lost control and burst out laughing. This lady was played by the prisoner Ivanov. Sirotkin, dressed as a girl, looked very charming. The verses were also well received. In other words, the play was greeted with complete and unanimous approval. There were no criticisms, and indeed there was no room for any.

Again the overture was played, and again the curtain rose. This was Kedril. Kedril is a sort of Don Juan figure; at any rate, both the master and his servant are carried off to Hell by devils at the end. A whole Act was performed—though it is clearly an extract, and the beginning and the end have been lost. It makes no sense whatsoever. The action takes place somewhere in Russia, at an inn. The innkeeper ushers a gentleman in an overcoat and round misshapen hat into the room. He is followed by his servant Kedril carrying a suitcase and a chicken wrapped in blue paper. Kedril is wearing a sheepskin and a footman's cap. He's supposed to be a glutton. He was played by Baklushin's rival, a prisoner called Potseikin. The master was rendered by Ivanov, who had taken the part of the Benefactress in the first play. The innkeeper—Netsvetaev—warns them that the room is haunted by devils, and leaves them. The master, gloomy and anxious, mumbles to himself that he has known this for a long time, and orders Kedril to unpack and prepare the supper. Kedril is a coward and a glutton. When he hears about the devils, he starts shaking like a leaf. He would like to run away, but he is too afraid of his master. Moreover, he wants to eat. He is a self-indulgent, silly character, cunning in his own way, cowardly, swindling his master at every possible opportunity, yet also afraid of him. He is a remarkable type of servant, with a faint touch of the characteristics of Leporello, and he was played absolutely superbly. Potseikin had real talent, and was, in my opinion, an even better actor than Baklushin. I did not, of course, express this opinion to Baklushin when I met him the following day. That would have upset him far too much. Ivanov as the master was also very good. His part was complete nonsense—I had never heard anything like it!—but his diction was correct and clear, and his gestures well chosen. While Kedril is messing about with the suitcases, the master walks pensively about the stage, announcing to anyone within hearing distance that the present evening marks the end of his travels. Kedril lends his ear to what is being said with curiosity, pulls faces, makes a few asides, and provokes laughter in the audience with every word. He does not feel sorry for his master; but he has heard about the devils; he wants to know what they are; so he strikes up a conversation with him, and starts asking questions. His master reveals that he has some time previously, while in trouble, turned to Hell for assistance; that the devils helped him and rescued him; that today is the end of his term, and perhaps today they will come for his soul, according to the conditions of the contract. Kedril begins to get cold feet. His master does not lose heart however, and orders him to prepare the supper. With the mention of supper, Kedril cheers up immediately, takes out the chicken and the wine, and every now and then tears off a little piece of the chicken and tastes it. The audience are laughing their heads off. Just then the door creaks, the wind rattles the shutters. Kedril begins to tremble, and quickly, almost without thinking, he stuffs an enormous piece of chicken, which he cannot even swallow, into his mouth. There is more laughter. "Is it ready then?" shouts the master, pacing up and down the room. "Just a moment, master ... I shall get it ready ... for you..." says Kedril; then he sits down at the table himself, and, calm as anything, he starts wolfing down his master's food. Clearly, the audience loved the servant's quick-wittedness and cunning, and the way the master is duped. (It has to be admitted that Potseikin deserved every praise. He delivered the line "Just a moment, master, I shall get it ready for you" really brilliantly.) Taking his seat at the table, Kedril begins to eat greedily, jumping at his master's every movement for fear he should notice what he is up to. As soon as his master turns round, Kedril dives under the table, taking the chicken with him. Finally, when he has satisfied his first pangs of hunger, he decides to think about his master. "How much longer will you be, Kedril?" shouts his master. "It's ready, Sir," Kedril answers smartly, suddenly realising that hardly anything is left for his master to eat. In fact there is only one chicken drumstick left lying on the table. His master, gloomy and anxious, takes his seat at the table without noticing what has happened, and Kedril stands behind his chair with his napkin. Each word and gesture of Kedril's, every face he pulls, as he turns to the public and nods at his simpleton of a master, is greeted by hearty laughter. But then, just as the master starts to eat, the devils appear. At this point, it was impossible to say what was happening, especially as the devils entered in a most peculiar manner. One of the doors opened in the wing and revealed something dressed in white, a lantern with a candle where its head should have been. Then another phantom appeared, also with a lantern on its head, and holding a scythe. Why they had lanterns, or a scythe—and why devils should be dressed in white—were matters which nobody could explain. However, it did not worry anyone too much. No doubt, that was how it should be. Then the master turns towards the devils rather courageously, and shouts that he is ready for them to take him. Kedril is scared out of his wits. He gets under the table, not forgetting, despite his fear, to take a bottle of wine along with him. For a second the devils disappear. Kedril comes out from under the table; but as soon as his master starts on the chicken again, three devils burst into the room once more, grab him from behind and carry him off into the nether world. "Kedril! Save me!" shouts the master. But Kedril is too busy to notice. This time he has taken the bottle, the plate, and even the bread, along with him under the table. Now he is alone—without the devils, and without his master. He scrambles out from under the table, and takes a look around. A smile spreads across his face. He mischievously screws up his eyes, sits down in his master's place, and nodding at the audience, says, half-whispering:

"So, I'm on my own now ... no master!"

Everyone laughs because he has no master. Then he goes on, in the same half-whisper, taking the audience into his confidence and winking at them, all the time growing more and more cheerful:

"The devils have taken my master!"

The delight of the audience knew no bounds. The words, good news in themselves, were spoken in such a mischievous manner, with such a mockingly triumphant expression, that it was impossible to do anything but applaud. Kedril's happiness is short-lived, however. He takes the bottle in his hand, pours himself a glass and is just about to drink when the devils return, creeping up on him from behind, and grabbing hold of him. Kedril screams at the top of his voice, but is too scared to look behind him. Nor can he defend himself, for in his hands he is holding the bottle and the glass which he will not part with. He sits there for half a minute, his mouth wide open in terror, staring at the audience, wearing such a hilarious expression of cowardly fright that he would make a very good model for a drawing. And then the devils carry him off. He clutches the bottle, kicks his legs in the air, and screams and screams and screams. His screams can still be heard from behind the wings. At this point, however, the curtain falls. Everyone is laughing in high delight... The orchestra strikes up the *Kamarinskaya* dance tune...

It begins very softly, hardly audibly, then the melody grows louder and louder, the tempo increases, the rhythm is accentuated by banging on the sounding boards of the balalaikas. This is the *Kamarinskaya* in full swing, and, honestly, I wish Glinka could hear how they played it[10] in our gaol. Then a mime began, to the music. The *Kamarinskaya* continued throughout. The interior of a country house was presented. On stage are a miller and his wife. The miller, in one corner, is repairing a harness; his wife, in another corner, is spinning flax. The wife was played by Sirotkin; the miller by Netsvetaev.

I must say that the props and the scenery were very poor. Both in this play, and in the previous one, and in all the others as well, much had to be added by your imagination to what there was actually to see. Instead of a back wall, there was a carpet or a horse-cloth. For the right-hand wings there were some rotten old screens. On the left side there was nothing at all, and the bed-shelves were visible. The audience were not too demanding though, and agreed to supplement reality with imagination—an activity at which prisoners are particularly able. "If you're told it's a garden, then take it for a garden, or a room if you're told it's a room, a house if you're told it's a house, don't be so fussy." Sirotkin, dressed as a young woman, looked very pretty. The audience started whispering compliments about her. The miller finishes his work, picks up his hat and a whip, crosses over to his wife and explains to her, with gestures, that he has to go, but that if, while he is gone, his wife receives any visitors, then ... and here he shows her the whip. His wife listens

185

to him and nods. This whip must be very well known to her—for she is a naughty young woman. The husband leaves. As soon as he has left the room, the wife shakes her fist after him. Now there is a knock at the door. The door opens, and a neighbour, who is also a miller, a bearded man in a kaftan, appears in the doorway. He is carrying a present—a red shawl. The young woman laughs, but as soon as the neighbour wants to embrace her, there is another knock at the door. Where can she hide him? Quickly, she hides him under the table, while she herself sits down at her spinning wheel again. Another admirer appears. This one is a clerk, in military uniform. Up to this point the mime has proceeded impeccably. All the gestures have been absolutely perfect. These hastily assembled amateur actors were really amazing, and one could not help thinking of the potential and the talent that perished in this Russia of ours, sometimes even for nothing, just wasted in thralldom and wretchedness! The prisoner who was playing the clerk, however, must have acted in a provincial or domestic theatre at some time in the past, because he had taken it into his head that all our actors without exception did not know the first thing about the profession and did not walk as they ought to on the stage. He himself strutted about as, they say, actors used to in the old days, when they were playing classical heroes. He took a long step, and then, before he had moved up his other leg, he suddenly stopped, leaned back with his whole body, threw his head back, gazed proudly around, and only then pulled his other leg up. However ridiculous this way of walking may look in classical heroes, when done by a military clerk in a comic scene, it is even more ridiculous. Our audience, however, thought that this was perhaps the way it should be, so they accepted the strutting of the lanky clerk without particular criticism, as a given fact. No sooner has the clerk managed to reach the centre of the stage, than another knock is heard. The wife again takes fright. Where should she put the clerk? Into the chest, which is very conveniently standing open. The clerk gets into the chest and the wife closes the lid. This time it is a special guest, also in love with her, but of a very particular kind. This man is a Brahmin, [11] and he is even in the right costume for it. The audience erupts

186

into uncontrollable laughter. The role of the Brahmin was played by the prisoner Koshkin, and he was really superb. He had the right figure for a Brahmin too. He explains the full extent of his love in gestures. He raises his hands skywards, then presses them to his chest and to his heart. But no sooner has he grown emotional, than a heavy knock sounds on the door. One can tell, from the nature of the knock, that it is the master. His frightened wife is at her wits' end. The Brahmin dashes crazily hither and thither, begging her to hide him. Hurriedly, she puts him behind the cupboard, and, forgetting to unlock the door, she runs across to her spinning wheel and begins spinning and spinning, oblivious to the knocking of her husband, twisting a thread which is not there, and spinning the wheel which she has forgotten to lift from the floor. (Sirotkin portrayed her fear with great success.) The master kicks the door in, and strides up to his wife, brandishing his whip. He has seen everything and has caught her red-handed. He indicates with his fingers that there are three men here, and he starts looking for them. The first one he finds is the neighbour, and he throws him out with a lot of pommelling. The frightened clerk, in an attempt to run for it, has given himself away by lifting the lid and showing his head. The master deals him a few lashes with the whip, and this time the enamoured clerk hops and jumps about in a most unclassical manner. Now only the Brahmin is left. The master looks for him everywhere, and in the end finds him hiding behind the cupboard in the corner. He bows to him politely, and then drags him out into the centre of the stage by his beard. The Brahmin, shouting "Damn you! Damn you!" (the only words which are spoken during the whole pantomime), tries to defend himself, but the husband does not listen, and makes very short work of him. The wife, seeing that it is now her turn, dashes from the room. The board she was sitting on clatters on the floor, and all the prisoners roar with laughter. Alei, without turning to me, pulled at my sleeve and shouted to me: "Look at the Brahmin! Look at the Brahmin!"—laughing so much that he could hardly keep his feet. The curtain falls. The next play begins.

There is no point in describing all these plays though. There were two or three more. They were all very funny and unaffectedly cheerful. Even if the prisoners had not composed them all themselves, they had certainly added something of their own to each of them. Almost every actor would improvise according to his own ideas, so that, on the following evenings, the same actor would play the same part slightly differently. The last mime, a fantasy, concluded with a ballet. A man was being buried. A Brahmin with his numerous attendants pronounced various invocations over the coffin, but to no avail. Finally, the strains of *The Sun Descending* were heard, the dead man came back to life, and everyone began to dance for joy. The Brahmin danced with the dead man, in a very special Brahmin manner. And that is how the performance ended, until the following evening. All our people left feeling cheerful and pleased, praising the actors and thanking the sergeant. No quarrelling was heard. Everyone felt inhabitually satisfied, almost happy, and they went to sleep, not as they usually did, but peacefully. Why, you may ask? But this is no fantasy of mine, it is the honest truth. Just for a little, these poor wretches were allowed to live as they wished, to enjoy themselves like real people, to live at least for an hour not as convicts, and this changed a man morally, even if only for a few minutes... Now it was already the dead of night. I started and woke up. The old man was still praying on the stove, and he would stay there praying until dawn. Alei was sleeping peacefully beside me. I remembered how he was still laughing just before he fell asleep, talking with his brothers about the theatre, and I could not help gazing at his calm and childlike face. Piece by piece I recalled it all: yesterday, the Festival, all of the last month... Fearfully, I raised my head, and in the dim trembling light of the prison candle, I looked around at my sleeping companions. I looked at their pale faces, their poor beds, and at all this utter shabbiness and poverty. I took a really good look at it, as though making sure that it was not the continuation of some terrible nightmare, but reality. Reality it was. Because at that very moment I heard someone groan, fling his arm heavily to one side, making his chains clank. Another one started in his sleep, and began to mutter something. The old man on the stove was still praying

for all 'Christians of the true faith', and I could hear his monotonous, quiet, sing-song prayer: "Oh Lord Jesus Christ, have
mercy on us!"

"I am not here forever, after all. Just for a few years, isn't
it?" I said to myself. And I lowered my head once more on to
my pillow.

End of Part One

PART TWO

I

The Hospital

Shortly after the Festival, I was taken ill and sent to our military hospital. It stood on its own, half a verst from the fortress. It was a long, one-storey building, painted yellow. In summer, when the repairs and redecorations were carried out, an extraordinary amount of ochre had to be used on it. In the enormous courtyard of the hospital, there were houses for the medical staff, and other buildings and outhouses. The main building, however, contained only wards. There were many wards, but only two of them were for prisoners, and they were always full, especially in summer, so it was often necessary to move the beds together. Our wards were filled up with all kinds of 'unfortunates'. There were people from our prison as well as soldiers who had been kept in different guardhouses, according to whether they were convicted, awaiting sentence or in transit; also men from the corrective battalion, a strange institution to which soldiers, who had committed some offence or were judged unreliable, were sent to have their behaviour corrected, and from which two or three years later they were usually discharged as the most full-fledged scoundrels you could meet anywhere. Prisoners who fell ill would generally tell the sergeant about it in the morning. Their names were immediately entered into a book, and they were dispatched, with this book and under guard, to the battalion infirmary. The doctor first examined all the sick people from the military units in the fortress, and those he found really ill he listed for admission to the hospital. I had my name entered in the book by the sergeant, and after the midday meal, when all the people in the gaol set off for work, I went to the hospital. A sick prisoner usually took as much money and bread with him as he could, knowing that no food was to be expected the first day in hospital, also a tiny pipe, a full tobacco pouch, a flint and a steel. These last items had to be concealed very carefully in your boots. As I entered the confines of this hospital, I was not totally devoid of curiosity for this new, and as yet unfamiliar variation in prison life.

It was a warm day, gloomy and overcast: one of those days when institutions like hospitals take on a particularly business-like, dreary, sour appearance. I entered the reception room, together with my guard. Inside, there were two copper baths and two patients—from among those awaiting their verdict, also accompanied by guards. The feldsher came in, looked us up and down lazily and haughtily, and then, even more lazily, went to report to the doctor on duty. The doctor appeared quite soon, examined us, treated us very kindly, and handed us our case histories, with only our names on them. The rest, such as filling in the regimen, the prescription and dosage of medicines, and so on, was left to the intern in charge of the prisoners' wards. I had already heard that prisoners could not praise their doctors highly enough. And when I was setting out for the hospital they said to me: "Who needs a father when they're around!" Meanwhile, we changed our clothes. The clothes and the underwear in which we had come were taken away from us, and we were dressed in hospital underwear; besides that, we were issued with long stockings, slippers, nightcaps and a thick cloth drab-coloured robe, lined with canvas or something like plaster. The robe was filthy, but how filthy I only appreciated fully when I was installed in my place. After that we were taken to the prisoners' wards, situated at the end of a long, clean, high-ceilinged corridor. The superficial appearance of cleanliness was very satisfactory all round; everything that first caught the eye was sparklingly clean. However, it may have looked so to me by way of contrast with the gaol. The two men who had come earlier went into the ward on the left, and I went into the one on the right. Beside the door, which was fastened with an iron bolt, stood a sentry with a rifle, and an assistant sentry with him. The lance corporal (from the hospital guard) gave the order for me to be let through, and I found myself in a long, narrow room, with about twenty-two beds—three or four of them unoccupied—ranged on either side along its length.

The beds were made of wood and painted green, a sight which is too familiar to each and every Russian: these are the kind of beds that seem predestined to crawl with bedbugs. I took one in the corner, on the side where the windows were.

As I have already mentioned, there were some of our prisoners here too, from the gaol. Some of them knew me already, or had at least seen me. But the vast majority were either people awaiting trial or prisoners from the corrective battalion. Only a few were seriously ill, and quite bedridden. The remainder, who had less serious ailments or were convalescing, were either sitting on their beds or walking up and down the room, along the wide enough aisle between the beds. There was a horribly stifling hospital smell. The air was redolent with all kinds of noxious evaporations and the smell of medicines, even though the stove was burning in the corner almost the whole day through and the flue was never closed. A striped bed cover had been spread across my bed. I removed it. Beneath the cover I found a cloth blanket lined with linen and coarse bed sheets in a rather doubtful state of cleanliness. There was a bedside table with a mug and a tin cup on it. All this had been covered for the sake of appearances with a small towel which had been issued to me. The table also had a shelf under it, where people who drank tea could keep their kettles, or else a kvass jug, and such things—though only very few did drink tea. The pipes and tobacco pouches which, on the other hand, almost everyone had (including those suffering from consumption) were hidden under the beds. The doctor and other staff hardly ever looked there, and even if they did find someone with a pipe, they pretended not to have noticed it. True, the patients were very careful not to be caught, and went over to the stove to smoke up the chimney. It was only at night that they smoked right where they were in their beds; but at night there was no one patrolling the wards, except sometimes the officer who was in charge of the hospital guards.

It was the first time I had ever been in any kind of hospital in my life, and so it was all quite new to me. I noticed that I was arousing some curiosity. People had already heard of me and were now looking me up and down without any ceremony at all, even with a hint of superiority, as schoolchildren look at a new pupil, or clerks at someone who has come with a petition. In the bed to the right of me there was a clerk, the illegitimate son of some retired captain, awaiting sentence. He was being tried for forgery, and he had been lying here now for about a year—not ill with anything, apparently, but assuring the doctors that he had an aneurism. He achieved his goal, being spared both hard labour and corporal punishment, and a year later he was sent to T—k to be kept in some place attached to a hospital. He was a stocky, robust lad, about twenty-eight years old, a great cheat and quibbler over points of law, and anything but stupid, extremely self-assured and presumptuous, and so painfully vain that he had seriously convinced himself that he was the most honest and truthful man in the world and in no way guilty of anything—an opinion which he upheld throughout his life. He was the first of them to start up a conversation with me. He asked me questions with curiosity, and gave me quite a detailed account of the hospital routine. The very first thing he told me, of course, was that he was the son of a captain. He very much wanted to be thought of as a nobleman, or—at the very least—as 'hailing from noble stock'. After him, one of the patients from the corrective battalion came up to me and announced that he knew a good many of the noblemen who had been in exile, referring to them by their first names and patronymics. He was already grey-haired, this soldier, and it was written in his face, as plain as daylight, that it was all a lie. His name was Chekunov. I think he must have been trying to curry favour with me, probably because he thought I had money. Noticing that I had brought a package containing tea and sugar, he at once offered his services, saying that he would procure a kettle for me and make my tea. I did not need a kettle because M—tsky had promised to send me one over from the gaol the very next day with one of the prisoners who regularly came over to the hospital to work. Chekunov, however, was not to be daunted. He got hold of a cast-iron pot somewhere, and a cup too, boiled some water, made tea, and, in short, waited on me with remarkable zeal, which provoked some caustic remarks from one of the other patients. This patient, who was called Ustyantsev and had consumption, was lying opposite me. He was the soldier who had been so frightened of his impending flogging that he had drunk a cup of vodka infused with snuff, and ended up with consumption. I have mentioned him previously. Up to this moment, he had lain silently, breathing heavily, staring at me gravely, and watching Chekunov's movements with indignation. His extraordinarily jaundiced, serious look lent a flavour of comedy to his indignation. Finally, he could bear it no longer.

"Look at this grovelling serf here! He's found himself a master!" he said slowly in a failing gasping voice. These were the last days of his life.

Chekunov turned to him angrily.

"Who's a grovelling serf?" he said, looking contemptuously at Ustyantsev.

"You are!" came the reply, delivered so confidently as though the speaker had every right to give Chekunov a good ticking off, and had even been appointed his companion for just that purpose.

"You say *I'm* a groveller?"

"That's right. It's you I'm talking about. Just listen to him, folks! He can't believe I'm talking about him. He's surprised!"

"But what's it to you? This gentleman has no one to lend him a hand. It's very difficult for them, when there's no servant around, and that's a fact. Why shouldn't I offer him my services, you fuzzy-mouthed fool?"

"Who's fuzzy-mouthed?"

"You are."

"I am, am I?"

"You sure are."

"And you think you're good-looking? If I'm fuzzy-mouthed—you've got a mug like a jug."

"Fuzzy-mouthed! That's what you are! God has already marked you for dead, so just lie there and pass away. Oh no, you still go blathering away. What's it all for?"

"What for! I'd show respect for a leather boot, but never a peasant bast shoe. My father never grovelled before anyone, and taught me not to either... I ... I..."

He wanted to go on, but he was seized by a terrible coughing fit, which lasted for several minutes, and during which he spat a good deal of blood. This so drained him of strength, that a cold sweat beaded on his narrow forehead. He would have gone on and on talking, but the coughing would not let him. You could see from his eyes how dearly he would have loved to rail at his companion for a little longer. Yet all he had the strength for was to wave his arm weakly. So at the end, Chekunov simply forgot about him.

I felt that the malice of this consumptive was aimed more at me than at Chekunov. Nobody would have been angry with Chekunov or looked down on him for his desire to be of service and in that way to earn a little money. Anyone would have understood that he was doing it purely for the money. The common people are anything but finicky about these matters, they know when it's business. The thing was that Ustyantsev had taken a dislike to me. He did not like me drinking tea, and he did not like it that, even in shackles, I acted like a lordship who could not do without a servant—though I did not seek help or even want any. I had really always wanted to do everything myself, and I was particularly anxious not to let anyone see that I was a ninny who was used to being mollycoddled and served. My self-respect depended partly on this, if I must be honest about it. And yet—and I really do not understand how it always happened—I was unable to turn down all kinds of fawners and underlings who thrust themselves on me and, in the end, gained such complete control of me that one might say they were the real masters, while I was their servant; whereas to all appearances I was a lordship who could not exist without servants. This was very distressing naturally. Ustyantsev had consumption, it must be remembered, and he was an irritable, sick man. The rest of the patients preserved an air of indifference, which even had an element of uppishness in it. I can remember how they were all preoccupied with one particular event. From their talk I gathered that later in the evening a man awaiting his verdict would be brought in, and that he was at that moment being beaten with sticks. The prisoners were expecting the newcomer with some curiosity. They said, however, that the punishment would be a light one—a mere five hundred strokes.

Little by little, I made a survey of my surroundings. As far as I could tell, the majority of the patients who were really ill had scurvy or eye diseases—endemic local illnesses in these places. There were several in the ward. Among the other really ill ones, there were those who had fevers, different kinds of skin ulcers, and lung trouble. In our ward, unlike the others, people ill with anything, even venereal diseases, were all lumped together. I said *really ill* because there were also a few who were not ill but had come *just like that*, to have a rest. The doctors readily admitted them into the hospital out of compassion, particularly when there were a lot of empty beds there. Conditions in the guardhouses and the gaol were so bad compared with the hospital, that a good number of the prisoners came for a stay in bed with pleasure, despite the stifling atmosphere and locked doors. Some had a particular liking for lolling in bed and for the hospital routine too. These were mostly from the corrective battalion. I surveyed my new companions with curiosity. I remember that one of them, another consumptive from our gaol who was already approaching death, and like Ustyantsev had only a few days to live, aroused particular curiosity in me. He too was almost opposite me, two beds down from Ustyantsev. His name was Mikhailov, and it was only two weeks since I had seen him in the gaol. He had been ill for a long time, and he should have gone to hospital long ago, but he had endured his illness with an obstinate and quite unnecessary patience, and he only went to the hospital during the holiday, to die from a most terrible consumption, within three weeks. He just burned up in front of our eyes. Now I was struck by the complete transformation in his face. It was one of the first faces I had noticed on my arrival in the gaol. For some reason it had caught my attention then. Lying next to him was one of the soldiers from the corrective battalion, a man who was already old, a horrid, disgusting sloven... There is no point in going through all the patients one by one, though... I recalled that unpleasant old man for the simple reason that he also produced an impression on me and, in one minute, managed to give me an understanding of some of the peculiar features of our prisoners' ward. This unpleasant old man had—as I now recall—a very bad running nose at that time. He could not stop sneezing, and for the whole of the next week he continued sneezing, even in his sleep, sneezing in bursts of five or six at a time, and adding very punctually after each burst: "Oh God, what a curse!" The very first time I saw him, he was sitting on the bed and avidly stuffing tobacco into his nose from a paper package, in order to secure as strong and as neat a sneeze as he could. He sneezed into his own cotton handkerchief, whose large checks were faded from a hundred washings, and as he sneezed, he screwed up his small nose in some strange manner, into millions of tiny wrinkles, revealing the stumps of old black teeth and his red frothy gums. When he had finished sneezing, he would immediately unfold his handkerchief, examine the snot that had accumulated there in large quantities, and then straightaway wipe it off on to his brown hospital robe, with the result that all the snot stayed on his robe, while his handkerchief was left just slightly wet, if that. He continued like this for a whole week. Such meticulous and miserly care for his handkerchief rather than the hospital robe did not arouse any resentment on the part of the other prisoners, even though one of them might well have to put this robe on after him. It is really strange how little squeamishness and queasiness there is in our common people. As for myself, I was completely horrified by what I saw at that moment, and I immediately began examining the robe which I had just put on, with a mixture of disgust and curiosity. I had noticed its strong smell from the first. By now it had warmed up on my body, and was reeking more and more strongly of medicines, plasters and what seemed to me was pus: which was hardly surprising as it had been worn by one patient or another for years. The canvas lining at the back had probably been washed once at some time, but I could not really be sure. At present, however, the lining was completely impregnated with all manner of lotions and nasty fluids after the application of blister plasters and so on. Besides this, the people who had been beaten with sticks were often brought into the prisoners' wards with bleeding backs. They were treated with various lotions, a robe was put on over their wet shirts, and as it absorbed all there was, it naturally went bad. Throughout all my time in gaol, whenever during these few years I happened to be put into hospital (and that was rather often), I would don my robe very fearfully and suspiciously. More than anything else, I disliked the very large, and remarkably fat-looking lice that one encountered in these robes. The prisoners loved executing them, and as one of the executed lice snapped beneath a thick, ugly prison nail, you could tell from the expression on the hunter's face how much pleasure he had derived from it. The patients also hated bedbugs and, occasionally, on a long, boring winter evening, the whole ward to a man would rise to exterminate them. So although on the surface our ward was passably clean, apart from the smell that is, there was no inner cleanliness in the underlining, shall I say, to be boasted of. The patients had grown used to it. They even considered it the right way for things to be, and then the rules did not dispose them to cleanliness either. I shall give an account of the rules a bit later though...

No sooner had Chekunov served me my tea (which was made, I might mention in passing, with water which was brought into the ward once in twenty-four hours and somehow went bad very quickly in our atmosphere) than the door opened rather noisily, and a soldier who had just run the gauntlet was led in under armed guard. It was the first time that I had seen someone after punishment. Later on, I was to see them very often. Some (the ones who had been punished too severely) were even carried in, and on every occasion the patients found it very diverting. These people were greeted with emphatically stern expressions and with an air so grave that it even seemed somewhat forced. The reception also depended on the gravity of the crime, and consequently on the extent of the punishment. A person who had been beaten severely and who was by reputation a big criminal enjoyed a greater degree of respect and attention than some escaped young recruit like the one who had just been brought in. In neither case were any especially commiserating or especially irritable remarks made. The sufferer was helped to his place in silence and looked after, especially if he was unable to manage without assistance. The feldshers already knew that they were delivering the man into experienced and skilful hands. The help usually consisted of frequent and necessary changes of a sheet or shirt soaked in cold water and placed across the mutilated back—particularly if the sufferer had no strength left to look after himself—and also in skilfully pulling out from the wounds the splinters which often lodged in the back from the sticks broken against it. This latter operation is usually very unpleasant for the patient, though by and large I was amazed at how resolutely these people endured the pain. I have seen many of them, very badly beaten, and yet hardly any of them groaned. Only their face changes—almost completely—and grows pale. Their eyes burn feverishly. Their glances become empty and anxious, and the lips of these poor people tremble so much that they bit them with their teeth—sometimes so hard that they make them bleed. The soldier who had just come in was a tall slim lad of about twenty-three, tough and muscular, with a swarthy skin and a handsome face. His back had taken quite a battering. His body was stripped right down to the waist. A wet sheet was thrown across his shoulders, making him shiver as in a fever. He paced nervously up and down the ward for about an hour and a half. I studied his face intently. It seemed that he was not thinking about anything at that moment. He just looked around him in a wild, strange way, his wandering glance seemed unable to stop and rest on any one thing. I fancied that he was staring at my tea. The tea was hot. Steam was rising from the cup. The poor fellow was cold and shivering, and his teeth were chattering. I offered him some to drink. He turned sharply towards me without saying a word, took the cup, drank it standing, without putting any sugar in it, hurrying terribly and not looking at me at all. When he had drunk it all, he put the cup down silently, without even nodding to me, and again began scurrying up and down the ward. He was past such niceties as words of thanks and nods. As for the other prisoners, they all avoided talking to the recruit when he was first brought in; and now, having helped him, they tried not to take any notice of him at all, perhaps wanting to give him as much peace as they could, and not to pester him with any further questions or with any 'condolences'. With this, he seemed to be completely satisfied.

Meanwhile evening had fallen and the night lamp was lit. It turned out that some of the prisoners—a very few—even had their own candle-holders. Finally, after the doctor's evening visit, the sergeant on guard came in and counted all the patients. He brought in the night bucket, and the ward was locked. To my surprise I discovered that this bucket remained in the ward all night, whereas the proper latrine was very near, only a couple of steps down the corridor. This was the established order. By day a patient could be let out of the ward, though for no longer than a minute; at night they would not let him out under any circumstances. Prisoners' wards were not like other wards, and a sick prisoner's punishment continued, even in his illness. Who introduced this rule I do not know. I only know that there was no real logic in this and that the useless rigidity of formalism was nowhere more glaringly evident than in this practice. This rule was not invented by the doctors, needless to say. I must repeat that the prisoners could not sing the praises of the doctors highly enough. They treated them as though they were their fathers, and showed great respect to them. Each prisoner had experienced nothing but gentleness from them, heard nothing but kind words from them. This is something that a prisoner, who is outcast by everyone, appreciates, because he sees that this gentleness and these kind words are quite genuine. It need not have been so; nobody would have rebuked the doctors if they had treated the patients differently, more rudely and more heartlessly. Their kindness, it follows, must have stemmed from real humanity. Doubtless they realised that any patient, whoever he may be—a prisoner or anyone else—needs the same amount of fresh air, for example, as any other, even a very high-ranking one. The convalescents in the other wards could walk freely along the corridors, taking all the exercise they wanted, and breathe air that was not so laden with infection as in the wards, where it was stuffy and always filled with stifling odours. It is terrible and disgusting to conceive how in our warm ward this air, which was already highly infected, grew even more so at night when the bucket was brought in, and there were men ill with certain diseases which demanded an outlet. Although I have just said that a prisoner carries his punishment with him even in his illness, I did not, of course, consider—and I still do not consider—that this was an order which had been established solely and deliberately to continue the punishment. This would undoubtedly have been a senseless and untrue claim for me to make. Sick people do not need any more punishment. If so, then obviously there must have been some strict and stern necessity that compelled the authorities to take precautions with such harmful consequences. What could that necessity be? Now, this is exactly what is so annoying: there is nothing that could at all explain the necessity of this measure and many other measures which are so inexplicable that it is impossible to even guess at their meaning, let alone explain them. How explain such unnecessary cruelty? By saying that a prisoner, having feigned illness and deceived the doctors, is going to enter the hospital, and then under pretext of going to the privy, will run away under cover of darkness? The complete nonsense of this reasoning does not need to be proved. Where would he run to? How would he run away? What would he wear when he ran away? By day, they let the prisoners out one by one. The same could have been done at night. There was a sentry with a loaded gun at the door. The latrine was literally only two steps further down the corridor, yet despite this the assistant sentry would accompany the patient and never take his eyes off him for one instant. There was only one window there—a double window because it was winter, with an iron grid over it. And under the window there was another sentry patrolling all night long very close to the prisoners' wards. In order to get through the window the prisoner would have to knock out the double window panes and the grid. Who would have allowed this to happen? How could that pass unnoticed—even supposing that he had killed the assistant sentry first, so that nobody heard the noise. And even accepting this absurd situation, he would still have to break the window pane and the grid. You must also note that the watchmen sleep very near the sentry post and that ten paces further on, outside the other prisoners' ward, there is another sentry with a gun, and his assistant and more watchmen next to him. And where can he run in the middle of winter, wearing stockings, slippers, a hospital robe and a nightcap? And if it is like this—if there is so small a danger that a prisoner might escape (none at all, in fact)—then what is this serious imposition on the patients really for, when they are perhaps living the last days or hours of their lives—these patients to whom fresh air is so much more essential than to healthy people? What for? I have never been able to understand it...

Now that I have raised the question 'What for?', and since I'm on the subject, I cannot help remembering another perplexing circumstance which for so many years confronted me as a most mysterious fact and for which I could never find any kind of answer. I must say a few words about it before I proceed with my story. I am talking about the shackles, from which no illness in the world will release a convict. Even the consumptives who died in front of my eyes, were still wearing their shackles. Everyone had grown used to it, however. It was considered a fact of life about which nothing could be done. Very probably no one had ever stopped to think about it, seeing that in all these years not even the doctors had once considered petitioning the authorities for permission to unshackle a prisoner who was seriously ill, the consumptives especially. Granted that the shackles are not so terribly heavy and usually weigh between eight and twelve pounds, for a healthy person a weight like that would not have been too burdensome to carry around, though I have been told that after several years the legs begin to waste away. I do not know whether this is true, but it sounds very probable. A weight—even a small one of just ten pounds—tied on to a foot forever, still increases the weight of the limb abnormally, and over a long period of time it no doubt causes harm... Let us assume, however, that for a healthy person it is no problem. Is it the same for a person who is ill? Even assuming that it is all right for an ordinary patient, can we assume that it is all right—I repeat—for someone who is seriously ill? Is it the same—I repeat—for those people who have consumption, whose legs and arms are withering away, so that even a straw seems heavy to them? Truly, if the medical authorities could obtain permission to unshackle just the people ill with consumption, even this would have been a real and considerable blessing. Of course, someone will say that this prisoner is a villain, and does not deserve any kindness. But is there really any need to exacerbate the punishment for someone who is already at death's door?

One surely cannot believe this is done purely to punish. Even the courts exempt consumptives from corporal punishment. There must therefore be some important and mysterious strategy concealed in this, whose aim is some safety precaution. But what kind of precaution can this be? It is impossible to understand. How can anyone be seriously afraid that a consumptive might run away? It would not even occur to anyone, especially knowing the stage to which the illness has developed. Faking consumption, deceiving the doctors in order to run away is out of the question. It is not that kind of illness; it can be discerned at first glance. And then surely a prisoner's legs aren't shackled for the sole purpose of preventing him from running away? Not at all. Shackles are degrading, shameful, and a moral and physical burden, which is all they are. At least, that is what they are meant to be. They could never prevent anyone from running away. Even the most unskilled, the clumsiest prisoner could very quickly and without much trouble manage to saw through the shackles or knock the rivet out of them with a stone. Shackles around the ankles are absolutely no precaution against escape. And if this is so and they are prescribed to a convicted man merely as a punishment, then I ask again why punish a person who is dying?

Just now, as I am writing this, I vividly remember one man dying of consumption. This was Mikhailov whose bed was almost opposite mine, not far from Ustyantsev. He died—as far as I remember—on the fourth day after my admission to the ward. That may be why I could not help talking about consumption just now: I was repeating the thoughts and impressions that occurred to me at the time in connection with his death. I knew Mikhailov only very slightly. He was still a very young man, about twenty-five, no more than that, tall and slim and extremely handsome. He was in the special category; his taciturnity verged on strangeness, and he was always very sad, in a quiet, calm kind of way. He was 'pining away' in gaol. That, at least, is how the prisoners, with whom he had left a rather pleasant memory, talked about him afterwards. All I can really remember of him now are his beautiful eyes, and I do not really know why he returns so vividly to my memory. He died at about three in the afternoon, on a bright, cold, frosty day. I remember how the strong slanting rays of the sun seemed to pierce the green, slightly frosted, panes of the ward windows. The sunlight poured on to the poor man. He was unconscious when he died, and he had been dying very painfully and slowly, over a period of several hours. From morning there was less and less recognition in his eyes of those who came up to him. The others wanted somehow to make it easier for him. They could see how he was suffering. His breathing was laboured, deep and wheezy. His chest rose very high, as though he were short of air. He had kicked off the blanket and all his clothes, and finally he started tearing off his shirt. Even that seemed too heavy for him. He was helped off with it. His unnaturally long body, the legs and arms withered to the bone, the hollow stomach, the raised chest, and the protruding ribs like a skeleton's, were horrible to see. On his whole body there remained only a wooden cross with an amulet and his shackles, through which he could easily have pulled out his withered feet now. About half an hour before he died, everyone in our ward grew quiet. They talked only in whispers. Anyone who had to walk anywhere, tried to step as noiselessly as possible. The men talked very little among themselves, and only about extraneous things. From time to time they glanced across at the dying man. He was wheezing more and more loudly all the time. Finally, with a wandering and unsure hand, he groped for the amulet on his chest and began tearing it off, as though even that were too heavy for him, hindering him, and weighing on him. They took the amulet off for him too. About ten minutes after that, he died. They knocked on the door to call the sentry. A watchman entered, looked dumbly at the dead man, and went to fetch the feldsher. The feldsher soon arrived, a kind young fellow who was rather too preoccupied with his appearance, though he was actually quite fortunate in that respect. He approached the dead man, his quick steps ringing out loudly in the hushed ward, and with a too casual air, which he may have invented especially for these occasions, he lifted the wrist, felt the pulse, waved his arm, and walked out. The sentries were immediately informed. The prisoner had been an important one, from the special category. Even to be certified dead some special formalities were needed.

While we were waiting for the sentries, one of the prisoners quietly suggested that it would not be a bad idea to close the dead man's eyes. Someone else, who had quietly heeded his words, walked up to the dead man and closed his eyes. Seeing the cross which was lying there on the pillow, he picked it up, examined it, and silently put it back around Mikhailov's neck. After doing this, he crossed himself. In the meantime, the dead face was already stiffening. A ray of light was playing over it. The mouth was half-open, and two rows of young white teeth sparkled under the thin lips, which were stuck to the gums. At last the sergeant on sentry duty arrived wearing a broadsword and a helmet, with two watchmen following on his heels. As he approached, he walked more and more slowly, looking around him in bewilderment at the silent prisoners watching him sternly from every corner. Coming close to the dead man, he stopped in his tracks, as though scared. The withered and stark naked corpse, dressed only in shackles, must have struck him very forcibly. He suddenly unfastened the neck flap of his helmet, took it off—which was not necessary at all—and crossed himself with a broad sweeping gesture. He was an old soldier, a stern, grey-haired veteran. I remember that Chekunov, who was also a grey-haired old man, was also standing there. He was looking silently and intently into the sergeant's face all the time, watching his every gesture with some strange attention. Then their eyes met, and for some reason Chekunov's lower lip began to tremble. He twisted it, bared his teeth, and, nodding towards the dead man, said hurriedly to the sergeant:

"He, too, had a mother!" And walked away.

I can remember how these words stabbed me... Why did he say that? Why did it cross his mind? The watchmen then started lifting up the corpse, and they lifted the bed along with it. The straw crackled. The shackles slipped to the floor with a clatter that sounded terribly loud in the surrounding silence. Someone picked them up. The corpse was carried out. Suddenly everyone started talking very loudly. In the corridor outside, the sergeant could be heard telling someone to fetch a blacksmith. The dead man would need unshackling...

But I have wandered away from the point...

II

Continuation

The doctors used to make their rounds of the wards in the morning. At a little after ten, they would all appear together accompanying the head doctor. The intern would have already been around about an hour and a half earlier. Our intern at that time was a young doctor who knew his job very well. He was a compassionate, amiable sort of fellow. The prisoners loved him very dearly, and could find only one shortcoming in him: he was 'too meek and mild'. As a matter of fact he was rather taciturn. It was as though he was embarrassed when he was with us, almost to the point of blushing. He would change the dosage of the medicines prescribed as soon as he was asked; in fact, he seemed ready to let the patients prescribe their own medicines. He was a nice young man. It must be admitted that, in Russia, there are many doctors who enjoy the love and respect of the common people. This, as far as I can tell, is absolutely true. I realise my words must seem paradoxical, especially considering the general mistrust of medicine, and even more so of medicine from abroad, shared by all the common people of Russia. A common person would rather suffer from a very serious disease for years and be treated by the local leech or try to cure himself with home remedies and folk medicines (though their efficacy cannot of course be ignored) than go to a doctor or to a hospital. Besides this, there is another extremely important circumstance, completely unconnected with medicine, namely the general distrust felt by all the common people for anything which bears the stamp of officialdom or formality. Apart from that, they are also frightened of hospitals and prejudiced against them, because of various hair-raising stories and old wives' tales, which are often absurd, but sometimes have a grain of truth in them nevertheless. Above all, the common people are frightened of the German style rules and regulations in hospitals, of having strange people around them throughout the whole length of their illness, of the strict diet, and of the stories they have heard about the unrelenting strictness of the doctors and their feldshers, how they open and disembowel the corpses, and so on and so forth. Besides, it's the gentry who will be treating them, because doctors are gentry just the same. On closer acquaintance with the doctors, however, usually all these fears (although there are exceptions) disappear quite quickly. This, in my opinion, redounds directly to the credit of the doctors, especially the younger ones. Most of them manage to win the respect and even the love of the common people. I am writing about what I saw with my own eyes and experienced many times and in many places, and I have no reason to suppose that in other places it was very different. There are places, of course, where the doctors take bribes, abuse their position, and practically ignore the patients, forgetting their knowledge of medicine almost completely. Such practices still continue; but I have been writing here about the majority, or—to put it another way—the prevailing spirit and direction of the medical profession of our time. Those others, the apostates of the cause, the rotten apples in the barrel, however they may justify themselves with fashionable excuses such as blaming their *environment* for leading them astray, will always be wrong, especially if even humaneness has also deserted them in all this. And humaneness, gentleness, and brotherly compassion are things a patient sometimes needs more badly than medicine. It is time for us to stop this apathetic moaning about the pernicious influence of the environment. Perhaps our environment does suppress many things in us, but still, it does not suppress everything, and very often a cunning rogue, fully aware of what he is doing, will skilfully disguise and explain not just his weaknesses but out-and-out foulness, by blaming the environment—especially if he has a gift for clever speaking or writing. I have wandered off my subject again, however. All I wanted to say was that the common people are more distrustful and hostile towards the medical administration than they are towards the doctors. Once having found out what the doctors are really like, they shed many of their prejudices. Even so the general atmosphere in our hospitals is in many respects at variance with the spirit of the people; the rules are still hostile to the customs of the common people and cannot win their full confidence and respect. At least that is how it seems to me, from some of the impressions that I gained.

Our intern usually stopped in front of every patient, examined him very thoroughly, asked him a lot of questions, and prescribed medicines. Sometimes he saw that the patient was not really ill at all, but the prisoner had come for a bit of a rest from work, or simply to lie on a mattress and not on bare boards, to be at least in a warm room and not in the damp guardhouse where dense crowds of pale and haggard men awaiting trial were kept crushed together (all over Russia people awaiting their verdict are almost always pale and haggard—an indication that the conditions they are kept in and their state of mind are even worse than is the case with those whose fates have already been decided), and so he wrote down with a clear conscience that the patient had *febris catarhalis* or something like that, and let him stay in the hospital, sometimes for as long as a week. It was a great joke in our place, this *febris catarhalis*. Everyone knew very well that it was an accepted formula for a feigned illness which had somehow been mutually agreed upon between doctor and patients. The 'reserve disease' was how the prisoners used to translate it. There were instances when a patient abused the doctor's kind-heartedness and stayed on in hospital until he was ordered to clear out. You should have seen our intern then. It was as if he were ashamed, afraid of telling the patient bluntly that it was time he recovered and asked to be discharged, although he had every right simply to discharge him without any cajoling or persuading, by writing '*sanat est*' into his case history. He would start by dropping a few hints, and then begin almost pleading with him. "It is time you were leaving us, isn't it? You're almost well again now, aren't you? The ward is full to bursting." And so on and so forth, until the patient also became embarrassed and started asking for a discharge himself. The head doctor, a humane and honest man (and the patients were very fond of him too), was incomparably stricter and more resolute than the intern; when necessary he was severely strict, which earned him more than ordinary respect. He would arrive after the intern's visit, accompanied by all the other doctors in the hospital, and he also examined each patient individually, dedicating a considerable amount of time to those who were seriously ill. He would always have something kind and reassuring to say to them, something heart-warming, and altogether made a very favourable impression. He never turned away the prisoners who had come in with the 'reserve illness', and he never sent them back to gaol either. If a prisoner thus admitted persisted with his feigned illness, the head doctor would simply discharge him. "Well, my friend, you've been here long enough, you've had your rest, now have the decency to go." The ones who persisted were usually either work-shy, especially during the busy season in summertime, or men still awaiting punishment. I remember one case where particular severity, even some cruelty, was used to persuade such a patient to apply for a discharge. He had been admitted with an eye disease. His eyes were red, and he complained of a strong, stinging pain in them. He was given a course of treatment with Spanish flies, leeches, smarting eye sprays, and what not, but still the disease would not go away, and still his eyes got no better. Gradually, the doctors began to realise that the disease was a feigned one. The inflammation was consistently quite mild in nature. It never got any worse, but it never got any better either. It was always at the same stage: a very suspicious case indeed. The other prisoners had known for quite a long time that his complaint was invented and that he was deceiving people, though he himself would never admit it to anyone. He was a young lad, quite good-looking, but somehow he produced quite an unpleasant impression on us all. He was secretive, suspicious and morose; he would not talk to anyone and only glared about him as though he suspected each and every man. I remember how some people even feared he might do something desperate. He had been in the army, he got caught in some serious theft, was sentenced to a thousand sticks and then the penal battalion. As I have already mentioned, men awaiting punishment sometimes take the most terrible chances trying to put off the dread moment. On the eve of the punishment, they will stick a knife into one of the authorities, or even one of their fellow prisoners, and in this way achieve their aim by ensuring that they will have to stand trial again, and have the punishment postponed for another two months or so. Never mind that in two months' time, the punishment will be two or three times more severe. All they want is to remove the threat that hangs over them, even if only for a few days. After that—come what may! This is how demoralised these poor wretches can become! In our place some people were already whispering that we should be careful of him for he might well murder somebody at night. Actually, this was only talk, and even those whose beds were alongside his took no practical precautions. They had noticed how at night he rubbed his eyes with the lime from the plaster on the walls, and with something else besides, making sure that they would be red again by morning. Finally, the head doctor threatened him to give him a seton. With persistent eye infections, when all other medical means have been tried, doctors sometimes take recourse to a very strong and painful remedy to save the patient's sight. They give the patient a seton, in the same way as they do to a horse. Even then the poor man did not agree to recover. What a stubborn character he was, or maybe just cowardly? Because although a seton is not actually as bad as the sticks, it is still very painful. A hand holds the scruff of the patient's neck—as much of it as possible—and pulls it together tightly. Then a knife is stuck right through this gathered skin, making a wide and long wound across the whole back of the neck, through which a linen tape, almost as broad as a finger, is then passed. Every day at a fixed time, the tape is pulled through the wound with the effect of re-opening it, so that it stays festering and does not heal. Although he was in terrible agony, the poor man endured this torture for several days, and only then agreed to be discharged. His eyes became perfectly well that same day, and as soon as his neck was healed he returned to the guardhouse from where, the very next morning, he would be sent out to receive his thousand sticks.

Of course, the moment before punishment is difficult, so difficult that I am perhaps offending against the truth to call this fear faint-heartedness or cowardice. It must be very hard indeed if a person risks being sent for a double or triple punishment simply to put it off. I have also mentioned, however, those people who of their own accord asked to be discharged as soon as possible, before their backs had healed after the first punishment, so they could take the rest of the sticks, and get the whole thing over. Being kept in the guardhouse awaiting punishment is, of course, incomparably worse than doing hard labour. Differences in temperament aside, the resolution and fearlessness of some people is augmented by the fact that they are used to sticks and punishment. Both the back and the spirit of a person who has been beaten many times become hardened, so much so that he comes to regard the punishment with a good deal of scepticism, rather as a minor inconvenience, and is no longer afraid of it. This is true, generally speaking. There was one of our prisoners, from the special category, a Kalmyk who had been baptised, Alexander or Alexandra as they used to call him, a strange, roguish, fearless, and very good-natured fellow, who told me how he went through the whole of his four thousand sticks. He laughed and joked about it, but told me very earnestly that he would never have survived it if he had not been brought up under the lash from his very earliest and tenderest childhood, the scars on his back never healing all the years he lived with his tribe. He told me this as though blessing this upbringing under the lash. "I was beaten for everything you can think of, Alexander Petrovich," he told me one evening before lights-out, sitting on my bed. "For everything and anything. I was beaten for about fifteen years running, every day from the very first day I can remember, sometimes several times a day! The only reason I wasn't beaten was because nobody felt like it. So in the end I grew completely used to it." I do not know how he was recruited. Maybe he told me, I don't remember. He had been forever on the move, a permanent wanderer. The only thing I do remember about his story is how terror-stricken he had been when he was sentenced to four thousand strokes for murdering his commander. "I knew I was going to be punished very severely, and very likely never come out from those sticks alive. I was used to lashes, but four thousand sticks is no joke. Besides, all the commanders were furious with me. I felt sure, positively sure they would get even with me, I wouldn't survive it, they wouldn't let me out alive. At first I thought maybe I ought to get baptised, maybe that would make them forgive me, though my own people told me there and then that nothing would come of it, and I wouldn't be forgiven. Still, I thought I might as well try it. They are bound to feel more pity for someone who has been baptised. So I was baptised—and in Holy Baptism I was given the name Alexander. But those sticks were still sticks. They might have given me one less. I felt really upset about it. Then I thought to myself: just you wait, I shall make fools of the lot of you. And do you know what, Alexander Petrovich? That's exactly what I did. I was very good at playing dead—well, not absolutely dead, but as though the soul was about to depart the body at any minute. I was led to the slaughter, and run through the first thousand. My back was burning, I was screaming. Then they started running me through the second thousand. This is my end coming, they've knocked my brains out, my legs won't hold me. And I flopped on the ground like a sack of potatoes; my eyes turned glassy. I was blue in the face, foaming at the lips, and not breathing. A doctor came up to me. Verge of death, he said. I was taken to the hospital, where I came back to life at once. They made me run the gauntlet two more times, and they were furious with me, really furious. But I managed to cheat them both times. I nearly croaked after going through the third thousand, and when I started on the fourth, every blow was like a knife in the heart, each blow felt like three, they were hitting me so hard. Vicious they were. That mean last thousand, damn it, was as bad as the first three put together, and if I had not died before the end, when there were only about two hundred strokes to go, they would have beaten me to death anyway. But I knew how to stand up for myself. I cheated them again and fell down dead. They believed it all right. What else could they do? The doctor believed it. So during the last two hundred, though they hit me with all their anger, so hard it was worth all of two thousand, but no fear, they did not beat me to death. And why didn't they? Because, just like I told you, I grew up under the lash. That's why I'm still alive today. Oh I've been beaten, I've been beaten pretty hard in my lifetime," he added at the end of his story in a sadly pensive voice, as if he were trying to remember and count all his beatings. "No," he said breaking his silence. "There's no counting the times I've been beaten, there aren't enough numbers." He raised his eyes to mine and burst out laughing with such good humour that I could not help smiling back at him. "Do you know, Alexander Petrovich, if I ever have any dreams at night, they are always about being beaten. I never have any other dreams." He did, actually, often shout out in his sleep at night, shouting so loudly that the other prisoners had to shake him awake. "What the hell are you shouting about?" He was a robust, rather short fellow, fidgety and cheerful, about forty-five years old. He lived in harmony with everyone, and though he loved stealing and would often get a beating for it, well who did not steal in our place, and who did not get a beating for it?

I will add one more thing to this: what always amazed me was the remarkable good humour and the absence of any malice with which these beaten men spoke about their beatings and the men who did the beating. Mostly I could not detect a single overtone of malice or hatred in their telling of the story, though it set my own heart pounding from anger. Telling their story, they sometimes laughed like children. This was not the case when M—tsky told me about the punishment he had received. He was not from the nobility, so he got five hundred. I had heard about this from the others so I asked him myself whether it was true, and how it had been. He answered somewhat brusquely, trying to avoid my eyes as though feeling some inner pain, and his face flushed red. Half a minute later he looked straight at me. Hatred was burning in his eyes and his lips were trembling with indignation. I felt that he would never be able to forget that episode of his life. The rest, however, almost all of them (though I cannot swear that there were no exceptions), looked at it quite differently. It could not be, I used to think sometimes, that they considered themselves so guilty that their punishment was deserved, especially when they had committed a crime against the authorities and not against their own kind. The majority did not regard themselves as blameworthy in the slightest. I have already said that I did not notice any pangs of remorse, even where the crime had been committed against their own kind, let alone crimes against the authorities. In this latter case it seemed to me that they had

213

their own practical, or better say factual way of looking at the matter. They accepted the irrefutable fact as fate, without trying to analyse it but submitting to it subconsciously, as an act of faith. Although a prisoner is always inclined to feel that he is in the right in his crimes against the authorities, so much so that any doubt here is completely out of the question, he does realise that the authorities take a totally different view of his crime and, therefore, he should be punished—and they are quits. Here the struggle is mutual. The criminal also knows, without any doubt, that he will be acquitted by his own kind, the common people, and that they will never, as he knows very well, denounce him completely. Most likely, they will absolve him completely, provided that his sin has not been against his own brothers, common people like himself. His conscience is untroubled, and this gives him his strength. He is not ashamed morally, and this is what really counts. He is aware that he has backing, and that is why he feels no hatred and accepts what has happened to him as an inescapable fact, which was not started by him and will not be brought to an end by him, which, once begun, will carry on for a long time into the future as part of an established passive but stubborn struggle. A soldier feels no personal hatred towards a Turkish soldier when he is fighting him, although the Turkish soldier is slashing at him, stabbing him and shooting at him. True, not all accounts were quite so cool and indifferent. Lieutenant Zherebyatnikov, for example, was always mentioned with even a shade of resentment. I made the acquaintance of this lieutenant during my first spell in hospital, though only through what the prisoners said about him, of course. Later I did see him in the flesh when he was on guard. He was a tall man of about thirty, rather fat and plump, with red bloated cheeks, white teeth and a deep rumbling laugh like Nozdrev's in *Dead Souls*.[12] You could see from his face that he was one of the least thinking people in the world. His greatest delight in life was whipping and caning people whenever he was appointed to administer the punishment. I should hasten to add that at that time I already regarded this Lieutenant Zherebyatnikov as a freak among his own kind, and that the prisoners regarded him in very much the same light. Of course, there had been other administrators of punishment who loved to carry out their task as zealously and diligently in times past, in those recent times of which, as Griboyedov writes, "the memory is still so fresh but it can hardly be believed".[13] Yet in their case it was done simply, without any particular enthusiasm. This lieutenant, however, where punishment was concerned, was something of a sophisticated gourmet. He loved punishment passionately, as an art. He revelled in it, and sated with pleasures like some decaying patrician of the Roman Empire, he would invent his own variations, different perversions, just to stir and tickle his fat and bloated soul. A prisoner, say, is brought out for punishment. Zherebyatnikov is in charge of administering it. One glance along the ranks lined up with their thick sticks is inspiration enough for him. Complacently, he inspects the rows and gives the emphatic order that each man should carry out his work zealously and conscientiously. Otherwise ... the soldiers already know what this 'otherwise' means. Now the prisoner himself is brought out. If he does not yet know Zherebyatnikov, if he has not heard the stories which are going round about him, then Zherebyatnikov will, for example, play the following trick on him. (This is of course just one little joke among hundreds; the inventiveness of the lieutenant knew no bounds.) While the victim is being stripped and having his hands tied to the butts of the rifles by which the sergeants will drag him past the lined-up soldiers, every victim, according to general custom, starts begging the administrator in a tearful and pitiful voice to punish him lightly and not be too severe. "Show mercy, Your Excellency," the poor man shouts, "spare me, be a father to me, I'll pray for you all my life, don't let me die, have pity!" This was the moment Zherebyatnikov was waiting for. Immediately he would bring the punishment to a halt and, with an appearance of compassion, strike up a conversation with the prisoner:

"Well, what do you think I should do with you, my dear fellow?" he would say. "It is not I who punishes you, it's the Law."

"Oh, Your Excellency, it is all in your hands. Have mercy on me."

"Do you think I don't feel sorry for you? Do you think it

gives me pleasure to see you being beaten? I am human, as you are. Am I human, or am I not? What do you say?"

"Of course, Your Excellency, naturally. You are as fathers to us and we are your children. Be a true father to me!" shouts the prisoner, beginning to feel there is some hope.

"But listen, my dear fellow, and judge for yourself. You have the brains to judge, haven't you? I know myself that, humanely speaking, I should look compassionately and mercifully upon the sinner you are."

"Oh yes, Your Excellency, that is the truth!"

"Yes, I should look upon you with mercy, however sinful you may be. But here it's not I, it's the Law. Think for yourself. I serve God and the motherland. I would take a grievous sin upon my own soul should I be lax with the Law. Think about it."

"Your Excellency!"

"Oh well, all right then. Just once, just for you. I know I am committing a sin but still ... so be it. Supposing I have mercy on you and punish you lightly. What, if by doing so, I do harm to you? I show mercy on you now, punish you lightly, and you, hoping it will be the same next time too, go and commit another crime. What then? It will be on my soul..."

"Oh no, Your Excellency. I won't do it again, and I'll make sure my friends and enemies never do it. As God is my witness, I'll..."

"Oh, all right, all right. Will you swear to me that from now on you will behave yourself?"

"Strike me down if I don't! May I never go to heaven..."

"Don't call heaven to witness. It's a sin. I can take your word for it. Will you give me your word?"

"Your Excellency!"

"Right then, now listen to me. I shall show mercy on you only for the orphan tears you shed. You are an orphan, I presume?"

"Oh yes I am, Your Excellency, cast out into the world, without mother or father..."

"Well, then, for the sake of your orphan tears. But mind you, it's the last time. Right then, take him through." He adds these last words in such a soft-hearted tone that the prisoner is overwhelmed with gratitude. The very next moment, however, the terrible procession starts to move, and they begin to lead him out. The drum begins to roll, the first sticks rise and fall... "Drag him through it!" yells Zherebyatnikov at the top of his voice. "Let him have it! Lay into him! Make it scorch him! Harder, harder! Make it hot for the orphan, the rogue! Lay into him! Let him have it!" So the soldiers hit him with all their might, until the sparks seem to fly from the poor man's eyes, and he starts to scream, while Zherebyatnikov runs along behind him down the line, laughing and laughing, fit to burst, holding his sides and doubling over, unable to straighten up, so that in the end you even feel sorry for him, poor chap. How happy he is! What fun he is having! Only very rarely is there a pause in those healthy roars of laughter, and his shouts are audible again: "Hit him! Hit him! Make it hot for the rogue, the orphan!"

Here are some other variations invented by him. A prisoner is brought out for punishment and again begins to plead with him. On this occasion Zherebyatnikov does not make a comic act of it, or jest at all, he simply delivers the following frank and open speech:

"You see, my man, it's like this. I am going to punish you very severely, because that's what you deserve. But there is one thing I think I'll do for you. I shall not have you tied to the rifle butts. We'll do it a new way, you'll go on your own, and run as fast as you can through the ranks. Now in this way, although each stick will still strike you, the whole thing will be over more quickly. What do you think? Do you want to try it?"

The prisoner listens to this in bewilderment and disbelief, and falls into deep thought. "Well," he thinks, "shall I do it? Perhaps it really will be easier. I'll run as fast as I can. The torture will be over five times as quickly, and maybe not all the sticks will even hit me."

"All right, Your Excellency, I agree."

"That's all right with me then. Off you go!" And to the soldiers he shouts: "Come on then, keep awake!" knowing all the time, of course, that not a single stick will miss its mark on the guilty back. A soldier who misses knows only too well what he is letting himself in for. The prisoner starts to run as fast as he

217

can, but he gets no further than the fifteenth man. The sticks come raining down on him like hail—suddenly, all of them together—and with a shout the poor fellow falls down flat on his face as though he has been shot. "Oh no, Your Excellency," he says, getting up slowly, pale and frightened, from the ground, "it's better to do it as it's laid down in the rules." Zherebyatnikov, meanwhile, who has worked out the trick beforehand and knows perfectly well what will come of it, laughs uproariously. He splits his sides laughing. It is not possible to describe all the entertainments he devised for himself, nor repeat all the stories that were told about him!

They also talked, in a slightly different way, about a Lieutenant Smekalov, who had been acting commander in the gaol before the present Major was appointed. When they talked about Zherebyatnikov, although their tone was rather indifferent and without much malice, yet they did not admire his deeds or praise him, and apparently despised him. They even looked down on him. Now, Lieutenant Smekalov, on the other hand, was remembered with joy and pleasure. He was not especially fond of beating people, and there was nothing of Zherebyatnikov's sadism in him. Still, he was not averse to giving someone a good flogging, but his beating was remembered by our people with a sweet tenderness. Such was the admiration he inspired in the prisoners. How did he do it? How did he win such popularity? It is true that our prison folk, like the entire Russian people perhaps, are prepared to forget all the torments they have endured for one kind word. I am stating this as a fact, without analysing it from one point of view or another. It is easy enough to win popularity among prisoners. But Lieutenant Smekalov won *especial* popularity, such that even his floggings were remembered with something like wistfulness. "You don't need a father when you've got someone like him around," the prisoners used to say; and they would sigh, comparing memories of this temporary commander and their present Major. "He had a heart, he did!" He was a simple man, perhaps even kind, after his own manner. But there are commanders who are not only kind but also generous. And yet what happens? They are not liked, and sometimes even laughed at. The thing is that Smekalov somehow contrived to make everybody feel that he 'belonged'. This takes skill, or rather talent, people who are born with it never give it a thought. Funny thing, but there are people of this type who are not kind at all but they win great popularity just the same. The reason lies, I think, in their not looking down squeamishly on the people in their charge, and not turning up their noses queasily. There is nothing of the young lordship about them, and no masterly airs, what there is about them is an aura of commonality, something they are just born with. And by God! How quick our people are to detect this aura! What will they not give for it! They are ready to swap the most kind-hearted commander for a hard-hearted one, if that latter one has something of their own earthy smell. And if this person, who has a trace of this odour of theirs, is also kind-hearted in some particular, individual way? Well, then he is second only to God. Lieutenant Smekalov, as I have already mentioned, could sometimes administer punishment very painfully, but he managed somehow to do this in such a way that not only did they hold no grudge against him for it, but quite the opposite—they even (and this was in my time when all that happened a long time ago) remembered his *tricks* during the beatings with a great deal of laughter and enjoyment. He did not have so many of these tricks: he lacked the artistic imagination for that. There had been, to tell the truth, only one single trick which he practised in our place during the space of almost a year. Maybe they held it so dear, exactly because it was the only one. It was really very simple and straightforward. The convicted man would be brought out, and Smekalov would come forward and, with a grin, ask him some question or other, jokingly, about something totally irrelevant, about his personal affairs, his life in prison—not for any particular reason, or in order to play up to him, but just like that—*because he was really interested in such things.* The rods would be brought out, together with a chair for Smekalov to sit on. He would take his seat, perhaps even light his pipe. His pipe was amazingly long... The prisoner would start pleading with him. "No, no, my friend, lie down. There's no point in kicking up a fuss now..." Smekalov would say. The prisoner would sigh and lie down. "Now, my dear friend..." and he would ask him if he could recite certain verses from the Gospel by heart. "Why not, Your Excellency, we're all good Christians; we've all known our Gospel since we were so high..." "Well then! Go ahead!" The prisoner already knows what he has to recite, and already knows what will happen to him while he is doing so, because exactly the same trick has been played on other prisoners about thirty times previously. And Smekalov also knows that the prisoner knows it. He also knows that the soldiers standing there with their birch rods raised above their prone victim have heard about it and known about it for a long time too. Yet he still repeats it again and again. That was how much he liked it, once and for ever, probably out of some artistic vanity, because he had invented it himself. The prisoner begins to recite, and the soldiers with the birch rods stand waiting, and Smekalov leans forward in his seat slightly, stops puffing on his pipe and raises his hand, waiting for a particular word. The prisoner comes to the words "Thy will be done" in the Lord's prayer. That is just what he is waiting for. "Stop!" the inspired lieutenant shouts, and turning to the man standing there with the raised rod shouts, with an inspired gesture: "Thy will be done! Let's have some fun!"

And he bursts into fits of laughter. The soldiers standing around grin too. The man doing the flogging smiles. Even the man being flogged almost smiles, although these words, *"Let's have some fun!"*, were the command for the birch rods to come whistling down through the air and cut like a razor into his guilty body. This delighted Smekalov. Delighted him because he could see how well he had devised it all, and he had invented it *all on his own*—"Thy will be done!" and "Let's have some fun!" fitted together so nicely, and rhymed so well. Smekalov leaves completely satisfied with himself, and the punished man is also pleased with himself and with Smekalov, and half an hour later he will be back in the gaol telling everyone how the joke, which has already been repeated thirty times, went this time, the thirty-first. "You've got to give it to him, he's got a heart, he has! A real jolly sort, he is!"

Occasionally the reminiscences of this kindest lieutenant became rather like those of Gogol's Manilov.[14]

"You would be walking along, mates, like this..." some prisoner would say, his whole face alight with the memory. "You'd be walking along, and he would be out there sitting under his window in his dressing-gown, drinking his tea, smoking that pipe of his. And you'd take your hat off to him. 'Where are you off to, Aksyonov?'

" 'To work, Lieutenant Smekalov sir, to the workshops to start with.' And he'd laugh, you know. That showed he had a heart! Oh yes indeed—what a man!"

III

Continuation*

I have now started to discuss punishments and all the various administrators of these fascinating duties, because it was actually only when I came to hospital that I received my first clear notion of these matters. Before that I only knew about these things from hearsay. To our wards came all the people who had been punished with sticks, persons awaiting their verdict from all the battalions, and all the penal units and other military companies, situated in our city and the surrounding district. During this time, while I was still avidly learning about everything that was happening around me, all these customs, which were very strange to me, and all the people, both those who had been punished and those awaiting punishment, naturally produced a very strong impression upon me. I was disturbed, confused and frightened. I also remember that this was the time when I suddenly and impatiently began to try and grasp all the details of these new phenomena, to listen to the other prisoners' conversations and stories on this theme, to ask them questions myself and strive to find a solution to these problems. I wanted, among other things to know how the sentences were classified,

*Author's note. Everything I write here about punishments refers to the time I was in prison. I have heard that it has now all changed, or is in the process of change.

how they were carried out, what variations were practised, and how the prisoners themselves felt towards them. I tried to imagine the state of mind of those going out to be punished. I have already mentioned how, just before a punishment, it is rare for anyone, even those who have been beaten many times before, to manage to keep calm. Some acute but purely physical fear—involuntary, irresistible and suppressing a person's whole moral being—takes hold of the condemned man at this moment. Later on, and throughout all my years in prison, I could not help observing how these men, having spent some time in hospital after taking the first part of their punishment, were released when their backs had healed in order to go through the second half of the sticks allotted to them on the following day. This splitting of the punishment in two is always dependent upon the verdict of the doctor who is present at the punishment. If the number of designated strokes is too much for the prisoner to endure, then the number is divided in two, or even three parts, according to the doctor's pronouncement (during the course of the punishment itself) as to whether it should be continued or whether this entails danger to the prisoner's life. Five hundred strokes, or even a thousand, or fifteen hundred strokes, are usually gone through all at once. If the sentence is two thousand or three thousand, however, the punishment is divided into two or even three parts. Those whose backs had healed after taking the first part, and who were waiting to be released from hospital in order to go through the second, were very gloomy, grim and taciturn on the eve of their discharge, and on the day itself too. A kind of stupefaction and unnatural absent-mindedness was evident in them. They did not join in conversation, and for the most part remained silent. The most curious thing is that the other prisoners never talked to them or tried to bring up the subject of what was in store for the condemned. There were no superfluous words of comfort. They even attempted to ignore the poor men and pay very little attention to them. This was by far the best thing for them. There were some exceptions, of course, like Orlov, whom I have already mentioned. All he complained about after the first part of the punishment was that his back would not heal quickly enough for him to be released, go through the remaining strokes, leave with a convoy for his place of exile, and escape on the way there. This dream was a source of diversion for him, and God knows what was really going on in his mind. His was a passionate nature, tenacious of life. He was very pleased with himself, and in a very excited state, for all his efforts to suppress his emotions. The fact of the matter was that even before the first half of his beating he was convinced that they would not let him escape the sticks alive, and that he was destined to die. Various rumours about the measures the authorities took had reached him while he was still on trial, and already then he prepared himself to meet his death. So he was considerably heartened that he had survived the first half. He was brought into hospital, beaten to within an inch of his life. I had never seen such sores in my life. Yet he came to us with joy in his heart, hope that he would survive and that the rumours had all been false since he had been let off alive, and he was already dreaming of the road, and how he would escape, of freedom and fields and forests... He died in the same hospital, in the same bed, two days after he was released, unable to survive the second part. I have already mentioned this.

Yet those selfsame prisoners, who spent such difficult days and nights beforehand, even the most fainthearted of them, would undergo the actual punishment very courageously. I rarely heard them moaning, even on the first night after they were admitted, even those who had been beaten the most severely. Generally speaking, the common people know how to endure pain. I used to ask a lot of questions concerning the pain. I was curious to discover just how strong this pain was, and what it could be compared to. To tell the truth, I do not really know why I was trying to get this out of them. I only remember that it was not idle curiosity. I should reiterate that I was disturbed and shaken at that time. Yet whoever I asked, I could never receive a satisfactory answer. It burns, it scorches like fire. This was the only answer any of them could give. It burns—that was all they could say. During those first days, I had grown rather close to M—tsky, and so I asked him about it too. "It's very painful," he answered, "and the sensation, well, it burns ... like fire. It's as though your back is being roasted over the hottest fire imaginable." Everyone, in other words, described it in the same way. I remember, however, how at that time I made one very strange observation, which I would not particularly insist upon. Yet the unanimity of the prisoners on the subject suggests, perhaps, that it is true. This was that birch-rod floggings, when administered in a large number of lashes, were the worst punishment of all. At first glance this seems impossible and absurd. Yet all the same, you can kill someone with five hundred, or even as few as four hundred lashes. More than five hundred means almost certain death. A thousand lashes cannot be endured in one go, even by someone of the strongest build. Five hundred stick strokes, however, can be survived without danger to life. A thousand strokes can be endured, without danger to life, even by someone who is not of particularly strong build. A person of average strength and medium build cannot be killed even by two thousand strokes. All the prisoners agreed that lashes with birch rods were worse than strokes with a stick. "They burn you worse; there's more of a torture in them!" they used to say. Lashes cause more agony than the sticks, of course. They affect the nerves more, jar them, shock them beyond endurance. I do not know how things are nowadays, but there have been ladies and gentlemen in recent times, to whom the opportunity of whipping a victim gave pleasure in much the same way as that reminiscent of the Marquis de Sade and the Marquise de Brinvilliers. There is something in this sensation which makes the hearts of such perverts contract with a sweet, pleasurable pain. There are men who, like tigers, crave for a lick of blood. Whoever has once experienced such power, such a boundless dominance over the body, blood and spirit of another man, who is in all respects like himself, created like him, his brother in Christ; whoever has experienced the power and the freedom to humiliate in the worst manner possible another human being, made in the image of God, that man is already powerless to control his sensations. Tyranny is a habit. It can develop. And it develops, in the end, into a disease. I must insist on this point, that the best person can become coarsened and stultified through this habit into bestiality. Blood and power befuddles the mind. Coarseness, corruption start to develop. The mind and the senses accept, and then finally enjoy, the most unnatural acts. In a tyrant, both the human being and the social being are killed forever, and the possibility of a return to human dignity, to repentance and to resurrection becomes almost impossible. The example and the possibility of such absolute power infect the whole of society like a disease; such power is tempting. A society which can regard such a phenomenon with indifference is already infected in its very foundations. In other words, the right to carry out corporal punishment, given to one person over another, is one of the ulcers of society, it is one of the most powerful ways of destroying in it any embryonic attempt to establish civic justice and forms all that is needed as a base for inevitable and irresistible decay.

Society shuns the official flogger, but not the gentleman-flogger. Far from it! It is only recently that any dissent has been uttered, and so far it has only been in books, that is to say as an abstraction. Even those who express this dissent have not all managed to extinguish within themselves this need to rule over others. Every factory owner and employer must doubtless feel titillated at the thought that his worker, with all his family, depends solely upon him. It must be so. A generation cannot so soon shake off the features it has inherited. A man cannot so quickly renounce what is in his blood, what he has drawn in with his mother's milk. Such hasty upheavals do not happen. It is not enough to recognise the guilt, the ancestral sin. It is very little. The habit has to be shed completely. And this does not happen so quickly.

I have started talking about the floggers. The qualities for this job are present, in embryo, in almost any modern person. The animal traits of a human do not, however, develop in the same way. If, in their development, they overpower all the other traits, then, of course, such a man becomes terrible and monstrous. There are two types of men who carry out public punishments: those who do it voluntarily, and those who do it under compulsion. The volunteer is, of course, much baser in all respects than the one who is compelled to do it, yet it is the latter who is despised and loathed by the people to the point of

225

horror, abomination, and an unaccountable, almost mystical fear. Where does it come from, this almost superstitious fear of one, and this indifference, and all but approval, of the other? There are some examples which are odd in the extreme. I have known people who were even kind, honest, respected in society, yet who could not take it calmly if the person being flogged did not shout under the rod, did not beg and scream for mercy. Screaming and begging for mercy is considered the decent thing to do. And when on one occasion the victim did not want to scream, the executioner—a man who was known to me and who could in all other respects be thought a rather kind man—took it as a personal affront. He had meant to punish the man lightly, but then, when he did not hear the usual "Oh Your Excellency! Have mercy on me! I'll pray for you till the day I die!" and so on, he lost his temper and ordered fifty extra lashes, to induce him to scream and beg. He got both. "Can't be allowed! There is something rude about it!" he told me very seriously in explanation. As for the flogger who is obliged and forced to do it, his situation is very well known. He is a convict, sentenced to exile, then left behind to administer public punishments. First he serves an apprenticeship under another flogger, and when he has learnt the skill from him, he remains in the gaol forever, kept apart from the other prisoners. He has a room to himself, even his own household, but he is kept almost continually under guard. A living person is not a machine, of course. Even though floggings are his everyday job, he does get excited sometimes, and while deriving some pleasure from it he hardly ever feels any personal hatred for his victims. The skill with which he delivers the blow, his knowledge of the art, the desire to show off in front of his mates and the public, stir up his vanity. He works hard for art's sake. Besides which, he knows very well that he is an outcast, that wherever he goes people look at him with superstitious fear, and it is impossible to be sure that this does not affect him, does not intensify the rage within him and all his bestial tendencies. Even little children know that he has 'renounced his father and mother'. One strange thing is that every flogger I have known has been a man with good brains and sense, and an incredible vanity, even pride. Whether this has developed in them as a rebuff to the general contempt in which they are held, or whether it has been intensified by the awareness of the fear they inspire in their victims, and the feeling of power over them—that I do not know. Maybe the very showiness and theatricality of the occasion on which they appear before the public contribute to the development of a certain arrogance in them. I recall a time when over a protracted period I had to meet and observe one of these public executioners. He was a man of medium height, lean, muscular, about forty years old, with rather a pleasant, clever face and curly hair. He always had a great air of importance and composure about him. Outwardly, he behaved in a gentleman-like manner, always answered questions curtly, reasonably and kindly, but this kindness was tinged with arrogance, as though he was showing off to me. The guard officers would often strike up a conversation with him in my presence and, truly, they seemed to feel a certain respect for him. He too could feel this, and deliberately enhanced his politeness, his curtness and his air of self-esteem. The kinder the way an officer spoke to him, the stiffer he seemed to become, and although he never transgressed the bounds of the most refined politeness, yet I am sure that at these moments he considered himself to be incomparably superior to the person in authority with whom he was talking. It was written on his face. It often happened, on hot summer days, that he was sent out under guard to beat the town dogs with a long thin stick. There was an extraordinary number of dogs in the town, strays which bred at an incredible speed. During school summer holidays they became dangerous, and on the instructions of the authorities an executioner would be sent out to exterminate them. Yet even this humiliating task did not seem to humiliate him in the least. You should have seen the pride with which he strode along the town streets with his wearied guard, frightening the women and children simply by dint of his appearance, calmly and even condescendingly surveying everyone he met.

However, these executioners in fact live in relative freedom and plenty. They have their own money. They eat well. They drink liquor. They take bribes. A civilian prisoner who is sentenced to a punishment by the court, will make a donation of some sort to the flogger beforehand, even if it is his last savings. From some people, the rich ones, they even demand the bribe themselves, naming a price according to their estimate of the victim's means. They sometimes take as much as thirty roubles, or more. They even bargain lengthily with the very rich ones. A flogger cannot administer the punishment too lightly, of course. He would pay for it with his own back. Still, for a certain sum, he promises the victim not to flog him too painfully. His terms are almost always accepted. If they are not, he administers the punishment in the most barbarous manner, as he is perfectly entitled to do. Sometimes he imposes a considerable sum even on a very poor person under sentence. Then the relatives come, bargain, bow and scrape, and woe to them if they cannot satisfy him. He is greatly aided, in cases such as these, by the superstitious fear that he inspires. There is no end to the strange tales they tell about these floggers! The prisoners actually assured me that a flogger is capable of killing with one blow. But I ask you! When and where did this happen? However, anything is possible. They sounded too positive. One flogger himself assured me that he could do it. It was also believed that he could administer a blow, with all his strength, right across the victim's back, but in such a way that it would leave no weal behind it afterwards, and that the man would feel no pain. There are too many well-known stories about these various tricks and subtleties. Even if a flogger does accept a bribe to administer the punishment lightly, he will anyway deliver the first blow with all his might, taking a good swing. This even became a custom among them. They would ease up on the blows that followed; especially if they had been paid to do so beforehand. The first blow, however, bribe or no bribe, was theirs. I really have no idea why such a custom should exist. Is it perhaps to accustom the victim at once to what will come afterwards, on the assumption that, after a hard blow, the lighter one will not seem so painful? Or is it simply a desire to show off in front of the victims, to cow them, to disconcert them at the outset, so that they know whom they are dealing with: in other words, a kind of boastfulness? Whatever the reason, an executioner, just before a punishment, is in a state of high excitement. He feels his power, he knows that he is king. At a moment like this, he is an actor on stage. The spectators marvel and gasp in horror, and obviously he enjoys shouting to his victim before the first blow: "Hold tight! This is going to scorch you!"—the customary and fatal words at this instant. It is hard to conceive of the extent to which human nature can be perverted.

During these first days when I was in hospital, I used to get carried away listening to all these prisoners' tales. We were all terribly bored by being confined to bed. Every day was so exactly the same as the last! In the morning we at least had the doctor's visit and then our main meal soon afterwards. Food, needless to say, in the midst of such monotony, was a welcome diversion. The rations were varied, worked out according to the patient's illness. Some got only soup made with cereal, others only a thin gruel, and still others only semolina, which was very popular. The prisoners were spoilt by their long stay in hospital and loved to pamper themselves. Those convalescing and those who had almost recovered were given a piece of boiled beef, or 'ox' as it was called there. The best food was served to the patients with scurvy: beef with onions, horseradish and so on, sometimes even a tot of vodka. The bread was well baked, brown or white, also depending on the patients' regimen. This formality and the fine distinctions in the diet only made the prisoners laugh. There were some illnesses, of course, when one did not want to eat anything. But those patients who had a good appetite ate what they liked. Dishes were swapped, so a dish suitable for one illness was passed over to someone with a completely different complaint. Men who were put on a weak diet, bought the beef dish or the scurvy patients' food, they drank kvass and the hospital beer, buying it from those for whom it had been prescribed. Some even ate two rations at once. The rations would be sold and re-sold for money. A dish of beef went for quite a high price: it cost five kopeks in notes. If there was no one to buy from in our ward, they sent the watchman to one of the other prisoners' wards, or even to one of the military wards, the 'free ones' as they called them. There was always someone to be found who was keen to sell his food.

It meant he would be left with only bread, but on the other hand would make a bit of money. The majority were poor, but those who did have a little money asked the watchmen to buy them buns, sweetmeats and so on at the market. Our watchmen ran all these errands for us without any self-interest. The most boring part of the day was after the midday meal. Some slept for want of anything better to do. Some chatted. Some squabbled. Some recounted something for all to hear. It was even more boring if there were no new patients entering the ward. A new arrival always created something of a stir, particularly if he was not already known to anybody. The patients would look him up and down, trying to find out what sort he was, where he came from, what he had been sentenced for. Convicts in transit aroused the most interest. Such a prisoner always had something to tell: not about his personal affairs, which, if he did not volunteer the information, nobody ever pried into. He was asked where he came from, who with, what the journey had been like, where he was bound for next, and so on. Some people, hearing a new story, recalled something from their own experience about transit points, convict parties and their commanders. By this time, in the evening, the men who had been through the sticks would also start arriving. These always produced a rather strong impression—as I have already mentioned. They were not brought every day however, and on the days when there were not any, the general mood in our ward sank very low, as if the men had grown so sick and tired of the sight of all the other faces that they could not help bickering. The prisoners were even glad to see a madman who had been brought in to be tested. The trick of feigning madness in order to avoid flogging was used by the prisoners once in a while. Some of those who did try it were soon found out, or—to put it another way—soon decided to change their tactics themselves; a prisoner who had been acting up for two or three days, would suddenly turn into a rational man, quieten down, and sullenly ask to be discharged. Neither the prisoners nor the doctor would reproach such a person, nor try to make him feel ashamed by reminding him about his recent tricks. He would be discharged in silence, seen off in silence, and—about two or three days later—he would appear back in our place, after flogging. Cases such as these were rather rare, true enough. Real madmen, on the other hand, brought to be tested in the ward, were like a curse on the whole ward. Some madmen, the jolly, lively, shouting, singing and dancing ones, were welcomed with something approaching delight. "Here's a bit of fun!" the prisoners would say looking at the newly brought in clown. For me, however, it was terribly painful to watch the poor wretches. I could never look calmly at mad people.

The endless grimaces and mad antics of the newcomer, who had at first been greeted with laughter, soon began to get on people's nerves, and tempers became frayed within a couple of days. One such man was kept with us for about three weeks. It was enough to make you run away from the ward. Then, as ill luck would have it, another madman was brought in at the same time. This second one made a particular impression on me. This was already during my third year in gaol. During my first year, or more accurately during my first few months in gaol, in the spring, I used to be sent out to the brick factory, about two versts away in a party of prisoners, to work as a brick carrier for the stove-makers. The stoves had to be repaired before the summer brick-baking began. On that particular morning at the factory, M—tsky and B. introduced me to the resident overseer of the works, Sergeant Ostrozhsky. He was a Pole, an old man of about sixty, tall, lean and very dignified in appearance, even rather grand. He had been in the forces in Siberia from time immemorial, and although he was of humble origins, he was loved and respected by both M—tsky and B. He was always reading his Roman Catholic Bible. I conversed with him, and he spoke to me very kindly and cleverly. His talk was so entertaining, and he had such a kind-hearted and honest expression too! This was about two years ago and I had not seen him since, and all I heard was that he had been tried for some offence or other. And, suddenly, here he was: brought into our ward as a madman. He came in howling and hooting with laughter, gesturing most indecently, and started dancing around the ward. The other prisoners were delighted, but I felt so sad... Within three days he drove us frantic, we simply did not know what to do about him. He squabbled and fought, screamed and sang songs, and even at night he went on getting up to such disgusting tricks that it made everybody sick. He was not afraid of anyone. He was put in a strait jacket, but that only made it worse for us, though when he was not in the jacket he picked quarrels and fights with almost everyone he could lay his hands on. From time to time, during these three weeks, the entire population of the ward would rise as one man and ask the head doctor to transfer our 'poor darling' into the other prisoners' ward. Within two days that ward would in its turn beg the doctor to have him transferred back to us. As at that time we had two troublesome madmen at once, the two wards would pass them backwards and forwards, taking each one in turn. Each one was worse than the other. When at last they were taken away somewhere else, everyone heaved a sigh of relief...

There is another strange madman I remember. It was a summer's day, and they brought someone into the ward. He was about forty-five, a healthy-looking and very clumsy man with a horribly pockmarked face, small, red, bloated slits of eyes, and a very sullen and gloomy expression. He was given the bed next to mine. He turned out to be a very quiet character who did not speak to anyone, and sat all the time as though meditating upon something. As night began to fall, he suddenly spoke to me. Straightaway, without so much as a 'how d'you do', and with the air of someone imparting a great secret, he began to tell me that one day soon he was to be given two thousand sticks, but that he wouldn't be because the daughter of a certain Colonel G. was intervening on his behalf. I looked at him with perplexity, and said that in a case like that, not even a Colonel's daughter had the power to do anything, I was afraid. I was still completely unaware of anything. He had not been brought in as a madman but as an ordinary patient. I asked him what illness he had. He answered that he did not know, that he had been sent here for some reason, that he was completely healthy, and that the Colonel's daughter was in love with him. One day, two weeks ago, she had been driving past the guardhouse, and just at that moment he had happened to look out through the barred window. She had fallen in love with him at first sight.

Since then she had found excuses to visit the guardhouse on three different occasions. On the first occasion she came accompanied by her father to see her brother, an officer who was on guard there. On the second occasion she came with her mother to give alms, and, as she walked past him, had whispered in his ear that she loved him and would rescue him. The degree of detail he gave as he recounted all this rigmarole—which was all the product of his poor deranged mind, of course—was very strange. He honestly believed in his deliverance. He spoke of this young woman's passionate love calmly and confidently, and absurd though his whole narration was, it was all the more amazing to hear the romantic story of a girl in love from a man hard on fifty, with such an ugly, gloomy and saddened face. What strange things the fear of punishment had wrought in this timid soul! Maybe he really had glimpsed someone through the window, and the madness which had been gathering inside him from fear, and growing with every hour, had suddenly found an outlet, a means of expression. This poor soldier, who had probably never in his life given a thought to young ladies, now invented a whole affair, clutching instinctively at this straw. I heard him out in silence, and then told the other prisoners about him. When they became curious he fell modestly silent. The next day he was questioned for a long time by the doctor. He told him that he was not suffering from any illness, and because the examination confirmed that this was true, he was discharged. But we only found out that 'sanat' had been written in his case history, when the doctors had left the ward, so it was too late for us to tell them what the matter with him was. At the time we ourselves did not quite understand, what had happened. It was a gross misunderstanding. Owing to a blunder on the part of the authorities, the man had been sent to hospital without an accompanying explanation. There had been some sort of negligence in this case. Though it may well be that they only suspected him of insanity from the rumours going about, but were not certain and wanted to have him tested. Anyway, the poor man was taken out to run the gauntlet two days later. It must have come as a great shock to him; it was so unexpected. He believed in his deliverance right up until the last minute, and when they began dragging him through the ranks, he screamed: "Help! Help!" This time he was not admitted to our ward, where there were no vacant beds, but to the other one. I made inquiries, and discovered that he did not say a word during his whole eight days there. He was very embarrassed and extremely depressed... Later, when his back had healed, they took him away somewhere. At least, I never heard any more about him.

With regard to medical treatment and medicines, as far as I could notice, the less serious cases hardly ever did what was prescribed for them or took their medicines. The serious cases and the people who were really ill simply loved being treated, and took all their potions and powders on the dot. Our patients were particularly fond of external medication. Such things as cupping glasses, leeches, poultices and blood-lettings which are so beloved and trusted by our common people, were taken by them with great eagerness and even pleasure. There was one odd aspect of this which aroused my curiosity especially. The very same people who so patiently endured the agonising pain inflicted by sticks and birch rods, complained, wriggled and even groaned when something as painless as cupping glasses were applied. Perhaps they had grown soft in hospital or were simply showing off, I really do not know how to account for it. It is true that our cupping glasses were of a very peculiar kind. The instrument which was used to make a quick incision in the skin had long been lost or broken by the feldsher and maybe he was not to blame, but in any case he had now to make the necessary incisions with a lancet. For every cupping glass there had to be about twelve cuts or so around it. It does not hurt when done with the proper instrument: its twelve tiny blades strike suddenly and simultaneously, and no pain is felt. Cutting with a lancet is quite another matter. A lancet cuts comparatively slowly, and it hurts. And as a hundred and twenty cuts have to be made for twelve cupping glasses, the whole procedure is painful, of course. I have been through it myself, it was both painful and annoying, but not so unbearable that I could not help groaning. It was even funny sometimes to see some hefty fellow writhing from the pain and whimpering. It is comparable to the way someone who is calm and resolute in some serious affair, starts moping and throwing tantrums at home when he has nothing to occupy him, refusing to eat what he is served, scolding and grumbling at everybody. He doesn't like this, and he doesn't like that, everybody gets on his nerves and is rude to him, everybody tortures him. 'He has it too easy,' it is said about such gentlemen, but the same applies to the lower classes, and in our gaol, with our communal living, such instances were all too common. Sometimes the man's own neighbours would start teasing him for his whimpering, or someone would simply curse him. And he would fall silent, as though a good telling off was all he had been waiting for to stop whining. Ustyantsev disliked such people more than anyone, and he never missed a chance to have a go at the softies. Generally speaking, he never missed a chance to have a fight with someone. It was his little pleasure, his need, because of his illness, of course, but also partly because of his stupidity. He usually began by staring at someone intently, and then, in a calm and convinced tone of voice, started lecturing him. He could not resist poking his nose into everything; he might have been put there to keep order and uphold moral standards.

"He can't keep out of anything," the prisoners used to say, laughing. They spared him though, avoided arguing with him, and only laughed at him now and then.

"You talk too much, you do! It'd take three carts to haul all the words you come out with!"

"What do you mean, talk! No one goes doffing his cap before a fool. What's he screaming blue murder about the lancet for? You must learn to take the rain as well as the shine. You've got to be patient in life."

"But what's it got to do with you anyway?"

"I'll tell you what, mates," interrupted another prisoner. "These cuppers aren't so bad. I've had them, so I ought to know. The worst pain is when someone grabs hold of your ear and keeps pulling it."

Everyone laughed.

"Has that been done to you?"

"Do you think it hasn't? It bloody well has!"

"So that's why your ears stick out like that!"

This prisoner—Shapkin by name—did actually have very long, sticking-out ears. He had been a tramp. He was still a young man, very sensible and quiet, and his words always had some serious and hidden humour in them, which lent comicality to some of his stories.

"And why should I suppose that you've had your ears pulled? Why should it occur to me, you thickhead?" interrupted Ustyantsev. He was speaking to Shapkin very indignantly, although the latter had not been addressing his words to him, but rather to everyone in general. Shapkin did not even bother to look at him.

"Who pulled them for you?" somebody asked.

"Who pulled them for me! The district police officer, who else. For vagrancy that was, mates. At that time, mates, we had just come into the town of K.—two of us, me and another vagrant, called Yefim Without-a-Name. We'd procured a few things from a fellow in Tolmino on the way. There is a village by that name—Tolmino. Well, we made our way in, and started taking a look around. We wanted to get our hands on something—and hop it. You feel free in the open country, and frightened in town. First thing, we went to an inn and took a look around. A fellow came up to us, he looked down-and-out, the sleeves of his German jacket torn at the elbows. We started talking about this and that.

" 'May I ask you if you have a passport?'* he asked.

" 'No, we don't have one of those,' we answered.

" 'Well, neither do we,' he said. 'I have two very good friends here with me. They're both in General Cuckoo's army too.** So, if I might make so bold ... we have been on a little spree, and are a bit out of pocket. Would you stand us a half-bottle of vodka?'

" 'Our pleasure,' we said. And we all sat down and had a drink together. And they started telling us about some job or

*Author's note. A travel passport.
**Author's note. This means: 'In the forests where the cuckoos sing'. He implies that they are also tramps.

other which was right up our street. There was a house, on the outskirts of the town, a wealthy tradesman lived in it amid great riches. So we fixed the time for our visit that same night. And we all got caught, all five of us, that very night, in that very house. We were taken down to the police station, and to the district police officer himself. 'I shall interrogate them myself,' he said. He came out, a huge hefty fellow with side-whiskers, a pipe in his mouth, and someone carrying a cup of tea after him. He took a seat. Another three men, also tramps, had already been brought in. Tramps are a funny lot, you know. They don't remember a thing. Try what you will, they've forgotten everything, they know nothing. The police officer came straight at me. 'What's your name?' he roared. Just like a gun going off! So I answered the same as all the others: 'I don't remember anything, Your Excellency. I've forgotten everything I knew.'

" 'You just wait, I'll talk to you later, your ugly mug seems familiar to me!' And he stared me right in the eye. As for me, I hadn't seen him before. Then he turned to one of the others.

" 'What's your name?'

" 'Skedaddle, Your Excellency.'

" 'That's your name, is it? Skedaddle!'

" 'That's right, Your Excellency.'

" 'Very well! So you're Skedaddle. And who are you?' (Turning to the third man.)

" 'Oh, I'm the one after him, Your Excellency!'

" 'But what's your name? That's what I want to know.'

" 'That is my name. I'm the one after him.'

" 'And who gave you that kind of a name, you scoundrel?'

" 'Kind, godfearing folk, Your Excellency. There are some such kind, godfearing folk in the world you know.'

" 'And who are these kind, godfearing folk?'

" 'I've forgotten, Your Excellency, forgive me kindly.'

" 'You can't remember any of them?'

" 'Not a one, Your Excellency.'

" 'But you must have had a mother and father! Surely you remember them, if nobody else?'

" 'I suppose I did have them once, Your Excellency, but they also seem to have gone clear out of my head. Maybe I did have them, Your Excellency!'

" 'Where have you been living until now?'

" 'Out in the forest, Your Excellency.'

" 'In the forest? All the time?'

" 'All the time.'

" 'In winter too?'

" 'I've seen no winter, Your Excellency.'

" 'Now you! What's your name?'

" 'Hatchet-Axe, Your Excellency.'

" 'And yours?'

" 'Look-Sharp-Eyes-Skinned, Your Excellency.'

" 'And yours?'

" 'Sharpen-up, Your Excellency.'

" 'And none of you remember a thing?'

" 'Not a thing, not a thing, Your Excellency.'

"He stood there laughing, and they stood there too, looking back at him and grinning. It's all a matter of luck, you know. Another time you'd just get socked in the teeth. They're all such huge fellows, beefy too.

" 'Take them to the cells,' he said, 'I'll talk to them later. As for you!' he addressed me. 'You stay here! Come over here and sit down.' There was a table there, paper and pen. I thought, 'What is he going to do?'

" 'Sit here, on this chair. Take the pen and write.' Then he caught hold of my ear and started pulling. I just gaped at him.

" 'I can't, Your Excellency Sir, I never learned.'

" 'Write, I'm telling you!'

" 'Oh have mercy, Your Excellency Sir!'

" 'Write any way you can!' And he was pulling at my ear all the time, pulling and pulling, and giving it a twist all of a sudden! Well, I'll tell you, mates: I'd rather he'd given me three hundred lashes. I started seeing stars I did. 'Write, I'm telling you!' "

"Was he crazy or something?"

"No, he wasn't. It was simply that one of the clerks in T—k had pulled a fast one not long before, running off with government money. And he had sticking-out ears, just like mine.

They'd circulated his description all over the place. I fitted it apparently. So what he was doing was testing me: to see if I could write, and if I could write, how well."

"Fancy that! Did it hurt?"

"You bet."

Everyone burst out laughing.

"Did you write anything?"

"What could I write for God's sake! I started moving the pen up and down the paper, and he gave up. He slapped my face about ten times, naturally, and on that he let me go, to gaol, I mean."

"But do you know how to write?"

"I could before, with a pencil, but when everyone started writing with pens, I forgot how..."

These were the sort of stories—or chat, to put it better—with which we sometimes whiled our boring hours away. Heavens, how bored we were! Each day was so long, so stifling, so exactly like the one before! If only one could have had a book of some sort. Any book would have done. And yet—especially in the early days—I used to go to the hospital quite often, sometimes because I was really ill, sometimes just to lie there—to get away from the gaol. It was hard back there, even harder than it was in this place—morally harder. So much malice and hostility, squabbling and envy, endless picking at us noblemen, such angry and threatening faces. While here, in the hospital, people lived on a more equal footing, in a more friendly manner. The saddest time of our whole day was always evening, when the candles were lit, and also when night fell. Everyone went to sleep early here. A faint night-light shone like a bright dot at one end of the ward, near the door; at our end it was dusky. The place became all the smellier and stuffier. Someone, unable to fall asleep, would get up and sit on his bed for an hour and more with his head, in the nightcap, drooping, as if he were deep in thought. And you would look at him for a whole hour, to while your own time away too, and try to guess what he was thinking about. Or you would start dreaming, remembering the past. Wide, bright pictures would be conjured up in your imagination, you'd see details which at other times you would never have remembered, and which would never have stirred you as they did now. Or else you would make conjectures about the future, when you came out of gaol. When would that be? And where would you go? Would you ever return home? You would think, and think, and hope would begin to glimmer in your heart... Other times you would just start counting: one, two, three ... and so on, to finally fall asleep, in the midst of these numbers. There were times when I counted up to three thousand and still no sleep came. Now, someone would begin to toss and turn, Ustyantsev would start coughing his phlegmatic consumptive cough, and then groaning quietly, adding with each groan: "Sinner that I am, oh Lord." It was uncanny, hearing this sick, broken, whining voice in the silence. Somewhere in another corner men were also not sleeping, talking in bed. One of them started recounting his story, telling about the things that were past: his wanderings, his wife, his children and old ways. You could feel just from the whispering that reached you faintly that what he was talking about was gone without recall, and that he himself, the storyteller, was a castaway. Another man was listening to him. Only this quiet and monotonous whisper was audible, like water murmuring in the distance, far away... I remember a story I overheard on a long winter night. At first I thought it was a delirious dream, that I was lying in a fever and raving...

IV

Akulka's Husband

A story

It was already late at night, after eleven. I fell asleep, and suddenly woke up. The dim, small flame of the distant nightlight barely illumined the ward at all... Almost everyone was already asleep. Even Ustyantsev. One could hear, in the silence, how difficult it was for him to breathe, and how the phlegm gurgled in his throat with every breath he drew... Far away, in the passage, there suddenly sounded the tread of heavy foot-steps as the change of guard approached. A rifle butt thumped on the floor. The ward door opened and the corporal, stepping very carefully, counted the patients. A minute later the ward was locked, a new guard was stationed at the door, the relieved guards went away, the same silence as before returned. It was only then I noticed that not far from me, over to my left, there were two people who were not sleeping, and who were apparent-ly whispering to each other. This did happen quite often in the wards: people would sometimes lie right next to each other for days or months without exchanging so much as a word, then quite suddenly one night, at an hour inviting confidences, they would start talking, and one of them would pour his soul out to the other, telling him everything about his past.

They must have been talking for some time already. I did not hear the beginning, and even now I was not able to hear every-thing; yet, little by little, I grew accustomed to the sound and began to make out every word. I did not feel like sleeping. What else was there for me to do but listen? One of the two was talk-ing passionately; he had propped himself on his elbows, his head raised, and his neck straining in the direction of his friend. He looked flushed and excited. He badly wanted to talk. His lis-tener was sitting on his bed, morose and completely indiffer-ent, his legs stretched out in front of him, just occasionally grunting in reply to indicate sympathy, but more for the sake of propriety than with real sincerity. Every other minute he would stuff his nose with tobacco. This was Cherevin, a soldier under correction, about fifty years of age, a gloomy pedantic man who philosophised coolly about everything and whose foolish head was swollen with vanity. The speaker, Shishkov, was still quite a young man, of about thirty, one of the civilian prisoners who worked in the sewing shop. I had paid little attention to him up till now, and even after this, throughout my time in gaol, I did not for some reason feel inclined to become too involved with him. He was a shallow person, erratic in his behaviour. Some-times he was moody and rude, and did not speak a word for weeks on end. Sometimes he got involved in some scandal or other, started spreading gossip, getting worked up for no reason, dashing backwards and forwards between one barrack and another, passing news, carrying tales and getting very hot under the collar. Someone then gave him a good hiding, and he had another of his silent spells. He was cowardly and seedy, and everyone treated him with scorn. He was short and thin; his eyes seemed full of strange anxiety, though they could also be rather thoughtful in a stupid kind of way. If he happened to be telling somebody something, he always started off passionately and heatedly, even gesticulating; then he would suddenly break off, or change the subject, becoming involved in new details and forgetting what he had started talking about. He quarrelled very often, and when he did he always accused the other man of having done him some wrong in a voice full of emotion, and all but weeping. He was quite good on the balalaika, and he enjoyed playing. On holidays he would even dance, and he danced well, when he was made to... It was very easy to get him to do things. It was not that he was so very obedient, he just thrust his friendship on everybody and tried to please.

For a long time, I could not get the gist of what he was saying. He seemed to be wandering away from the point all the time, letting himself be sidetracked. Maybe he had noticed that Cherevin showed almost no interest in his story, yet he apparently wanted to persuade himself that his listener was all ears, and he would perhaps have taken it very badly had he become convinced that, in fact, this was the opposite of the truth.

"...When he came to the market," he continued, "everybody bowed to him and paid their respects to him, a moneyed man, no other word for him..."

"He was in trade, you say?"

"Why yes, he was in trade. There weren't many of that sort among us. We were all beggars. The women used to carry water from the river, all the way up the hillside, to water the vegetable plots there. They sweated their guts out at it, but they didn't even grow enough for that watery cabbage soup of theirs. None of it came to anything. As for him, he had a large homestead, he had hired labourers, three of them, who did the ploughing, and on top of that he kept his own bees. So he used to trade in honey, and cattle, and he was greatly respected in our backwoods for it. He was very old then, in his seventies. A big hulk of a man he was: his hair had gone grey and his bones had grown heavy. You should have seen him come to the market there, in his fox-lined coat, with everyone paying their respects to him. He was really somebody, and everyone felt it. 'Good morning to our dear father Ankudim Trofimovich, sir,' they used to say to him. 'Good morning to you too,' he would answer. He never looked down his nose at them, not at anyone. 'May you be with us for many years to come, Ankudim Trofimovich!' 'How's life with you?' he would ask them. 'Could be worse, I suppose,' they would answer. 'But how is it with you, dear Ankudim Trofimovich?' 'Well, I'm still living, for all my sins. The sun shines on all of us, I suppose.' 'Well, I hope you'll be with us for a good deal longer, Ankudim Trofimovich.' So he never looked down his nose at any of us. Every word he uttered was worth its weight in gold—he spoke in such a way. He was a great reader, he was always reading holy books. He used to sit his old woman down in front of him. 'Now, wife, you listen to me, and get this into your head,' and off he would go, explaining things to her. She was not so old as a matter of fact, his old woman. He had married a second time to have children because his first wife had borne him none. Well, this second wife of his, Maria Stepanovna her name was, she gave him two sons. He was already sixty when he begot the boy Vasya, the younger one. The oldest of the children was the daughter, Akulka, who was only eighteen."

"That's your one, is it? Your wife?"

"Hold on a minute. The first thing was all that muckracking of Filka Morozov's. 'Give me my share,' said Filka to Ankudim Trofimovich one day. 'Give me my four hundred roubles. I'm not just your labourer you know—I don't want to go into business with you, and I won't marry that Akulka of yours either, I'm having a spree now,' he says. 'My parents are dead and gone. I shall spend every kopek I have on drink, then I'll hire out as a soldier[15] and come back to you as Commander-in-Chief in ten years' time.' So Ankudim gave him the money. He paid him off completely. Filka's father, you see, had been the old man's partner, and they'd gone half-half. 'You're a finished man,' he said to him; and Filka answered back: 'Well, that's as may be, but if I stick around here with you, I shan't learn anything but how to skin a flint. Look at you squeezing every kopek dry, collecting all sorts of rubbish, maybe you can put it in your porridge. I don't give a damn for any of it. You'll save and save, and like hell you'll buy anything. I'm a man of character I am! And as for your Akulka, I wouldn't marry her whatever you say. I've been to bed with her already anyway...'

" 'How dare you cast shame on an honest father and an honest daughter!' cried Ankudim. 'When did you sleep with her, you shark's spawn, you snake?' And he started shaking all over. Filka told me about it himself.

" 'And it's not just me she won't be marrying! I'll see to it that your Akulka won't marry anyone now. Who'd want her? Not even Nikita Grigorievich would take her now, she's so disgraced. I was already going with her last autumn. And now I wouldn't marry her, not even for a hundred crayfish.* You can bet your life on it. Offer me a hundred crayfish now and see me spit on the money!'

"He started really drinking hard! Painted the town red, set the ground trembling, he did! He got a band of mates together, with his piles of money, and then he set off on a three-month spending spree—blew every kopek he had! He used to say: 'When I've gone through this lot, I shall sell the house, spend the last kopek, then hire out for a soldier or turn into a tramp.' He was drunk as a lord from morning to night, and rode around with two horses in harness, bells jingling. My, how the wenches fell for hir, something terrible! He played the *torba* very well too!"

"You mean he'd been carrying on with Akulka before then?"

"Now you hold on a minute. At that time I had already buried my father; my mother baked honey cakes, we worked for Ankudim, you see. That's how we made our living. We were very poor. We also had our little plot of land behind the forest and sowed a bit of rye, but all went to the dogs when my father

*Ten-rouble notes, red in colour.—*Ed.*

244

died. That's 'cause I also took to drinking, you see. I used to beat the money out of my mother..."

"That's bad that is, doing it with beating. A terrible sin."

"I'd be drunk from morning till night. The house we had was all right: a hovel but still home, but there wasn't a scrap of food in the larder. We used to sit around there starving for a week on end sometimes, chewing on a piece of cloth. My old mother would nag, nag, nag at me. I didn't give two hoots. At that time I followed Filka Morozov wherever he went. Day and night I'd be with him. 'Play something on the guitar,' he'd say to me. 'Dance for me. I'll just lie back and toss money at you, because I'm the richest man there is.' There was nothing he wouldn't do. Though he wouldn't take anything stolen. 'I'm not a thief, but an honest man,' he used to say. 'Let's go and paint Akulka's gates with tar, because I'll not have her marrying Mikita Grigorievich, you see. That's the most important thing of all to me now.' You see, the old man had wanted to marry Akulka off to Mikita Grigorievich before all this trouble. Mikita was a widower, he was already old, wore glasses, and was also in trade. Well, as soon as he heard all the rumours going round about Akulka, he at once backed out. 'This would be a terrible disgrace for me, Ankudim Trofimovich,' he said. 'Besides which, I have no desire to marry in my old age.' So we went and daubed the gates of her house with tar. Oh, what a thrashing she got for that! What a thrashing! 'I'll make you sorry you were ever born!' Maria Stepanovna screamed at her. 'In ancient times,' said the father, 'I would have taken an axe to her and thrown her on a pyre, but there's darkness now and corruption in the world.' All down the street the neighbours could hear Akulka howling the livelong day. She was flogged from sun-up to sun-down. Filka would stand in the market-place where everyone could hear him, yelling: 'Such a nice girl, called Akulka, comes a-drinking with me. Looks so neat and clean, you ask her what's the name of her true love! I've tweaked the noses of all of them, they'll remember me for the rest of their lives.' I met Akulka one day carrying pails of water. 'Good day to you!' I shouted. 'My respects, Madam. Look how neat and clean you are, who's your lover, might I ask?' That was all I said. She just looked at me. She had such big eyes, and she'd become very thin—as thin as a rake. When she looked at me, her mother thought she must be smiling at me, so she shouted through the gates: 'I'll wipe that grin off your face, you shameless hussy!' And that very day she flogged her again. She'd go on flogging her for a whole hour. 'I'll flog her to death,' she used to say. 'She's no daughter of mine any more!' "

"A hussy she was, you mean?"

"Well, you listen to what I'm saying. I was drinking with Filka all the time, and once my old mother came to speak with me, and there I was lying around. 'You good-for-nothing. What're you lying around like that for? You wretch!' And she started swearing at me. 'You go and get married,' she said. 'You go and get married to Akulka. Even you will be a welcome suitor now, and for dowry we'll get three hundred roubles, besides everything else.' So I said: 'She's disgraced before the whole world.' 'You're a fool,' said my mother. 'Make an honest woman of her and she'll be indebted to you for life. And with the dowry we'll get back on our feet. I've already had a word with Maria Stepanovna about it. She listened to what I had to say all right.' And I answered: 'Give me twenty roubles now, and it's a bargain.' And believe it or not, I was drunk from that moment right up to the wedding. And that was when Filka started threatening me as well. 'Akulka's husband, are you! I'll break every bone in your body! And I'll sleep with your wife every night if it suits me too!' 'You lying cur,' I told him. And here he slung mud at me for the whole street to hear. I came running home shouting: 'I don't want to get married, not unless they give me another fifty roubles for it, on the nail.' "

"And were the parents keen to marry her off to you?"

" 'Course they were. Why shouldn't they be? We weren't disgraced in any way. My father was ruined because of a fire. Before that happened, we lived even better than they did. 'You're the lowest of the low,' said Ankudim. 'Well, your gates have been tarred a good few times if I'm not mistaken,' I answered back. 'Why do you keep harassing us?' he said. 'Where's the proof that she's dishonoured? It's all gossip, idle tongues will wag. If you don't want to take her, don't, but return me the money I've given you.' That was when Filka and I decided to send him word with Mitri Bykov that I would really disgrace him good and proper now, and I was drunk—I can tell you—right up to the moment of the wedding. I only sobered up in time to go to church. And when we were driven back from church and seated at the table, Mitrofan Stepanovich—who is an uncle of mine—said: 'Well, it wasn't done honestly, but it's done nonetheless, and finished with.' Old Ankudim was drunk too, and burst into tears, and sat there with the tears running down his beard. Well, this is what I did then. I'd brought a whip in my pocket, I'd bought it before the wedding, and I decided that now was the time to have my fun with Akulka, for getting a husband by deceit, and so people should know that I hadn't been fooled into marrying her..."

"Good idea! You mean, so she'd behave in future..."

"You sit tight, and hold your tongue. In our place the custom is to take the newly-weds into the bedchamber, leaving the guests to go on drinking at the table. So they left us on our own in the bedchamber. She sat there, white as a sheet, with the blood all drained from her face. Scared out of her wits, in other words. Her hair was practically white too, like flax. And you'd never believe what big eyes she had. And she sat there the whole time in silence, without a sound. It was like having a deaf mute in the house. But you'll never guess what happened. I'd got my whip ready, and I put it down next to the bed. And—do you know what, it turned out she was absolutely pure and innocent!"

"You don't say!"

"Absolutely innocent, pure as the driven snow. An honest girl she was, from an honest household. Then why did she have to suffer such torment? Why did Filka Morozov disgrace her before the whole world?"

"That's true, why?"

"I knelt down in front of her, right there, by the bedside, folded my hands, and said: 'My dear love, forgive me, fool that I am, for thinking you were that kind of girl. Forgive me for my cruelty.' She sat on the bed looking at me. Then she put both her hands on my shoulders and laughed, she cried and laughed at the same time. Then I went out to the assembled guests. 'Well now,' I said, 'just let me get my hands on that Filka Morozov. He won't have much longer in this world.' Her old folks, they did not know who to beg forgiveness from. Her mother almost fell down at Akulka's feet, she was crying so much. The old man said, 'If only we had known, dearest daughter, we would have found you a better husband than this one.' And when we went out together to church on our very first Sunday—I in my astrakhan hat, a fine caftan, and velveteen trousers, and she in a new hareskin coat and a silk scarf—it was as much as to say, 'Here we are, I'm worthy of her and she's worthy of me.' That's how we went. People admired us both: me—that goes without saying, and her—they couldn't say she was better or worse than other girls, but she was with first ten anyway for beauty..."

"Well, that's good."

"Now, you listen to the next bit. After the wedding—on the very next day—although I was drunk I gave the guests the slip, went outside and started running: 'Bring me that no-good Filka Morozov! Bring me that bastard!' That was how I shouted in the market-place. I was drunk as a lord besides. Three people managed to grab me just outside the Vlasovs' house and bring me home by force. A rumour started going round the town. The girls passed it around as they chatted in the market: 'Do you know, dear girls, Akulka turned out to be a virgin.' Filka, however, not long afterwards, said to me in front of several other people: 'Sell your wife to me. I'll keep you in money for drink, if you will. We've got a soldier here called Yashka who got married for that very purpose. He never slept with his wife, but he walked around drunk for three years on end.' 'You're a bastard,' I told him. 'And you're a fool,' he told me. 'They married you off while you were drunk. You couldn't have known what was going on, you were in such a state.' So I went home and started yelling: 'You married me off while I was drunk!' My mother set up a screech. 'They've blocked up your ears with their gold, mother,' I told her. 'Bring me Akulka, right now.' And I started beating her. I beat her and beat her for about two hours, till I was so tired I couldn't stand up. She had to stay in bed for three weeks after that."

"Well, that's the way," remarked Cherevin phlegmatically. "If you don't beat women, they'll... Why, did you catch her with a lover?"

"No, I did not," said Shishkov after a silence, and with apparent difficulty. "I just couldn't stand people taunting me all the time, and Filka was always the ringleader, too. 'You've only got a wife for show—so don't go thinking we don't know.' He had some guests at his house one day, and he really laid into me. 'His wife,' he said, 'is a fine lady—noble, obliging, polite, good in every respect. At least that's how he has it now. He's forgotten how he tarred her gates with his own hand.' I was sitting there drunk, and he grabbed me by the hair—just like that—and pulled my head right down. 'Dance for us, Akulka's husband. I'll keep hold of your hair, and you dance and entertain me!' 'You bastard!' I shouted. And he: 'I'll be coming round to your place with some friends of mine, and I'll flog that wife of yours, right in front of you, to my heart's content.' Well after that, believe it or not, I was afraid to go out of the house for a whole month. Scared he would come and disgrace me. It was because of all this that I started beating her..."

"What's the good of beating them? Hands can be tied, but not tongues. Too much beating is no good either. Punish her, teach her a lesson, and then fondle her. That's what wives are for."

Shishkov fell silent for a while.

"I was very hurt by it all," he started again, "and besides ... I got into the habit. Some days I would beat her from morning till night. I didn't like the way she stood, or the way she walked... I felt bored when I wasn't beating her. She would sit there, silently, looking out of the window, crying... She was always crying. I did feel sorry for her—but I still beat her. My mother was always cursing, taking her side against me, calling me a villain and a gaolbird. And I'd answer: 'I'll kill her if I want to, and nobody dare stop me. It's only through your trickery I got married off.' The old man Ankudim also stood up for her at the beginning. He'd come round saying, 'You're not such a bigwig that I can't find some way of putting the curb on you.' Later he just gave up though. Maria Stepanovna put up with it all along. She came to me once, in tears, bowing to me and begging me. 'I have a great favour to ask of you, Ivan Semyonovich. It's not much I ask, but with all my heart. Let her live, my lord. Subdue your anger, find it in your heart to forgive her. Bad people have been talking about our daughter, but you know the truth ... that she was chaste when you took her...' And she bowed low to me, crying. But I just went on taunting her. 'I won't even listen to you,' I said. 'I can do just what I want with you all, because I cannot help myself any more. As for Filka Morozov, he's my best and dearest friend...'"

"You'd started drinking together again then?"

"Not a bit of it! There was no getting near him. He never sobered up. He'd run through all his money and been hired by some townsman to serve in the army in place of his eldest son. And according to the custom of our parts, if you do that, then right up to the day that you're taken off everything in the house must be yours for the asking, and you're the lord and master. You get all the money due to you the day you're taken off, and until then you live in the house of the person who has hired you. Some live like that for half a year and more, and there's nothing they don't get up to during that time. They bully their hosts, and do things that would make the saints blush. It's all a way of saying: 'Here I am, going into the army instead of your son. I am your benefactor, and you must all show respect to me if you don't want me to change my mind.' Well, Filka turned the man's household upside down. He slept with his host's daughter, and dragged him about by the beard every day after dinner. He did everything he fancied. He wanted the bathhouse heated every day, he demanded that spirits should be poured over the hot stones to make more steam, and that the women of the household should carry him into the bathhouse in their arms. When he returned to the house, drunk, he'd stand in the street outside, yelling: 'I don't feel like coming through the gates tonight! Make a hole in the fence for me.' So they broke down the fence in yet another place, to make a way in for him, and that was where he would go through. Well it all came to an end one day, of course. Soldiers came to take him away, and that sobered him up. You should have seen it.

The street was packed with people wanting to see how Filka Morozov would be taken. He bowed to right and left. Akulka was walking home from the vegetable plot at that moment, and when Filka caught sight of her, right near the gates of our house, he shouted: 'Wait!' He jumped down from the cart and bowed down to the ground before her. 'Oh my dear heart, my flower, I have loved you these two long years. Now they are taking me off to be a soldier. Forgive me, if you can find it in your heart to do so. You are an honest daughter of an honest father, and I have been a scoundrel to you, the guilt is all mine.' And he bowed down to the ground before her again. At first Akulka just stood there stock-still, as though frightened. Then she bowed low to him in return and said: 'Forgive me too, good man. I bear you no grudge!' I followed her into the house and said: 'What did you say to him, you rotten piece of dog's meat?' And believe it or not, she just looked at me and said: 'I love him more than my own life now.' "

"Get away with you!"

"I did not say another word to her that whole day. It wasn't till evening that I said: 'Akulka, I'm going to kill you.' I couldn't sleep all night. Just as dawn was breaking, I stepped out into the entry to get myself a drink of cold kvass. Then I came back into the room. 'Akulka, get ready to go to the farmstead.' I had been planning to make a trip out there for a long time, as my mother was well aware. 'Glad to hear it,' she said, 'just what you should be doing. It's harvest-time now, and I hear the labourer there has been ill for the last three days.' Without saying a word, I harnessed the horse to the cart. As you drive out of our village, there's about fifteen versts of pine forest, and our farmstead was behind that. We had gone about three versts through the forest when I stopped the horse. 'Get down, Akulka. This is the end for you.' She stood in front of me silently, looking at me in fear. 'I'm sick and tired of you,' I said. 'You had better say your prayers!' Then I caught hold of her hair. She had long thick plaits and I wound them round my fist. I pressed my knees into her back from behind, took my knife out, pulled her head back towards me and slit her throat with it. She gave a wild scream. The blood came spurting out. Then I threw my knife away, grabbed her in my arms, lay down on the ground beside her, embracing her, weeping over her, wailing like anything. She was wailing, and I was wailing. She was trembling all over, and jerking out of my arms. Blood was spurting all over me, over my face and hands, gushing and gushing. I left her there, and the horse as well, I was frightened and started running and running towards my home, through the back lanes, making for our old bathhouse. We had a bathhouse there which was not used any more. I climbed onto the top steam shelf, and lay low till nightfall."

"And what about Akulka?"

"They say she also got up afterwards and set off home. They found her later, a hundred paces away from the place."

"You didn't finish her off then?"

"No, I..." Shishkov halted momentarily.

"There's one vein which is like that," remarked Cherevin. "If you don't cut it straightaway, then the person will go on thrashing about. And however much blood comes out of them, they still don't die."

"But she did die. They found her in the evening. The police were informed. A search was started. And they found me before nightfall, hiding in the bathhouse... I've been here over three years now," he added after a pause.

"Well... Naturally, if you don't beat your wife, you can't expect her to stay good," Cherevin observed coolly and methodically, taking out his tobacco pouch once more. He began sniffing tobacco, and he sniffed it for a long time, in a very leisurely manner. "But there again, my lad, you yourself appear to be a very silly man indeed. I once caught my own wife with a lover. I took her into the barn, folded a rein in half. 'Who is your master? Who is your master?' My, what a beating I gave her with that rein, I beat her and beat her, about an hour and a half, till she started screaming: 'You are! I'll wash your feet and drink the water.' Ovdotya her name was."

V

Summertime

Here we are at the beginning of April already, and Easter is approaching. Little by little, the summer jobs are starting too. The sun grows brighter and hotter with every day. The air smells of spring and has a disturbing effect upon one. These glorious days stir even the hearts of people in shackles, arousing vague desires, yearnings, and misery too. One misses freedom even more under the rays of a strong summer sun than on overcast winter or autumn days, and this is apparent in all prisoners. It is as though they are glad to see the bright days, but at the same time they grow more impatient, restless. I really did notice that the arrival of spring brought a higher incidence of quarrelling. You would more often hear outbreaks of noise, and shouting, and yelling, and there were more breaches of discipline too, but at work you would notice somebody gazing pensively and intently into the hazy bluish distance, somewhere out yonder, at the opposite bank of the Irtysh, where the free Kirghiz steppe begins, stretching away, on and on, for one and a half thousand versts; or else you would observe someone drawing a deep sigh, as if yearning to breathe that distant air of freedom, and with that to soothe his crushed, broken soul. "Ah well," the prisoner would say finally, and then suddenly, as though shaking off his dreams and his thoughts, he would impatiently and gloomily go back to shovelling, or carrying bricks from one place to another. A minute later he would have forgotten this momentary feeling, and would already be laughing or cursing again, depending on his character, or he would even start upon the 'task'—if that was what he was doing—with a fervour quite out of proportion to the demands of the job. He would put everything he had into it, and work as though he wanted to stifle something within himself with the arduousness of work, something that pressured and pushed him from inside. They are all strong men, and the majority of them are in their prime ... and at the peak of their strength too... How heavy their shackles feel in spring! I am not being poetic when I say this—I am convinced of the truth of this observation. Quite apart from the fact that in the warmth and the bright sun, when you can hear and feel with your entire being that Nature is coming back to life all around you with enormous force, being locked up, with guards, and forced to obey the will of others, becomes even harder—quite apart from all this, in Siberia and all over Russia, springtime heralds, with its first larks, the season of vagrancy, when men escape from prisons and seek refuge in the forests. After the suffocating incarceration, after the trials, the shackles, and the sticks, they wander where they want and as they want, where it's better and safer, drinking and eating what they find—what God sends to them—and at night falling peacefully asleep somewhere in the middle of the forest or in a field, free of care, without the heartaches of prison life, and like forest birds, bidding good night. only to the stars in the sky, alone, under God's watchful eye. There's no denying that it is sometimes hard and hungry and tiring, this 'serving under General Cuckoo', going without food for days, hiding from everyone, lying low, compelled to steal and rob and even murder, if the worst comes to the worst. "Exiles are like children, what they see they take," they say in Siberia, and it also applies, even more so, to tramps. It is a rare tramp who is not a bandit, and almost always he is a thief, needless to say more from necessity than from inclination. There are some diehard tramps. Some people run away from the exile settlements, even after their term is over. One would think they would be content to stay there with a household provided with everything, but no! They still have this craving to go somewhere, to answer the call of the road. Life in the forest is hungry and frightening, but it is free and full of adventure, and it holds an alluring, mysterious attraction for those who have already experienced it once; it may entice away even a modest and organised man who was already promising to make a good, permanently settled farmer. There were some who had even married, had children, lived for no less than five years in the same place and then suddenly, one fine morning, disappeared, leaving behind them a puzzled wife, children, and the district in which they were registered. One such fugitive was pointed out to me in our gaol. He had not committed any particular crimes—at least none that I heard talk of—but he just kept running away. He spent his whole life running away. He had been on the southern border of Russia beyond the Danube, in the Kirghiz steppes, in eastern Siberia, in the Caucasus—everywhere. Who knows—perhaps in different circumstances, he, with his passion for travelling, might have become as famous as Robinson Crusoe. All of this I was told by the others; he spoke very little himself in the gaol, and then only when absolutely necessary. He was a tiny little man, about fifty years old, incredibly quiet, with a very calm, even rather stupid face—calm, in fact, to the point of idiocy. In summertime he loved sitting in the sun, and he was forever humming some song or other, but so quietly that even five paces away you could hardly hear anything. His face had something woodenish about it. He ate very little—bread mostly. He had never bought a single bun or measure of liquor, and it seems unlikely that he had any money at all, or even knew how to count. He took everything absolutely calmly. He sometimes fed the prison dogs out of his hands, but nobody in our place ever fed them at all. Russian people do not generally like feeding dogs. It was said that he had been married, even that he had been married twice. He had children somewhere too... What he was put into gaol for I have no idea. Everyone in our place was expecting him to run away from us too. Yet either his time had not yet come or had already gone, for he went on living with us, observing this strange environment in which he found himself with an air of a bystander. You could never tell for certain though. Really, why should he run away, what would he gain from it? On the whole, of course, a tramp's life in the forest is paradise compared to life in gaol. There's no comparison. "It's a hard life, but it's your own," as they say. That's why all prisoners in Russia, wherever they may be, become restless in spring, with the first welcoming rays of spring sunshine. It is by no means everyone who means to run away. One could say, quite definitely, that there are only about one in a hundred who dare to do it, because of the difficulty and the terrible consequences for those who are caught. Nonetheless, the other ninety-nine anyway dream of how they would run away and where they would go; they at least ease their hearts with wishing, and just imagining how it could be. Some of them might find consolation in recalling the escapes they had made long ago... I'm talking about those whose fates were already decided, of course. In fact it was much more often the ones awaiting punishment who would try to make a break. The sentenced convicts, if they are going to run away, do it at the beginning of their term. Having done two or three years of hard labour, they begin to value these years, and little by little, they decide that it is better to serve their term to the end and then be sent to one of the exile settlements, than to take such a big risk and ruin everything by failing in the attempt. And failure is very likely indeed! Perhaps only one in ten manages *to change his fate*. More often than not it is the convicts with too long sentences who risk running away. Fifteen or twenty years can seem like an eternity, and even if he has already done half his term he keeps on dreaming of changing his fate. Finally, being branded also discourages people from risking a run. *Changing one's fate* is in fact a technical term. Even under the interrogation which follows an unsuccessful attempt, a prisoner always answers that he had wanted to change his fate. This somewhat bookish turn of phrase can be applied to this situation quite literally. No runaway thinks that he can find absolute freedom, for he knows that to be almost impossible. He wants either to be sent to a different institution, or to one of the exile settlements, or to be tried again for a new crime, already committed as a tramp. He wants, in other words, to go anywhere other than back to the prison that he has grown so thoroughly sick and tired of. All such runaways who have failed during the summer to chance upon some godsend of a place in which to spend the winter—for example, someone who gives refuge to runaways for his own profit—or who have failed to procure (perhaps through murder) some kind of passport which will enable them to live where they please—all these people, the ones who have not been caught, turn up in droves at the towns and gaols, presenting themselves as vagrants, to weather the winter in prison with the hope to escape again the next summer.

I too was affected by the spring. I can remember how I would sometimes look very avidly through the chinks between the pales and stand for a long time leaning my forehead against them, gazing persistently, insatiably, at the green grass sprouting on the earthwork of our fortress, and the distant sky becoming deeper and deeper blue. My restlessness and my misery increased with every day, and the gaol grew more and more hateful to me. The hatred towards me for being a nobleman, which I experienced all the time from the other prisoners during my first years, was becoming unbearable, poisoning my entire life. I would often go away, during these first years, to the hospital, solely in order to avoid being in gaol, to escape this persistent hatred which nothing could subdue. "It's iron beaks like you that have pecked us all to death," the prisoners used to say to us. How much I envied the common people who came into the gaol! They immediately became everyone's friends. And that is why spring, the vision of freedom, the general cheerfulness of Nature, all had a sad and irritating effect upon me. Towards the end of Lent, during the sixth week I think, I had to do my fasting. The inmates of the entire gaol had been divided by the senior sergeant into seven shifts for fasting, corresponding to the seven weeks of Lent. There were thus about thirty men in each shift. I enjoyed the week of fasting immensely. Those who were fasting were released from work. We went to church, which was quite close to the gaol, two or three times a day. I had not been in church for a very long time. The Lenten service was so familiar to me from my childhood in my parents' house. The solemn prayers, the deep bows, all stirred up in my heart this faraway past, brought back to me the feelings of those childhood days, and I remember how I loved those mornings when we were taken, under guard, to the house of God, walking on ground which had frozen over during the night. The guards, however, did not come into the church themselves. Inside the church we would form a tightly packed group near the doors, in the very back rows, and so all we could hear was the resonant voice of the deacon and now and then, through the crowd, catch a glimpse of the priest's black cassock and balding head. I remembered how, when I was a child, I would sometimes look back at the common people crowding near the entrance, humbly stepping aside for a gold epaulette, a fat landlord, or a

257

dressed up but exceedingly devout lady, as these gentry made their way to the front, all but quarrelling over the best places. It seemed to me then that there, near the entrance, people prayed differently from us, up front. There, they prayed humbly, fervently, with a full awareness of their own humbleness.

Now it was I who stood in such a place—well, not even so far forward as that. We were chained and branded. Everyone shrank from us, everyone was afraid of us, and always we were given alms. I remember that I even derived a certain degree of pleasure from this, and that there was something refined and very special in this strange pleasure. "Let it, if that's how it has to be!" I would think. The prisoners prayed very devoutly, and all of them every time brought the little money they had with them to the church, and either bought a candle with it, or placed it into the collection box. "I too am a Christian," were perhaps their thoughts or feelings as they gave it away. "We are all equal in the sight of God, are we not?" We received Communion at the early morning service. When the priest, with the chalice in his hands, recited the words "Oh Lord receive me, even as a thief", then almost all of them—shackles ringing—fell to their knees, as though they took these words quite literally meaning themselves.

Finally Easter came. Each of us was presented with an egg and a slice of rich white bread as a gift from the authorities. Once again, gifts poured into the gaol from the town. Once again, we were visited by a priest with a cross and by the authorities. Once again, there was rich cabbage soup with meat, once again, there was drunkenness and idle wanderings. It was all exactly as it had been at Christmastime, with the sole difference that we were now able to walk out in the yard and bask in the sunshine. Somehow it was brighter and more spacious than in winter, and more heart-rending too. The endlessly long days of summer were somehow even harder to bear during the holiday. At least the working days were made shorter by our labour.

The work in summer turned out to be much harder than in winter. Most of it had to do with engineering construction. The prisoners did the building, dug the earth, laid the bricks. Others were busy with metalwork, or else they did the carpentry and painting jobs involved in repairing the prison buildings. Still others went to the brickworks to make bricks. This last task was considered the hardest of all. The brickworks was about three or four versts away from the fortress. Every day, throughout the summer, a party of about fifty men set off at about six o'clock in the morning to make bricks. Unskilled workers were chosen for this job. They took some bread with them, because it was too far to return for the midday meal, an extra eight versts, and had their big meal in the evening, after their return. The 'task' was assigned to them for the whole day, and could not have been finished in less time. Each man had first to dig out the clay and bring it in himself, fetch enough water, then tread the clay in the claypit with his own feet, and, lastly, make a large number of bricks, about two hundred, I believe, or maybe even two hundred and fifty. I only went to the brickworks twice. The workers from there would return late in the evening, dead tired, practically exhausted, and all summer long they hold it as a reproach to the others that theirs was the hardest work of all. This seemed to be their consolation. Still, there were some who were even quite keen to go there. For one thing the work was outside the town, in the open, on the banks of the Irtysh. At least they could look around them at something more cheering than the inside of the prison fortress! They could smoke when they wanted to, and even have a lie-down for half an hour or so. For my part, I was still sent to the workshops or to the alabaster kilns, or to the construction site as a brick carrier. There was one time when I had to carry bricks from the banks of the Irtysh over the rampart to the barrack which was being built about a hundred and sixty yards away; this work continued for about two months. I even grew to like it, although the rope sling, in which I carried the bricks, chafed my shoulders terribly. What I liked about this work was that it was obviously building up my strength. Each brick weighed about ten pounds, and at first I was only able to carry eight at a time. Later I got up to twelve bricks, then to fifteen, and this gave me a feeling of immense happiness. Physical strength is needed in gaol quite as much as moral strength, if one is to endure all the material hardships of that accursed life...

I also wanted to go on living after my release...

As a matter of fact, I liked carrying bricks not only because this built up my body, but also because the work was done on the bank of the Irtysh. I mentioned this bank so often because only from there we could see the free world. The clear, bright distances, and the emptiness of the free and uninhabited steppe produced in me the strangest of sensations. It was only here, on the bank, that one could turn one's back on the fortress and completely cut it off from view. All other places of work were either inside the fortress or alongside it. I had come to detest this fortress from my very first days, and certain of its buildings in particular. The Major's house struck me as a cursed, disgusting place, and every time I passed it I looked at it with hatred. Out on the riverbank, however, one could forget about everything. I peered into this vast and empty space, like a prisoner peering at the free world from the window of his cell. Everything there was dear and precious to me: the bright, hot sun in the fathomless blue sky; the distant Kirghiz song carried by the wind from the Kirghiz bank of the river. Peering intently for a long time, you would at last make out the poor smoke-stained yurt of a Kirghiz nomad. Then you would see a tiny trickle of smoke nearby, and a Kirghiz woman bustling around her two rams. Such a poor, primitive life, but a free one nonetheless! High up in the blue transparent sky, your eyes would seek out a bird, and follow its flight for a long time. There it was, skimming above the water, then disappearing into the blue, then reappearing as a tiny, barely flickering speck... Even a poor sickly-looking flower that I found in a hollow of the rocky bank in early spring attracted me poignantly. The misery of the whole of this first year in gaol was unbearable, and had a disturbing and bitter effect upon me. There were many things around me during my first year which I failed to notice because of this. I closed my eyes to things—I did not want to study them too intently. I did not distinguish between my nasty, spiteful companions, and those who were good people, capable of thinking and feeling, despite the hatefulness with which they were encrusted. Among all the caustic words, I did not notice the occasional kind and welcoming one, so much more valuable for being said without any selfish motive, and sometimes coming straight from a heart that had suffered and endured far more, perhaps, than I had. But why dwell on this! I used to feel extremely happy if the work had tired me out, as it would help me to fall asleep— with luck! It was torture sleeping in that place in summer, almost worse than in winter. Things were sometimes very pleasant in the evening however. The sun, which had not left the yard for a moment through the whole day, finally set. The air cooled, and then came a cold (relatively speaking) steppeland night. The prisoners, before they were locked up, usually walked around the yard in great numbers. The biggest crowd, however, gathered around the kitchen. In there, some urgent issue of the day was always being raised, talk was going on about this and that, some rumour or other was being discussed— often something quite ludicrous—but one which really caught the attention of these wretches cut off from the world. Maybe there would be news that the Major was to be given the boot. Convicts are credulous folk—like children. They know very well that a certain piece of news is gibberish, as it has been brought over by Kvasov, a notorious windbag whom all of them have long since decided to ignore since his every word is a lie, and yet they eagerly clutch at the news, start discussing and chewing it over for their own gratification, and it all ends with them losing their tempers, ashamed of themselves for having ever believed Kvasov.

"And just who is going to chuck the Major out?" shouts one of them. "He's tough, he'll hold tight."

"But there's somebody above him, isn't there? Someone in charge of him?" objects a hot-tempered, far from stupid fellow who has seen a lot, but is given to arguing to an unimaginable degree.

"Ravens don't peck out other ravens' eyes," remarks a third man sullenly, as though talking to himself. This man is already grey-haired, and is sitting alone in the corner, finishing off his cabbage soup.

"And the higher-ups will come and ask you if they should replace him or not," a fourth one remarks indifferently, brushing the strings of his balalaika.

"Why shouldn't they ask me!" objects the second fellow violently. "And if they start asking you must all speak up; it'll mean the whole poor lot of us are of one mind. 'Cause there's a lot of bragging here, but when it comes down to business you all start backing out."

"What do you expect? This is a prison, isn't it," said the balalaika man.

"Just the other day," said the hot-tempered fellow, too excited to listen, "there was a bit of flour left over. We scraped every last speck of it together—every last teardrop as they say. And we sent someone out to sell it. But that chap went and told on us, and the flour was confiscated. For the sake of economy. Well I ask you! Is that fair?"

"Who do you want to complain to?"

"Who to? To this Inspector-General who's coming."

"What Inspector-General?"

"It's true you know, he is coming," said a young, lively-looking fellow, who had been a scribe and had read a book called *The Duchess Lavalier* or some such thing. He was always cheerful and making the others laugh, but they respected him for being knowledgeable and experienced. Ignoring the general curiosity excited by the forthcoming visit of the Inspector, he went straight up to the *stryapka* (that is to say, the cook) and asked him for some liver. The *stryapkas* were in the habit of doing a bit of trade now and then. They would buy a big piece of liver with their own money, fry it, and then sell it in slices to the prisoners.

"For half a kopek or one kopek?" asked the *stryapka*.

"Make it for one kopek! Let the others envy me!" came the answer. "Yes, mates, there's a general coming, a general from Petersburg, and he's out to inspect the whole of Siberia. And that's the truth. I've heard them talking about it at the Commandant's."

This piece of news produced the most remarkable excitement. There were so many questions that wanted answering, and the talk went on for about a quarter of an hour. Who was he exactly? What rank? Was he superior to the local generals or not? The prisoners were very fond of talking about ranks among the authorities—who was whose senior, who would unsaddle whom, and who would get unsaddled himself. They even used to get into quarrels and arguments, almost fights, about the generals. What could there be in it for them, you might wonder. The thing is that the extent of a prisoner's worldly wisdom, intelligence, and his former standing in society are all measured in terms of his knowledge of generals, and of the authorities as a whole. In prison, conversations about people in the highest positions of authority are generally considered to be the finest and most important conversations of all.

"So it's true that they are going to come and change our Major over," said Kvasov, a reddish little man, excitable and extremely muddle-headed. It was he who had brought the news about the Major in the first place.

"He'll bribe his way out of it!" countered the morose-looking man with grey hair who had now finished his soup.

"That's just what I'm saying—he'll buy them off," observed another. "You think he hasn't filched a lot of money? He had a battalion command before he came here. And just the other day he was going to marry the archdeacon's daughter."

"All right! But he never did marry her. He was shown the door. Not rich enough. What kind of match would he be! All he's got is what he stands up in. He lost all his money playing cards during Holy Week. Fedka was telling me about it."

"That's the way it goes. No money coming in, but plenty going out."

"I was married once, too, you know, mates," remarked Skuratov, taking the opportunity to jump back into the conversation. "It's no joy for a poor man to marry. The nights are always too short."

"You don't say! We've been talking about you all the while, I suppose," observed the former scribe. "And you listen to me too, Kvasov. You're a big idiot you are! Do you really think that a general like that could be bought off by our Major? Do you think he'd come all the way out here from Petersburg just to inspect our Major's doings? You're stupid, fellow, that's what."

"And why not? You think that if he's a general he won't

take money?" a voice from the crowd remarked sceptically.

"Of course he won't, or if he does, it has to be a lot."

"Naturally. According to his rank."

"Generals never refuse money," said Kvasov, very decisively.

"How do you know? Have you been giving him something?" Baklushin, who had just come in, asked with a sneer. "I don't suppose you've ever even seen a general."

"Of course I have."

"Liar!"

"Liar yourself."

"All right, if he has seen a general, let's hear him tell everyone here exactly who this general he knows is. Come on, let's hear you, because I know them all."

"I've seen General Zibert," Kvasov answered hesitantly.

"Zibert! There's no such general. You must have seen him from behind while he was still a lieutenant-colonel, this Zibert of yours, and you took him for a general because you were so scared."

"Now you listen to me!" Skuratov shouted out suddenly. "I'm a married man I am. And I tell you there really was a general named Zibert, in Moscow. A Russian of German descent. He used to go to a Russian priest for confession every year. And he drank water without stopping, like a duck. He used to drink forty glasses of Moskva River water a day. They used to say he was treating himself for some disease that way. It was one of his footmen told me, personally."

"And I expect he had a few carp swimming round in his belly as a result, did he?" remarked the balalaika man.

"Shut your mouths! This is serious talk here. And you!.. Well now, mates, what kind of Inspector-General is it going to be then?" asked Martynov with great concern. He was a very fussy old man, who had once been in the hussars.

"How people do lie!" said one of the sceptics. "Where do they get the news from, or how do they make it up? I bet it's all nonsense."

"No, it is not nonsense," Kulikov, who had so far remained grandly silent, asserted very dogmatically. He was a man not to be taken lightly, about fifty years old, with an extremely dignified face and a somewhat contemptuously grand manner. He knew this very well himself, and was very proud of the fact. He was part gypsy, a veterinary surgeon who earned money in the town by treating horses, and in the gaol by trading in liquor. He was a clever chap, and he had seen the world. He was sparing of words, as though he valued them highly.

"It's all true, mates," he calmly continued. "I heard about it a week ago. A general is coming—a very high-ranking one—and he is going to inspect the whole of Siberia. Naturally, bribes will be offered him too, only not by our old eight-eyes, he wouldn't even dare to try. There are generals and generals, mates. There are all kinds. But I can tell you one thing for sure. Our Major will be staying where he is, whatever happens. That is absolutely certain. We have no say, and none of the people in authority will inform on their own kind. The Inspector will take a look at the gaol, and that will be that. Later on he'll file a report saying everything was in good order..."

"You hear that, mates, but our Major is scared all right. He's been tanked up since morning."

"He'll go on drinking in the evening too. Fedka told me."

"Well, you can't make a black crow white. It's not the first time he's been drunk."

"What kind of pass have we come to if even a general cannot do anything about it? We've stood their foolery long enough!" the prisoners were exchanging comments excitedly.

The news of the Inspector-General spread quickly through the whole gaol. Prisoners, walking about the yard, eagerly passed it on to one another. Some made a point of saying nothing and kept very cool, thereby trying to make themselves look more important. A third reaction was to remain indifferent: prisoners with balalaikas seated themselves on the porches of their barracks. Some just went on chatting. Some started singing songs, but, in general, the whole place was in a state of great excitement that evening.

After nine o'clock we were counted, herded into the barracks, and locked in for the night. The nights were short at that time. We were roused soon after four in the morning, but we never went to sleep before eleven, people would still be pottering about, chatting, and sometimes playing cards, in summer as well as in winter. At night it became unbearably hot and stuffy. Even though there was a refreshing draft of cold night air from the slightly open window, the prisoners tossed and turned feverishly all night long. There were fleas by the thousand. They bred there in quite large numbers in the wintertime too, but from spring onwards they multiplied to an extent which, although I had heard about it, I had been loath to believe, not having had a taste of it. And the nearer we came to summer, the more and more vicious they became. It is true that one can grow used to fleas, I know this from personal experience, but it is a difficult attitude to acquire. They reduced you to a state when you seemed to be lying in a sick fever, not sleeping, but in some kind of delirium. Finally, just before dawn, when the fleas settled down at last and stopped pestering you, and in the cool morning air you fell into a sweet sleep, suddenly the pitiless rat-a-tat-tat of the drum near the prison gates sounded reveille. Snuggling down deeper into your sheepskin, you would curse those loud, clear beats, almost counting them, and an unbearable thought would tease your sleepy mind that it would be the same again tomorrow, and the next day, and every day for years to come, right up until the day you were released. When will it be, you think, this freedom? And where? Meanwhile it was time to get up. The hustle and bustle that went on every day had already started... People were dressing, hurrying off to work. True enough, there was also an hour or so in the afternoon when you could sleep.

What had been said about the Inspector was true. The rumours were confirmed more and more with every day that passed, until at last it became definitely known that an important general was coming from St. Petersburg to carry out an inspection of the whole of Siberia, that he had in fact already arrived and was at the moment in Tobolsk. Every day some new rumour reached the gaol. News came in from the town as well. They said everybody was worried there, making a great to-do, and wanted to put their best foot forward. There was talk of people in high places making preparations for grand receptions, balls and fêtes. Large gangs of prisoners were dispatched to level out the fortress roadways, dig up the bumps, paint the fences and the fence posts, touch up the plaster, fill in a few cracks, and in other words, quickly give everything that would be seen a presentable appearance. Our folk understood this kind of business very well, and they discussed the impending visit with mounting excitement and enthusiasm. They soared to new heights of bizarre imagination. They even planned to submit a *petition* to the General when he started asking them about their conditions. Their usual quarrelling and squabbling continued unabating. The Major had grown extremely edgy. He came to the gaol more often, shouted a lot more often, went for people more often, sent people to the guardhouse more often, and demanded that everything should look clean and proper. There happened, at that time, as though on purpose, one unpleasant little event which did not worry the Major as one might have expected, but on the contrary—seemed to give him a great deal of pleasure. In a fight, a prisoner stabbed another one in the chest with an awl, right under the heart.

The prisoner who had committed this crime was called Lomov; the other was called Gavrilka, one of the diehard tramps. I don't recall whether he had any other name or not. Everyone just called him Gavrilka.

Lomov had been a well-do-do peasant in T—, in K—sky uyezd. The Lomovs lived as one large family: the old man, three sons, and an uncle. They were rich peasants. All over the gubernia people said that they had as much as three hundred thousand roubles in capital. They tilled the soil, tanned skins, engaged in trade, but their main occupation was pawnbroking, sheltering vagrants, receiving stolen goods, and doing other suchlike business. Half the uyezd was in debt to them or in bondage. They had the reputation of being both clever and cunning, but they became too conceited, particularly when a very important person took to staying with them when he passed through, became closely acquainted with the old man, and took a strong liking to him for his resourcefulness and cleverness. The Lomovs suddenly began to think that there was no longer anything which could keep them in check, and they began taking bigger and bigger risks in various illegal exploits. Everyone around had some kind of grudge against them. Everyone wished the ground would open up and swallow them. But they just stuck their noses higher and higher into the air. They didn't give two hoots about either the uyezd police officers or the uyezd assessors. In the end they went too far and came to grief: not, however, on account of their wicked doings, nor for their secret crimes, but because of a wrongful accusation. Ten versts away from the village where they lived, they had a large farmstead. In early autumn they had half a dozen Kirghiz labourers living there, all of whom had long become bonded labourers to them. One night, all these labourers were murdered. An inquiry began, and continued for a very long time. In the course of the inquiry, many other crimes came to light. The Lomovs were accused of murdering their labourers. This was how they told the story themselves, and as it was known to the whole gaol: they were suspected of owing these labourers a good deal of pay in arrears, and since, despite their enormous wealth, they were extremely mean and stingy, they murdered the Kirghizes so as not to pay them what they owed them. Their entire fortune went down the drain during the course of the investigation and the trial. The old man died. The sons were all imprisoned in different places. One of the sons and the uncle were given twelve-year sentences in our gaol. And what do you think? They were completely innocent of the Kirghizes' murder. Some time later Gavrilka, a cheerful and bright fellow, a famous rogue and vagrant, appeared in our gaol, and he took the responsibility for the murder upon himself. Now, I did not hear him actually confessing as much, but the entire gaol was convinced that the Kirghiz killing was his doing. Gavrilka had had some dealings with the Lomovs before the murder. He came into the gaol for a short time, as an army deserter and vagrant. He and three other vagrants had killed the Kirghizes expecting to make off with a lot of booty and money from the farmstead.

The Lomovs were unpopular in our place. I do not really know why. One of them, the nephew, was a fine young man—intelligent, and easy to get along with. The uncle—the one who stabbed Gavrilka with an awl—was a stupid and quarrelsome man. He had been in a lot of fights before that, and he had received a good number of beatings. Gavrilka, on the other hand, was loved by all for his cheerful disposition and easy ways. Though the Lomovs knew that he was the murderer and that they had been sentenced for his crime, they did not quarrel with him, nor come into contact with him either. He, for his part, ignored them completely. Then suddenly he had an argument with the uncle over some ghastly whore. Gavrilka started boasting of how she fancied him. The other man grew jealous, and then—one sunny afternoon—he stabbed him with an awl.

Though the Lomovs had been ruined by the trial, still they lived in the gaol like rich folk. It was clear that they had money. They kept a samovar, and drank tea. Our Major knew of this, and he hated both the Lomovs wholeheartedly. Everyone could see how he was always picking holes in them, and always trying to get at them. The Lomovs' explanation for this was that the Major was angling for a bribe from them—but they would not give him one.

Needless to say, if Lomov had pushed the awl just a little bit harder, he would have killed Gavrilka. Luckily, the whole incident ended with a mere scratch. It was reported to the Major. I can remember clearly how he came, panting for breath, and apparently delighted. He was surprisingly tender towards Gavrilka, almost fatherly.

"Tell me, dear boy, can you make it to the hospital on your own or not? No, I think we should harness a horse for him. Harness a horse! Immediately!" he shouted to one of the sergeants.

"But really, sir, I hardly feel a thing. He's just stabbed me slightly, that's all, sir."

"You can't tell, dear boy, you can't tell. You'll see... It's a very dangerous place, that. Everything depends on where the awl went in. He stuck it right under your heart, the villain! And as for you," he roared, turning to Lomov, "as for you ... I'll get at you now, all right. To the guardhouse with him!"

He really did get at him too. Lomov was tried, and although the wound turned out to be only skin-deep, the intention behind it was clear to all concerned. The criminal had his term of hard labour increased, and given a thousand sticks. The Major was absolutely delighted...

At last, the Inspector arrived.

The day after he arrived in the town, he came to visit our gaol. This took place on a holiday. A few days earlier everything had been scrubbed clean, washed, and ironed. The prisoners' heads were all freshly shaved. Their clothes were clean and white. According to the regulations, in summer they wore white linen jackets and trousers. A black circle, about eight centimetres across, was sewn into the back of the jacket. For a whole hour the prisoners were instructed on how to answer if the dignitary should speak to them. There were rehearsals. The Major was jumping about like a madman. An hour before the General made his appearance, everybody was standing at attention in his place like a statue. Finally, at one o'clock in the afternoon, the General arrived. He was a very important General, so important that his arrival had to make every official heart quake all over Western Siberia. He entered in a stern and majestic manner, followed by a large retinue of local dignitaries and a scattering of generals and colonels. There was a civilian with them too, a tall handsome gentleman wearing a frock-coat and shoes, who had also come from St. Petersburg and who behaved in an extremely free and independent manner. The General very often turned to him, and addressed him most politely. This intrigued the prisoners enormously: here was a civilian, yet held in such esteem, and by such a General! They later found out his name and what he was, but there was a lot of talk about him just the same. Our Major, in his tight-fitting uniform with the orange collar, with bloodshot eyes, and purple, pimply face, did not seem to make a very favourable impression on the General. Out of respect for the important visitor, he was not wearing his spectacles. He stood at attention over to one side, desperately watching with his entire being for a chance to make himself useful, to dash to do the General's bidding, but nobody seemed to need him. The General inspected the barracks in silence, also went into the kitchen as well, and I believe, tasted the cabbage soup. I was pointed out to him. This is so and so, a former nobleman.

"Oh yes," replied the General. "And how does he behave himself here?"

"Satisfactorily so far, Your Excellency," came the reply. The General nodded. About two minutes later, he left. The prisoners were, of course, dazzled and stunned, also somewhat bewildered. Needless to say, making any complaints against the Major had been out of the question. And the Major himself had known this beforehand.

VI

Prison Animals

The prisoners found the purchase of a replacement for Gnedko, which occurred soon afterwards, far more preoccupying and entertaining than this visit from on high. According to the regulations, there had to be a horse in the gaol, for bringing in water, carrying out the sewage and so on. One prisoner was detailed to look after it. He drove it too—always under guard, of course. Morning, noon and night, there was always plenty of work for this horse of ours. Gnedko had already been working in the gaol for a considerable while. He was a fine horse, but rather past it. Then one fine morning in late June, just before St. Peter's Day, after bringing in the barrel for the evening, Gnedko fell down and died. It was all over in a couple of minutes. Everybody felt sorry for him. They gathered around him, talking and arguing. Those who had been cavalrymen, horse thieves, veterinary surgeons etc., displayed their specialised knowledge about everything to do with horses, and even had words, but that did not bring old Gnedko back to life. He lay there dead, with a swollen stomach which everyone, for some reason, felt in duty bound to poke with a finger. This act of God was reported to the Major, and he immediately decided that a new horse should be bought at once. On St. Peter's Day, when everyone had assembled after the church service, horses that were for sale were brought into the gaol. The purchase of a horse should have been entrusted to the prisoners themselves, of course. There were some real connoisseurs among us, and besides, it is hard to swindle two hundred and fifty people who have spent their lives swindling other people themselves. Horses were brought in by Kirghizes, dealers, Gypsies and townsmen. Each new horse was waited for impatiently by the prisoners. They were happy as boys. More than anything else they felt flattered that in this situation they, too, were like free people, buying a horse *for themselves* out of *their own* pocket, and they had every right in the world to do so. Three horses were brought in and taken out again, before they finally settled on the fourth. As each dealer came in, he looked round in amazement, almost in fear, and sometimes even glanced back for the guard who had brought him in. The more than two hundred strong crowd that confronted them—a crowd of shaven-headed, branded, chained men who seemed to feel quite at home in their prison over whose threshold nobody ever steps, inspired some sort of awe. Our people really excelled themselves with the cunning tricks they employed to test out each horse. There was nowhere they did not look, no part they did not feel and poke at, and, what is more, they did everything in such a businesslike manner, with an air of such seriousness and concern, as if the well-being of the entire gaol depended on their choice. The Circassians, eyes shining and teeth flashing, even mounted the horse, chattering away in their incomprehensible dialect and nodding their dark aquiline-nosed faces. A Russian would try to follow what they were saying, riveting his attention on their faces. Not understanding a word, he wanted at least to guess, from the expressions in their eyes, whether they thought the horse would do or not. An outside observer would have found this poignant attention rather odd. What could there be, they might wonder, that was worth so much trouble to some poor prisoner, a submissive, downtrodden man at that, who hardly dared open his mouth even among his own sort. It was as though he was buying the horse for himself, as though it really did matter to him which one would be bought. All the former horse thieves and horse dealers also made their mark, as well as the Circassians. They were given pride of place and first say. There was even a kind of noble sparring match, especially between two individuals—the prisoner Kulikov, who had previously been a horse thief, horse trader, and a self-taught horse doctor, and a cunning Siberian who had come only recently to the gaol but had already managed to take almost all of Kulikov's practice in town away from him. The fact of the matter was that these self-educated horse doctors of ours were held in the highest esteem in the town, and not only among the middle classes and the tradespeople, but even among the upper classes, who turned to the gaol for help when their horses fell ill, despite the fact that the town boasted several proper veterinary surgeons. Before the arrival of this Siberian horse doctor—whose name was Yolkin—Kulikov had no rivals. He had a large practice, and naturally received a fee. There was a lot of cheating and trickery in his vetting, of course, because he knew far less than he laid claim to. His income made him an aristocrat among us. His experience, his intelligence, his boldness and resoluteness had long since won him the respect of all the other prisoners. They listened to what he said, and did what he bade them. He actually spoke very little. He would deliver his judgement only on the most important issues, and present it very cleverly, as something of great value. He was certainly a show-off, but there was also a lot of real, genuine energy in him. He was already quite advanced in years, but extremely handsome, and extremely clever. He treated us noblemen with a kind of refined courtesy and at the same time with extraordinary dignity. I really think that if he were dressed up and taken to some club in the capital as a count, he would not lose his presence of mind at all, he would play a hand of whist, talk well, sparingly but with aplomb, and no one would guess that he was a tramp, and not a count at all. I really mean it, because he was so clever, bright and quick-witted. In addition he had the superb manners of a dandy. He must have seen a good deal of life. His past, however, was shrouded in dark mystery. He was one of the special category prisoners. Yet with the arrival of Yolkin—a man of around fifty, an Old Believer, who was a muzhik, but one of those extremely cunning muzhiks—Kulikov's veterinary career went into decline. Within two months Yolkin had taken away most of Kulikov's practice in the town. With great ease, he cured even the horses which Kulikov had long since given up as hopeless. He even cured the ones which the town veterinary surgeons had abandoned. Yolkin had come to the gaol as a member of a gang involved in forgery. Whatever could he have been thinking of, to become involved in such business at his age, I do not know! He told us—laughing at himself—how it had taken them three real gold coins to make one forged one. Kulikov was rather hurt by Yolkin's success in the veterinary world, and even his reputation among the other prisoners began to wane. He had kept a mistress living in the suburbs, worn a long velveteen waistcoat, a silver ring and an ear-ring, and his own pair of smartly trimmed boots. Suddenly, for lack of money, he was forced to become a vintner, and now, during the purchase of the new Gnedko, everyone was thinking that the two rivals might fight. They awaited it with curiosity. Everyone had taken sides with one or the other. The leaders of each side were already growing excited, now and then hurling a few swearwords at each other. Yolkin's cunning face was already creased up into the most sarcastic grin imaginable. Things turned out quite differently though. Kulikov had no intention of squabbling, but chose an extremely clever tactic instead. He began by deferring to his rival and even listening respectfully to his criticisms and judgements; then, picking on one word, he modestly and insistently pointed out to him that he was mistaken, and before Yolkin could collect his wits and defend himself, Kulikov had proved conclusively that he was wrong on this and that point. Yolkin, in other words, was tripped up quite unexpectedly and ingeniously, and though he had the last say, Kulikov's supporters were satisfied all the same.

"You won't get a fellow like that muddled easily, mates. He knows how to stand up for himself, he does," said one group.

"Yolkin knows more," insisted the others, but half-heartedly, as though ready to withdraw. Suddenly, both groups began talking in a very conciliatory manner.

"It's not so much that he knows more, but he's got a lighter touch. When it comes to animals, Kulikov knows what he's doing too..."

"Oh, he knows what he's doing all right!"

"You're right there..."

At last the new Gnedko was chosen and paid for. He was a fine horse, young and good-looking, strong, and with a nice cheerful sort of air about him—and doubtless he had passed on every other score as well. The bargaining began. The seller asked thirty roubles, our people offered twenty-five. They bargained very passionately and at great length, bringing the price down, making concessions, until at last even they began to see the funny side of the situation themselves.

"Is the money coming out of your pocket or something? Why d'you haggle so over the price?" said one of them.

"Why should we care about spending prison funds?" some others shouted.

"But still it's our community money, mates..."

"Community money, hell! It's a true saying that fools like us grow without watering..."

The deal was finally closed at twenty-eight roubles. The Major was informed and the purchase was agreed to. Needless to say the traditional bread and salt were immediately produced, and the new Gnedko was led into the gaol in triumph. There did not seem to be a single prisoner who did not pat his neck or stroke his muzzle. He was harnessed up to carry the water on that very day, and everybody watched curiously to see how he would haul his barrel. Roman, our water-man, looked at the new horse very complacently. He was a man around fifty, of a silent, steady disposition. All Russian coachmen are of such a silent and steady disposition as a matter of fact, so it must be true that by being in constant contact with horses a man acquires sedateness and even a special dignity. Roman was a quiet man who was kind to all and sundry, spoke very little, sniffed tobacco, and had looked after the prison Gnedko since time immemorial. This newly acquired horse was, in fact, the third. All our people were absolutely sure that another bay horse was right for the gaol, and that this was somehow the colour which suited our home. Roman confirmed this judgement. They would never, for example, have purchased a skewbald. The job of water-man was for some reason permanently Roman's, and no one had ever thought of disputing this. When the last Gnedko died, there was no one—including the Major—who even thought of blaming Roman for it. It was God's will, that was all, and Roman was a good driver. Gnedko quickly became the gaol's darling. The prisoners, for all that they were such hard-bitten characters, often went up to him to stroke him. When Roman came back from the river, he had to go and lock the gates behind him—which the sergeant had opened for him—and meanwhile Gnedko stood in the yard waiting for him and watching him out of the corner of his eye. "Go on without me!" Roman would shout at him, and Gnedko would immediately set off towards the kitchen, and stop there, waiting for the *stryapki* (the cooks) and the *parashniki* (cleaners) to come with pails for water from the barrel. "Clever boy, Gnedko!" they would shout. "All on his own he's brought it. Always does as he's told."

"He's only a beast but he understands!"

"Good boy, Gnedko."

Gnedko would nod his head and snort, as though he really did understand everything, and was pleased with the praise he was given. And someone would always bring him a piece of salted bread. Gnedko would eat it, then start nodding his head again, as much as to say: "I know who you are too! I'm a fine horse, and you're a good man!"

I also loved giving him bread. It was so pleasant to look at his handsome muzzle and feel his soft, warm lips quickly taking what I offered him from my palm.

Our prisoners on the whole could have loved animals, and if they had been allowed to, they would have gladly bred a large number of domestic animals and birds in the gaol. And really, what better way could there be of softening and ennobling the hard, savage character of prisoners? But it was not allowed. Neither the regulations nor the institution would permit it.

Nevertheless, there were several animals which—by chance—came to live in the gaol during my time there. As well as Gnedko, we had dogs, geese, Vaska the goat, and—for a short while—an eagle.

As permanent gaol dog we had Sharik, as I have already mentioned, a clever, kind dog, with whom I was always good friends. But because the common people generally consider dogs to be dirty animals which are best ignored, so Sharik was, for the most part, ignored in our gaol. This dog lived and slept outside, ate the scraps from the kitchen, and though he aroused no interest whatsoever in anyone, he still knew everybody and regarded each of them as his master. When the prisoners came back from work and he heard the cry "Call the corporal!" from the guardhouse, he would treat it as a signal, and dash over towards the gates, greeting each party of prisoners with great affection, wagging his tail and looking with a welcoming expression into the eyes of each man, as though expecting some tenderness, however small, in return. Yet throughout the years, no one had ever fondled him, except perhaps me. That was why he loved me most of all. I cannot recall now how the second dog, Belka, appeared in the gaol. The third one, Kultyapka, I brought home from work myself, when he was only a puppy. Belka was a strange creature. He had been run over by a cart, and his back had caved in, so that when he ran, it looked from a distance as though there were two white animals, which had somehow grown together into one. Apart from this deformity, he also had scabs all over him, and eyes full of mucus. His tail was tatty and almost devoid of fur, and held permanently between his legs. Mistreated by fate, he had apparently decided to submit. He never barked or growled at anyone. It was as though he did not dare. For the most part he lived by scavenging for food behind the barracks. If he saw any of our people coming, he would roll over onto his back while they were still several paces off, doing this as a sign of submission, as much as to say: "Do anything you want to me. You can see I have no intention of resisting." And the prisoner, for whom he had rolled over on his back, would inevitably jab him with his boot, and say: "Look at the scabby thing!" Belka, however, did not dare so much as whimper; if the pain became really unbearable he would howl, in a muted, piteous sort of way. In the same way, he would roll over in front of Sharik, or any other dog, if he happened to leave the territory of the gaol on some business of his. He would roll over and lie there submissively, while some huge floppy-eared dog came bounding up to him barking furiously. Dogs, however, are rather fond of submission and resignation among members of their own species. So the ferocious animal would immediately calm down and, coming to a halt beside Belka, would look down thoughtfully at this dog lying there meekly with his paws sticking up in the air, and then slowly and very curiously would start sniffing him over, examining every part of his body. What could Belka have been thinking at these moments as he lay there quivering? "What if this monster suddenly rips me with his teeth?" must surely have been the thought that was passing through his mind. Yet, the other dog, having sniffed him carefully all over, would finally abandon him, feeling that there was nothing of any special interest here. Belka would lap to his feet immediately and set off again, hobbling along, and tagging on to the end of the long line of dogs running after Zhuchka or some other bitch. And although he knew too well that he would never become intimately acquainted with this Zhuchka, he could at least hobble along some way behind her—and this was already something of a compensation for his other misfortunes. Obviously he had stopped worrying about his honour long ago. With no future, the dog lived only for food, and was fully aware of it. On one occasion I tried to show some tenderness to him. This was so unexpected, and such a totally new experience, that Belka suddenly sank down to the ground on all fours, shuddering, and whining loudly with emotion. I often used to stroke him, out of pity, and he would always greet me with this same whining. He would catch sight of me from far away, and start whining painfully and tearfully. In the end Belka was torn to death by some dogs out on the rampart outside the prison.

Kultyapka's character was completely different. What it was that had induced me to bring him into the gaol while he was still a blind puppy, I really do not know. I enjoyed feeding him and rearing him. Sharik immediately appointed himself Kultyapka's guardian, and they used to sleep together. When Kultyapka grew a little older, Sharik allowed him to bit his ears, tear at his fur, and played with him as adult dogs usually play with puppies. The strange thing was that Kultyapka did not grow in height, but only in length and breadth. His fur was fluffy and a sort of mousey grey. One of his ears flopped down, and the other stuck up. He had a passionate and ecstatic temperament, and like any other puppy, whose joy at beholding his master expressed itself in squealing, whimpering and licking your face, he was unable to control himself in other respects either: "Let only my joy be

278

clear, never mind manners." No matter where I was, when I shouted "Kultyapka!" he would suddenly appear round some corner, as though from under the ground, and fly towards me with his delighted whimpering, rolling along like a ball, and somersaulting as he came. I grew awfully fond of this little horror. Fate seemed to be planning only pleasure and happiness for him. Then one fine day, Kultyapka caught the eye of the prisoner Neustroyev, whose business was making ladies' boots and treating animal skins. Some idea suddenly struck him. He called Kultyapka over, fingered his fur, and rolled him over on his back playfully. Kultyapka suspected nothing, and he lay there whimpering with pleasure. The very next morning he disappeared. I searched for him for a long time. He had vanished into thin air. It was two weeks before the truth came to light. Kultyapka's fur had caught Neustroyev's fancy. He had skinned him, treated the fur and used it to line the velvet calf-length boots when they were ready. The fur looked beautiful. Poor Kultyapka!

Quite a few prisoners in the gaol treated skins and they often used to bring in dogs with good fur, all of whom disappeared immediately. Some of these dogs had been stolen, others had been bought. I remember seeing two prisoners on the other side of the kitchens one day. They were conferring together, busy discussing something. One of them was holding a large and splendid dog—obviously some expensive breed or other—on the end of a rope. Some scoundrel of a servant had apparently stolen it from his master and sold it to our bootmakers for thirty silver kopeks. The prisoners were about to hang it. This was done very easily. The animal was skinned, and the carcass thrown into the large, deep rubbish pit in the furthermost corner at the back of the gaol, a place which stank horribly in the summer during hot weather, and which was rarely cleaned out at all. The poor dog seemed to understand what was in store for it. Inquisitively and anxiously it looked at each of the three of us in turn, and only now and then did it dare to wag its fluffy tail slightly, holding it down low, as though hoping somehow to mollify us with this sign of trust in us. I went away, and the other two no doubt saw the business through to a successful conclusion.

The geese also came to live in the gaol almost by accident. Who started breeding them, or whose indeed they were, I do not know, but they amused the prisoners for quite a while, and they even became well known in the town. They had been hatched out in the gaol and they were later kept in the kitchen. When the brood grew up, all of them—the whole gaggle of them—acquired the habit of accompanying the prisoners to work. As soon as the drum began to beat and the convicts to move towards the gates, the geese would come running and honking along behind us, spreading their wings slightly to jump, one after the other, across the high doorstep of the gate, and then—without fail—go to the right flank of the company and line up, waiting for the roll call to finish. They always tagged along with the largest party of prisoners, and while the men were working, they would be grazing somewhere close by. As soon as the party set off on the return journey to the gaol, they would start off too. The news soon spread through the garrison that the geese went out to work with the prisoners. "Look! There's the convicts and their geese!" the passers-by would say. "How on earth did you teach them to do that?" "That's for the geese," someone else would say, offering us alms. Yet, despite their faithfulness, the geese were all killed for one of the feasts, to mark the conclusion of a fast.

Vaska, our goat, would never have been killed if it had not been for one circumstance. As with the geese, I do not know where he came from or who brought him. Suddenly, one day, this pretty little white kid appeared in the gaol, as though from nowhere. We all fell in love with him during the next few days, and he became a source of general amusement, and even comfort for everyone. The prisoners invented a reason to keep him, saying that surely it was necessary to have a goat in the prison stables. He did not, however, live in the stables, but first in the kitchen, and then later all over the gaol. He was the most graceful and mischievous of animals. When called, he always came running, he jumped up on to the benches and the tables, and butted the prisoners playfully. He was unfailingly cheerful and amusing. Once, after his horns had sprouted to quite a size, Babai, a Lezghin who was sitting on the barrack porch with a crowd of other prisoners, took it into his head to have a butting match with him. They went on banging their foreheads together for some time (this was the game the prisoners loved to play with him most of all) when Vaska suddenly jumped onto the top step of the porch and the moment Babai turned away from him, reared up, and drawing his hooves in close against his chest, butted Babai as hard as he could on the back of his head. Babai was sent sprawling on the ground, to the delight of everyone present and himself too. Everyone, in other words, adored Vaska. When he began to grow up, there was a serious discussion among all the prisoners, the outcome of which was that a certain operation was performed on him by our vets, who knew how to do it very well. "The whole place'll smell of goat otherwise," said the prisoners. After this Vaska started to grow terribly fat. The prisoners overfed him too. In the end he grew into a beautiful, big, but enormously fat billy goat with very long horns. He waddled around all over the place. He also got into the habit of accompanying us to work, entertaining both the prisoners and the people they met. Vaska, the prison goat, was known to all and sundry. Sometimes, when the work was on the riverbank, the prisoners would pick some supple rose-willow twigs from one place, some leaves from another and some flowers from the prison rampart, and bedeck Vaska with them. His horns were braided with twigs and flowers, and garlands were wound around his body. On the return journey to the gaol, Vaska was always out in front, bedecked and adorned, for all to see, and the prisoners followed behind him, letting the passers-by see how they prided in him. This adulation of our goat reached such proportions that some even got the childish idea into their heads to gild his horns. It was a suggestion, however, and it was never carried out. I remember asking Akim Akimovich, who was our best gilder after Isai Fomich, whether it was really possible to gild a goat's horns. At first, he looked at the goat very carefully, made some serious calculations, and then said that it probably was possible, but that it would not last and was, in any case, completely useless. That was as far as it went. So Vaska might have lived on in our gaol for long years and perhaps died only from a shortage of breath, had it not been that one day, when returning from work fully adorned and decked out at the head of a party of prisoners, he crossed the path of the Major as he was driving along in his carriage. "Stop where you are!" bellowed the Major. "Who does this goat belong to?" It was explained to him. "What do you mean, a goat in the gaol without my permission! Get me the sergeant at once!" The sergeant arrived, and was immediately ordered to kill the goat, skin it, sell the skin in the market, add the money to the prison funds, and put the meat into the prisoners' cabbage soup. The prisoners were sorry for the goat, they grieved over him, but nobody dared to disobey. Vaska was slaughtered over the rubbish pit. One of the prisoners bought up all the meat wholesale, and put a rouble and a half in the gaol funds. The money was used to buy buns, while the purchaser proceeded to sell the meat in pieces to the prisoners for roasting. The meat, as it turned out, was unbelievably tasty.

At one time, there was also an eagle (a *karagush*—a species of small steppe eagle) in the gaol. It had been brought in wounded and exhausted. All the inmates of the prison clustered round it. It was unable to fly. Its right wing was dragging along the ground and one of its feet was dislocated. I can remember how aggressively it surveyed the curious crowd and how it opened its aquiline beak, ready to fight to the death. When people had had their fill of looking at it and began to disperse, the eagle hobbled away, limping, hopping along on one foot and flapping its one good wing, until it reached the furthest end of the gaol, where it huddled into a corner, pressed up tightly against the pales. It lived in this place for nearly three months, and never once left the corner during the whole of this time. At first people came to look at it often, and they even sicked one of the dogs on it. Sharik jumped at the eagle angrily, but was apparently scared to come any closer. This amused the prisoners no end. "He's a wild thing," they said, "he won't let himself be taken easily." Later, even Sharik learned how to hurt the eagle badly. His fear passed, and when he was let loose on the bird, he contrived to grab hold of its bad wing. The eagle defended itself as well as it might with its beak and claws, and like a wounded king, glared proudly and wildly at the curious crowd. In the end everyone grew bored with the eagle. They all abandoned it and forgot about it. Yet every day there would be pieces of raw meat, and a crock with water on the ground beside it. Somebody must have been caring for it. At first the eagle refused to take any food, and did not eat for several days. At last it began to take food, but it would never eat out of anyone's hand, or in anyone's presence. Several times I happened to be watching it from afar. Seeing no one around and imagining itself to be alone, it would risk moving a short distance beyond its corner, and hobble along the pales for about twelve paces, then return to its original position, then sally forth again, as though it were walking for exercise. When it saw me it would hurry, limping and hopping back towards its place, its head thrust back and its beak open, ruffled and preparing for battle. No cajoling could pacify this bird. It bit me and thrashed about angrily; it refused to take meat from me, and while I stood over it, stared straight into my eyes with the same vicious and penetrating glare. Angry and alone, it awaited its death, trusting nobody, resenting everybody. Finally the prisoners did remember it, and although none of them had taken any care or notice of the eagle for about two months, all of a sudden they felt terribly compassionate. The bird had to be taken outside somehow. "Let it die if it must, but don't let it die in prison," said some of them.

"That's right," said some of the others. "This is a free bird, a tough bird, it could never get used to imprisonment."

"It's not like us then," someone added.

"That's a stupid comment to come out with. We're people. This is a bird. That's what."

"An eagle, mates, is the king of the forests..." Skuratov began, but this time nobody listened to him.

Then one day, after the midday meal, when the drum was sounding the return to work, they took the eagle out of the gaol. Its beak had to be held firmly in somebody's hand as it had started to struggle violently. They went as far as the rampart. The twelve people in that particular work party were all fired with curiosity to see where the eagle would go. The strange thing was that each one of them seemed to be happy about something, as though it were a part of himself which had suddenly gained its freedom.

"Just look at the bastard. You try your best to help it, and it goes on biting your bloody hand," said the man who was holding it, looking at the cruel bird almost lovingly.

"Let him go, Mikita!"

"No keeping him locked up. He wants freedom, real freedom."

They threw the eagle off the rampart and into the steppe. It was the middle of autumn and the day was cold and overcast. The wind whistled across the barren steppe, stirring the yellow, shrivelled, ragged grass. The eagle set off in a straight line, flapping its bad wing, apparently not caring where it went in its hurry to escape us. The prisoners curiously followed its head, as it appeared and disappeared among the grass.

"That's that then," someone said, thoughtfully.

"It don't even look back!" added someone else. "Not once, mates! He don't even look back once. He just keeps running..."

"Did you expect him to come and say thank you to us?" remarked another.

"That's what freedom is. He can feel the freedom."

"Yes, that's it. Liberty."

"No sign of him any more, mates."

"What are you hanging about there for?" shouted one of the guards. "Get a move on!"

And, in silence, everyone trudged off to work.

VII

The Grievance

Before embarking upon this chapter, the editor of these notes of the late Alexander Petrovich Goryanchikov considers it his duty to inform his readers of the following:

There was mention, during the first chapter of these *Notes from the Dead House* of a certain patricide, a former member of the nobility. Amongst other matters, he was presented as an example of the heartlessness with which some of the prisoners recount their crimes. It was also said that this murderer did not admit his guilt to the court, but that—judging from the testimony of others, who knew all the details of the case—the facts spoke for themselves, and it was quite impossible not to believe in his crime. These same people had told the author of *The Notes* that the criminal had led a most dissolute life, had fallen deeply into debt, and had killed his father in the hope of a speedy inheritance. In fact, the entire town, in which the patricide had previously been employed, recounted the tale in exactly the same way. On this last point, the present editor has access to quite reliable information. In conclusion, it is stated in *The Notes* that this murderer was continually in the happiest and most cheerful frame of mind, that he was unbalanced, light-minded, unreasonable to the utmost degree, though without being a fool, and that the author of *The Notes* never once noticed the slightest degree of cruelty in him. The following words were also added: "I did not, of course, believe in this crime."

The present editor quite recently received official notification from Siberia that the criminal in question had indeed been telling the truth, and that he had unjustly served ten years of hard labour. His innocence was established officially, in court. The real criminals had been found, and had confessed, and the poor wretch referred to above, had already been released from the gaol. The present editor has no reason to doubt the truthfulness of this information.

There is nothing more to be said, no point in discoursing further about the depth of the tragedy, about a young life wrecked by such a horrible accusation. The facts of the matter are too clear, too striking in themselves.

We also think that if such a fact proved possible, then this possibility in itself adds a new and extremely eloquent feature to the picture of the Dead House.

But let us continue.

I have already mentioned how I finally grew accustomed to my life in gaol. Yet this 'finally' came too slowly and painfully, little by little. In fact it took a whole year—a year which was the most difficult one in my life. That is why it remains in my memory in its entirety. I believe I can remember every single hour of that year in chronological order. I have also mentioned that there were other convicts who also could not *get used* to prison life. I remember how, during my first year, I often wondered about the others: "What do they feel? Surely they haven't become used to this? Can they really take it so calmly?" Such questions concerned me a great deal. I have already mentioned that all the prisoners behaved as though they were not really domiciled in prison but were in some wayside inn for a short stay, or on the march, *en route* somewhere else. Even the people who had been put away for life were unsettled and homesick, and I feel quite positive that each was weaving some quite impossible daydream. This permanent sense of unrest, unspoken but nevertheless obvious, the strange and passionate impatience sometimes revealed in involuntarily voiced hopefulness, more often than not so groundless that one thought the man was raving, and the fact, which was particularly striking, that such hopes took hold of what seemed to be the most realistic minds, all this lent an unusual feeling and atmosphere to the place, to so great an extent that it was perhaps its most characteristic feature. You felt, almost immediately, that it was something which did not exist outside the prison. Everybody here was a daydreamer. It was something that struck you immediately. One felt it poignantly, precisely because this daydreaming gave a grim, brooding, unhealthy air to the gaol, or anyway the majority of its inmates. The vast majority of the convicts were taciturn and spiteful to the point of hatred, and they did not like to put their private hopes on show. The open and the simple-hearted were held in contempt. The more unreal the hopes of the prisoner were, and the more conscious the dreamer was of their unreality, the more stubbornly and chastely he kept them secret, but he could never abandon them. Who knows? Maybe he was ashamed of them. The Russian character has so much soundness and sober-mindedness, such readiness to mock at itself in the first place... Perhaps it was this constant sense of self-dissatisfaction that was the source of such impatience in

these people's everyday relations with each other, such implaca-
bility and such jeering at each other. If occasionally, for
example, one of the more naive and impatient prisoners should
happen to stick his neck out, allowing himself to be carried
away by his hopes and dreams, voicing the thoughts that were
on the minds of all the others, he would immediately be rudely
cut short and jeered at. Yet I believe that the people who were
most passionate in this persecution, were the very ones who had
themselves carried their dreaming to far greater extremes. The
naive and simple types were—as I have already mentioned—held
in the deepest contempt in our place, and regarded as the silliest
of fools. Most of the men were so sullen and vain that they immediately began to despise anyone who was kind or lacking in
vanity. Apart from these simple-minded chatterboxes, the
others—the silent others—could be sharply divided into those
who were kind and those who were mean, and those who were
gloomy and those who were easy-going. The gloomy and mean
kind were by far the most numerous. If any of them also happened to be talkative by nature, they were certain to be
worriedly gossipy and nervously jealous. They stuck their noses
into everyone else's business, but never disclosed their own secret doings or opened their hearts to anyone. That simply was
not done. The kinder types—who were very small in number—
stayed silent, quietly guarding their private hopes, and naturally
enough were more inclined than the gloomy ones to believe in
their dreams. It seems to me, however, that there was still
another category: those who were utterly desperate. The old
man from the Starodubye settlement was of this type, for
example. Such characters were at any rate very rare. This old
man was outwardly quite calm (I have already spoken about
him) but there were some signs which led me to believe that his
inner emotional state must have been quite terrible. He had
his own salvation, however, and his own escape: prayer and a
philosophy of martyrdom. The prisoner I have already mentioned who went mad after becoming over-absorbed in his Bible
reading, the one who lunged at the Major with a brick, was
also very probably from this last group of desperate people,
those whose last hope had deserted them—and as no one can live

utterly without hope, he had found a way out for himself in his voluntary and almost artificial martyrdom. He declared that it was not from anger that he had lunged at the Major, but solely because he craved martyrdom. Who knows what psychological process had taken place in his soul at that instant. Every living person needs some kind of aim and a desire to attain it, if he is to go on living. A person who has lost this aim and this hope, is turned into a monster by despair... The aim of each one of our people was to attain freedom and be released from prison.

On the other hand, I am now trying to consign every individual in our gaol to a category ... but is it really possible to do this? The diversity of reality, compared with even the most shrewd conclusions of abstract thought, is infinite, and it does not allow large and rough categorisation. The tendency of reality is towards fractionation. Even we prisoners had our own individual lives, not much to speak of, of course, but anyway our own inner lives and not just our official lives.

Yet as I have already spoken of partly, at the beginning of my gaol term I was unable to penetrate the inner depths of this life, and so its outward manifestations tortured me, causing me inexpressible anguish. There were times when I simply hated the people around me, sufferers like myself. I was even envious of them, and cursed my own fate. I envied them for being at least among their own kind, part of a brotherhood who understood each other, even though they were in fact, like me, sick to the teeth of this brotherhood, enforced by the lash and the stick. The eyes of each man were secretly turned away from the others. I must emphasise again that this envy, which seized me in moments of anger, had its own legitimate basis. Indeed, anyone who claims that a nobleman, an educated man, is no worse off in our prisons and fortresses than a peasant, is most decisively wrong. I have heard such views put forward in recent times; I have even seen them in print. The basis of the idea is correct and humanitarian. The prisoners are all people, human beings all. But the idea is too abstract. Many practical factors, which can only be understood through experience, in actual reality, are left out of consideration. I do not say this because I think that noblemen and educated people feel things more subtly and painfully, or that they are in some way more developed. The development of a soul cannot be consigned to some designated level or other, and even education can be no yardstick in cases such as these. I would be the first to testify that even among the most uneducated sufferers, and among people from the lowliest milieu, I saw evidence of the most sophisticated emotional development. In gaol, it was sometimes the case that you would know someone for several years and thoroughly despise him, regarding him more as a beast than a human being. Then suddenly, by chance, there would come a moment when some impulse would open up his soul to you, and you would see before you a heart so rich in feeling, with such clear understanding of both his own and another's suffering, that it was as if a film had dropped from your eyes, and for a moment you could not believe what you had just seen and heard. The reverse was also sometimes true. Education is sometimes the bedfellow of terrible barbarity and cynicism; it makes you sick with disgust, and in your heart you are unable to find either excuses or justification for it, however kind you may be, or prejudiced in favour of it.

I am not talking here about the change of habits, way of life, food, and so on, which is undoubtedly harder to bear for a man from the higher layers of society than for a peasant, who has known hunger in his previous existence and here, in gaol, he at least gets enough to eat. I do not want to argue this point. Let us assume that for a person who possesses any strength of character, such inconveniences as these are mere trifles when compared with others; although changing one's habits is not a trifling matter at all, nor the least important one. Yet there are other inconveniences beside which all these others pale into insignificance, so much so that you no longer notice the filth around you, your shackles, or the frugal, sloppy food. After a full day of sweating toil, of the kind he had never done in his free life, even the most pampered, the most fastidious man will eat both rough brown bread and cabbage soup with cockroaches. These are things one can grow used to, as it says in the comic prison song about a man who led a life of luxury, and then ended up in gaol:

They give me cabbage floating in water,
But I guzzle it down all the same.

The most important factor of all is that any new arrival in gaol becomes the same as everyone else within the space of a couple of hours. He is *at home*, he has the same rights as all the others. Everyone understands him; he understands them. The prisoners are familiar with men like him, and they accept him as *one of themselves*. But if it's a *nobleman*, a member of the upper classes, it is a completely different matter. However fair and kind and clever he may be, he will be hated and despised by everybody, *en masse*, for years. No one will understand him, and—what is more important—will not believe him. He is no friend or comrade to them, and even if, after many years, he does achieve security from their perpetual insults and slights, he will anyway remain forever an outsider, eternally and painfully aware of his alienation and his solitude. The estrangement to which his fellow convicts subject him is not always malicious, but just instinctive. He is not one of us—and that's all there is to it. Nothing can be more awful than having to live in an alien milieu. A peasant, exiled from Taganrog to Petropavlovsk, will immediately find another Russian peasant exactly like himself; they will at once strike up some kind of mutual understanding and relationship, and within a couple of hours perhaps, settle down to live together in the same wooden hut or shelter. Not so with the gentry. Between them and the common people lies the deepest abyss: a nobleman only becomes *fully* aware of this when by force of external circumstances he is deprived of his privileges and turned into one of the common people. You may have known the common people all your life, even have associated with them daily for forty years in the course of your work, say, in some administrative capacity or other, or even perhaps simply in a friendly manner, as their benefactor, but you will never have really known them. It will have been an optical illusion—no more. I know, of course, that when people read this, everybody—absolutely everybody without exception—will say that I am exaggerating. But I am convinced that I am right. I was convinced not by books, nor by abstract speculation, but by life itself, and I had ample time to test my conviction. Maybe eventually everyone will realise how right I am...

As if to confirm the truth of this observation, it was borne out by the events of my very first days in prison, affecting me in a most painful and distressing manner. That first summer, I used to wander around the gaol totally alone. As I have already said, I was in such a terrible state of mind that I was even unable to appreciate and distinguish among the prisoners those who might grow fond of me and did in fact show affection to me later, but never on an equal footing. I had some comrades, also former noblemen, yet even their comradeship failed to lift the whole burden from by soul... Everything was too loathsome, but there was no escape. Let me tell you, for example, of one instance that right away brought my alienation and my peculiar standing in the gaol clearly home to me. Soon after twelve o'clock one bright, hot weekday during the summer I have been speaking of, with August already hard upon us, when everyone was having a rest before going back to work after the midday meal, all the convicts suddenly rose to their feet as one man and began lining up in the prison yard. Until that very moment, I had no idea that there was something going on. I was sometimes so deeply absorbed in myself at this hour of rest that I hardly noticed what was happening around me. Actually, there had been some discontent brewing in the prison for about three days. It is possible, as I realised much later when I thought back over some of the prisoners' conversations I had overheard, their marked belligerence, their glumness and especially their irascibility, that it had already been brewing for quite some time. I had previously ascribed it to the hard work, the long and tedious summer days, insuppressible dreams of the forests, of freedom, and to the short nights when it was so difficult to get enough sleep. It may be that all these factors came to a head and exploded; but the pretext for the explosion was something else: the food. For several days now complaints had been voiced out loud; indignation was expressed in the barracks and most angrily, when everyone assembled in the kitchen for the midday and evening meals. The prisoners were dissatisfied with the cooks, they even tried to change one of them, but quickly

291

sacked the new man and reinstated the old one. In short, they were all in an extremely restless state of mind.

"We break our backs working, and then we're fed with tripe," was how the grumbling would start up in the kitchen.

"If you don't like it, order a *blanc-mange*!" someone else would answer.

"Cabbage soup with tripe is good, I love it," took up a third.

"And if you get nothing but tripe every day, you'll still love it?"

"This is the meat season, of course," said a fourth one. "Slaving away all day in the factory, you get real ravenous, and it's not food—this tripe!"

"And if it isn't tripe, it's *hurts*."*

"That's it. Take this heart here. Tripe and heart day in, day out. D'you call it food? Is there any justice in the world or isn't there?"

"Sure, the grub's pretty poor!"

"He's filling his own pockets, I reckon."

"That's none of your business."

"Well, whose business is it? It's my belly, isn't it? If we all complained together, that would do the trick."

"Make a complaint?"

"Sure."

"They can't have flogged you hard enough last time. You and your bloody complaints!"

"It sounds good, of course, but won't wash," another prisoner, who had sat in silence up to this point, suddenly added grumpily. "Tell us first, you wiseacre, what you are going to say in your complaint?"

"I'll say something all right. If we all go together, I shall say it together with everyone else. All us poor ones, anyways. There are some here who have their own food, and others who have to make do with just the prison stuff."

"Look at you now! Bursting with envy!"

"The grass is always greener on the other side!"

Author's note. By this they meant 'heart', the prisoners sarcastically referred to it as 'hurt'.

292

"Is that so! I'll stick to what I've said till I'm old and grey. You must be rich then, if you don't want to take part in this."

"Rich, my foot."

"Really, mates, what's the use of sitting around and just talking? We've borne their tricks long enough. They're fleecing us, that's what. So why not go and complain?"

"Why? Because this is hard labour prison, that's why. You want it all chewed up for you, you're used to eating chewed-up stuff."

"To put it in a nutshell: while the dog fights the cat, the master grows fat."

"That's right. Old eight-eyes has grown fat at our expense. He's bought himself a pair of greys."

"He doesn't mind a drink, either."

"He had a fight with the vet at cards the other day."

"They played all night. The light lasted for two hours, our Major getting the worst of it, Fedka told me."

"That's why we get cabbage soup and *hurts.*"

"Listen to me, you bloody idiots. We aren't in a position to go taking chances."

"Why not, if we all come out together we'll see what excuse he makes. We must stand firm, that's what."

"'What excuse'! You'll get your teeth pushed in, and that'll be the end of that."

"And you'll stand trial besides..."

Everyone, in other words, was terribly disturbed. We really did have very bad food at that time. Grievances kept mounting up. But the main cause of the discontent was the general mood of misery, the anguish each man was suffering in secret. Prisoners are grumpy and rebellious by nature, but they rarely rise to mutiny in large numbers. This is because they continually disagree with one another. Each one felt this to be true, and as a result there was more squabbling than action. This time, however, the restlessness had certain consequences. Prisoners started congregating in groups, holding discussions in the barracks, quarrelling, angrily recalling the entire length of the Major's reign, and getting together what evidence they could against him. Some of them were particularly agitated. In any business of this kind, there are always instigators and ring-leaders who put themselves forward. Ring-leaders in these instances—that is, in all cases of malcontent—are as a rule remarkable people, not only in gaols but in any kind of community, in work gangs, and so on. They are a particular type, alike no matter where you find them. They are passionate people, they crave justice and are convinced, in the most naive and honest way, that it is certainly, indisputably and—what is more—immediately possible to attain. It is not that they are less intelligent than the others—there are even some very clever men among them—but they are too hot-headed to be cunning and calculating. In all cases such as these, even if there are people capable of manipulating the crowd and scoring a victory, these constitute a different type of natural popular leader, a type extremely rare in this country. The people I am talking about at the moment, on the other hand, the instigators and ring-leaders of complaints, almost invariably lose their case and end up in our gaols. They lose because they are so hot-headed, but it is also because they are hot-headed that they can influence the masses. And when all is said and done, people follow them readily. Their passion and honest indignation affect everybody, and finally inspire even the most indecisive to join them. Their blind confidence in success infects even the most sceptical, despite the fact that this confidence sometimes has such a flimsy and infantile foundation that one cannot help wondering how anyone could have followed them at all. Most important of all is that they go first leading the way, and are not afraid of anything. Like bulls, they charge straight ahead, often blindly, incautiously, with none of that prevarication with which even the most vile and imperfect character can sometimes win the day, achieve his aim, and come out unscathed. All the ring-leaders I'm talking about do, is break their horns. In ordinary, day to day life these people are bitter, peevish, irritable and intolerant. More often than not they are extremely narrow-minded, although this partly constitutes their strength. What is most irritating is that instead of going for the centre of the target, they often rush over to one side, missing the main issue and getting tangled up in trivialities. That is their destruction. Yet they are understood by the masses, and that is their strength. I ought really to say a few words here, about what exactly 'complaint' means...

In our gaol, there were several men who were here for submitting 'complaints'. They were the ones who were particularly agitated now, especially one of them, by the name of Martynov, a former hussar, and a man of a fiery, restless and suspicious nature, though honest and truthful too. Another was Vasili Antonov, who became irritated in a strangely cool manner, and had an insolent glance and sarcastic smile. He had a highly developed intellect, and was also honest and truthful. It is not possible to list all these people, however. They were numerous. Petrov, by the way, was busy scurrying from group to group, listening to everything that was said, saying very little himself. Obviously he was extremely excited, and was the first to dash out of the barrack when they started forming up outside.

Our prison sergeant, who fulfilled the duties of sergeant-major in our place, appeared immediately, greatly alarmed. When the prisoners had lined up, they politely asked him to go and inform the Major that the prison wished to speak to him personally, and ask him to amend certain regulations. The invalid soldiers also came out after the sergeant-major, and lined up in the other side, opposite the prisoners. The mission with which the sergeant-major was entrusted was, of course, extraordinary, and it plunged him into a fit of terror. All the same, he did not dare suppress the request and not report to the Major immediately. Firstly, seeing that the gaol had risen, something much worse could be expected. All the authorities were very cowardly in their relations with the gaol. And secondly, even if nothing happened and all the prisoners immediately regained their sense and peaceably dispersed, the sergeant-major would still be obliged to report the details of the incident to his superiors immediately. Pale and trembling with fear, he hastened off to see the Major, without even attempting to question and remonstrate with the prisoners first himself. He could see that they would refuse to talk to him.

Not knowing anything at all of what was happening, I too went out to line up. I only learned the details of the affair much later. At the time I thought there must be some extra roll call, though I was surprised when I did not see the guards who always conducted such roll calls, and started to look around me. The convicts looked nervous and irritated. Some were even quite pale. They were all worried and silent, thinking of how they would have to talk to the Major. I noticed that many of them glanced at me with amazement, and then silently turned away. They must have found it strange to see me lining up with them. They obviously did not believe that I, too, was going to support their complaint. Very soon, however, almost everyone started turning round, and looking at me inquisitively.

"What the hell are you doing here?" Vasili Antonov, who was standing further away from me than the others, asked me loudly and rudely. On previous occasions he had always addressed me rather formally and politely.

I looked at him in confusion, trying to understand what he meant by this, and already beginning to guess that something extraordinary was afoot.

"Yes, you! Why should you stand here? Get back in the barrack, it's none of your business." This was a young lad, a kind and quiet fellow, a former soldier, with whom I had never exchanged a word before.

"But everybody's lining up," I answered. "I thought it was some kind of roll call."

"Look what's crawled out of the woodwork!" someone shouted.

"Yeah! Iron nose!"

"Fly squasher," added another, with inexpressible contempt. This new nickname made them all burst out laughing.

"He is in great favour with the cooks," said another.

"His sort always are in clover wherever they go. Here they are in prison, but they eat white bread and sucking pig all the time. You eat your own food, don't you? So keep out!"

"This is no place for you," said Kulikov, coming up to me in a self-assured manner. He took me by the arm and led me out of the ranks.

His face was pale, his dark eyes were flashing, and he was biting his lower lip. He was not waiting for the Major at all composedly. I should mention, by the way, that I always immensely enjoyed looking at Kulikov in situations such as these, where it was necessary for him to show the stuff he was made of. He was a terrible poseur, but he did what had to be done, nevertheless. I think he would have gone to his own execution with style and flamboyance. Now that all the others were so rude to me, he seemed purposely to address me with redoubled politeness, but at the same time his words sounded haughtily insistent, brooking no objections.

"We've come to talk about our own affairs, Alexander Petrovich, and it is no concern of yours. Go somewhere else, and wait till it's over... All your sort are sitting inside in the kitchen. Go and join them."

"Yes ... in the deepest pit of Hell..." someone else added.

One of the kitchen windows had been slightly raised and I really could see our Poles there. There seemed to be quite a few others in the kitchen as well... Puzzled, I went over to the kitchen. Laughter, cursing and cat-calls followed me all the way.

"He couldn't take it! Boo! Boo! Sic him!"

I had never been subjected to such a barrage of insults in the gaol before, and it pained me terribly. I made a good target for their pent-up excitement. The first person I met in the entrance to the kitchen was T—vsky, a former nobleman, a staunch, generous-hearted and not very well educated young man, who was particularly fond of B. The common prisoners singled him out among us, and even liked him to some extent. His bravery, valour and strength were evident in his every gesture.

"What's up with you, Goryanchikov?" he shouted. "Come over here, will you?"

"What is going on out there?"

"They're presenting their complaint. Didn't you know about it? Nothing will come of it, of course. Who's going to believe what prisoners say? A hue and cry will start for the ring-leaders, and if we're among them, we will be the first to be blamed for inciting a riot. Remember what we are here for? They will simply be flogged, but we will be tried. The Major hates us and would be only too pleased to destroy us. He will use us to clear himself."

"The prisoners would also be the first to betray us," added M—tsky, as we went into the kitchen.

"Don't worry, they aren't going to feel sorry for us," agreed T—vsky.

There were quite a few people in the kitchen apart from the noblemen: altogether about thirty. They had all stayed behind there, because none of them wished to participate in presenting the complaint: some out of cowardice, others because they were strongly convinced of the complete ineffectiveness of any such complaint. Akim Akimovich was there, an inveterate and natural enemy of all such actions which only disrupted the normal run of prison routine. He was waiting in silence for the end of the affair, not ruffled in the slightest about the outcome, sure of the inevitable triumph of order. Isai Fomich was also there. He looked bewildered as he listened to our conversation with a kind of cowardly eagerness. He was extremely worried. Also present were all the common Poles who had attached themselves to the noblemen. There were several timid Russian convicts, the downtrodden, silent kind. They did not dare go out with the rest, and were now waiting sadly for the outcome. And then there were some morose, tough prisoners, who were anything but timid. They had stayed behind because they felt stubbornly and scathingly certain that the whole thing was nonsense and would end in nothing but trouble. But it seemed to me that they too were rather uneasy at this moment, and lacked their usual self-confidence. Although they knew they were right, and indeed later proved to be correct, they nevertheless felt like renegades who had deserted the community, and betrayed their comrades to the Major. Yolkin was also there, that very cunning Siberian muzhik, who had been sentenced for making counterfeit money and had then taken Kulikov's veterinary practice away from him. The old man from the Starodubye Settlement was also there. All the cooks had remained in the kitchen, presumably regarding themselves as part of the administration and so considering that it would be improper for them to come out against it.

"Apart from these people almost everybody is out there," I said, addressing M—tsky hesitantly.

"Yes, but what is it to do with us?" grumbled B.

"We would have been taking a risk a hundred times greater

than theirs, if we had come out. And what for? *Je hais ces brigands.* Do you really imagine even for a moment that their complaint will be accepted? Why get involved in this lunacy?"

"Nothing will come of it," said a stubborn and bitter old man.

Almazov, who was also here, hurried to add: "Nothing except that about fifty of them will get flogged."

"Here comes the Major!" someone shouted, and everyone rushed excitedly to the windows.

The Major was in a blind rage, red in the face, and wearing his spectacles. Silently and resolutely, he went up to the lined-up prisoners. He was really brave in such situations, and did not lose his presence of mind. True, he was almost permanently only half sober. At that moment, even his greasy cap with the orange peak and his tarnished silver epaulettes had something threatening about them. Behind him came the clerk, Dyatlov, an extremely important person in the life of our gaol, who actually ran the whole thing, and could even exert considerable influence over the Major. He was a cunning, self-interested fellow, but not a bad person really. The prisoners were generally quite satisfied with him. Then came our sergeant, who had evidently received a good tongue-lashing already and was expecting ten times worse to come; then three or four of the guards, no more. The prisoners, who had been standing with their hats in their hands since the sergeant had gone for the Major, now straightened up, shifted their weight from one foot to another, and finally all froze to attention, waiting for the first word—or better to say the first scream—from their superior.

It came immediately. With his second word, the Major began yelling at the top of his voice, which rose to a screech because he was so furious. From our windows, we could see him running up and down the line, jumping at people, interrogating them. Owing to the distance, however, we could hear neither his questions nor the prisoners' answers. All we could hear was the shrill cry:

"Rebels! You'll all run the gauntlet!.. Ring-leaders! You're the ring-leader, are you? You're the ring-leader!" he screamed at someone.

We could not hear the answer. A minute later we saw one prisoner detach himself from the others and set off towards the guardhouse. In another minute, a second man followed, then a third.

"You'll all be tried for this! I'll teach you! Who's that over there in the kitchen?" he shrieked, seeing us at the open kitchen windows. "Bring them all out! Herd them over here!"

Dyatlov, the clerk, came into the kitchen. Here, he was told that we had no complaint. He immediately returned and reported this to the Major.

"Oh! They don't!" he said. His voice had dropped a couple of tones, and he was obviously pleased. "Never mind that though, bring them here all the same."

We went out. It seemed somehow shameful for us to come out, somehow embarrassing. Everyone walked with his head hung low.

"Oh, Prokofiev! And Yolkin as well! Can this be you, Almazov... Stand over there, in a group," the Major said in a hurried softer voice, looking at us with twinkling eyes. "So you're here too, M—tsky. Right! Take all their names down, Dyatlov. Make separate lists of all those who are satisfied and all those who are dissatisfied—every man Jack of them—and bring the lists to me at once. I shall take you all to court for this! I'll have you, scoundrels, for this!"

Talk of the lists had an immediate effect.

"We are satisfied!" one of the dissatisfied suddenly shouted out in a glum but not very resolute voice.

"Satisfied, are you? Who's safisfied? Those of you who are satisfied, step forward."

"Yes, we're satisfied, we're satisfied," came more voices.

"Satisfied, are you? You must have been suborned then. There must be ring-leaders, rebels! The worse for them!"

"Oh God, what is this?" a voice came from the crowd.

"Who was that? Who shouted out?" bellowed the Major rushing to where the voice had come from. "Was that you, Rastorguyev? Did you shout that? Off to the guardhouse with him!"

Rastorguyev, a tall, bloated-looking young man, came forward, and shuffled off towards the guardhouse. He was not the one who had shouted, but—as he had been singled out—he made no protest.

"It's this easy living!" the Major yelled after him. "Look at his fat mug, a three days' shitting couldn't cover it. I'll get the lot of you! Step forward, all those who are satisfied!"

"We're satisfied, Your Excellency." Dozens of glum voices responded. The others remained stubbornly silent. That was just what the Major wanted. Clearly, he needed to bring the whole affair to a close as soon as possible, and somehow end it peacefully.

"Aha!" he said quickly, "so we're *all* satisfied now, are we? I could tell that straightaway actually... I knew it! All the doing of ring-leaders. There are ring-leaders among them, of course," he continued, turning to Dyatlov. "We must be sure to find out who they are! And now ... now it's time for work. Sound the drum!"

He attended the roll call in person. The prisoners drifted off to their various work places sadly and silently, glad to be out of the Major's sight. Immediately after the roll call the Major went over to the guardhouse and had the ring-leaders punished. He was not, however, too severe. He even seemed to be in something of a hurry. There was one of them, they said afterwards, who had asked his forgiveness, and the Major had granted it at once. The Major was a little ill at ease and maybe even scared. A complaint is a very unpleasant business, and although this time it could not really be called that, since the prisoners had not submitted it to the higher authorities, but only to the Major himself—even so, it was disturbing and bad. What was particularly disturbing was that the prisoners had risen up almost as one man. The Major had to quash the affair at all costs. The 'ring-leaders' were soon released. The food on the following day was somewhat better, though this improvement was rather short-lived. The Major began to visit the gaol more and more frequently, and more and more frequently he uncovered instances of disorder. Our sergeant went about looking worried and perplexed, as if still unable to recover from his shock. As for the prisoners, they did not calm down for a long time after that, though they were not agitated as before, but rather appeared to be silently disturbed and nonplussed. Some even lost heart completely. Others talked about the whole incident grumpily, though not at any great length. Many sneered at themselves loudly and bitterly for failing to present their complaint.

"We were too big for our boots," one of them would say.

"We've cooked our goose, so now we've got to eat it," said another.

"They never did find the mouse to bell the cat," said a third.

"The stick's the only language we understand. That's clear. Luckily he didn't have us all flogged."

"In future you should think first, and open your mouth afterwards. That'll make more sense," someone else remarked spitefully.

"You think you're a teacher or something?"

"I'm teaching you sense."

"And who are you anyway?"

"I'm still a man and what are you?"

"You're a dog's arse, that's what you are."

"I thought that was you."

"Come off it, you two. Stop squabbling will you!" This came from every corner.

That very evening, I met Petrov behind the barracks as I was returning from work. He had already been looking for me. He mumbled something as he came up to me, which sounded like vague exclamations, and then became absent-mindedly silent and fell into step beside me, automatically. The whole incident was still preying on my mind, and I thought Petrov might be able to explain some things to me.

"Tell me, Petrov," I said. "Are you people angry with us?"

"Who's angry?" he asked, awakening from his reverie.

"The prisoners, with us—the noblemen."

"Why should we be angry with you?"

"Well, for not joining you in the complaint."

"But why should you want to complain?" he asked, as though straining to understand what I meant. "You eat your own food."

"Well yes, of course, but there are some of your people who eat their own food too. They still came out with you though.

And that's what we should have done ... as a mark of comradeship."

"But ... what sort of comrade can you be to us?" he asked in dismay.

I shot a glance at him. He really could not understand me. He could not understand what I was driving at. But then I understood him completely at that moment. For the first time, the thought that had been stirring vaguely in my head for a very long time and haunting me became finally clarified for me, and all at once I saw what I had so far only partly guessed at. I realised that I would never be accepted as their comrade, even if I were in gaol all my life, even if I were in the special category. The look Petrov gave me at that moment I shall never forget. Nor the sincere naiveté and the simple-hearted dismay when he asked: "What sort of comrade can you be to us?" It occurred to me that there might be some irony, some malice, some mockery in these words. But there was nothing of the sort. I could not be a comrade, and that was all there was to it. You go your way, we'll go ours. You have your business, we have ours.

I thought that after the fiasco with the complaint, the other prisoners would make our life not worth living. There was nothing of the kind, though. There were no reproaches at all, not even a single hint of one. There was no additional malice. They just continued nagging at us every time they had a chance, just as they had always done, and that was all. In fact, they even were not angry with those of their own kind who had stayed behind in the kitchen, nor with those who had been first to shout out that they were satisfied with everything. Nobody even mentioned it. This last fact, in particular, was something I have never been able to understand.

VIII

The Fraternity

Of course, I was more attracted to my own kind—that is to say 'the noblemen'—especially at the beginning. Yet from among the three former Russian noblemen who were in our prison (Akim Akimovich, the spy A—v, and the one who was thought to have been a patricide), the only one I had anything to do with was Akim Akimovich. I approached him, I must confess, out of despair, at moments of the worst boredom, when there was no choice. In the last chapter I made an attempt to divide everyone up into categories; now, remembering Akim Akimovich, I think I might add one more such category, of which he would be the sole member. This would be the category of totally indifferent prisoners. Of course, there cannot be—and indeed among us there were not—people so totally indifferent that they do not care whether they live in prison or at large, and yet Akim Akimovich seemed to be an exception. He even organised his life in the prison, as if he planned to spend the rest of his days there. Everything around him—his mattress, pillows and household utensils—was arranged so compactly and solidly, obviously for long usage. There was nothing of the bivouac or temporary life here. He still had many years to serve, and I do not suppose he ever thought about his release. But even if he had resigned himself, he had done it not at the bidding of his heart, but rather through subordination, which in his case was really one and the same. He was a kindly man and even helped me at the beginning with advice and with a few favours. I must admit, however, that there were times when he unwittingly drove me to desperation, especially at the beginning, when he only exacerbated my state of depression which had been quite bad enough without him. Yet it was because of my depression that I had started talking to him in the first place. One longs for a sincere word, even an acrimonious or impatient one, even for a bit of spite. We could at least have cursed our fate together. But Akim Akimovich just remained silent, pasting his little lanterns together, or else describing some parade or other in such and such a year telling me who had been commander of the division, his name and patronymic, whether he had been pleased with the parade or not, and how the signals and skirmishing excercise had been changed and so on, all delivered in the same even, prudish tone, like water dripping, a drop at a time. He hardly ever got excited, even when telling me of the Saint Anna sword decoration which he had been awarded for his participation in one of the Caucasian campaigns. His voice simply grew extraordinarily important and weighty. As he said the words 'Saint Anna' he let his voice drop slightly, to a sort of mysterious hush, after which he remained pointedly silent and sedate for about three minutes... There were some rather silly moments during that first year when I would almost—and always very suddenly—start to hate Akim Akimovich, for no reason at all, and silently curse my fate for having put me head to head with him on the bed-shelf. Within an hour I was usually reproaching myself for this. This only happened during the first year, however. Later I managed to reconcile myself completely to his personality, and I felt ashamed of my earlier silliness. There were never—as far as I remember—any open quarrels between us.

Apart from these three Russians, there were about eight other nobles in the prison during my time there. I became quite close friends with some of them, though not all, and was glad to do so. However, even the best of them were rather morbid, exclusive and extremely intolerant. At a later date I stopped talking to two of them completely. Only three of them were well educated: B—sky, M—ky and the older man Zh—ky, who had at one time been a professor of mathematics somewhere. He was a good and kind old man, extremely eccentric, who despite his education seemed to be very narrow-minded. M—ky and B—sky were completely different. I grew very close to M—ky almost immediately. I never quarrelled with him and I had great respect for him; yet somehow I never really came to love him or become permanently attached to him. He was a profoundly suspicious and embittered character, with an amazing ability to keep himself under very tight control. And it was this too superb ability that I did not like in him. I could sense that he would never really bare his soul in front of anyone. I may be wrong, however. His was a strong and very noble personality. His deep and hidden scepticism was revealed by his extraordinary, even somewhat Jesuitical, skill and caution in his dealings with others. Yet he suffered inwardly from this very duality: from the conflict of his scepticism with his deep and unshakeable belief in some very particular convictions and hopes. Despite his considerable worldly cunning he lived in a state of irreconcilable enmity with B—sky and his friend T—sky. B—sky was in bad health, susceptible to consumption, irritable and nervous, though actually very kind, and even great-hearted. His irritability sometimes developed into extreme intolerance and peevishness. I could not bear this side of his character, and I later broke off with him completely, but I never ceased loving him; whereas, although I never argued with M—ky, yet I never loved him. Having parted company with B—sky, it so happened that I also had to part with T—sky, the very same young man whom I mentioned in the previous chapter in connection with the complaint. I was very sorry about this. Though T—sky was not an educated man, he was kind and courageous—a nice young man in a word. The thing was that he loved and respected B—sky so much, and held him in such reverence that anyone who disagreed with him even slightly immediately became an enemy in his eyes. I believe it was also over B—sky that he broke off with M—ky, although he tried not to do this for quite some time. They were all, however, morally ill, bitter, irritable and suspicious. This is understandable: it was much harder for them than it was for us. They were all far from their homeland. Some had been sent here for long terms—for ten or twelve years—and, what is more important, they regarded the people around them with deep prejudice. In the other prisoners they saw only brutality and nothing more; they could not, and did not even want to see any goodness or anything human in them whatsoever, which was also quite understandable as it was force of circumstances and fate that had compelled them to adopt this unfortunate attitude. Naturally, they felt utterly wretched in prison. They were kind and friendly towards the Circassians, the Tatars and Isai Fomich; but they avoided all the other prisoners with disgust. The only other person they respected was the Old Believer from Starodubye Settlement. It was a remarkable fact, however, that never, during my whole time in gaol, did any of these other prisoners ever reproach them with their origin, or beliefs, or their way of thinking. This is sometimes—though very rarely, in fact—the attitude of our common people towards foreigners, particularly Germans. They laugh at the Germans actually—and that is all. To our common Russian people, a German represents something extremely comic. And yet they treated the Poles with much more respect than they had for us, their fellow Russians, and they never *went for them* at all. The Poles, though, did not deign to take any notice of this fact or take it into account. I started to talk about T—sky. He was the man who, when these people were first brought to our fortress from their first place of exile, carried B—sky in his arms for almost the entire journey after the halfway stage, when the latter, who was both sickly and physically weak, began to grow tired very quickly. Their previous place of exile had been U—gorsk, where they lived well, as least much better than here in our fortress. They had, however, begun a correspondence, which was actually quite innocent, with some exiles in another town, and for this three of them were transferred to our fortress, where they could be kept more closely under surveillance by the higher authorities. Their third friend was Zh—ky. M—ky had been alone in our gaol before they arrived. How bitterly miserable he must have been during that first year!

This Zh—ky was the old man I have already mentioned who was always praying. All our political prisoners were young, some very young; only Zh—ky was over fifty. He was an honest man, of course, but somewhat queer. His companions B—sky and T—sky disliked him so intensely that they would not even talk to him, and attested him as stubborn and quarrelsome. I do not know how true this was. I think that in prison—like in any other place where people are brought together against their will—quarrels and even hatreds start sooner than in places where people are free. There are many fomenting circumstances. Zh—ky was indeed rather stupid and narrow-minded, and perhaps even unpleasant. None of the rest of the fraternity got on with him. I never quarrelled with him, but neither did I grow particularly close to him. He seemed to know his own subject of mathematics very well. I can remember to this day how he was forever struggling, in his broken Russian, to explain to me some special system of astronomy which he had invented. I was told he had published it some time ago, but it had only evoked ridicule in scientific circles. I think he was not quite right in the head. All day long he would be down on his knees praying. This won him the respect of the whole prison, and this respect lasted until the day he died. He died in the prison hospital, before my very eyes, after a grave illness. He had in fact enjoyed the immediate respect of the prisoners from the day he came into the prison, owing to his encounter with the Major. He and his companions had not been shaved on the way from U—gorsk, and their beards had grown, so when they were taken up to see the Major, the latter flew into a rage at this insubordination—although they were in no way responsible for it.

"What on earth do they look like?" he roared. "Vagrants! Tramps!"

Zh—ky, who did not understand Russian very well, and who thought the Major was asking them if they were tramps or vagrants, answered:

"We are not tramps. We are political prisoners."

"Wha-a-at! Talking back, are you!" bellowed the Major. "To the guardhouse with him! Give him a hundred lashes this minute!"

This punishment was carried out. The old man took it without a word, biting his hand, but not uttering a single cry or moan, and not even moving. B—sky and T—sky had meanwhile been brought into the gaol. M—ky was already waiting for them near the gates, and he flung his arms around the two and hugged them, even though he had never known them before. Still chafing from the reception given them by the Major, they told M—ky everything about Zh—ky. I remember how M—ky told me about it. "I was beside myself," he said. "I could not understand what was happening to me, I was shaking all over. I waited for Zh—ky at the gates. He was to come straight from the guardhouse where they were flogging him. Suddenly the gate opened and Zh—ky, without looking at anyone, his face pale and his bloodless lips trembling, made his way through the prisoners who had assembled in the yard when they heard a nobleman was being flogged. He entered the barrack, went straight over to his place and, without saying a word to anyone, knelt down and started to pray. This amazed the prisoners and even moved them.

"When I saw that grey-haired old man, who had left his wife and children behind him in his motherland," said M—ky, "when I saw him down on his knees praying after his shameful punishment, I rushed out of the barrack and for two solid hours I could not come back to my senses. I was in a frenzy..." From that moment onwards, the prisoners began to treat Zh—ky with great respect, and they always behaved towards him with deference. What they particularly liked was that he had not cried out while he was being beaten.

One must tell the whole truth though. One must not judge the way exiles from noble families—whether Russian or Polish—were treated by the Siberian authorities from this episode alone. All this example shows is that it is possible to come up against a vicious character, and naturally if this vicious character happens to be an independent and high-ranking authority somewhere, and particularly if he takes a personal dislike to an exile, then the fate of that exile will be very difficult indeed. One has to admit, however, that the highest Siberian authorities—who set the tone for all the lower commanders, are very discriminating about exiled noblemen, and sometimes they even grant them privileges which prisoners from the lower classes do not enjoy. The reasons are clear enough. First, these highest authorities are themselves noblemen; second, there had been instances of noblemen who refused to submit to the birch rods and attacked the floggers with various ghastly consequences; last—and most important in my view—about thirty-five years ago, a large party of exiled nobles had arrived in Siberia all together,[16] and in the course of these thirty odd years they built up so splendid a reputation for themselves and gained such recognition throughout Siberia that the authorities of my time from long-established habit automatically regarded convicted noblemen belonging to a certain category not as they did all other prisoners. Following this example of the higher authorities, their subordinates also became accustomed to this attitude, modelling it submissively and obediently on the opinions of those higher up. Many of these subordinate commanders, however, took a dim view of this; mentally they criticised the instructions from higher up, and would have been only too pleased if they had been allowed to do things as they saw best themselves. They were not really allowed to, however. I have good reason to say this, and here is why. The second category of convicts to which I belonged, and which was made up of prisoners who were kept in the fortress under military jurisdiction, was incomparably harder than the other two: that is to say the third category (in the factories) and the first (in the mines). It was harder not only for noblemen, but for all the other prisoners as well, because the authorities and the organisation of this category were military, much the same as in the penal companies in Russia. The military authorities are stricter; the discipline is stiffer. Prisoners are always in chains, always guarded, always locked up. In the other two categories this is not done to the same degree. This, at least, is what the prisoners in our gaol used to say, and there were some real experts among them. They would happily have gone over to the first category, which the law regards as the hardest; they even dreamed about it. Those who had been in the penal companies in Russia, on the other hand, talked of them with horror, and assured us that there was no worse place in the whole of Russia than those penal companies in the fortresses, and that compared to them Siberia was paradise. Consequently, if prisoners from the nobility were regarded in a slightly more favourable light than the other prisoners under a regime as stern as ours, with its military authorities, under the watchful eye of the Governor-General himself, and taking into account that there were (occasionally) cases when officious outsiders, out of spite or zeal, stealthily informed the pertinent quarters that such and such an 'unreliable' commander was letting a certain type of prisoner take things too easy, then they must have been given even more preferential treatment in the third category and the first category. Consequently, from my knowledge of the place where I was, I believe I can form a general judgement of this matter as regards the whole of Siberia. All the rumours and exiles' stories which reached my ears on this subject from the prisons for the first and the third categories confirmed my opinion. In fact, in our gaol, the authorities did pay particular attention to all the nobles and treated us more cautiously. But as regards work and general conditions no allowances were made for us whatever. We did the same jobs, wore the same shackles, and were kept under the same locks as all the other prisoners. Actually, it would not have been possible to make life easier for us. I know that during this *long ago but not-so-distant past* there were so many informers in the town, so many intrigues, so many people plotting behind each others' backs, that the prison authorities were quite understandably afraid of being denounced. And in those days what could have been worse than someone saying they were giving a certain category of prisoners an easy life! So they all lived in fear, and we were treated like the other prisoners. True, some exception was made in the case of corporal punishment. Certainly they would have flogged us with a clear conscience had we done anything to merit it—committed some misdemeanour or other. Their sense of duty and equality where corporal punishment was concerned would have demanded it. Still, they would not have flogged us for no reason, for a whim, as they sometimes flogged the other prisoners, especially if the commander was some junior officer who was eager to show his authority and make an impression whenever the opportunity presented itself. We heard that the Commandant grew terribly angry with the Major when he heard the story of the old man Zh ky, and reprimanded him, asking him if he would be so kind as to keep a tighter rein upon himself in the future. Everybody told me this. They also said that even the Governor-General himself, who trusted our Major and liked him for his executive zeal and abilities, had also told him off when he learned of this story. And the Major took this into consideration. Much as he wanted to get his hands on M—ky, whom he hated because of A—v's slandering of him, he simply could not give him a flogging, though he searched hard for a pretext, victimised him, and tried to get under his skin. Soon the whole town knew the story of Zh—ky, and the general feeling was that the Major was in the wrong; many rebuked him, and even said unpleasant things to him. I can remember my own first meeting with the Major. They had already frightened us—myself and another prisoner from the nobility who entered the prison with me—with stories of the man's unpleasant character while we were still in Tobolsk. Some noble exiles (old hands who had been there for twenty-five years) who greeted us with deep sympathy and kept in touch with us during our whole period in the deportation gaol, warned us against our future commanding officer, and promised to do everything in their power, through various connections, to protect us from his persecutions. The Governor-General's three daughters who had come from Russia to visit their father had received letters from these exiles, and I believe they spoke to him about us. What could he do though? He only mentioned to the Major that he might be a little more scrupulous with us. We (that is to say, my friend and I) arrived in the town after two in the afternoon, and were straightaway taken by the guards to see our liege lord. We stood and waited for him in the entrance hall. Meanwhile the prison sergeant had already been sent for. The Major came in immediately after him. His mean red face, covered with blackheads, had an extremely depressing effect on us. He made me think of a cruel spider about to pounce on an unfortunate fly caught in his web.

"What is your name?" he asked my friend. He talked quickly, sharply and abruptly, in a way that was clearly intended to impress us.

My friend told him.

"And yours?" he went on, addressing me now, and staring at me through his spectacles.

I told him.

"Sergeant! Take them over to the gaol this minute! Have them shaved in the guardhouse for the civilian category: straightaway, half the head. See that they're re-shackled by tomorrow, at the latest. What sort of overcoats are these? Where did you get them from?" he asked us, suddenly noticing our grey coats with yellow circles on the back which had been given us in Tobolsk, and in which we came into his presence. "This must be some kind of new uniform? Still in the design phase in Petersburg ... I suppose!" he said, turning each of us around in front of him. "Have they got anything with them?" he said suddenly, addressing the escort who had brought us.

"They have their own clothes, Your Excellency," answered the gendarme, instantly drawing himself up with a slight jerk. The Major was well known to everybody; everybody had heard of him. He struck fear into them all.

"Take it all away from them. Return only their under-clothes to them—and even then only the white ones. If they've any coloured underwear, you can take that away from them too. The rest must be sold at auction. Put the money in the prison fund. Prisoners," he continued, looking at us severely, "do not have their own property. Now, look here you two, make sure you behave yourselves! Make sure I don't hear any reports of you! Or else ... it'll be cor-por-al pun-ish-ment for you, for the smallest offence ... birch rods!"

Unused to being greeted in such a manner, I felt quite ill all evening. This feeling was, of course, enhanced by what I saw in the gaol. I have already given an account of my entry into the prison, however.

I have just mentioned that the authorities did not make any allowances for us in work and did not dare to do so. There was however one occasion when they tried to do this. For three whole months B—sky and I went to the engineering office as scribes. This was arranged on the quiet by the engineering authorities. Or rather, everyone else who needed to know, in fact, probably did know—but feigned ignorance. This happened when G—kov was in command. This Lieutenant-Colonel G—kov came to us out of the blue, spent only a very short time with us—six months or less if I remember correctly—and then left for Russia, having made an extremely strong impression on all the prisoners. To say the prisoners loved him would be an understatement, they adored him—if such a word can be used in this context. How he achieved this, I do not know, but he won them over from the very beginning. "Father! Father! No one needs a father with this man around!" the prisoners used to say all the time he was in command of the engineering department. He was a terrible debauchee, I believe, a rather short fellow with an arrogant, self-assured look. He was very kind to the prisoners, almost tender, and really loved them like a father. Quite why he loved them so much I cannot say, but he would never pass a prisoner without saying some kind, cheerful word to him, or cracking a joke with him, and, what was most important, he managed to do this without any hint of superiority, with none of the inequality of a commander dispensing favours from on high. He was their comrade, one of themselves. Yet despite this instinctively democratic conduct of his, the prisoners were never once guilty of displaying undue familiarity or lack of respect. Quite the opposite. A prisoner's whole face would light up as he met his Commander, and taking his hat off, he would already be smiling as G—kov approached. And if the Commander actually spoke to him—he was the happiest of mortals. That is how popular people can be! He had the air of a brave, his posture erect, his shoulders thrown well back. "An eagle of a man!" the prisoners used to say. He could not make their lives easier in any way, of course. He was only in charge of the engineering works, which followed its own daily routine—fixed forever by the regulations—under him as under any other commander. When he came across a party of prisoners whose work was finished he might perhaps let them leave early before the drum sounded, without keeping them unnecessarily late. But it was his trust in the prisoners that most attracted them to him, the absence of any pettifogging, irritability, and any other insulting forms practised by men in his position. If he had lost a thousand roubles and the worst thief among us had found the money, he would have returned it to him, I do believe. Yes! I am certain that is how it would have been. And how deeply sympathetic our prisoners were when they discovered that their Commander—their eagle!—had fallen out forever with their detested Major. This happened during his very first month here. The two men had worked together before. They met as good friends who had not seen each other for a long time, and went on a spree together. Then suddenly they fell out. They quarrelled and G—kov became the Major's mortal foe. There was even talk that they had come to blows, which (knowing how often our Major got into fights) may well have been true. When the prisoners heard about it, their joy knew no bounds. "You wouldn't expect old eight-eyes to get on with a fellow like that, you know. He's an eagle is that one, whereas ours is a..." and here they usually called him a short unprintable word. They were terribly curious to know which of the two men had beaten the other, and if the story of the fight had turned out to be only a rumour (as may well have been the case) our prisoners would have been most disappointed. "Well, surely the Commander would have got the upper hand..." they would say. "He's a little fellow, but nippy, whereas that other one, I bet, he hid under the bed." It was not long before G—kov left, however, and the prisoners again fell into despondency. As a matter of fact all the engineering commanders in our place were fine men. There was a changeover three or four times during my sentence. "There'll never be one like him though," said the prisoners. "Like an eagle he was. An eagle and protector." Well, this G—kov was very fond of us noblemen and gave orders for B—sky and me to be given work in the office from time to time. After his departure, this was put on a more regular footing. There were people among the engineers—one in particular—who were very well disposed towards us. We used to go to the office and copy various papers, even our handwriting improved, and then, without warning, an order came from the higher authorities to send us back to our previous jobs at once. Someone had already informed on us. But it was really for the best; the office was beginning to get on our nerves. After that, for about two years, B—sky and I were almost always detailed to the same place of work, more often than not to the workshop. We used to chat together a lot: talking about our hopes and ideas. He was a nice man, but his convictions were sometimes most peculiar and extreme. It often turns out like that with one particular type of person: they are very clever, but they sometimes have utterly paradoxical notions. They have suffered so much for their convictions in life, paid so dearly for them that it is too painful and almost impossible for them to tear themselves away from them. B—sky was hurt by each of my objections and retorted with some cutting remarks. In some things, perhaps, he had more reason on his side than I did—I do not know. Finally we had to part company, and this was very painful for me. We had been through so much together by then.

Meanwhile M—ky was growing ever sadder and gloomier as the years went by, sinking deeper and deeper into the slough of misery. During my first years in the gaol, he had been more communicative, and giving much more of himself, quite freely and openly. When I came into the gaol, he had already been living there for more than two years. At first he showed considerable interest in what had been happening in the world during those two years and which he knew nothing about. He asked me a lot of questions, listened to my answers, and was obviously stirred. Then, as the years passed, an inner tension began to build up in him, burdening his heart. Ash was covering the coals. Bitterness was welling up inside him more and more. *"Je hais ces brigands,"* he repeated to me ten times over, looking with hatred at the prisoners—whom I had already come to know more closely. No argument that I put forward in their favour had any effect. He did not seem to understand what I was talking about. Sometimes, however, he would agree with me absent-mindedly, then on the very next day, repeat: *"Je hais ces brigands."* We often talked French by the way, and there was one works supervisor, a private called Dranishnikov, who from some obscure line of reasoning, christened us 'the medics'. The only occasion when M—ky showed any sign of emotion was when he remembered his mother. "She is old," he used to say to me, "and she is ill. She loves me more than life itself. And here I am, not knowing whether she's alive or dead. It was enough for her to be told how I had been made to run the gauntlet..." M—ky was not a noble, and he had been given corporal punishment before being sent into exile. These memories made him clench his teeth and look away. He had recently begun to keep more and more to himself. One morning, shortly after eleven, he was summoned to the Commandant. The Commandant came out to greet him with a cheerful smile.

"Well, M—ky," he asked him, "what did you dream about last night?"

("I started, as if a sword had pierced me to the heart," M—ky told me when he came back.)

"I dreamt I had a letter from my mother," he answered.

"Much better news than that," said the Commandant. "Much, much better! You're free. Your mother put in a plea for you, and her plea was granted. Here's the letter from your mother, and here's the order concerning you. You shall leave the gaol immediately."

He returned to us, looking pale and still dazed by the news. We congratulated him. He shook hands with us. His hands were trembling and cold. Many of the other prisoners also congratulated him. They were happy that fortune had smiled on him.

He was released from prison but had to live in a district designated for exiles. He stayed on in our town. A job was soon found for him. At first, whenever he could, he used to come over to the gaol and tell us the news. He was mostly interested in political news.

Of the four others, apart from M—ky, T—sky, B—sky and Zh—ky, two were still very young and had been given very short sentences. They were uneducated men, but they were honest, simple, and straightforward. The third, A—chukovsky was too simple and had no particularly interesting traits, but the fourth, B—m, who was already middle-aged, produced the rottenest impression on all of us. I do not know how he came to be included with this category, and he himself denied any connection with the others. He was a crude, petty-bourgeois sort of character, he had the habits and code of a shopkeeper who had made his money by overcharging his customers—one kopek here, three kopeks there. He was completely uneducated and showed no interest in anything except his own trade. He was a house painter, an exceptionally good one, a marvel of a house painter. The authorities came to hear of his abilities, and he was soon in demand the whole town over as a painter of walls and ceilings. Within two years he had painted almost all the houses and flats provided for the officials who paid him out of their own pockets, so he was anything but hard-up. The best part of it was that some of his companions were sent along with him to help with the work. Of the three who were always sent, two learned the trade from him and one of them, T—zhevsky, became as good as B—m. Our Major, who occupied one of these houses, also demanded, in his turn, that B—m should paint all his walls and ceilings. And B—m did his very best. It was better done than even the Governor-General's house. The Major's house was a dilapidated one-storey wooden building, very shabby on the outside. But inside it was painted like a palace, and the Major was absolutely delighted... He rubbed his hands together in glee, and talked about how he must definitely get married now. "A man simply must marry with quarters such as these!" he added, terribly seriously. He grew more and more pleased with B—m and—because of him—with the others who worked with him. The work continued for a whole month. During the course of this month the Major quite changed his opinion of every one of us, and took on the role of our benefactor. It reached such a point that one day he suddenly summoned Zh—ky from the gaol and said to him:

"Zh—ky! I insulted you. I had you flogged for no reason. I know it, and I am truly sorry. Do you understand what I am saying? I am sorry, *I myself*!"

Zh—ky answered that he did understand.

"Do you understand that I, your master, have summoned you here to ask you forgiveness? Do you feel this? What are *you* compared with me? You are a worm! Less than a worm! A prisoner! While I, through the grace of God,* am a major. A major! Do you understand what I am saying?"

Zh—ky answered that he understood that too.

"Well, now I am going to make up with you. But do you feel ... do you feel this fully ... in all its significance? Are you capable of understanding this, of feeling it? Just think about it ... a major..."

And so on.

Zh—ky recounted this scene to me. So there must have been some human feelings in that drunk, quarrelsome, and unstable man. Considering his notions and level of development, such behaviour might be considered almost generous. On the other hand, it may be that a great deal of all this could be accounted for by his drunkenness.

The Major's dream did not come true. He did not marry, although he had quite made up his mind to do so when his house had been fixed up. Instead of getting married he was put on trial, and ordered to resign. During the prosecution all his

*Author's note. 'Through the grace of God' is an expression which was often used quite literally during my time in prison, not only by the Major, but also by the junior officers, particularly those who had risen from the ranks.

old sins were dragged out into the open. He had once been the governor of this town, as far as I remember... The blow fell quite unexpectedly. The news about his downfall cheered everyone up immensely, and was the pretext for a holiday and celebration in the gaol. The Major was said to have wept buckets of tears, like an old woman. But there was nothing for it. He resigned, sold his pair of greys and then his estate, and even fell upon hard times. We used to come across him, at a later date, wearing a threadbare civilian coat and a peaked cap. He would look maliciously at the prisoners, but his aura had deserted him completely once he took off his full dress uniform. In his uniform he was a holy terror, a god. Now in an ordinary civilian coat, he suddenly became a nonentity and looked a bit like a footman. It is truly amazing how much a uniform means for these people.

IX

An Escape

Shortly after the Major's replacement, some fundamental changes were made in our gaol. Hard labour was abolished and a penal company under military command established in its place, along the lines of the penal companies in Russia. This meant that second category convicts were no longer sent to our gaol. From now on it received only military prisoners, that is people who had not been deprived of their civic rights, but were soldiers, the same as any others, with the difference that they were serving short terms of imprisonment (up to a maximum of six years) and upon release they would rejoin the ranks of their battalions. Those who committed a new crime and were returned to prison for a second term, would be given twenty-year sentences, just as before. We had actually had a category of military prisoners even before this change, but they were only with us because there was no other place to put them. Now, however, the entire gaol was given over to this military category. It goes without saying that the existing prisoners—the civilian convicts who had been deprived of all their civic rights, who had been branded, and had half their heads shaved, remained in the prison until the end of their terms; but there were no new-comers, so gradually people would be leaving and in ten years' time there would be not a single regular prisoner in our gaol. The special category also remained in the gaol, and occasional-ly men sentenced for serious military crimes were transferred here, until the opening of the more rigorous hard-labour pris-ons in Siberia. Thus, life actually continued much as before for us: the same provisions, the same work and almost the same rules and regulations. It was only that the authorities had changed and the structure became more complicated. A Staff Officer and a Company Commander were appointed, and also four senior officers, who took it in turn to be on gaol duty. The duties of invalid soldiers were taken over by twelve sergeants and one quartermaster-sergeant. Divisions were set up in tens, with corporals appointed from among the prisoners themselves (only nominally, of course), and naturally Akim Akimovich immediately became one of them. The whole of this new organi-sation, and the entire gaol with all its officers and prisoners, remained under the overall control of the Commandant just as before. This is all that happened. Naturally, the prisoners were very agitated at first, and talked about it a great deal, making wild guesses and trying to see through their new commanders. When they saw that it would all, in essence, remain as it had been, they immediately calmed down again, and life continued the same as ever. The most important thing was that everybody was freed from our Major; everyone drew a sigh of relief and cheered up. They no longer wore a cowed look. They all knew that they could, if necessary, explain things to those above them, that the innocent might be punished instead of the guilty only by mistake. Liquor continued to be sold in the gaol, on the same old terms as before, despite the fact that the invalid sol-diers had now been replaced by sergeants. The majority of these sergeants turned out to be decent sorts, they were quite bright and understood the situation. At first some of them showed a tendency to swagger and thought, from inexperience, of course, that they could treat the prisoners like soldiers. But they, too, soon came to realise how the land lay. For the few who refused to mend their ways, the situation was made clear by the prisoners themselves. There were some rough clashes. Prisoners would tempt a sergeant with liquor, get him drunk, and then tell him afterwards, without ceremony, that he had been drinking with them, so... It all finished with the sergeants turning a blind eye or looking the other way when the intestines full of vodka were smuggled in and sold. There was more to it than that though. The sergeants now went to the market, just as the invalid soldiers used to do, and brought back buns and beef and anything else, in other words ran errands that were not too shameful for their official position. Why all these changes took place or why a penal company was organised at all, I simply do not know. It all happened during the last years of my term. But I still had another two years to live out under the new regime...

Should I recount my whole life in gaol, though, year by year? I do not think so. If I were to write it all down in sequence and recount everything that happened, everything I saw and experienced during those years, I would produce three or four times as many chapters as I have already. Such a description, I am afraid, would inevitably grow tedious. All the happenings would sound monotonous, especially to a reader who has already succeeded in forming some sort of satisfactory notion of prison life for the second category, as I have described it in the chapters so far. My aim was to present the entire gaol and everything I lived through during those years in one clear and graphic picture. I do not know if I have achieved this aim. And it is not really for me to judge. I am convinced, however, that I could end on this. Besides, I myself am sometimes seized by anguish when remembering... And I could hardly remember everything anyway. The years that followed seem to have become erased from my mind. I am sure there are many things that have completely disappeared from my memory. I remember, for example, that each year, exactly like the one before, passed so slowly and so miserably. I remember that those long boring days were as monotonous as the sound of rainwater dripping from a roof, drop by drop. I remember that it was only my passionate longing for resurrection, rejuvenation, and a new life that gave me the strength to wait and to hope. In the end, I managed to steel myself: I waited; I counted off every day; and although there were still a thousand of them in front of me, I counted off each one of them with pleasure, saw it off, buried it, and with the beginning of another day felt happy that there were now not one thousand days, but nine hundred and ninety-nine. I remember how, all this time, despite having hundreds of fellow prisoners, I was most dreadfully alone, and how at last I grew enamoured of this loneliness. Alone in my heart, I reviewed my former life in its entirety, turned it over in my mind right down to the smallest detail, thought over my past, and passed my own harsh and inexorable judgement upon myself. There were even times when I blessed my fate for sending me this solitude, without which neither this trial of myself, nor this harsh revision of my previous life, would have come about. How hopefully my heart beat in those minutes! I thought—I resolved—I swore to myself that there would be no more such errors in my life in future, no more downfalls like before. I mapped out a programme for my entire future life, and resolved to follow it resolutely. A blind belief that I could and would carry all this out was born inside me... I waited. I wished my freedom would come sooner. I wanted to test myself anew, in a new struggle. At moments a feverish impatience gripped me... It pains me to remember what went on in my soul at that time... Of course, all this concerns just me alone... But I have written it all down because I think that everyone will be able to understand it, because the same would happen to anyone if he were put in gaol for a certain term in the prime of life.

But what point is there in talking about this? I had better give an account of something else, so as not to break off abruptly.

It has occurred to me that somebody might well ask: is it really impossible to escape from the gaol, and did nobody actually escape from your place in all those years? I have already explained above how a prisoner who has already spent two or three years in gaol, begins to value those years and comes involuntarily to the conclusion that it is better to live out the remainder of his term without inviting danger or trouble and then be legally released for settlement. True, such calculations only enter the heads of prisoners who do not have to serve a very long term. Someone with a long sentence may well be prepared to take the risk... Somehow it just did not happen in our place. I do not know whether the prisoners were too scared, or too closely watched with military strictness, or whether the terrain around our town (open steppe) did not favour it. It is very difficult to say. I think all these factors played their part. It really was very hard to run away from our place. Yet there was one case during my time there. Two prisoners—both very serious criminals—decided to take the risk.

After the replacement of the Major, A—v (the prisoner who had been his informer about the whole gaol) was left completely out in the cold, without any protection whatsoever. He was still very young, but with the years his character was growing stronger and more stable. Generally speaking, he was bold, resolute and very bright. Had he been set free, he would no doubt have continued as an informer and made a living in various underhand ways but without foolishly allowing himself to be caught and sentenced to hard labour again. While he was in our place, he tried his hand at making fake passports, but I am not really sure about this. It is something I heard the other prisoners saying. They said that he had been doing something of the kind when he was the Major's informer, and that, naturally, he had made some money from it. It seemed, in other words, that he was prepared to take any risk to change his fate. Once I happened to catch a glimpse of his inner self. He was cynical to the point of the most outrageous arrogance and the coldest mockery, which was intolerably repulsive. I believe that if he badly wanted a drink of vodka, and there was no way of getting it except by stabbing someone, he would have certainly committed the murder if only it could be done quietly, and no one would ever know. In prison he learned to be prudent and calculating. And it was this man who attracted the particular attention of Kulikov, a prisoner in the special category.

I have already said something about Kulikov. He was no longer young, but he was a passionate, vigorous, strong man of extreme and varied capabilities. He had reserves of strength in him, and he wanted to go on living. Such people as he still want to go on living even when they are very old. If I had set my mind to wondering why no one ran away from our place, then my thoughts would have turned primarily to Kulikov. Kulikov did take the risk. Which of the two had more influence upon the other, A—v on Kulikov or Kulikov on A—v, it is very difficult to say. They made a pair, and were extremely well suited to each other for such an enterprise. They became friends. Kulikov, I imagine, relied on A—v for faking the passports for them. A—v was a former nobleman, who had moved in high society, and this promised some variety in their future adventures, if they could only get as far as Russia. Who knows what agreement they reached or what hopes they had, but their hopes must have been a cut above the usual dreams of wandering about Siberia... Kulikov was a born actor, capable of playing many different roles in life. He had reasons to hope for a great deal, and for variety at the very least. Prison life must have weighed heavily on such people. So, they arranged to escape.

It was, however, impossible to escape without a guard. And so they had to persuade one of the guards to join them. In one of the battalions stationed in our fortress, there was a Pole: an energetic kind of man—middle-aged, brave, and serious—who had perhaps deserved a better fate in life. In his young days, just after being posted out to Siberia, he had deserted because he was so miserably homesick. He was caught, flogged, and sentenced to about two years in one of the penal companies. When he returned to regular military service he had a change of heart, and dedicated himself to the service with all the zeal he had in him. For exemplary conduct, he was promoted to corporal. He was ambitious and vain, and knew his own worth. This showed even in his appearance and in his manner of talking. I came across him among the other guards several times during the course of these years. I had also heard some things about him from the Poles. I imagine that the misery and homesickness he once felt had been transformed inside him into a hidden, repressed, but constant hatred. He was a man who might agree to anything, and Kulikov had made no mistake in picking him out as an accomplice. This guard's surname was Koller. An agreement was reached, a day was fixed. This was in June, when the weather was hot. The climate in this town of ours is pretty stable. In summer the weather stays much the same, very hot, in answer to a tramp's prayer, as they say. The fugitives could not just set out from the fortress, of course. The entire town is situated on the crest of a hill in open country. There is no forest for quite some distance. They had to change into civilian clothes, and for this they had to get into the suburbs, where Kulikov had long had a kind of hideout. I do not know if their suburban friends had been in league with them. I would have thought so, although during the investigation which followed, it was not absolutely clear. That year, in a corner of the suburbs, a young and very comely hussy who went by the name of Vanka-Tanka, was just embarking upon her career. She showed great promise of rising to better things—as indeed she did later on. The other name she went by was 'Hotsy'. Apparently she also played some part in the operation. Kulikov had been lavishing his money on her for a whole year. So our two braves appeared for the roll call in the morning, and very cleverly contrived to be sent off to work with Shilkin, the stove-maker and plasterer, to give a coat of plaster to the empty battalion barracks, from which the soldiers had departed for their summer camp. A—v and Kulikov went along to act as assistants. Koller appeared as the guard at just the right moment, and—as two men were required to guard three people and Koller was a corporal and an old hand at the business—a raw recruit had been sent along with him to learn the ropes. So apparently our two fugitives had the strongest influence over Koller and he must have really believed in them, if he—a clever, staid and prudent man, with many years of army service behind him—successful years too, especially recently—had decided to risk everything and go along with them.

They arrived at the barracks. It was about six o'clock in the morning, and there was nobody there but themselves. After working for an hour or so, Kulikov and A—v told Shilkin that they were going over to the workshop, firstly to see someone, and secondly to collect some tools which, as it turned out, they did not have with them. They had to be very cunning with Shilkin there, and behave as naturally as possible. He was a Muscovite, a stove-maker by trade, a wily and clever man, not given to talking. In appearance he was puny, and haggard-faced. He should by rights have lived out his days like a true Muscovite, walking about in a waistcoat and caftan, but fortune had had other plans for him, and after a lot of wandering here and there he had ended up permanently in the special category—the section for the most dangerous military criminals. What he had done to bring such a plight upon himself I do not know, but I never noticed any signs of discontent in him. He behaved very quietly and consistently. From time to time he got drunk as a lord, but even then he continued to behave very well. He did not know what was afoot, of course, but he had very keen eyes. Kulikov gave him a wink and a sign to tell him that they were really going to fetch the vodka that had been laid up in the workshop since the day before. This won Shilkin over. He let them go without suspecting anything, and stayed behind with only the recruit, while Kulikov, A—v and Koller set off into the suburbs.

Half an hour went by and the three had still not returned. Suddenly, with a flash of hindsight, Shilkin began to wonder. He'd been through the mill had this Shilkin. He began remembering. Kulikov had been in a strange sort of mood and he'd twice seen him whispering together with A—v, and Kulikov had winked at him a couple of times; he'd seen that clearly enough. He remembered all this now. There'd been something odd about Koller as well. That is, when he was leaving, he had started giving the recruit instructions about how to behave while he was gone. That was not really natural somehow, especially from Koller. To put it in a nutshell, the more Shilkin thought about things, the more suspicious he became. Meanwhile more time went by and they still did not return. Shilkin's anxiety reached breaking point. He knew very well what a risk he was running: the suspicions of the authorities might turn on him. They might think he had let his companions go, by mutual agreement, knowing full well what they were up to, and if he put off reporting their disappearance, these suspicions would only be reinforced. There was no time to lose. At this point he remembered how Kulikov and A—v had been growing very close recently, how they often whispered together, and often walked about together behind the barracks out of everybody's sight. He remembered how already then he had begun to think that they

326

were up to something... He looked hard at the recruit: he stood there leaning on his rifle, yawning and picking his nose in such an innocent manner that Shilkin did not even think it worth the bother to tell him what was in his mind, but simply ordered him to follow him into the engineering workshop. He wanted to find out if the others had been there. It turned out that no one had seen them there. Any doubts that Shilkin had entertained now vanished. He thought: "They couldn't have just gone into the suburbs to have a drink and a bit of fun as Kulikov sometimes did. They would have told me, that was nothing to make a secret of." Shilkin abandoned his work, and without returning to the barrack, went straight over to the gaol.

It was already close on nine o'clock when he came to the sergeant-major and reported the matter. The sergeant-major was frightened and refused to believe it at first. Shilkin, of course, had only recounted it all as a surmise, a suspicion that had crossed his mind. The sergeant-major immediately dashed off to see the Major. The Major went at once to the Commandant. Within a quarter of an hour, all necessary measures had been taken. The Governor-General himself was informed. The two criminals were important convicts and there might be serious trouble from St. Petersburg. Whether rightly or wrongly, A—v was classed as a political prisoner; Kulikov was from the special category, an arch-criminal, and a military one to boot. There had never been a case of someone escaping from the special category. It was also remembered that according to the rules with prisoners from the special category there should be two guards, or at least one guard for each prisoner, watching them at work. This rule had not been observed. Therefore there might well be trouble. Messengers were dispatched to every region and all the towns and villages in the vicinity, to make known the news of the escaped prisoners and to leave descriptions of them. Cossacks were also sent in pursuit. Letters were written to all the neighbouring uyezds and gubernias. In short, everyone panicked.

Meanwhile, inside the gaol, a different sort of anxiety was spreading. The prisoners, returning from work, heard about the escape at once. The news had already reached everyone. Everyone took it with a feeling of immense secret joy. Everyone's heart sort of jumped. Besides breaking the monotony of gaol life, an escape, and especially an escape like this one, evoked a response from every heart and touched long-forgotten chords— and something like hope, daring, and the possibility of changing one's fate began to stir in everyone's mind. "Some people have escaped, haven't they. So why not?.." And each man, heartened by this thought, looked challengingly at the others. At least, they all suddenly grew proud, and started looking down their noses at the sergeants. Of course, all kinds of officers immediately started arriving at the gaol. The Commandant came in person. People in our barrack felt braced, and their looks were bold, even contemptuous, and there was some firm and silent importance about them, as much as to say: "When we do a thing, we do it properly..." It goes without saying that a general inspection by the authorities was immediately predicted. There would be searches, naturally, and so everything was hidden away in good time. People always locked the stable door after the horse had bolted. That was, in fact, exactly what happened. There was a great deal of fuss and bustle. For all the searching and rummaging through everything, nothing incriminating was found, of course. The prisoners were sent back to their afternoon work under double guard. In the course of the evening, the guards came poking their heads into the barracks every couple of minutes. They made an extra count of the prisoners and there were twice the usual number of miscounts. That created an even greater fuss. Everybody was herded into the yard and counted again. Then the prisoners were counted one more time, inside the barracks. There was quite a hullabaloo, in other words.

The prisoners did not give a damn, though. Each one of them looked incredibly self-confident, and as always happens at times like these, they behaved in a markedly proper manner for the remainder of the evening. "You won't find anything to get at us for." No doubt it had crossed the authorities' minds that there might still be some accomplices of the fugitives left behind in the gaol, and they gave orders that all eyes should be kept open and all ears to the ground. The prisoners, however, simply laughed at this. "Who'd ever leave accomplices behind?" "Things like this are kept hush hush." "And anyway A—v and Kulikov aren't the kind to leave clues behind them. They did the job in a masterly fashion, kept it dark. People like them have gone through fire and water; they could go through locked doors too." The reputation of Kulikov and A—v was growing by the minute, in other words. Everybody was proud of them. Everyone felt that their heroic deed would be passed down generations of prisoners, and would survive the very prison walls themselves.

"Masterminds, they are!" said some people.

"People thought no one would ever run away from here! But they did, didn't they!" added some others.

"Who ran away, who?" said a third man, joining in, and surveying everyone authoritatively. "You a match for them?"

At any other time, a prisoner to whom words such as these were addressed, would most certainly have taken up the challenge and defended his honour. In this case, he stayed modestly silent. "Well, it's true, we aren't all like Kulikov and A—v. You have to prove your worth first..."

"I tell you what, mates! I don't see what keeps us here," a fourth prisoner said, interrupting the silence. Until then he had been sitting modestly in the corner near the kitchen window. He sat with his chin resting in the palm of his hand and spoke in a sing-song voice that seemed to come from some relaxed and self-satisfied inner emotion. "What are we here? We're not like the living when we're alive, and we're not like the dead when we're dead!"

"Shackles aren't shoes, you know—you can't take them off, just like that!"

"Yeah, but look at this Kulikov..." butted in some excitable young greenhorn.

"Kulikov!" one of the others joined in screwing up his eyes contemptuously at the boy. "Kulikov!"

This was his way of saying that there are not many such Kulikovs in the world.

"And that A—v too, mates! He's a slick character he is! Slick as they come!"

329

"You're right there. He could even twist that Kulikov round his little finger. He's too tricky by half."

"I wonder how far they've got now, mates. That's what I'd like to know..."

With this comment, a heated discussion started at once about how far they could have got. Which direction had they gone in? Which would be the best places to pass through? Which volost was the closest to ours? It immediately transpired that there were some who knew the area intimately. They were listened to avidly. Then the talk turned to the kind of people living in the nearby villages; it was agreed they were all no good. Living close to the town, they knew what was healthiest for them. They couldn't be expected to help the fugitives. They'd catch them and give them up.

"The peasants in these parts are nobody's friends. My, they're hard!"

"Unreliable types!"

"Sly characters, these Siberians. You don't want to get caught by them. They'll string you up as soon as look at you."

"That's right, but our fellows'll..."

"Yes, we'll see who comes out on top. Ours are nobody's fools."

"Well, we'll hear what happens, if we're not dead by then."

"You think they'll catch them?"

"They'll never be caught. Not on your life!" shouted another of the young hotheads, banging on the table with his fist.

"Well, we'll wait and see."

"As for me, mates," said Skuratov. "They'd never catch me if I were a tramp."

"Oh wouldn't they now!"

There was an outburst of laughter, but some of the others pretended that they were not interested and would not even listen. But Skuratov was getting quite worked up.

"They'd never catch me!" he went on hotly. "I often think about it, mates, and it makes me quite surprised at myself. I could squeeze through the crack in the door. They'd never catch me."

"Go on with you. When you got hungry you'd go running to the peasants for bread."

Everybody laughed.

"I'd never do that!"

"Oh, shut your mouth! You and your Uncle Vasya did murder for a cow's death,* and that's what you're here for."

The laughter grew louder, with the more serious ones looking on even more indignantly.

"That's a lie!" shouted Skuratov. "That's one of Mikita's tales about me—and it isn't even about me anyway, it's about Vasya. He just dragged me in to spin it out a bit. I'm a Muscovite I am, and I've lived a vagrant's life since I was so high. When the deacon taught me to read and write, he used to pull me by the ear and say: 'Repeat after me, *O Lord, have mercy on me...*' and so on. I used to repeat it after him like this: 'Have mercy on me, policemen, when I'm hauled in.' And I've carried on like that ever since I was a little nipper..."

Everyone burst out laughing again. That was exactly what Skuratov wanted. He could not help playing the fool. They abandoned him pretty soon and resumed the serious conversation. The discussion was mostly between the old men and real experts in these matters. The younger ones and the quieter ones contented themselves with simply looking on and listening with their heads thrust forward the better to hear. There was a large crowd gathered in the kitchen, and there were naturally no sergeants among them. In their presence they would not have said everything they did. Among the people who were particularly pleased, I noticed one Tatar called Mametka, a short man with high cheekbones, an extremely comical character. He spoke hardly any Russian, and could understand almost nothing of what the others were saying, but still craned his neck from the back of the crowd, and listened with great eagerness.

"What, Mametka, *yakshi*!" Skuratov addressed him. Abandoned by all the others, he had attached himself to Mametka for want of anything better to do.

"*Yakshi, ah yakshi,*" Mametka mumbled, brightening up con-

---

*Author's note. In other words, murdered a man or a woman suspected of sending a curse on the wind that killed cows. There was one prisoner convicted of such a murder in our prison.

siderably, nodding his funny head towards Skuratov. "*Yakshi*."

"They no catch them, *yok*?"

"*Yok, yok!*" Mametka started mumbling again, this time waving his arms around as well.

"Me no understand. You no think that true, Mametka?"

"True, true. *Yakshi!*" agreed Mametka, nodding furiously.

"Well, if you say so. Let it be *yakshi*!"

And Skuratov, slapping down the Tatar's hat so that it almost covered Mametka's eyes, went out of the kitchen in a most cheerful mood, leaving a bewildered Mametka behind him.

The strictness continued in the gaol for a whole week, as did the raids and searches into the surrounding countryside. I do not know how, but the prisoners always obtained correct and immediate information about all the steps taken by the authorities outside the gaol. For the first few days all the reports seemed to favour the fugitives. They had vanished into thin air, without leaving a single trace. Our people just grinned at the news. All the anxiety for what would happen to the fugitives evaporated. "They won't find a thing. They won't catch nobody," the prisoners would say with satisfaction.

"It's like trying to catch a flying bullet!"

"Goodbye, don't cry!"

It was well known in the prison that all the peasants in the surrounding area had been told to keep their eyes peeled, and that all likely places in the forests and ravines were watched.

"It's all daft," said our people, jeering. "They've obviously got someone who's hiding them."

"No doubt about it," the others added. "They aren't stupid. They'll have had it all worked out in advance."

They went even further in their wishful thinking, and were now saying that the fugitives were perhaps still somewhere in the suburbs, hiding in some cellar or other, waiting for the all-clear and their hair to grow. They would be there for six months or even a year, then off they would go... They were all in a romancing mood.

Then suddenly, about eight days after the escape, a rumour spread that the authorities were on the fugitives' trail. Of course, such a ridiculous notion was immediately and contemptuously dismissed. Then, the very same evening, it was confirmed. The prisoners started worrying. The next morning there was talk in the town that they had already been caught and were being brought in. After the midday meal there were even more details. They had been caught in some village or other, seventy versts away. Finally there was definite news. The sergeant-major who had just been talking to the Major, confirmed that they would be brought in that evening, straight into the prison guardhouse. This left no room for doubt. It is very difficult to convey the effect of this news on the prisoners. At first, they all seemed to be angry, and then crestfallen. Some attempts were made to sneer. People started laughing, not at the catchers now, but at the caught. Only a few people laughed at first, but then almost everybody joined in, apart from the more stolid and serious-minded, who thought for themselves and would not be driven off course by such mockery. They held this shallow behaviour of the majority in contempt, and kept their own counsel.

To put it bluntly, the prisoners now denigrated Kulikov and A—v to the same degree that they had previously glorified them, denigrating them with relish. It was as though these two had done the others a wrong. They talked contemptuously about how the two fugitives had felt hungry and, unable to stand it, had gone to the village to beg the peasants for some bread. That was the lowest a vagrant could stoop to. These stories, however, had no truth in them. The fugitives had been tracked down while they were hiding in the forest, with the place surrounded on all sides. Then, seeing there was no hope of escaping, they had given themselves up. There was nothing else for it.

Yet when they were actually brought in, bound hand and foot, with an escort of gendarmes, the entire gaol crowded up against the fence to see what would be done to them. They did not, of course, see anything, other than the Major's and Commandant's carriages near the guardhouse. The fugitives were locked in a cell there, in chains. On the following day they were tried. The other prisoners' mockery and contempt very soon subsided of its own accord. They found out more details, and how there had been nothing left for them to do but surrender, and then started following the trial compassionately.

"They'll give them a thousand sticks I reckon!" some asserted.

"What's a thousand!" said some of the others. "They'll just beat them till they're dead. They might give A—v a thousand, but the other fellow'll be beaten till he's dead. Because, mates, he's from the special category."

Their guesses were not right though. A—v was only given five hundred sticks. His previous good behaviour and the fact that this was his first offence were both taken into account. Kulikov was given—as far as I know—fifteen hundred. The punishments were not carried out too harshly. The two fugitives, being sensible men, did not involve anyone in the case at the trial. They testified clearly and precisely, saying they had just run right away from the fortress, without stopping in any other place at all. The person I felt most sorry for was Koller. It meant the end of everything for him, and he lost even his last glimmer of hope. He was punished more severely than the other two, with two thousand sticks, if I remember correctly, and sent off to another gaol to serve time. A—v was punished leniently, mercifully, thanks to the doctors. Still he swaggered about it and talked very loudly in the hospital that he was now ready for anything, he would stop at nothing and it wasn't the last they'd hear of him. Kulikov behaved as he always did, with propriety and dignity, and back in the gaol after his punishment, he acted as if he had never been away. The other prisoners, however, could never look at him in the same way again. Although Kulikov could always stand up for himself in any situation, yet the other prisoners, in their heart of hearts, ceased to respect him, and treated him somewhat patronisingly now. To sum up, Kulikov's reputation started to decline after his escape. Success means so much to people...

X

Leaving Prison

All this took place during my last year in prison. I found this final year almost as memorable as my first, particularly the very last period. But why go into detail? I shall mention only that despite my impatience to leave gaol as quickly as possible, I found life easier during that year than during all my previous years there. For one thing, I had by then many friends and comrades among the other prisoners, who had reached the conclusion that I was a decent fellow after all. Many of them were devoted to me and loved me sincerely. The 'sapper' almost wept when he saw me and my friend off, and afterwards, when for about a month we lived in one of the houses maintained by the authorities in town, he came to see us practically every day, simply to look at us. There were some characters who remained grim and unfriendly to the end. These people, it seems, could not bear to exchange even a few words with me—God knows why. It was as though there was a wall between us.

During my last months, I received more privileges than at any other time during my life in prison. I discovered that there were acquaintances and even former schoolfriends of mine serving in the army in the town. I re-established contact with them. Through them I was able to receive more money, to write home, and even have some books. I had not read a single book for several years, and I cannot describe in words the strange, moving impression made upon me by the first thing I read in the prison. I remember that I began reading it in the evening when we were locked up in the barrack, and I read the whole night long, until daybreak. What I had been given to read was a magazine. It was like news flashed to me from the outside world. My former life passed before my eyes, radiant and bright, and I tried to imagine, from what I read, how far behind I was, how life had progressed without me, what the major issues of the day were, and what problems occupied people's minds. I sifted every word, I tried reading between the lines, I sought out hidden meanings, and hints about past events. I sought traces of those issues that had interested people in my own time. It was terribly sad for me to realise how alienated I was from the modern world. I would have to adjust to this new world, and become acquainted with a new generation. I pounced hungrily upon an article if the author was someone who had been a close friend of mine in times gone by... But there were many new names in the magazine. New people had appeared on the scene and I sought avidly to make myself familiar with them. It was annoying that books were so few in number and so hard to come by. Previously, under the rule of the Major, it had been dangerous even to bring books into the prison. Questions would no doubt have followed a search. "Where are these books from? Where did you get them? You must have contacts outside." How could I have answered such questions? So without books, I had involuntarily withdrawn into myself, posing questions to myself and trying to answer them, torturously sometimes... None of this can be simply told, of course...

I had been admitted to the gaol in winter, so I also had to leave in winter, on exactly the same day of the month. How impatiently I waited for that winter, how joyfully I watched the leaves shrivelling on the trees, the grass withering in the steppe. Summer was well over, the autumn winds started wailing. Then the first snowflakes came drifting down... At last the longed-for winter came! At moments my heart began to pound with a great presentiment of freedom. Yet strange to say, the more time passed and the closer came the day of my release, the more patient I became... Towards the very end this truly amazed me and I rebuked myself for growing totally cool and indifferent. Many of the prisoners whom I came across in the prison yard during their free time would talk to me and congratulate me.

"You'll be out then soon, free as a bird, Alexander Petrovich sir. You'll be leaving us old fellows behind you."

"And will you be released soon yourself, Martynov?" I would ask.

"Me? Well, let's see now... I'll be stewing in here for another seven years." And he would sigh, stop, and look around absent-mindedly, as if he were trying to catch a glimpse of the future... There were many who gladly and sincerely congratulated me. Everyone seemed to have become more friendly. Probably this was because I was already ceasing to be one of them. They were already bidding me goodbye. Like me, K—chinsky, one of the Polish noblemen, a quiet, self-effacing young man, also enjoyed walking around the yard during his time off. He hoped that fresh air and exercise would keep him in good health and repair the harm done by nights passed in the stuffy barrack.

"I can't wait for you to be set free," he said to me with a smile, when he met me one day. "When you go, then *I shall know for certain* that it will be exactly one year until my own release."

I should remark here in passing that because we dreamed of freedom so much and had become so unused to it, the thought of freedom seemed somehow *freer* than real freedom, that is to say, than the freedom which exists in the real outside world. The prisoners had an exaggerated notion of real freedom, and this is completely natural, so typical of every prisoner. Any officer's shabby batman was in our eyes a king, almost an ideal of the free man when compared with us, prisoners, simply because he could go about unshaven, unshackled and unguarded.

On the eve of my release, at dusk, I walked around the pales of the fence *for the very last time*. How many thousands of times I had walked around them during all those years. Here, behind the barracks, during the first year of my imprisonment, I had wandered all alone, forlorn and crushed. I remember counting how many thousands of days I had left in prison. Heavens, how long ago that seemed to me now! In this corner here lived our captive eagle. This is where I often met Petrov. He did not leave my side now either. He ran up to me and, as though sensing what was passing in my mind, walked along silently beside me, pondering over something. My thoughts were busy bidding farewell to the blackened beams of our barracks. How unwelcoming they had seemed to me at *that* time, when I first arrived. They were even older now than they were then, yet I never noticed. How much youth was interred here between these walls for no purpose, what great forces had perished in here to no avail. This has got to be said, all of it, openly: the people here were extraordinary people. Perhaps they possessed the most talents and the greatest strength of all our people. Yet this great strength perished here, and perished unnaturally, unlawfully, irrevocably. Who is to blame for this?

That is the question. Who is to blame?

Early the next morning, when it was just beginning to grow

light, I went all around the barracks to say goodbye to the prisoners before they left for work. Many strong and calloused hands were held out to me in friendship. Some shook me by the hand as a sign of real comradeship: but these were few. The others knew only too well that I would now become a completely different kind of person from them. They knew that I had friends in the town, and that upon leaving the gaol, I would immediately go to these *lords* and sit among these lords as an equal. They understood this, and, though they said goodbye to me in an amiable and kindly manner, yet it was not as they would have parted from a friend, but as they would have parted from a master. Some coldly turned their backs on me and would not answer my goodbye. Some even looked at me with something like hatred.

The drum sounded, and they all left for work, while I remained behind. Sushilov had been almost the first to get up that morning, and was making a great fuss about making tea for me before he left for work. Poor Sushilov! When I gave my prison rags—my shirts, my thongs and some money—to him as a present, he burst into tears. "That's not what I want! That's not what I want!" he said, trying to control his quivering lips. "How can I do without you, Alexander Petrovich! How will I go on here without you!" I also said goodbye to Akim Akimovich.

"You'll be out soon too," I said to him.

"No, I shall be here for a long time yet, a very long time indeed," he mumbled, shaking my hand. I flung my arms around his neck and kissed him.

About ten minutes after the prisoners had left for work, I also left, never to return—together with the friend who had entered prison at the same time as I did. We had to go straight to the blacksmith's to have our shackles taken off. There was no guard with a rifle accompanying us this time—only a sergeant. We were unshackled by our own fellow prisoners in the engineering workshop. I waited for my friend's shackles to be taken off, and then went up to the anvil myself. The blacksmiths turned me round so that I had my back to them, lifted my leg from behind, and placed it on the anvil... There was a lot of bustling, for they wanted to do it neatly and well.

"Turn the rivet—the rivet, I said—first," ordered the man in charge. "Just there. That's it. Now give it a knock with the hammer!"

The shackles dropped to the ground. I picked them up. I wanted to hold them in my hand, to look at them one last time. Amazing that they had just been around my ankles!

"Well, God speed! God speed!" The prisoners' voices sounded gruff and abrupt, but they seemed to be pleased about something too.

Yes. God speed. Freedom. A new life. Resurrection from the grave... What a moment!

The End

NOTES

Included in this volume is the story *Notes from the Dead House*, written by Fyodor Dostoyevsky in 1860-1862 after doing his term of hard labour in Siberia, service in the army as a private, and then exile, to which he was sentenced in 1850 for participation in Petrashevsky revolutionary group.

The newspaper *Russky Mir* (Russian World) published the preface and the first four chapters of this book in 1860-1861. The full text first appeared in *Vremya* (Time), a magazine edited by Fyodor Dostoyevsky and his brother Mikhail, in April-December 1862.

[1] p. 45

...one of the Old Believers, who had come to us from the Starodubye Settlement, formerly known as Vetkovtsy... —The Old Believers formed a religious sect in Russia which had not adopted the church reforms, concerning certain rituals, carried through in the 17th century, and had thus become hostile to the official Russian Orthodox Church.

Starodubye, a village in the south of Russia, was a major centre of Old Believers.

[2] p. 56

...a fugitive from the Nerchinsk mines...—a group of hard-labour prisons in the south of Eastern Siberia.

[3] p. 64

...was sentenced to the full number of strokes...—according to the law of 1839, the highest corporal punishment was six thousand sticks, but according to an unwritten law their number was reduced to four thousand. The sticks were actually pliant osier twigs about 2 metres long and 4 cm thick.

[4] p. 77
The Poles, however, were a separate and exclusive group...—these were political prisoners who had taken part in the Polish military revolt in 1850 against the Russian tsar.

[5] p. 77
...Gogol's story Taras Bulba...—an episode from the story by Nikolai Gogol (1809-1852).

[6] p. 90
...a truly remarkable painter, something of a Briullov...—Karl Briullov (1798-1877)—a Russian painter, noted for his portraits.

[7] p. 95
This book and the money inside it had been given to me as a present while I was still in Tobolsk...—Dostoyevsky here recalls how on his way to the hard-labour prison he met the wives of the 'Decembrists', the Russian nobles who rose against the autocracy in December 1825, were sentenced to hard labour, and after doing their term were doomed to permanent exile in Siberia.

[8] p. 119
...a book about the Countess Lavalier...—the book meant here is *Vicomte de Bragelonne* by Alexandre Dumas père (1802-1870).

[9] p. 171
'The Rivals Filatka and Miroshka'—a very popular vaudeville by P. Grigoryev (1807-1854), a Petersburgian actor.

[10] p. 185
This is the Kamarinskaya *in full swing, and, honestly, I wish Glinka could hear how they played it...*—Mikhail Glinka (1804-1857), an outstanding Russian composer, had written a symphonic fantasy based on this folk song.

[11] p. 186
This man is a Brahmin...—one of the characters in the play was a Russian priest, but for reasons of censorship Dostoyevsky called him a Brahmin.

...*white teeth and a deep rumbling laugh like Nozdrev's in* Dead Souls...—a character in the novel by Nikolai Gogol (1809-1852).

[13]p. 215
...*as Griboyedov writes, "the memory is still so fresh but it can hardly be believed"*...—words from the play *Wit Works Woe* by Alexander Griboyedov (1795-1829).

[14]p. 220
...*like those of Gogol's Manilov* —Manilov is a character in *Dead Souls* by Nikolai Gogol.

[15]p. 243
...*I'll hire out as a soldier*...—in the 19th-century Russia, men were recruited into the army for 25 years. A recruit could hire someone else to serve in his stead.

[16]p. 309
...*about thirty-five years ago, a large party of exiled nobles had arrived in Siberia all together*...—this large group of prisoners comprised 121 Decembrists sentenced to hard labour and subsequent exile.